Boardroom

Baby

Mixing business with pleasure…and babies!

Boardroom
Baby

THE FATHER OF HER CHILD
by
Emma Darcy

AFTER HOURS
by
Sandra Field

THE SEDUCTION SCHEME
by
Kim Lawrence

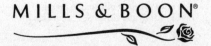

MILLS & BOON®

*MILLS & BOON and MILLS & BOON with the Rose Device
are registered trademarks of the publisher.
Harlequin Mills & Boon Limited,
Eton House, 18-24 Paradise Road, Richmond, Surrey, TW9 1SR*

BOARDROOM BABY © by Harlequin Enterprises II B.V., 2003

The Father of Her Child, After Hours and *The Seduction Scheme*
were first published in Great Britain by Harlequin Mills & Boon Limited
in separate, single volumes.

The Father of Her Child © Emma Darcy 1996
After Hours © Sandra Field 1996
The Seduction Scheme © Kim Lawrence 1999

ISBN 0 263 83589 8

05-0403

*Printed and bound in Spain
by Litografia Rosés S.A., Barcelona*

Initially a French/English teacher, **Emma Darcy** changed careers to computer programming before marriage, motherhood, and the happy demands of keeping up with three lively sons and the very social life of her businessman husband, Frank. Very much a people person, and always interested in relationships, she finds the world of romance fiction a thrilling one and the challenge of creating her own cast of characters very addictive.

**Emma Darcy's latest book is out next
month in Modern Romance™.**

**Don't miss this passionately provocative story
THE BILLIONAIRE BRIDEGROOM**

THE FATHER OF
HER CHILD

by

Emma Darcy

CHAPTER ONE

"LAUREN says…"

Michael Timberlane's jaw clenched. His friend and client, Evan Daniel, continued talking, blithely ignorant of the effect of those two explosively evocative words…*Lauren says*. Michael didn't hear anything else. His mind filled with brooding resentment.

He couldn't count the number of times his ex-wife had thrown those words at him as though Lauren Magee was the font of all knowledge and wisdom on how a marriage should work. *Lauren says, Lauren says*…a long litany of feminist claptrap that had given Roxanne the encouragement to indulge herself in single-minded selfishness. Any sense of give and take had flown right out the door under Lauren Magee's influence.

It was a black day when that woman had accepted the position as publicist at the publishing house where Roxanne worked in marketing. Why the Sydney branch of Global Publications had to import a career woman from Melbourne to head its publicity department was beyond Michael's comprehension, but the word in the industry was that Lauren Magee was a fireball. She obviously didn't mind whom she scorched, either.

Michael grudgingly conceded he had not been averse to the idea of divorce by the time Roxanne decided it was what she wanted. His ideal of a true partnership within a love relationship had been comprehensively whittled away. Nevertheless, Evan's inadvertent reminder of the interfering judgments by a woman who didn't even know him stirred a vengeful wish to turn Lauren Magee and her insidious list of women's rights upside down and inside out.

Would that he could!

It was undoubtedly a waste of energy even thinking about it. The woman had to be a man hater with a brick-wall temperament, totally closed to logic or reason. She would probably have Evan's balls for breakfast if he stepped out of line on this promotional tour she had organised for him. A male author who liked an alcoholic lunch would not be her cup of tea at all.

Michael unclenched his jaw, relaxed his facial muscles and dutifully tuned back into Evan's flow of excitement over his jam-packed schedule of interviews with the media. Global Publications, via Lauren Magee, was certainly doing him proud in their efforts to launch his new historical novel on the Australian reading public. Michael hoped it would sell well, not only for his friend's sake, but also for his own satisfaction as Evan's literary agent.

He silently congratulated himself on getting Evan an extremely good deal for the book, though he would have privately preferred the highest bidder to have been any other publishing house than Global

Publications. But business was business. The best interests of all the authors on his list had to be served. That was one of the principles by which he'd gained his reputation as an agent whose judgment could be trusted.

He knew books. He knew what they were worth and where their market was. Evan Daniel's sweeping saga of early colonial days in the convict settlement of New South Wales was a rattling good story and had the elements for solid, commercial success. All it needed was the right push to bring it to public attention.

"I need your help, Michael."

Evan's excitement seemed to have faded into a sudden fit of anxiety. Michael raised his eyebrows, inviting elaboration on whatever problem was troubling his friend. This had to be the underlying reason for his visit this morning. It was a long drive from Evan's home at Leura in the Blue Mountains to Michael's apartment-cum-office at Milson's Point in the very heart of Sydney. Enthusing over his promotional tour hardly constituted a strong enough motive to bring him here.

All the signs of inner agitation were evident. Evan shifted his somewhat roly-poly body uncomfortably. He tugged at the frizzy brown curls above his ears, pulling them out into tufts. With his round face and big, dark, soulful eyes, Evan frequently reminded Michael of a cuddly koala bear. Despite his rotund shape, women were attracted to him. There was some-

thing very appealing about Evan. His bright and benevolent personality reached out to people.

"Could you take the time off to come with me on
the tour to Melbourne and Brisbane?" he finally
blurted out.

"You don't need me to hold your hand, Evan.
You'll do fine. Your natural enthusiasm about your
book..."

"It's not that. I'm not scared of the interviews,"
came the hasty assurance. His ensuing grimace held
both apology and an appeal for understanding. "It's
Tasha. She's going to be rabidly jealous of Lauren
the moment she lays eyes on her."

Michael was astounded. "Lauren Magee?"

"You know how gorgeous she is. And I'll be staying in the same hotels with her."

"Lauren Magee...gorgeous?" Michael couldn't
believe it. In his mind's eye Lauren Magee was a
sexless martinet, as thin as a matchstick with every
bit of feminine sweetness squeezed out of her.

Evan looked puzzled. "Haven't you met her?"

It would be pistols at dawn if he did, Michael
thought darkly. "I can't say I've had the pleasure,"
he drawled with deliberate carelessness.

"I thought you knew everyone in the publishing
industry."

Evan's surprise was comical. Michael had to smile.
"The publishers and the commissioning editors, yes.
I haven't met every single person on their staffs."

"But Lauren... Oh, well, you can meet her at the

party tonight. I'll introduce you. Then you'll see why I need you to come with me on the tour. I know it's asking a big favour, Michael, but…''

"I won't be there tonight," Michael stated flatly.

It was Global's launching party for all its new books for the coming year. Roxanne would be swanning around with her second choice of husband, who was, Michael thought cynically, quite perfect for her. Her preening didn't bother him, but she made such a pointed show of it in front of him he felt sorry for the other guy. It was distasteful. Such comparisons always were.

Michael prided himself on being civilised. Most of the time he was. Very civilised. Extremely civilised. The combination of Roxanne on parade, trying in her perverse vanity to make a fool of him, plus Lauren Magee on the sidelines with her feminist cant, just happened to bring out the savage in him. It was not a feeling he liked.

Evan looked hurt. "I'm one of the speakers."

"I'm sorry, Evan, but you don't need me to applaud your speech."

"I do need you. Not for applause. If I could stand you between Tasha and Lauren, it would save me a power of trouble. Tasha wouldn't get any funny ideas with you around. It's perfectly obvious that any woman with two eyes in her head would go for you, not me."

That wasn't necessarily true, Michael thought. Superficially, he supposed, he fitted the tall, dark and handsome tag, but in a savage mood, he knew he could look more intimidating than attractive.

"And if you came on tour with me," Evan pressed, "Tasha would have no reason to get upset."

The impassioned plea tried Michael's patience. "Your marital problems are none of my business, Evan. If you can't assure your wife of your unbreakable fidelity, take her with you."

"You know Tasha is eight months pregnant," came the plaintive protest. "Can you see her manoeuvring into an economy-class seat on one of those small intercity planes? Not to mention her doctor's orders to rest and take care. We're not taking any chances with this baby. Not after two miscarriages."

Michael frowned. He had forgotten Tasha's delicate condition and the trouble she'd had in carrying a child to full term. Evan was right. It was stupid to take any risk. If it was his wife and baby Michael knew he'd be cocooning them in cotton wool.

His desire to have children had been frustrated by Roxanne's deceptions, and he wondered now if he'd ever get to be a father. Finding the right woman had to come first. He assured himself that at thirty-four, he was still in his prime and his choices in life were wide open. He was not restricted by time.

"Surely Tasha can trust you," he offered. "It's only for a few days."

Evan sighed. "Normally, yes, but she's in a very fragile mood, feeling all lumpy and undesirable. We've had to refrain from sex because... Well, I don't want to go into that.'' He flushed. ''Anyhow, she's not going to be happy about me flying off with a woman as gorgeous and sexy-looking as Lauren Magee.''

Lauren Magee sexy-looking? Michael shook his head incredulously. That was wrapping a wormy apple in a glossy skin.

The glum, discomforted face of his friend stirred sympathy. Evan and Tasha were going through a tough time. The successful launching of this book was important to them financially, so it couldn't be dropped, and Evan was quite likely to fumble the interviews and get smashed on double gins if he was upset.

''Please?'' he begged. ''There's no one else I can turn to. If you don't help me...'' He rolled his eyes and gestured despairingly.

Michael's curiosity was piqued. ''Do you like her, Evan?'' he asked pertinently.

''Who? Lauren?'' He looked innocent. ''She's a lovely girl, but I'm a married man, Michael. I love my wife and I'm not about to stray.'' Hotly earnest.

''Does she like you?''

Uncomfortable shifting again. ''Well, er, only in a friendly kind of way. I just don't want Tasha to misunderstand. If you're with me, everything will be all right.''

A nasty little troublemaker, amusing herself by coming between husbands and wives, Michael thought with considerable venom. Not this time,

Lauren Magee, he silently vowed. *Lovely girl*...huh! She might be gorgeous and sexy-looking, but she clearly had the sting of an asp, poisoning other people's relationships.

Michael decided it would give him immense satisfaction to do a bit of stinging of his own. Besides, Tasha deserved to have peace of mind during this difficult period. The strain of an advanced and possibly threatened pregnancy was more than enough for her and Evan to cope with. Protecting them from any capricious harm by Lauren Magee was the decent thing to do.

"Okay, Evan, I'll run interference for you," he said, a dangerous little smile lurking on his lips.

Relief burst over his friend's face. "At the party tonight? And the tour?"

"Yes. You can count on me for both."

And to hell with Roxanne and her ridiculous gloating with her new husband! He could stomach that if he had to for one evening. It was in a good cause. As for Lauren Magee, well, he was beginning to look forward to locking horns with her.

Evan surged out of his chair and reached over Michael's desk to grab his hand and shake it vigorously with both of his. "You're a true, true friend and I thank you from the bottom of my heart. It means I can relax and enjoy everything, and Tasha will, too. She's been looking forward to tonight's launching party. Wouldn't miss it for anything."

"Then I hope she'll have a happy evening."

Evan grinned. "Champagne on tap. I love free drinks."

"Don't forget you have to drive," Michael warned dryly.

"Uh-uh. We're staying in the city overnight. Taxis both ways."

"What hotel? I could pick you up. Best if we arrive together, don't you think?"

"Great!" Evan heaved a huge, contented sigh. "I won't forget this, Michael. Any time you want a favour, you've got it."

"I'll remember that. Do you have a list of the tour details with you...dates, times, flights, hotels?"

"Sure do. With all the telephone numbers for you to make your bookings."

Evan was probably right about no-one else being able to help him, Michael reflected a few minutes later. The cost of this safeguard venture would prohibit most people. Money meant nothing to him, never had, and Evan knew it. Real friendship did. All the wealth in the world couldn't buy that. If a couple of thousand dollars could prevent Tasha and Evan from being messed up by Lauren Magee, Michael was only too happy to supply the necessary.

That lady had a few things coming to her.

Michael figured he was just the man to deliver them.

He could feel the primitive savage stirring inside him, and this time he didn't try to suppress the feeling. He revelled in it. Being civilised could definitely be overrated. He had the taste of revenge in his mouth. It was sweet.

CHAPTER TWO

"COME on, Lauren," Graham Parker urged. "It's peak hour, remember? The traffic across the city is bound to be horrendous, and I want to make it to Rose Bay by six."

"I'm coming." The last page of the publicity flyer started rolling through the fax machine. Confident there'd be no problem with the transmission, Lauren turned to her desk, snatched up her handbag and flashed a smile at the head of the marketing department. "Ready to go."

Graham was in his mid-forties, solidly married to his wife, family and computer and nicely avuncular towards her. Lauren knew he read nothing personal into her asking him for a lift to the launching party. It was simply a convenience between two coworkers. She always felt in a comfort zone with Graham. It was a pleasant feeling.

"Snazzy belt," he commented appreciatively.

She grinned, pleased with the compliment. The belt was a recent purchase, featuring a large gold bow set on a wide, black, elasticised band. "Nothing like a good accessory to turn day wear into glitz."

He shook his head in bemusement as she joined

14

him. "Do you turn your whole life into a time and motion study?"

"Have to with my job, Graham."

"I don't know how you can stand the pace. Always on the go. It would give me a coronary."

"I like it."

It filled her life. She needed that. She didn't like having too much time to dwell on the empty spaces. It was good to keep busy. Besides, she was doing what she did best, organising schedules, taking care of people, sorting them out, fitting everything and everyone into a workable and effective pattern. It seemed to Lauren she had been doing that as long as she could remember, having been the eldest child in a family of nine.

Once she had dreamed of having someone take care of her and do all the looking after. Big mistake. Her stomach clenched in recoil at the memory of the prison her ex-husband had made of their marriage. Never again, she vowed. Obsessive possessiveness had no place in Lauren's concept of love. It was both frightening and crushing.

As she rode the elevator to the ground floor with Graham, she consciously banished those shadows from her mind. These days she lived life on her own terms, and the party tonight should be fun. No responsibilities for her apart from chatting to a few authors, making them feel welcome and introducing them to other guests. Champagne was to flow freely and a band had been booked to provide dance music after the speeches. Lauren loved dancing.

She adjusted the new belt so the gold bow was set closer to her hip line. It looked brilliant on the bright violet of her ribbed knit sweater. She was really pleased with the overall effect, the wide black elastic accentuating the black of her skirt and tights and the bow picking up the gold trim on her black suede shoes.

She still had to do her hair. It was in a bit of a tangle from being loose all day. Lauren grinned to herself as she recalled her hairdresser calling it a wild animal. The copper-red hue did not come out of a bottle and the natural curls bounced from her scalp and rioted over her shoulders and halfway down her back.

Once she was in Graham's car she would pile up her unruly hair and clip on the black and gold earrings. That would certainly put the finishing touch to her cocktail-hour appearance.

Graham hustled her out of Global's office building to the car park, clearly anxious to be on his way. By Lauren's calculation, from where they were in Artarmon, the express route to the bridge and the Harbour Tunnel to the Eastern Suburbs cut the trip to Rose Bay to forty minutes at most, even through peak hour traffic. The party didn't start until six, and it was only just past five now.

''Why the hurry?'' she asked. Accustomed to travelling to a tight schedule, Lauren disliked the waste of time involved in arriving anywhere too early.

"I want to check the display table before anyone arrives."

"I thought Roxanne was doing that."

She had told Lauren so this morning, pleased with the task of setting up a display of the new titles catalogue and the gift T-shirts.

"She tripped down the steps out there and sprained her ankle," Graham stated flatly.

Lauren rolled her eyes. Another drama in Roxanne's life to be endlessly recounted to every ear she could find!

"I don't know if she finished the job first," Graham added with a grimace.

"I take it she won't be at the party with her new husband tonight," Lauren said dryly.

"Into each life some rain must fall."

Lauren couldn't help laughing at his droll intonation. Since Roxanne worked in marketing, Graham was even more a victim of her *confidences* than Lauren was. His responses were invariably short, pithy sayings. He let the rest float over his head.

They were probably being unkind, Lauren thought, as they settled into the car. Spraining an ankle was no joke. It should evoke sympathy. The problem was that Roxanne was such a sympathy gobbler, one's natural store of it ran out. This past year Lauren had taken to actively evading Roxanne and her self-indulgent wallowing in real or imagined woes.

She ruefully reflected that when she had first arrived at Global Publications, she had been sucked right into being a listener. Like a sponge, she had absorbed a steady stream of complaints about the demands and unreasonable expectations of Roxanne's first husband. It had hit on wounds from her own miserable marriage, drawing what might have been, in hindsight, unwarranted sympathy, as well as the best advice she could give.

She hadn't known then that advice was not really what was wanted. Roxanne soaked up advice from everyone who would give it. She went looking for advice constantly because it gave her the excuse to talk about herself. Roxanne Kinsey was the most self-absorbed person Lauren had ever met.

All the same, Roxanne was probably well rid of her first husband. He had sounded as though he was tarred with the same brush as Lauren's big mistake. Men who wanted to own women were innately insecure. No trust. Rabid jealousy. Demanding accountability of every moment away from them. Forcing their will on every little thing.

Nightmare alley, Lauren thought, and was glad to be out of it. Although she did miss living in Melbourne. All her family were there. Unfortunately, so was Wayne, and she didn't trust him to stay out of her life. Despite their divorce, he wouldn't let go. Coming to Sydney had effected a solid break from him, and that had been necessary for her peace of mind, but she did find it lonely up here.

At least she would have a chance to visit her mother during her stay in Melbourne with Evan Daniel. A smile broke through her brooding as she thought of the upcoming promotional tour. Some authors were highly touchy and temperamental, but Evan Daniel was a real sweetie, cheerful, obliging, appreciative of everything she had arranged for him, a lovely, warm, huggable bear of a man. She wished she could find someone like him for herself.

Her mobile telephone beeped, and she quickly drew it out of of her handbag.

Graham threw her a twinkling look. ''That thing will be growing out of your ear if you don't watch out, Lauren.''

''It would be handier if it did,'' she returned lightly.

She knew Graham's remark was not a criticism, yet coming on top of her thoughts about Wayne, it scraped a highly sensitive area. The night she had walked away from her marriage, Wayne had ripped her mobile telephone from her ear and hurled it against the wall in a jealous rage. The memory lingered darkly as she answered the call.

It was from the producer of a television daytime chat show. She had tried to reach him earlier this afternoon, but he had been too busy to take the call. He was returning it now. This frequently happened with the media people she had to deal with. It was not until they had wrapped up the business of the day that they gave their attention to anything relating to tomorrow or next week or a fortnight from now. Calls were made after normal working hours had ended.

That was one of the reasons Lauren had a mobile telephone. It was necessary to gain a successful result from her initiatives. She worked to other people's convenience, not her own. If she wasn't available to take calls, to instantly follow up on opportunities offered, they could all too easily be lost.

A promotional campaign had to be effected within a certain limited time. Media interest was often a chain reaction. It was also fickle. If she didn't strike while the iron was hot, she was not doing her job properly. It was as simple as that.

It wasn't as though Wayne hadn't known she loved her job before they were married. It had come as a shock when he had expected her to give it up for him within weeks of their honeymoon. She might even have done so if that had been the only problem emerging between them, but his attitude towards her work permeated everything else, too. It was like having married Dr. Jekyll, then finding herself living with Mr. Hyde.

By the time she had talked through arrangements with the television producer, Graham had driven past King's Cross and was well on the way to Rose Bay. She tucked the mobile phone in her handbag and decided to postpone putting her hair up until they arrived at the restaurant. It would be easier to do it in the ladies' powder room, and they would certainly be arriving ahead of the guests.

"When do you take off with Evan Daniel?" Graham asked.

"Next week. Wednesday."

"You've drummed up a lot of interest in him."

"Good subject."

"He's a nice guy."

"Very likeable," Lauren agreed warmly. "I think he'll come over well. I hope you've got good supplies of his books in the shops, Graham."

"Best-seller status."

"Great!"

He shot her a curious look. "Is Evan Daniel your kind of guy, Lauren?"

"Why do you ask?" she returned teasingly, aware there was considerable speculation about her love life amongst Global's staff.

Graham shrugged. "I know you date occasionally but you don't stick with anyone for long."

"It's difficult to maintain a relationship in my kind of job."

"I notice you shy off really good-looking guys."

"Do I?"

"Yes. And that's odd for a good-looking girl like you."

"Maybe I want more than what's on the surface."

"That's why I asked about Evan."

"He's married, Graham."

"That doesn't seem to stop anyone these days," he observed dryly.

"His wife is pregnant. Do you think I'd respect a

man who played around when his wife is expecting his baby?''

''Ah, respect! Yes, there has to be respect.'' He nodded sagely, then threw her a smile of approval. ''I've got to hand it to you, Lauren. You've got your head on straight.''

She hoped so. She'd certainly lost her head completely over Wayne. He was so handsome he'd melt most women in their shoes. And he had a body to drool over. Pure pin-up material. Her chemistry had led her badly astray, and that was something to be wary of. Graham was very perceptive. She did shy off good-looking guys.

Maybe, Lauren reflected, that wasn't being fair. One shouldn't make generalisations from one bad experience. She resolved to give the next really attractive man who showed an interest in her at least half a chance to show he had some decent substance, too.

They drove past the marina at Rose Bay and through the gateway to the park where the Salamander Restaurant held a prime position on the shoreline. Global was holding its launching party in real style. Lauren felt a bright lilt of anticipation. Perhaps tonight she would meet someone interesting, a stranger across a crowded room.

She grinned.

Did hope never die?

CHAPTER THREE

LAUREN saw him arrive—the stranger.

She didn't know why her gaze was drawn to the restaurant foyer at that particular moment. She was out on the deck overlooking the bay, chatting with a small circle of associates. People were milling around in the dining room, which had been cleared of its normal furniture for freedom of movement. For some reason the groups of guests had shifted, leaving an unobscured channel of vision. And there he was.

It gave Lauren a weird feeling, as though she had conjured him up herself, somehow waving a mental magic wand, making the people part, and there in the spotlight—one tall, dark, handsome stranger. But the illusion was incomplete. His eyes didn't meet hers. He didn't even glance her way. His attention was directed to his companions. He was smiling, a warm, kindly, reassuring kind of smile.

"Lauren, what did you think of…?"

It took an act of will to draw her gaze to her companions and focus her mind on what was being said. She gave her opinion on the question directed at her and tossed the conversational ball into the general ring, disinterested in pursuing a discussion.

People had moved when she looked again. She surreptitiously changed her position, scanning the crowd in an idle manner, half wondering at herself that she felt so drawn to find him, place him. Hadn't she told herself a thousand times it was the person inside who really counted, not superficial attraction?

It was the smile, she decided. She'd liked his smile. A smile could say a lot about the inner person. She was curious about him. That was perfectly natural.

She spotted him in a group she quickly identified. Evan Daniel was talking to his editor, Beth Hayward. The pretty blonde between Evan and the stranger was probably Evan's wife, Tasha. She had a proprietal air as she watched him speak. *My husband,* it said, with pride and pleasure.

The stranger bent and whispered something in the blonde's ear. She nodded and threw him a grateful look. He moved away. Lauren followed his progress across the room to a set of glass doors that opened to the other end of the deck from where she stood. He didn't look around him as most people did, seeking familiar faces, ready to greet or respond. From the moment he set off alone, his face wore a closed, forbidding look.

Lauren was intrigued. It was a total shutdown of charm. He exuded an air of single-minded purpose. Not a party animal, she concluded, more a man with a mission. She wondered why he was here this evening and what he intended to achieve.

His classy, dark grey suit had the stamp of a conservative professional, as did his shirt and neatly styled black hair. In contrast to that image, a blue shirt and a brightly patterned silk tie made a vivid splash of individualism that denied any easy pigeonholing of this man.

His face was pleasingly proportioned, cleanly chiseled, unmistakably male, although a full-lipped mouth softened and sensualised it. Another interesting and endearing feature was surprisingly small and neat ears. His eyebrows were straight, with a slightly downward slant. It was impossible to discern eye colour at this distance, but Lauren decided it would probably be brown. Dark chocolate. She loved dark chocolate.

He stepped onto the deck. He didn't glance in her direction or pause to admire the spectacular view of the harbourside around the bay. He headed straight to where tables and chairs were stacked in the far corner. With brisk economy of movement he separated a small table and two chairs, then took them inside, choosing to set them against the glass wall in a protected alcove beside a serving bench.

It was interesting to watch the animation of his face as he returned to Evan and Tasha Daniel, breaking into their chat with Beth Hayward to usher them all over to the place he had prepared for them. As they moved, Lauren saw how heavily pregnant Evan's wife was and realised it was her comfort that was the stranger's prime consideration.

A thoughtful, caring man. Also a man of action. As soon as Tasha Daniel was settled on a chair, he signalled one of the waiters over to offer his tray of drinks. He selected champagne for Tasha but took orange juice for himself. A non-drinker, Lauren speculated, or a man bent on keeping all his wits about him? It would be interesting to know his connection to Evan and Tasha Daniel.

Lauren waited until Beth Hayward took her leave of them, then went straight into action, intent on having her curiosity satisfied. With the ready excuse of having to see an author, she moved inside and collected two of the gift presentation packs from the display table. Armed with these to sweeten the introduction to Evan's wife and their friend, she headed across the room to them.

Evan saw her coming. His genial face broke into a welcoming smile. He spoke to his wife, clearly identifying Lauren for her, and Tasha Daniel's gaze zeroed in on the woman who would be taking her husband on a promotional tour. Shock was the first reaction. Lauren could almost see, *Her?* flashing into Tasha's mind, surrounded by neon-red lights zigzagging danger signals.

She'd met the reaction before and hoped to defuse it quickly. Few women liked the idea of having Lauren look after their men. She was too vividly female, almost spectacularly so with the contrast of pearly pale skin, copper-red hair and cornflower-blue eyes. But she was not a predatory rival for their affections. Usually she managed to project that, given a few minutes in their company.

After leaving Wayne, she had gone through a period of downplaying her physical attributes, covering up her figure, wearing no make-up, even having her red curls cropped to within an inch of her scalp and dying her hair brown, hating the idea of any man seeing her only as an ornamental possession.

Eventually she had realised she was damaging herself, feeding fears and repressing her natural exuberance for life and all its joys. It was much better to simply maintain a balanced sense of self-worth and let the rest of the world sort itself out.

Lauren felt the stranger watch her approach, too. Maybe it was only the effect of her heightened awareness of him, but she was conscious of all her sensory levels rising, sharpening, as though she was moving into a highly dangerous zone. Suddenly she felt wary of him, reluctant to pursue the interest he had sparked in her.

A spurious, fantasy interest, she told herself, bound to bring disappointment. Now that she was so close, it was silly not to look and assess the man more directly, yet some deeply protective instinct tugged on her mind, wanting to shun the influence he had already unwittingly exerted on her. She switched on a bright smile for Evan Daniel and his wife, but didn't include the stranger in its warm sweep. He was, after all, a stranger.

"Hi, there!" she greeted them with casual friendliness. "I collected these souvenirs for you before they're all taken."

"I didn't realise they were being given away," Evan remarked in surprise. "Thanks, Lauren. Good of you to think of it." He turned quickly to his wife, who began to struggle up from her chair. "This is Tasha. Lauren Magee, Tasha."

"Please don't move," Lauren protested. "It's good you've found a place to sit. It's a long night on one's feet."

"Yes," Tasha agreed, subsiding again. "I'm pleased to meet you, Lauren," she added somewhat stiffly.

"Likewise. I've heard so much about you from Evan. And the coming baby. I'm very happy for you both."

Tasha flushed. "Thank you."

"And please remember, if you're worried about anything while Evan is away on tour, just ring me on my mobile telephone number, and I'll cancel interviews at a moment's notice. You come first, Tasha."

The wariness left her eyes. "Oh, I'm sure everything will be all right."

"That's great! Your husband has written a top-line book, so we hope to let every reader in Australia hear about it."

"I'm amazed at the number of interviews you've lined up for him."

Lauren laughed, placing the catalogue and T-shirt packages on the table for Tasha to take as she shared her amusement in a woman-to-woman confidence. "He'll be complaining to you about being run off his feet and how exhausted he is, but it will be worth the effort if the sales zoom. That's the whole point of the exercise.''

''How soon will you know if it's worked?'' she asked curiously.

Having successfully refocused Tasha's mind, taking it off her and moving it squarely onto the job in hand, Lauren relaxed. ''Give it a month.'' She moved her gaze to Evan. ''If you contact Graham Parker, of marketing, he should have figures for you by then.''

''Oh, good! Uh, Lauren...'' Relief and pleasure beamed from Evan's face. With the eagerness of an overgrown puppy wanting everyone lapped with goodwill, he pressed on. ''Someone I want you to meet.''

She braced herself. Against what, she wasn't sure. Even as she'd been addressing Tasha, working at winning her over, she had been acutely conscious of the man standing to the right of her, waiting, listening, watching.

Evan gestured for her to turn and meet the stranger head on. ''My friend and literary agent, Michael Timberlane.''

Lauren's mind buzzed with that information as she slowly swung towards him. Michael Timberlane was, by renown, the most trusted literary agent in the business, his judgment of books being proved commercially sound so many times it overrode doubt. She knew he handled Evan's work and that of many other successful authors, but their paths had never crossed.

His work was done before she was called in to help the books sell. She hadn't been curious about him, since his field of expertise didn't touch on hers. But she was curious now. The combination of a highly perceptive mind in a highly attractive body was an irresistible draw.

Still an instinctive caution held her back from showing eagerness. She fixed a polite smile on her face, one she would turn on for an introduction to anyone. Her gaze, she was sure, reflected only a friendly interest as she lifted it to acknowledge him.

Choong! Two laser beams piercing her eyes and attacking her soul with lightning-bolt force!

Lauren felt like a stunned butterfly, pinned to a board for minute examination under a powerful microscope and utterly helpless to do anything about it. She had not braced herself enough. She vaguely sensed a declaration of war—*you cannot hide from me*—and the assault from his eyes—silver-grey eyes, like luminous stainless steel slicing through all her defensive levels—left her mind quivering and her body a mass of jangling nerve ends.

She must have offered her hand because she felt it being taken, hard warmth enclosing hers, male touching female, igniting an electric sense of sexuality, linking, testing, while his eyes still staked their claim on her, riveting in their concentrated quest for knowledge. And she couldn't tear her own away.

Lauren had never experienced anything like it in her whole life. Some tiny logical strain in her brain recited that this cataclysmic moment would pass. It had to. Time did move on. Soon she would make sense of this.

Soon...

CHAPTER FOUR

MICHAEL fought grimly against being completely thrown by the woman who stood before him. His first sight of her had been like a punch in the gut. Lauren Magee was everything Evan had said she was, and more—gorgeous, sexy, vibrant, vital, and that was before she had even opened her mouth and displayed the adept mind that could assess a situation, seize it and act positively to gain the result she wanted.

Tasha was now putty in her hands. Evan's fears were demolished. It was perfectly plain he was tickled pink by the attention Lauren Magee was giving to both of them. And it was such clever attention, striking the right note of caring and liking for Tasha and a delightfully open camaraderie with Evan.

Michael had clutched at cynicism to reduce her effect on him. Lauren Magee was exerting control over her impact, exercising manipulative skills, showing she was a superior being who could handle anything and anyone. Not him, he had fiercely vowed as she had turned to encompass him in her powerful radiance. He knew her for what she was!

With every atom of his brain and will he had penetrated the deceptive mask of polite interest, denying the distraction of her stunning blue eyes, seeking for the truth, scouring her soul for it. There had to be some trace of antagonism towards him, some sense of malicious triumph. She knew who he was now. She had to know what part she had played in ending his marriage.

Nothing! Nothing except a mesmerised wonder that tugged at his heart, making him feel like a marauding savage for not treating her tenderly. That had to be wrong. She was tricking him somehow.

He took hold of her hand, grasping it firmly, expecting at least a twinge of recoil. If she was true to her inner beliefs and judgments she had to react negatively to his touch. Yet her hand lay submissively in his, soft, delicately boned, seductively feminine, stirring sensations he didn't want to acknowledge.

Still that clear luminosity in her eyes. Nothing to hide. But there had to be. Unless…

She didn't know he was Roxanne's ex-husband.

It seemed incredible to Michael that Lauren Magee was ignorant of the connection, yet it was the only answer that made sense of her total lack of any discernible rejection of him. Had Roxanne been so disaffected that she hadn't bothered to identify him as the husband she sought advice about?

Keeping her precious maiden name of Kinsey might have muddied the tracks, or Roxanne could have assumed it was common knowledge she was married to Michael Timberlane. She had been proud to own him for the first year or two, though by the time Lauren Magee arrived in Sydney from

Melbourne, the shine had worn off that pride under the burden of trying to make their relationship gel in a workable fashion.

Easier for Roxanne to slide out of putting the effort in, Michael reflected cynically, and Lauren Magee had given her all the excuses to justify doing so. Yet she looked at him so innocently, so openly and honestly, waiting for him to write on the blank sheet that the meeting of strangers always offered, to give her a cue for what might develop between them from this moment, a moment cut free of any past and offering all the choices of possible futures.

He was tempted.

In any rational, objective sense, Lauren Magee was an anathema to him.

Yet he wanted her.

He wanted to empty her mind of all its clever reasoning and drive her insane with desire for him. He wanted to unpin the fiery mass of curls she had swirled into a topknot and see them spilling over a pillow in riotous abandonment. He wanted to tear off her sweater and fill his hands with the lush softness of those delectably rounded breasts that were thrusting so provocatively against the stretchy knit fabric.

And that sexy belt accentuating the feminine smallness of her waist and the sensual curve of her hips... He imagined stretching her white-skinned arms above her head, winding the wide black elastic around her wrists with the gold bow on top, holding her hands together so she couldn't weave her female magic on him while he took his fill of her.

Lauren Magee, submitting to the man she had reviled, giving herself to him, her long, elegant legs wrapped around him in supplication, in need, wanting him... Oh, yes, that would be sweet vengeance. And ravishing her luscious mouth, purging it of all the unjust words she'd said against him, replacing them with the intensely satisfying sounds of cries and gasps of pleasure.

His loins tightened. His heart thudded with the violent force of the warring feelings she stirred. His body zinged with shots of adrenaline as his mind played through one scenario after another, all of them erotic, all of them feeding the highly aroused savage inside him.

It took all of Michael's formidable willpower to clamp down on that rampant beast. Basic common sense insisted he play the civilised man. Fantasies were fantasies. Realities wiped out any chance of them happening anyway.

He might be a blank page to Lauren Magee right now, but the moment Roxanne turned up, he'd be history in her book. Roxanne would make certain of it. He only had a very limited time to play the game he had set out to play, getting in a few pointed shots that might just puncture Lauren Magee's confidence in dabbling with other people's lives.

It should be amusing to draw her out, to watch her natural response to him before Roxanne's axe fell.

And afterwards she would remember. Oh, yes, that keen, clever mind of Lauren Magee's would remember everything said between them, spoken and unspoken.

Michael told himself he would be satisfied with that. The trick was to keep his mind focused on the desired result, the only result that was really open to him.

CHAPTER FIVE

"I'M IMPRESSED."

Michael Timberlane's voice seemed to harmonise with the feelings he stirred, sliding to Lauren on a low, penetrating, intimate level.

"What by?" The words tripped from her tongue, breathless, husky, unconsidered, revealing how deeply she was caught in the thrall of possibilities pulsing between them.

"Your professionalism," he answered.

Did he know intuitively what was important to her? Excitement tingled through a welling of intense pleasure. Lauren wished she knew more of him. Was he married?

"Thank you," she returned warmly. "I do my best. As you do, by reputation."

"There are some who would say my best falls short of their expectations. Haven't you heard that, Ms. Magee?"

His hand slid away from hers. The withdrawal highlighted the unexpected formality of his address to her. Lauren felt confused. Why was he suddenly being off-putting?

"I'm sorry if you've been a target of ill will, Mr.

Timberlane,'' she said with a touch of sympathy. ''People's expectations are sometimes unrealistic.''

''And unreasonable,'' he shot back.

She hesitated, uncertain of where he was coming from or leading to. Wayne and his unreasonable expectations flitted through her mind. Maybe Michael Timberlane was still smarting from some personal or professional contretemps. With someone at Global? Was that what had made him look so forbidding earlier?

Lauren fell back on one of Graham Parker's pithy sayings, offering it with an ironic little smile. ''Well, Mr. Timberlane, I guess into each life some rain must fall.''

''You being the rainmaker?''

She laughed and shook her head. ''I like to think I spread sunshine.''

''The giver of light.'' He nodded, his silvery eyes gleaming satisfaction. ''Yes, that would be how you think of yourself.''

''And how do you think of yourself, Mr. Timberlane?''

He smiled, but it was a secretive, private smile, not an open, sharing one. ''Oh, I'm the sword of justice, Ms. Magee.''

Definitely on some personal high horse, Lauren thought, wanting to pull him down from it. ''Then I hope your balancing scales are in good order. Justice is so often blind,'' she said, tilting at him.

''How true!'' he agreed. ''It's unfortunate that so

many people's eyes aren't open to both sides of a situation before making judgments.''

"Are yours?''

"I always look at the big picture, Ms. Magee.''

"Never missing a piece of the jigsaw, Mr. Timberlane?'' she queried, niggled by his assumption of having all-seeing eyes. Nobody saw everything.

"Oh, for heaven's sake!'' Evan broke in jocularly. "What's all this Mr. and Ms.? We're at a party, not a stuffy reception.''

"One must be careful not to assume too much these days, Evan,'' Michael Timberlane answered his friend good-humouredly. "How do I know I'm not meeting a raging feminist who'll take offence at inappropriate familiarity?''

Evan laughed. "I'd think it's obvious Lauren isn't a raging feminist.''

"Appearances can be deceptive.'' Michael raised his eyebrows quizzically at Lauren. "Would you be so kind as to shed some light on the matter?''

Why did she have the sense he was playing out some secret agenda, toying with her, waiting to pounce if she didn't keep on her toes?

"You have my permission to call me Lauren,'' she said with a disarming smile, neatly sidestepping any argument about feminism.

"Then I shall not stand upon dignity,'' he replied with mock gravity. "Please feel free to call me Michael.''

Lauren laughed at him. There was a certain spice

to the game, a challenge. She couldn't recall any man ever having put her quite so much on her mettle before, certainly not at first meeting.

"I've never liked Ms.," Tasha remarked artlessly. "It sounds like a mosquito."

"I think that's spoken from the complacency of being a Mrs., Tasha," Michael reproved lightly. "Lauren may feel differently."

Another test, another nudge.

Tasha flushed, her brown eyes shining an apologetic appeal. "I'm sorry. I didn't think. I guess it has its place."

There was a fragile vulnerability, a simple innocence about Tasha Daniel that automatically touched Lauen's protective instinct. She was not street-wise, and with Evan as her husband had probably never had the need to become so. In a way, Lauren envied that, never having to confront the darker games men and women played.

"It saves making a mistake with Miss or Mrs.," she gently explained. "Like Mr., it doesn't carry the label of being single or married."

"Will you keep Ms. when you do marry?" Tasha asked curiously.

"That's assuming she wants to marry," Michael pointed out. "Many career women choose not to take on a commitment that could interfere with their life goals."

"Oh, dear!" Tasha pulled a rueful grimace. "I'm really putting my foot in it, aren't I?"

Lauren smiled to set her at ease again. "Being politically correct can be carried too far. I don't mind your questions, Tasha. I've been married, and I was very happy to be a Mrs. then."

Michael's face jerked towards her. Surprise. Reappraisal. Lauren had a sense of factors being shifted, energy zapping through him as his inner vision was rearranged.

"Now I'm divorced," she went on matter-of-factly, "the title of Miss is fine by me."

Tasha looked pained. "Another broken marriage. Michael's been through it, too. So sad…"

One revelation had bought another.

Michael Timberlane was divorced—single—free! The equation zipped through Lauren's brain, and she didn't feel sad at all. She felt as though wonderful fireworks were exploding in fabulous cascades of brilliant colour, lighting up a world that had been empty of dreams.

She was twenty-nine, looking down the barrel of thirty. Unattached, intriguing and attractive men like Michael Timberlane weren't exactly thick on the ground. Attractive was far too weak a word, she swiftly corrected. He was dynamite. He had both her mind and body shaken to acute awareness of all sorts of exciting possibilities.

Hope was definitely not dead!

"No reason to be sad, Tasha," Michael said. "It's a matter of statistics in today's society. Two out of three marriages end in divorce. You and Evan are the lucky ones. You should let us in on the secrets of your success.''

Tasha smiled and reached out her hand to her husband. ''It's wanting the same things,'' she said with moving simplicity. ''Isn't it, Evan?''

''Yes,'' he agreed, beaming his love at her as he took her hand and fondled it indulgently.

Lauren fought down an emotional lump in her throat. They were lucky to have found what they wanted in each other. She wondered what had gone wrong with Michael Timberlane's marriage. Who had left whom, and why?

''I didn't know you'd been married, Lauren,'' Evan commented with a look of puzzlement at her.

She shrugged, inwardly recoiling from that bad time. ''Does anyone like talking about their mistakes?''

Evan shook his head. ''I can't imagine why any man wouldn't fight tooth and nail to keep you with him.''

''I'll take that as a compliment,'' she said, smiling to hide the bitter irony behind it. Wayne had certainly fought to keep her with him. Abusively. On a sudden wave of fear, she turned to Michael Timberlane and bluntly asked, ''Did you fight to keep your wife?''

For one fleeting moment she saw a turbulent core of savagery flash through the windows of his soul. It sent a shiver down her spine. Then the silver screen of his extraordinarily compelling eyes clicked into place again, glistening with outward interest in her, reflecting nothing of what was within.

"It's difficult to fight a saboteur," he said with a sardonic twist. "The damage is done behind one's back."

He'd hate that, she thought.

"Besides, when the illusion of love and commitment has proven false, why fight to keep it?" he went on. "I'm a great believer in facing realities and moving on."

"Yes," she agreed, elated that he shared her attitude and convictions.

But it was one thing to leave the experience behind, another to forget. She wondered what damage he carried, what his wife had been like, why she had taken a lover? The reference to a saboteur pointed to another man in her life, and infidelity certainly destroyed the illusion of love and commitment.

"Do let's get off this painful subject," Tasha pleaded. "I wish I hadn't brought it up. This is a happy night."

"Indeed it is!" Lauren quickly supported her, switching on a bright smile. She didn't want this electric sense of anticipation tarnished by memories of relationships that had failed to bring the happiness they had initially promised. Determined not to brood on her past or Michael's, she turned teasingly to Evan. "I'm looking forward to your speech. It's your first public tryout, and I don't expect you to disappoint."

Evan pulled a doleful look. "Pressure, pressure.

My editor said the same thing. My wife wants me to shine. Michael thinks I don't need his applause…''

"I promise to clap if no one else does," Michael interposed.

"It's a wonderful speech," Tasha declared. "I know, because he's been rehearsing to me."

"Such loyalty is the voice of love, my darling," Evan said, almost purring. "And I appreciate it. I truly do."

They bantered on in light party style. Waitresses circulated with fancy finger food, Melba toast with smoked salmon, fish cocktails, spicy chicken legs, mini croissants with savoury fillings. Both Evan and Tasha helped themselves liberally, enjoying the novelty. Lauren wondered if Michael's stomach was in the same state as hers. Both of them declined everything offered.

"Dieting?" Michael asked at one point.

"No." She looked directly into his eyes. "Are you?"

"No."

There was a magnetic flash of unspoken but unmistakable recognition and understanding. Their hunger was for other things.

But would it be answered?

Lauren stayed at his side, wanting to know more of Michael Timberlane.

He was charm itself to Tasha and obviously a supportive friend to Evan, yet for the most part, he remained a tantalising enigma to her. The sexual attraction was strong and mutual. Nothing else could explain the vibrant energy field being generated between them. But she'd felt an awareness akin to this with Wayne and knew it could be treacherous. Perhaps Michael had similar thoughts, reflecting on his experience with his ex-wife.

Was the control he was exerting simply caution on his part, or did it conceal something darker? Was she flirting with danger? Was she willing to take a risk on pursuing this fascination with a stranger? Handsome men were usually spoilt men, she reminded herself, their egos too well fed from always getting their own way.

But Michael had shown consideration to Tasha.

Lauren found herself pushing caution aside and justifying the case for ignoring it altogether. For so long now she had trodden a safe path, and where had it led her? She was lonely. It was not a happy state, being lonely.

She wanted this excitement, this sense of being on the brink of something special. It was exhilarating. She felt so alive. She wanted to turn to Michael Timberlane and say, *Don't hide from me,* but she wasn't quite bold enough to do it. Besides, if he was the man for her, he would decide to involve himself further without any pushing.

She willed him to want to.

"Evan…" Beth Hayward, Evan's editor, broke into their foursome. "They're getting ready for the speeches.'' She smiled at the glass in his hand. ''Had enough drinks to fortify you?''

She was six years older than Lauren, a striking brunette, stylish and very much a woman of the world. She wore a long grey skirt and a cowl top in black and white and grey. It was a smart, fashionable, sophisticated outfit. Lauren glanced at Michael, sensing a sudden coiling of tension in him.

His face had hardened, wearing the same closed expression she had noted earlier when he had left Beth with the Daniels to collect the table and chairs. Was there some conflict between them? They would have done business together many times, since Beth was a commissioning editor for Global.

''I feel warm and convivial but definitely not fuzzy,'' Evan declared. ''Where am I wanted?''

Beth nodded towards the bar. ''Up that end of the room.'' She smiled at Michael. ''Perhaps you could bring a chair for Tasha, because they'll probably go on for a while.''

''We'll look after her comfort,'' Lauren assured Evan, coupling herself with Michael.

Beth darted a sharply speculative look between Lauren and Michael, then frowned as though niggled by some problem. Her gaze fell on the gift packages, still lying on the table. ''I see you've collected your souvenirs. Better not leave them behind,'' she advised. ''They're all gone from the display table.''

''I'll take them with me,'' Tasha said, quickly gathering them up.

Beth looked directly at Lauren with a curious expression that seemed to convey some loaded meaning. "A pity Roxanne sprained her ankle this afternoon and couldn't come to the party. Do you know—"

Crash! Broken glass and spilled wine scattered and splashed across the floor right next to Michael. A drinks tray had toppled from a waiter's hand, and the people closest to the disaster area scuttled back with cries of shock and dismay at being spattered.

Michael wheeled and gestured an apologetic appeal at the hapless waiter. "I'm so sorry! Did I bump you?"

"Not to worry, sir. These things happen with a crowd."

"Let me help." He crouched to pick up the tray.

"No, please leave it, sir," the waiter protested emphatically. "Staff will be here in a moment to do the necessary."

"Damn! Red wine on my skirt!" Beth muttered in vexation. "Excuse me, I'm off to the powder room. Evan, don't dally. It's time to move." She didn't wait for him, frustration and impatience with the mishap getting the better of courtesy.

Michael straightened and pulled a rueful grimace. "Not my best party trick."

"Well, it can't be helped now," Tasha said sympathetically. "Do go on, Evan. Michael and Lauren will see to me."

"Front row seat," Michael promised. He clapped his friend on the shoulder. "Off you toddle, and mind you do us proud.'' He grinned, his face lighting up with undiluted good humour. ''You can hold up the bar until you're wanted for your party piece.''

Lauren couldn't help staring at the startling trans-formation a wicked grin made to Michael Timberlane's face. She had thought him handsome before, certainly enough to spark her interest at first sight of him. But the difference now was heart-stopping. A grin like that would cause any woman considerable internal havoc. Lauren was no exception.

She vaguely heard Evan and Tasha exchange a few words, then Evan started weaving his way through the crowd and Michael turned to her, the grin still lurking, his silver eyes gleaming with some wild and reckless satisfaction that instantly encompassed her.

Her pulse kicked into a faster beat. Her mind throbbed with the knowledge he was going to ride the current that flowed between them. No more stand off. No pulling back. He had decided.

She felt the glow of a wild and reckless satisfaction grow inside herself. She had willed this from him. *So let it be,* she thought, *wherever it might lead.*

She repressed the thought that it could be danger-ous.

She didn't wonder, Why now? What had changed from a few moments ago?

She made no connection whatsoever between Michael Timberlane's decision and the accidental tip-ping over of a tray.

She forgot about Beth Hayward and whatever she was going to tell her about Roxanne.

She was brilliantly, vibrantly, idiotically happy!

CHAPTER SIX

MICHAEL could barely tear his eyes away from her to make the coffee. Lauren Magee in his apartment, not wanting the night to end any more than he did. Not the Lauren of *Lauren says*. It was utterly absurd to even vaguely relate this woman to Roxanne's ally in castrating men.

False impressions, lies… He shook his head, dismissing them all. The reality was this magical enchantress who offered him everything he'd ever dreamed of in a woman. Her openness delighted him. Her intelligence, her uninhibited sexuality, her honest expression and acceptance of her feelings made her incredibly special.

Maybe he should tell her about Roxanne, get it out of the way. But Lauren hadn't brought up her ex-husband. Those marriages were mistakes. Neither of them had known what it could be like with the right person. As Lauren had said to Evan, nobody likes talking about their mistakes. Why waste time that could be better spent exploring what was happening between them?

''You are so lucky to have such a fantastic view! she said with a long, appreciative sigh.

Yes, he thought, looking at her drinking in the harbour vista through the floor-to-ceiling windows in his sunken living room. The opera house, the bridge, the watercraft in and out of Circular Quay provided a feast of glittering spectacles, but she outshone them. Her shoes were off, her glorious hair unpinned, the seductive curves of her femininity silhouetted in soft lamplight, and he whimsically wondered if she'd ever been painted. He mentally ran through the artists he knew. Who could do her justice?

She turned to look at him behind the kitchen counter on the mezzanine level. "Are you terribly rich, Michael?" she asked.

No-one had ever asked that question quite so frankly. He grinned at her, amused by her total lack of artfulness. "Should I admit it or conceal it?"

"Are you wondering what effect your reply will have on me?"

"I suspect, none."

She laughed. "I'm not here for your money. I said yes to your invitation before I even knew you drove a BMW. But such an expensive car and this apartment, both of which you seem to take for granted…"

"Does that offend you?"

"No." She shrugged. "I just want to know about you."

He pressed the plunger on the coffee grains as he considered how best to answer.

"Does it bother you, Michael?" she asked quietly.

"I guess rich is the wrong word. I have never felt rich…until tonight." He met her gaze and spoke the truth as he knew it. "To be rich is to have things of great value, Lauren. I've never valued wealth because I've had it all my life and it can't give you what you really want."

"Are we talking great wealth here?"

"Mmm…" He poured out the coffee, picked up the tray he'd set and carried it down to the living room. "Goes back to the last century. The Timberlanes were highly successful merchants. Owned ships and docking yards and auction houses. Lots of investments in city property and businesses."

Lauren frowned. "But you're not a high-profile family. I've never heard or read about you in that sense."

"A very quiet establishment family," he agreed. "Besides, I'm the only one left living in Australia. I have a brother who prefers Monaco and an aunt who has long been settled in Italy."

She looked appalled. "What happened to the rest of your family?"

"Wealth does not prevent death." He set the tray on a glass table. "Cream? Sugar?"

She helped herself. They settled on one of the leather chesterfields and she regarded him pensively. "Why a literary agent?"

"I like encouraging authors and getting their books published. They give a lot of pleasure to others."

He would never have survived his boyhood without books and the escape they provided, not with any sanity, but he didn't want to rake over those old nightmares. He didn't want her sympathy. He wanted her warmth, the total inner essence of Lauren Magee.

"Do you come from a large family?" he asked.

"Yes." She laughed. "Five brothers and three sisters, plus innumerable aunts and uncles and cousins. You could say the Magees went forth and multiplied at a profligate rate. They all have big families."

"Then you can count yourself as very rich, indeed."

"Yes. Though I…" She checked herself. "Well, I'll get to see them soon. I'm glad you're not an idle playboy. I like my work, too."

"Tell me how you got into it," he invited, genuinely interested in knowing.

"Communication, public relations…"

She talked about the various jobs she'd held, moving up to publicist for a publisher. A natural progression, Michael thought, and pondered the one telling comment that her ex-husband had disliked her work. The man could not have really loved her. Anyone with eyes could see that Lauren lived and breathed the publicity mill. Using it as brilliantly as she obviously did was an expression of herself, her unique talents and abilities.

She was such a joy to watch, so vital, her eyes the blue of summer skies bathing him with sparkling sunshine, heating him with a simmering brew of desires he could barely contain. The right woman. Coming from a big family, she would be sure to want children herself. Beautiful breasts. Voluptuous hips. Long, elegant, sexy legs. She could even match him dancing. Everything right.

The urge to reach out and pull her into full body contact with him made his hands itch. She had to feel the need, too. The coffee was cold in their cups, forgotten, untouched by either of them. If she wanted to leave, she would have said so by now. Was it assuming too much to want everything on the first night?

Let there be truth between us, he thought with passionate intensity as he stood and took her hands, drawing her to her feet and into a loose embrace that didn't demand or presume. Her eyes were wide, waiting for him to speak his mind, her body softly pliant, no resistance. The desire raging through him could not be denied.

"I want you, Lauren," he said, his voice raw with urgency.

"Yes," she answered with a soft expulsion of breath.

"Are you protected?"

"No."

"I'll take care of it."

"I'd appreciate that."

So direct, so honest in her desire for him. It almost blew Michael's mind, as well as other strained parts of his anatomy. He lifted a hand to touch the softness of her cheek, trailed his fingers into the silken curls of her hair. Her lips parted invitingly. Her eyes swam with hopes and dreams.

"Not here," he said gruffly, barely recognising his own voice. "Come all the way with me, Lauren."

"Yes."

He led her upstairs to his bedroom.

Her mouth was passion.

Her hair was erotic sensuality.

Her breasts were intoxicating.

Her hands were hypnotic pleasure.

Her legs were seductive silk.

And the inner essence of Lauren Magee…was ecstasy.

Michael loved her as he'd never loved a woman before, with unbridled passion, uninhibited fervour, wild exultation and the freedom—the amazingly sweet freedom—of fulfilling his every desire and meeting always the most exquisite response. Perfection. Bliss. Pleasure on a scale he had never imagined possible. And she gave it him. Lauren. The woman of his dreams.

It made up for everything else—the neglect of his parents who had never been there for him and his younger brother, Peter, even when they were alive; the oppression of his childhood under the cold domination of his grandmother; the loneliness of boarding school; the sense of not belonging at Oxford and Harvard; the alienation from his brother, who saw no point in working at anything; the bitter disillusionment of his marriage to Roxanne.

He should tell Lauren about Roxanne.

Tomorrow.

Tonight belonged to them. The future belonged to them. He could see it, taste it, feel it. And it was right.

CHAPTER SEVEN

THE morning after... The phrase flitted through Lauren's mind as she rode to work on the bus, and she almost laughed out loud at its connotations of shock and regrets and subsequent blues. None of it applied to how she felt.

It was as though her bloodstream was bubbling with joy. A sparkling zest for life sharpened all her senses. She was in love—madly, deliciously, wonderfully in love—and she didn't regret one moment of the risks she had taken. Not one.

This time yesterday, if someone had told her she would meet a man, fall head over heels in love and go to bed with him, all on the same night, she would have responded to the prediction with outright disbelief. No chance. She wasn't that kind of woman. She had her head on straight. Impulsive sexual adventures were not her style, never had been, never would be. Making love should be something special with someone special.

And it had been. Lauren closed her eyes and hugged the memory of all the marvellous sensations Michael had made her feel. He was a fantastic lover, wildly passionate, incredibly sensual, erotic and tender, powerful and playful. Lauren had never

55

known a night like it. Wayne… But she wasn't going to think about her ex-husband any more. Her life had definitely taken an upward turn with Michael Timberlane.

She wondered if she should have woken him before leaving his apartment this morning. It had been tempting, just to share a last kiss, a last smile, the mutual knowledge of how incredibly magical their coming together had been. But he would have delayed her, and she'd barely had time enough to whiz to the house she shared at Chatswood, change her clothes for work and catch her usual bus to Artarmon. Besides, the note she had left him said it all.

The bus came to a ponderous halt. It was her stop. Lauren leapt from her seat and pushed quickly past the standing passengers to the opened door. She alighted on the sidewalk with a spring in her step and only just suppressed the urge to skip and twirl down the street to her office building.

Michael had danced her off her feet last night. He was the best. The very best. At everything! She was so lucky to have met him, lucky the attraction was mutual, lucky to be alive and sharing the world Michael Timberlane occupied.

A song started playing through her mind. It was ''I Feel Pretty'' from *West Side Story*. Only last week she'd seen the revival of the original stage production, currently showing at the Capital Theatre. She remembered the exhilaration coursing through Maria following her meeting with Tony, the high spirits that had fired the song with its lovely lilt of exhuberant happiness. It was precisely how Lauren felt.

She was still singing it in her head as she entered Global's foyer and walked jauntily to the elevators. The receptionist, Sue Carroll, spotted her and called out, "Hey! That was some hot dancing last night, Lauren. How did you latch onto Michael Timberlane?"

"He was with Evan Daniel," Lauren answered offhandedly, unwilling to feed Sue's penchant for gossip.

"Of course. Your current project." Sue's smile was a twist of irony. "Well, the macho Michael sure surprised me, loosening up like that. The few times he's come through here, you'd think he was encased in ice. Cold, forbidding and untouchable."

His manner had undoubtedly piqued her. Sue enjoyed a bit of chitchat and loved to know everybody's business. Apart from that, no attractive young woman, even married as Sue was, liked to be frozen out by a handsome man. With her chic pageboy bob and shiny brown eyes, pretty face and petite figure, Sue tended to court male attention and usually got it.

"Maybe the party atmosphere thawed him," Lauren suggested tactfully as the elevator doors opened.

"Or something more basic."

Lauren laughed off the dry comment and hurried into the compartment, waving to Sue while pressing the button for her floor and exulting with private certainty that it was she who had melted the ice. It was interesting, though, that Sue had been subjected to the forbidding look Lauren had observed last night. Obviously Michael didn't open up to many people, but when he did… Lauren breathed a sweet sigh of satisfaction. Dynamite!

She walked briskly from the elevator to her office, happy to return greetings from fellow workers but not encouraging any discourse about last night's party. No-one would understand what had happened between herself and Michael, and she didn't want to make light of it. There would inevitably be comments like Sue Carroll's to field. For the moment, however, Lauren preferred to defer them.

Once in her office, she switched on her computer, collected the faxes that had come in and settled at her desk. Her inner happiness bubbled up again at the memory of Michael's appreciation of her work. He knew how important good promotion was in launching a new book on the market. Far from denigrating or resenting or dismissing her job, as Wayne had, Michael had shown he would be right behind her in everything she tried to achieve.

To be able to talk freely about it, to share ideas with someone who was receptive and constructive in bouncing ideas back…that was sheer heaven to Lauren. It was wonderful to have books in common. For Michael, too, it was surely more pleasurable to be with a woman who comprehended what his business entailed.

Though there were plenty of women in the publishing industry who would be attuned to it. Like Beth Hayward. Recalling Michael's tension at Beth's approach last night, Lauren wondered if there had been something between them. Not that it mattered now.

Having dismissed the speculation, Lauren skimmed through the faxes, noting replies that had to be made and appointments that had to be changed. She was updating her schedules when Graham Parker dropped by, bringing her a cup of coffee.

"Nursing a hangover?" he asked, looking somewhat seedy himself.

She smiled. "No, but thanks for the thought."

He set her mug carefully on the desk then sagged slowly onto the spare chair, holding his own mug gingerly. "Oh, to be young and full of boundless energy," he intoned.

"I take it you overindulged."

"They were serving a very good red."

Lauren knew his wife was to have met him at the party, so no doubt she had driven him home. "Well, so long as it was worth it," she said, barely repressing outright amusement at his hangdog expression.

He gave her a doleful look. "I hope it was for you, too."

"I'm not suffering," she reminded him.

"You will. Believe me, you will."

His conviction puzzled her. "How so?"

"I know Roxanne. The classic dog-in-the-manger attitude will click in the moment she hears."

"Hears what?"

He frowned at her as though she was definitely thick in the head. "Correct me if I'm wrong, dear girl, but were you not tripping the light fantastic with Michael Timberlane last night? Or should I say, exploring the modern boundaries of dirty dancing?"

Lauren grinned. "He's certainly got rhythm."

"Yes. My wife considered him as good as John Travolta. A high accolade, indeed, considering how many times she's watched what she calls classic Travolta movies."

The sardonic comment did not enlighten her. "So what point are you making, Graham?"

"Oh, far be it from me to question chemistry. If you want to get involved with Michael Timberlane, that's entirely your business. I merely perceive the thunderclouds gathering on the horizon." He sighed. "I guess I'm going to get rained on again."

"Why should you?"

"Because Roxanne won't like it, and she'll pour out her umpteen million reasons, and as her closest associate, I'll cop it more than you will. She might not have any use for her ex-husband, but I very much doubt she'll take kindly to—"

"Her *ex-husband*?" Shock and incredulity billowed through Lauren's mind.

"You didn't know he was He Who Demandeth Too Much?" Graham was startled out of his air of bleak resignation.

"Michael Timberlane is Mikey the Monster?" Lauren squeaked, her voice rising uncontrollably as her mind fought to relate the man she had met last night to the husband who had made Roxanne miserable. The two images simply did not mesh in any shape or form.

"The Dump Merchant," Graham expounded, nodding gravely.

"How could she call him Mikey?" It was a cry of protest against what she didn't want to accept.

"A need to diminish him. The guy is formidable. Roxanne couldn't live up to him. Simple psychology," Graham answered in his best pithy style.

"But…" Lauren floundered, shattered by her ignorance. "Her name is Kinsey."

"Maiden name. It's still Kinsey, even though she's married again," Graham pointed out. "Roxanne clings to it because it has status. Being from Melbourne, you're probably not aware that generations of Kinseys have held high office in the New South Wales government. Kinsey equals power. Timberlane is also old establishment, but most of that family has died off. Not very useful for Roxanne, who got her job here because someone who knew someone…"

Lauren groaned, appalled that probably everyone on Global's staff had been titillated by her social involvement with Roxanne's ex-husband, doubly appalled that she could have been so completely misled by a man who, according to Roxanne, was every bit as soul-crushing as Wayne.

"Sorry." Graham offered a rueful grimace. "I thought you were being brave."

"Stupidly reckless, you mean."

"Not necessarily. Horses for courses. You're made of sterner stuff than Roxanne."

"Not that stern." Her eyes flashed bitter determination. "I'm through with fighting to be me. I don't need another bout of it, thank you very much."

"Oh, I wouldn't take too much notice of Roxanne's self-serving diatribes against him," Graham said dryly. "She didn't really want a man. She wanted a sugar daddy. And that's precisely what she's married now."

Lauren was not consoled. The blissful confidence she'd had in her response to Michael Timberlane was in tatters. Gone were her buoyant spirits. Gone were her high hopes. Was she doomed to be attracted to the wrong kind of man? Perhaps it was Roxanne who had her head on straight, choosing a sugar daddy who was happy to give her everything she wanted in return for simply being herself with him.

Graham pushed himself up from the chair and gestured apologetically. "I didn't mean to drop a bombshell on you, Lauren."

"That's okay. Best that I know," she said flatly.

"One man's meat is another man's poison. Same with women. Forget Roxanne and go with your gut feeling," he advised kindly, then gave her a crooked smile. "I can weather the storm in my department."

"Thanks, Graham." Her smile was wry. "Unfortunately, my experience tells me my gut feeling isn't wonderfully trustworthy.''

''Up to you,'' he said with a shrug, and left her to mull over the madness that had consumed her last night.

Or was it madness?

She was older, wiser now than she'd been in the dizzy days of being swept along by Wayne's ardent courtship. Last night with Michael, she hadn't overlooked any false notes or responses that grated on her sense of harmony with him. There had been none. That was what had been so marvellous about everything. All those hours together and every minute of it sheer pleasure, once he had made up his mind to take a chance with her.

She could understand his wariness about associating with anyone at Global, apart from what his business necessitated. Global was Roxanne's stamping ground. Lauren acknowledged that she would certainly be reluctant to involve herself with anyone who worked with Wayne. Broken marriages did create conflict of interests areas.

It was little wonder he assumed a forbidding demeanour to anyone attached to Roxanne's milieu. No doubt he had only gone to Global's party out of friendship's sake, to provide company for Tasha Daniel while Evan gave his speech. Lauren had to respect him for that gesture alone. He couldn't have known beforehand that Roxanne wouldn't be there.

Though he did know she was not about to turn up

after Beth Hayward had mentioned Roxanne's sprained ankle. Lauren remembered the sudden change in him, the casting aside of any inhibitions about showing he was attracted to her. Perhaps it was because the possible threat of Roxanne causing an unpleasant scene had been removed.

Lauren began to question Roxanne's version of her ex-husband's behaviour. Last night, when Michael had spoken of a saboteur, Lauren had assumed his ex-wife had taken a lover. If Roxanne had been unfaithful, there could be reason for him to demand an account of her time. Which had come first, the sense of oppression from Michael or the betrayal of his trust?

Lauren could well imagine Roxanne justifying her own behaviour by heaping blame on Michael. Probably the only way she could feel good about herself was by gaining sympathy for her course of action. When it came to the bottom line, Lauren readily conceded that Roxanne would never qualify as a bosom friend, whereas Michael could be the right man for her.

Hope dusted off the bleak desolation that had descended at Graham's revelation, but the bubble of undiluted happiness did not bounce back. A sense of caution kept it tightly confined. Despite her intense desire to dismiss all Roxanne's complaints against Michael, Lauren couldn't quite do it. The seeds of doubt had too much fertile ground to feed on from the hurts and disillusionment that had ended her own marriage.

She would give her gut feeling a chance to prove correct. After last night, it would be cowardly not to. Graham was right. She had to trust her own judgment. It wouldn't be fair to Michael otherwise.

Her telephone rang.

Satisfied she had sorted out her mind concerning Michael, Lauren focused her concentration on work as she picked up the receiver. "Lauren Magee," she said expectantly.

"Are you completely mad, Lauren?" Roxanne sounded peeved, pettish and sniping full bore.

"I beg your pardon." Some dousing dignity was called for.

"I can't believe you let Michael Timberlane sweep you off after all I've told you about him," Roxanne raged.

"I'm sorry. I've never heard you mention Michael Timberlane, Roxanne." And that was the cold, hard truth.

Silence. Some heavy breathing. "You didn't know he was my ex-husband?"

"How could I? We've never met before last night, and you always referred to your ex-husband as Mikey." Lauren screwed up her nose at the inappropriate little-boy name.

"Oh, my God! Did he know you didn't know?"

"I would think it was obvious. To me he was a perfect stranger." Maybe that had influenced his decision, too, knowing she wasn't prejudiced against him.

"Lauren, you didn't go to bed with him, did you?"

She bristled. "Aren't you being highly personal, Roxanne?"

"This *is* personal. He hates you, Lauren. Nothing would give him more satisfaction than to seduce you and have you begging for more."

A horrible chill crawled down Lauren's spine at the vehement conviction in Roxanne's voice. "Why?" she asked brusquely. "Why should he hate me?"

"We used to have fights over what you said."

"What do you mean? I never said anything to him. I didn't know him."

"I mean when I threw your advice at him. He just couldn't take it. He started calling you the feminist saboteur in his sneering, superior way. Believe me, he hates you, Lauren. If you could have seen the savage look in his eyes whenever I brought up your name. Pure venom."

Shock didn't roll through Lauren's mind this time. It hit like jackhammer punches.

Feminist! Saboteur!

She felt sick. That was what had been going through Michael's mind during all that talk with Tasha and Evan. The savage flash in his eyes—it had been directed at her, not a memory. And once he realised Roxanne would not be coming to the party—the accident with the waiter, stopping Beth from blurting out his connection to Roxanne, was a very timely party trick, clearing the path to put his vengeful plan into action.

No, her heart screamed.

But it all added up.

"Look, I understand if he got to you," Roxanne went on. "He's a very sexy male animal when he decides to put out. But I'm warning you, Lauren. He'll turn on you as fast as look at you when it suits him. I hope you didn't let him have his rotten triumph over you."

Lauren gritted her teeth and swallowed the bile that had surged up her throat. "Triumph?" she repeated raggedly.

"He reckoned what you needed was a real man who'd knock all the feminist starch out of you and melt you into a human being. He would have gone all out to achieve that, and if he did…"

"I see. Well, thank you for calling, Roxanne," she managed stiffly and hung up, hating the thought that Michael might boast he had made her melt. Over and over again.

The perfect stranger. She should have realised he was too perfect to be real. Anyone could sustain an act for a night, especially if he knew what would strike a false note with her. Michael Timberlane was a highly intelligent man. He'd sucked her right in with his blend of sexiness and sensitivity to her desires and needs.

The telephone rang again. She hesitated, then berated herself for letting him affect her so deeply that she didn't want to take what might be an important call. Work was work, and it was far more reliable than people, she thought fiercely. At least she could count on herself to get it as right as she could in that area of her life. She picked up the receiver, but her voice was momentarily disconnected because of the miserable muddle in her mind.

"Lauren? It's Michael." Said with a soft lilt of anticipation.

Her stomach clenched. The arch-deceiver himself! If he thought she was about to rush in and beg for more, he could think again. "Yes?" she queried, her mind suddenly cold and clear.

"I found your note. It was a great night for me, too." Purring with pleasure.

"I'm glad it was mutual," she replied silkily, waiting for the perfect line to turn the knife.

He laughed. "Couldn't be more so. When do you think you'll finish work tonight?"

"Oh, I don't know. What do you want, Michael?" That was a good question. Let him beg!

"To be with you again as soon as you're free."

She deliberately heaved a sigh. "Look, Michael, it was a great night. A really great night. Let's leave it at that, shall we?"

Silence. "Come again?" He sounded puzzled, disbelieving.

Lauren went for the kill. "Well, the fact of the matter is I don't go in for repeat performances. Why spoil a perfect memory?"

"Performance?" he repeated harshly.

Got you, you rat!

"Mmm." It was the hum of satisfaction. She injected some warmth into her voice. Warm poison. "I've got to hand it to you, Michael. You certainly delivered. Thanks again. It was great."

She hung up to punctuate the finality of her farewell. And if that didn't turn the tables on his rotten triumph, she didn't know what would. A savage little smile curled her mouth. Vengeance could be sweet.

CHAPTER EIGHT

THEIR taxi was cruising towards Mascot. Lauren checked her watch. The flight to Melbourne was scheduled to leave at five. Domestic aircraft rarely departed on time. They would have a good twenty-five minutes to collect their tickets, check in their luggage, get their seat allocations and relax with a drink in the Golden Wing lounge.

It had been a long, exhausting day, racing between the ABC studios at Ultimo for the radio spots and the other venues for magazine interviews. Evan Daniel had performed well overall, gaining confidence and a dash of panache as he became more practised at handling the questions thrown at him. He was riding a high. Lauren felt totally limp.

It was as though last week's highly charged encounter with Michael Timberlane had drained something vital out of her. She wasn't sleeping well. Doing anything required a conscious effort. She forced herself to follow the schedules she set, but somehow she couldn't lift herself out of this…this slough of despondency. Sometimes she even wished she was dead.

The taxi was beetling along, the driver seemingly unconcerned that the cars in front of him were stopped at a red traffic light. Did he expect it to change? Alarm shot through Lauren's nerves. Couldn't he see?

"I say," Evan started weakly.

Lauren screamed.

The driver snapped alert, slammed on the brakes and the tyres burnt rubber to a squealing halt, millimetres from the stationary traffic ahead of them. Brakes shrieked from the car behind them as it narrowly avoided crashing into the back of the taxi.

"Sorry," their driver mumbled.

Evan turned from the front seat to check on Lauren. "Are you okay?"

"Yes," she replied shakily, then with a dark look at the back of their driver's head, added, "I would like to get to the airport in one piece though."

"I think I need a double gin," Evan said with feeling.

It didn't sound like a bad idea to Lauren, either, although the adrenaline kick of the near accident had proved one thing to her. She definitely didn't want to be dead. There was life after inattentive taxidrivers and Michael Timberlane. It was up to her to make the best of it. And she would. Somehow.

It had only been a week since the disastrous morning after. Perhaps she had been subconsciously grieving a lost dream. This trip to Melbourne should lift her spirits. Tonight she would visit her mother and whatever family was at home. It was always heartwarming to be with people whom she cared about and who cared about her. Lauren didn't want anything to do with hatred. It was a destructive emotion.

It was a relief to leave the errant taxi and enter the bustle of the terminal. Here were people on the move, going somewhere, doing something, excitement, adventure, change… Lauren loved the mood of airports. The check-in went smoothly, and anticipation began to tingle through her as they rode the escalator up to the waiting areas. She was flying home.

The Golden Wing lounge seemed packed when they entered. "I'll look for some seats while you get your drink, Evan," Lauren offered.

"No problem. Michael should have bagged a table somewhere."

"Michael?" Her heart fluttered.

"Ah, there he is!" Evan said with satisfaction, pointing to a window table across the room from the bar.

Lauren's heart dropped to the floor. The dark, striking figure of Michael Timberlane, lounging at ease, idly perusing a business magazine, burned through her retinas and stamped itself on her quivering mind. Her peripheral vision took in the two chairs grouped with his, one occupied by a flight bag, the other by a newspaper. He was expecting them, waiting for them.

Goosebumps broke out on Lauren's skin. She wasn't finished with him. He wasn't going to let her be finished with him. Just like Wayne. He had his own agenda, and to hell with what she wanted!

Rebellion stirred, pumping her heart into its rightful

place. If Michael Timberlane thought he could get at her again, he was in for a big surprise. The trick was to act as though this meeting was totally inconsequential to her. Which it was. She would get that message across to him if it killed her.

She forced her legs to follow Evan as he picked his way towards his friend. *Head high,* she advised herself, and fiercely wished she'd pinned her hair up this morning. It was wildly afloat around her shoulders, and Michael had made almost a fetish of it in their lovemaking. Such a reminder was unwelcome, but it had to be borne with an air of carelessness.

She was glad she was wearing a tailored slacks suit. If Michael Timberlane wanted to make something feminist of that, let him. At least it didn't mould her body in any overt way, not even with the jacket off. She had added a jazzy little vest featuring white reindeers on bands of mustard and black, and it neatly skimmed the curves her black skivvy and slacks would have outlined. Except for her hair, she presented a smartly professional appearance.

''We got here!'' Evan announced, alerting Michael to their arrival. ''No thanks to the taxi driver who gave us one hell of a fright.''

''Oh?'' Michael queried as he put his magazine aside and rose to his feet, looking sleek, dangerous and disturbingly virile in blue jeans and a black leather jacket.

''If Lauren hadn't screamed, I reckon we would

have crashed for sure,'' Evan went on with the relish of a storyteller.

A sardonic smile was directed at her. ''I congratulate you on your timely screaming, Lauren.''

''It took siren strength to wake the driver,'' she said, jollying the story along, pretending his presence had no import to her.

His silvery eyes swept a glittering glance over her hair, then shot piercing derision at her as he observed, ''When it comes to siren quality, you certainly have it in quantity.''

So the knives were out, Lauren thought. No intent to seduce again. This was counter-kill time. Which suited her just fine. Where Michael Timberlane was concerned, she was armour-plated.

She smiled at Evan. ''If you're going to have a drink…''

''You bet I am.'' He grinned and patted his stomach. ''Needs some settling down. What will you have, Lauren? You can fill Michael in on our drama while I get our medicinal measures.''

''A lemon squash will be fine for me.''

''You're joking!''

''No. I find alcohol drying on flights.''

''There's an easy solution to that. Drink more.'' Evan advised.

She shook her head. No way was she going to fuzz her brain in the present circumstances. If she'd drunk less champagne the last time she was with Michael

Timberlane, she might not have lost her head in a cloud of rosy dreams.

"Lemon squash," Evan conceded with mock disgust. "What can I get you, Michael?"

"I'll join you in a gin."

"Double?"

"Why not?"

Evan grinned at the ready camaraderie from his friend. "A Waki special coming up," he promised and headed to the bar.

Michael leaned over and lifted the flight bag off the chair opposite his. "Have a seat," he invited.

"Thank you."

It was a comfortable tub chair, and Lauren deliberately struck a relaxed pose, settling back against the cushioned upholstery, laying her arms openly on the armrests and crossing her legs. If Michael Timberlane was adept at reading body language, the message she was projecting was as easygoing as she could get. Lauren was not about to show him any sign of tension.

He adopted a more casual posture, elbows on the armrests, hands dangling loosely, one foot resting on the other knee. He surveyed her slowly from head to toe, a deliberate stripping, meant to shame and unsettle her. Lauren wished she could do the same to him but found she couldn't carry it off.

The blue chambray shirt he wore was open-necked. When her eyes hit the springy black curls nesting below the base of his throat, the memory of their intimacy was triggered too forcefully. She didn't want to face it. She turned her gaze to the window and looked at the aircraft lined up at their boarding tunnels. Baggage was being loaded into the closest one. Watching that process was pleasantly mind-numbing.

"Do you have business in Melbourne?" she asked when it became obvious he did not intend offering any conversation. If he had some battle plan against her she preferred some warning of what to expect.

Silence.

She directed a look of polite enquiry at him, determined to show his rudeness did not affect her.

"No," he answered, a mocking challenge in his eyes.

"But you are flying with us," she persisted, wanting at least the present situation clarified.

"Yes, I'm coming along for the ride."

"Why?"

"I guess you could say I'm riding shotgun for Evan and Tasha."

She frowned. "You think they need protecting?"

"Yes. You may consider it rather quaint of me, but I care about them. They're meaningful people in my life. And God knows I've found few enough of them."

The sarcasm cut. It was difficult to ignore. "Who would want to hurt them?" she asked. None of the interviews she had lined up were in the go-for-the-jugular category. It was all human-interest fare; easy, informative, entertaining.

"You."

"Me?" She stared incredulously at him.

"Don't come the innocent, Lauren," he said harshly, his eyes flashing contempt. "I've been there with you and know what's at the end of it. If Evan is chalked up as your next dalliance, I aim to prevent it."

Hatred, hard and violent, coming at her in heart-jolting, throat-constricting, mind-jamming waves. Lauren had never been subjected to anything like it before. For several moments she could do nothing but sit in mesmerised horror at what had been wrought in him by her act of vengeance.

She collected herself with difficulty. He hated her before she even met him, she reasoned. He deserved everything she had handed out for having played so falsely with her. There was no cause for guilt or shame on her part.

Nevertheless, it was frightening that her ego wounding had fired his hatred to such a high level of intensity. Would he do her harm if he got the chance? More harm than he had already done with *his* act of vengeance? Had he poisoned Evan's mind against her?

No. The answer was swift and certain. Evan was treating her no differently. His personality was too open to cover up any harbouring of ill will towards her. There had been no confidences. This was a private thing, a deep festering of wounds that cut to the innermost core of Michael Timberlane.

"I don't dally with married men," she stated flatly, wanting at least that part of his picture of her corrected.

"What a nice distinction." Pure acid. "If true."

She shrugged. "Believe what you like, Michael." Her mouth twisted with irony. "You will, anyway."

"I keep thinking of your poor sucker of a husband. No wonder he didn't like your job," he drawled. "All those convenient hotel rooms and a quick change of authors to provide variety. How many notches have you got on your belt, Lauren?"

He was so far off beam she could let his offensiveness float over her. She raised a taunting eyebrow. "Hurt pride, Michael?"

"Curiosity." His thin-lipped smile deflected the hit. "As a specimen of the modern female, you're quite an interesting study, Lauren."

"I do hope you're open-minded enough to take response to stimuli into consideration," she said sweetly. "You were—" she fluttered her gaze from his chest to his thighs in a deliberate parody of his sexual survey "—very stimulating."

She saw the powerful leg muscles tauten against the stretch denim of his jeans and felt a savage triumph at having affected him, despite his contemptuous attitude towards her.

"But you prefer a change of flesh," he said, rushing to the worst judgment again.

She raised her gaze, subjecting him to a mocking challenge. "Do I? Leaping to conclusions from faulty assumptions does not strike me as a sound way of conducting a study. Where's your body of evidence, Michael?''

His mouth curled. ''You gave it to me, Lauren.''

She forced a tinkling laugh. ''How marvellous it must be to confidently extract the pattern of a person's life from one incident.''

''Hardly an incident,'' he drawled. ''More a revelation.''

''Indeed?''

His deceit burned through her, igniting energy resources that had lain dormant for days. One thing could be said for Michael Timberlane's unwelcome intrusion in her life again. He generated an electricity that had her firing on all cylinders.

She leaned forward and gave him an earnestly questioning look. ''Could there possibly be a vital piece of the picture missing? Something critical that the genius has overlooked in his summing up?''

His eyes narrowed.

She flopped back in her chair in careless dismissal of whatever answers he came up with, scorning his arrogance in judging her so meanly when the meanheartedness was all his.

He leaned forward, his eyes hypnotically luminescent in their need to know. ''Enlighten me, Lauren. Tell me the missing factor.''

''You don't recall the factor you so deliberately left out of the equation, Michael?'' she tossed at him. She couldn't quite keep the contempt out of her voice as she added, "Neat trick with the drink waiter. Very timely."

He reeled, face tightening as though she had slapped him. He shook his head. His mouth thinned. Another more vehement shake of the head. With a startling burst of explosive energy, he jackknifed forward, his eyes riveting hers in a blaze of sizzling emotion.

"Are you telling me you let Roxanne influence you?" It was a blistering hiss. "After what we shared?"

She felt the memories if that night pulsing from him, bombarding her mind, curling around her heart, squeezing it. And the thought came to her that hatred was the reverse side of love…love betrayed, belittled, abused. Had she leapt to all the wrong conclusions?

Lauren was so paralysed by this appalling possibility she could make no response. Inwardly she retreated from the assault of his eyes, closing up, guarding herself from making any further mistakes. Confusion, emotional turbulence, a deep, dark sickness in her soul.

"Here we are!"

Three glasses clinked onto the table. Evan Daniel back from the bar, a lemon squash for her, double gins for the men. She wished she'd ordered something with the kick of a mule. It might have anaesthetised the painful chaos of trying to evaluate where she was and what she should do about Michael Timberlane.

"Thanks, Evan," he said, picking up his glass,

composing himself in a flash. He smiled at his friend, master of himself, master of the situation, and lifted his glass in a toast. ''You did yourself and your book proud today.''

''You listened to the radio spots?'' Evan's grin was pure delight.

''With keen attention. You warmed up very nicely. Tomorrow should be a breeze for you.''

His comments echoed Lauren's assessment of Evan's performance, reminding her how closely in tune they had seemed to be, the sense of real sharing. It gave her a hollow feeling, knowing she had rejected it all. What if there had been no malevolent intent to deceive and seduce?

She picked up her glass, sipping the sharp tangy drink while Evan rehashed the interviews, inviting Michael's opinion on various aspects of them. It was obvious he valued and respected Michael's judgment, hanging on his words as though they were pure gold.

No gold for her, though, Lauren caustically reminded herself. His judgments where she was concerned had been downright nasty, making her out to be a promiscuous siren, luring men to her bed for one-night stands. And that totally uncalled for crack about her husband being a poor sucker… Lauren gritted her teeth in bitter resentment. What right did he have to paint her so black? He knew nothing, absolutely nothing about her marriage!

On the other side of the ledger, she didn't really know what had gone on in his marriage. She only had

Roxanne's word for how he had behaved, what he had thought and felt and said. Graham Parker was sceptical of Roxanne's version of the truth, yet what she had told Lauren about Michael's attitude towards her struck a few truths with Lauren.

His quickness to make harsh judgments was not a trait that endeared him to her, no matter that she had given him some cause to think badly of her. He had jumped right in and thought the worst. No benefit of the doubt. No pause for reflection. No wondering if he had done something wrong.

Lauren didn't need that.

Destructive.

She'd been through one destructive relationship. She certainly didn't need another. She wanted…how that one night with Michael had been. But he'd shown her the other side of the coin of love, the blind passion of hatred.

A shudder ran through her.

As though his sensory perception was acutely tuned to her, Michael snapped his attention from Evan, his laser eyes sweeping Lauren like searchlights, determined on pinpointing what she was feeling and thinking.

No. No more, she thought.

The memory was spoiled.

Irrevocably.

''Ansett Flight AN37 is boarding now. Would passengers please proceed to the departure lounge?''

Lauren set her glass down and stood. She was going home. The only person she wanted right now was her mother.

CHAPTER NINE

REGRETS savaged Michael's stomach as they moved out of the Golden Wing lounge. Roxanne! His teeth gritted at the name. So many times during that magical night with Lauren the warning had rung in his mind—*Tell her now. Tell her about Roxanne.* And he had put off doing it because he hadn't wanted to break the incredibly exhilarating and soul-lifting rapport flowing between them.

And that critical piece of communication had become less and less important as the night wore on. Their intimacy had been too precious, too intensely felt to admit any third party. To have introduced the subject of Roxanne would have been crass. It could be done in the morning before Lauren left, he had told himself.

If only he hadn't slept on.

If only Lauren had woken him before going.

Yet would he have told her?

If he was ruthlessly honest with himself, the answer was almost certainly no. Roxanne had become totally irrelevant, lost in the wonder of all Lauren promised. He hadn't even given her a fleeting thought when he had rung Global that morning, eager to speak to Lauren, ebullient with a happiness so intense and pervasive there hadn't been room for any thought but renewing the link with Lauren.

A link that had already been broken.

A link he had just comprehensively smashed, probably beyond repair, in his bitter attack on her supposed lack of morality and callous using of people.

He didn't have to look at Lauren to know how effective he'd been in destroying the special bond they had shared. The three of them were heading towards the departure lounge together, but they weren't together. She walked with them but apart. Michael keenly felt the separation.

He'd seen the decision crystallise in her eyes, the vulnerable bright blue of cornflowers hardening, glinting into the cold, hard surface of sapphires, shutting him out. The walls were up, forbidding any entry to her space. She walked alone.

And it was all his own damned fault! No, not all. His precious ex-wife had a few things to answer for. Couldn't keep her nose out of his business despite having bagged a husband who pandered to her self-centred little soul. But, of course, the idea of him and Lauren together wouldn't sit well with her, not after all she'd said about both of them. It would show her up for the shallow, selfish, two-faced person she was.

God! Couldn't Lauren see that?

They turned into the nominated departure lounge, he and Evan automatically hanging back for Lauren to hand in her boarding pass first. She went ahead without demur. No feminist stand about equality when it came to traditional courtesy. There rarely was, Michael reflected. Not that he classed Lauren as a rabid feminist anymore. She was an intelligent woman who wanted her intelligence respected. Nothing extreme in that attitude.

She picked up a packet of headphones on her way into the boarding tunnel. It was an ominous sign. Headphones would provide a communication block during the flight. He needed to talk to her, needed to get things straightened out between them, needed to apologise for the rotten things he'd said. And thought. And done.

His gaze was drawn to the sensual undulation of her buttocks as her long legs put more distance between them on the short walk along the tunnel to the aircraft. He could feel the imprint of their softly cushioned roundness pressed against his groin in the aftermath of lovemaking. It reawakened the wanting that had hit him the moment he had seen her again. He wrenched his eyes up, but the vibrant bounce of her glorious hair made the ache of desire worse.

Damn, damn, damn! he could feel himself bulging, stretching the crotch of his jeans. *Think cold,* he commanded. If he couldn't match Lauren's coolness, he was a dead man. He was probably dead anyway. At the present moment, he doubted she would touch him with a barge pole. How he was going to recapture what he'd lost he didn't know, but he had to start somewhere and he'd better get it right.

The stewardess smiled a greeting, her eyes sparking

female interest at him. It irritated him. Unreasonably. Hadn't he been instantly and strongly affected by Lauren's physical attractions? Still was. Yet what was inside her head and heart was far more important to him. And more than anything he wanted a woman who could see and share what was in his head and heart. With honesty. Not the pretence Roxanne had given him in the beginning.

Lauren. Her openness had delighted him, enthralled him, entranced him. He followed her down the aisle the stewardess directed them to, determined to break through the barriers that now shut him out. Lauren Magee was the woman he craved in every sense there was…his other half. Or certainly the closest he'd ever come to it. He had to win her back.

She stopped by two vacant seats on the window side. A third vacant seat was directly across the aisle in the middle section of the plane. She looked at it and Michael knew it would be her choice if he didn't do some fast manoeuvring.

''There's some space in the overhead lockers a bit further along, Lauren,'' he directed.

She glanced up and moved, intent on storing her briefcase and jacket out of the way.

Michael turned to Evan who was behind him. ''Better take this seat,'' he advised, steering him straight into it. ''Easier to catch the drink waiter's eye right here on the aisle.''

Evan cheerfully obliged. Lauren cast a sharp look over her shoulder, saw the fait accompli, and with a word proceeded to stow her excess belongings into a locker. Michael jammed his flight bag in beside them, then backtracked to allow her to move in to the window seat ahead of him.

She stopped by Evan. "The view over Sydney is so lovely, like a fairyland with all the lights on, Evan," she said persuasively. "You really should take the window seat. I've seen it dozens of times. Besides, if I sit here, you'll be seated right next to Michael and can talk to him more easily."

Evan clearly wavered for a moment. Then he had the good sense to look at Michael and get the message in no uncertain terms. "No, no, I'm fine here," he declared, waving magnanimously as he added, "You and Michael sit together."

Done! And she knew it was done. She didn't bother to argue. With a nod of compliance she moved to the seat allocated to her by Michael, but if she felt trapped by the situation he had engineered, she didn't show it. Not a hint of frustration, vexation, resignation or surrender. She sat down with an air of insular dignity, fastened her seat belt, folded her hands in her lap and turned her face to the window.

He settled beside her.

She ignored his presence as steadfastly as though he didn't exist.

He had to strike now, Michael decided, before she put the headphones on and blocked her hearing. "I apologise," he said, his voice low, throbbing with sincerity.

There was no indication she had heard. She remained wrapped in stillness, her face obscured by her hair so he couldn't see if there was some change of expression on it. He stared at her hands, their long elegant fingers quiescent, as withdrawn from him as the rest of her. They could be part of a marble statue, he thought, so white and lifeless, yet the memory of their warm, erotic touch set his skin tingling with the want and need to feel it again.

"What for?"

Flat words, disembodied, ejected without any physical accompaniment to reflect that she had spoken them, but they were a response. Michael's mind went into a spin, like a roulette wheel bouncing the ball around until it stopped at what he hoped was a winning number.

"For not trusting what I'd felt with you."

That was the core of it. She hadn't trusted it, either, letting Roxanne colour her natural response to him, cutting him off without even granting him a fair hearing. A sense of injustice welled up, rekindling the frustration and fury that had fed the false image she had given him in brushing him off like the used mate of a black widow spider after she'd devoured all she wanted of him.

How could she have been so ruthless, so destructive? On the spurious strength of Roxanne's self-serving view of him? Michael was working himself up to a fine sense of justification when Lauren spoke, shattering any feeling of self-righteousness.

"You judged." Hard, implacable words, delivered without inflexion, without a trace of bending movement.

He heard the black hood of condemnation in her voice, felt the sentence of death hovering over him and instantly fought it. "You did, too, Lauren."

A slight shake of the head. Slowly she turned to look at him. Sapphire eyes. No quarter given. "I let it go, Michael. No rancour, no nastiness, no coming after you with guns blazing."

Guilty heat burned across his cheekbones. He'd wanted to reduce her to nothing. She'd left him feeling like nothing. But he'd had no real evidence to suggest she might play dirty with Evan. Or that she'd ever been unfaithful to her husband. That had been pure bile on his part, pumped out of the turbulent feelings she stirred with her apparent indifference to him.

"I'm sorry. What I said was unwarranted and undeserved," he acknowledged.

"Yes, it was. It's indicative of what I can expect from you if your desires are thwarted," she coolly added.

"No." The glittering scepticism in her eyes urged him to more vehement emphasis. "I swear it won't be like that. I know better now."

The scepticism didn't waver. "I'm sorry. I won't take the risk. Just let it go, Michael. Gracefully."

She turned away and stared out the window again. Everything in Michael rebelled against her edict.

Before he could think of any effective argument against it, the in-flight intercom came on, announcing imminent departure. The stewardesses directed attention to the television screens showing the usual safety procedures in the event of various mishaps occurring. The advice floated over Michael's head. He was facing death of a different kind, and all his concentration was bent on changing the path of his future.

As the aircraft taxied towards its take-off runway he struggled with the most compelling urge to reach across and grasp Lauren's hand, forcing a physical link between them. Yet she might interpret it as an aggressive act, overriding her wishes. Which it was. But if it recalled and reinforced the intimacy they had known together, might it not weaken the reservations she had against him? Would touch achieve what words could not?

The last resort, he sternly told himself. He was not under extreme time pressure. If he couldn't break through to Lauren this evening, he still had tomorrow. He would make plenty of opportunities to wear down the rigid barriers she had erected. Each moment spent with her would be an information-gathering exercise. Sooner or later he would find the key that would open her door again. In the meantime, he had to appear to respect her wishes.

The aircraft gathered speed and lifted off. The stewardess came by taking drink orders. She provided Michael with a legitimate and inoffensive reason to draw Lauren's attention away from the window.

''Lauren, the stewardess is asking about drinks,'' he said matter-of-factly.

She turned her head, her gaze shooting straight past him. ''Nothing for me, thank you.''

So much for a companionable drink, Michael thought, and echoed Evan's order of a gin and tonic for himself. He needed something to occupy his hands and keep them out of temptation, and gin did soothe the beast inside him.

Lauren started tearing open the pocket containing the headphones.

''Is conversation with me anathema to you?'' he asked.

She paused and lifted a wary gaze to his.

He gave her an appealing smile. ''I promise to be civilised.''

''It won't do any good, Michael,'' she said quickly. ''We're each carrying baggage that won't go away.''

His smile turned rueful. ''Are you referring to Roxanne?''

''Amongst other things.''

''I assure you Roxanne is totally expunged from my life.''

Her eyes derided his assertion. ''Feminist, saboteur, hatred…'' A succinct list, delivered with deadly aim.

''I threw away that load before I bumped the drink waiter's arm at the party.''

''Deceit,'' she added, shooting at his integrity.

''I didn't tell you about Roxanne because I wanted

what happened between us to be free of prejudice. Was that unreasonable, Lauren?''

''It was wrong not to give me a choice. You chose, Michael. You should have trusted me to choose, too.''

He couldn't answer that. Excuses were useless. She had cut straight to the heart of the matter and laid it bare for him.

''You see?'' Her smile was a wry twist. ''You judged. You did what suited you. And I'm sure you'll justify it. Men like you always do.''

''Men like me?''

''That's my baggage, Michael.'' Her eyes had changed again. Bleak winter blue, dull and flat. ''Now, if you'll excuse me, I'm very tired. I don't want any refreshments.''

She put the headphones on, plugged into the sound system, relaxed in her seat and closed her eyes. He let it go…for now. She'd given him a lot to think about.

His mind circled around honesty and trust. It was what he wanted in a relationship. Lauren was right in saying he had denied her that. And he had justified it. He could see how wrong he had been not to let her know about Roxanne straightaway, giving her a fair chance to make up her own mind about him. He had played to his own advantage.

However, she was wrong in thinking he would keep justifying it. He was not in the habit of repeating mistakes once he had been shown where he had erred.

Doing what suited him… Roxanne would have fed

that line to Lauren until she was brainwashed with it. Roxanne twisted everything around to suit herself. It wasn't true of him. Or was it?

Leaving Roxanne and her lies out of consideration, how had he come across to Lauren?

It had suited him not to reveal that Roxanne was his ex-wife. It has suited him to come on this trip. He had used the excuse of protecting Evan and Tasha, but the real reason was he wanted to face Lauren with what she had rejected. It had suited him to manoeuvre her into the window seat. Selfish and self-serving. That was the truth of it.

Yet the memory of their night together was the driving force behind his pursuit of her, and it wasn't only his future happiness at stake. Lauren had been just as committed to total involvement. He had to convince her it wasn't a mistake, for both their sakes. He had to prove he wasn't like the men she was comparing him to in her mind.

How many other men, he wondered?

Her ex-husband for a start. Something must have gone badly wrong there. The others were probably irrelevant, he decided. Her marriage would have been the crucible that had cemented her attitude towards what she did and did not want in a man. His marriage had certainly sorted him out about what was important to him and what wasn't.

Tasha's recipe for a happy marriage slid into his mind. *It's wanting the same things.*

He looked at Lauren. Did she want what he wanted? Her magnificent hair frothed around the constriction of the headphones. Her profile in repose had a purity of line and proportion that would have appealed to any artist. There was a translucence to her pale skin, giving an impression of fragility. Under the sweep of her lashes lay shadows he hadn't noticed when her eyes were open. The result of sleepless nights? Had she lain awake, mourning the despoiling of a dream?

He wished he could cradle her in his arms, wished they could go back a week and start again. He gathered every shred of willpower he had and drove it into a telepathic message.

Give me another chance, Lauren. That's all I ask. Another chance.

CHAPTER TEN

"THE Como Hotel, Chapel Street, South Yarra," Lauren said to the taxidriver, hoping he was capable of giving them a problem-free trip.

"Going to be slow, I'm afraid," he informed them cheerfully. "Lot of traffic tonight. Big rugby league match on at the MCG."

"Of course. Queensland against New South Wales in the second of the State of Origin matches," Evan cried, his face lighting up with eager interest. "What's the betting here in Melbourne?"

"The money's on New South Wales, but most people I talk to want Queensland to win." The driver grinned. "Sorry if that's against your home state, but that's how it is."

They chatted on about state rivalries as the driver stowed their luggage in the boot of the taxi. Michael, she noted, did not join in the conversation. He moved around to the far passenger side, leaving her and Evan to take their places in the car wherever they willed. No direction from him this time. Had he let go? Given up?

She frowned, knowing it was positively perverse of her to feel disappointed. If he was respecting her decision, she should be approving his restraint, glad to be relieved of the stress involved in resisting continual pressure to change her mind. Best to make a clean break of it. Perhaps he saw it was the wisest course, too.

Lauren hesitated over whether to sit in the front or the back of the taxi. It was easier for Evan to carry on his football chat with the driver if he sat beside him. It didn't really matter where she sat. Michael Timberlane would still be sharing the same space as herself, and she wouldn't escape being aware of him. Even with her eyes shut and music playing in her ears on the flight to Melbourne, she had been unable to block him out.

Michael was already settled on the back seat when she chose to join him. His eyes flashed with surprise, then kindled with warm pleasure. His mouth curved into a slow, teasing little smile that somehow expressed both hope and self-mockery.

"Does this mean my sins are forgiven?"

The smile and the soft lilt of his voice played havoc with her composure. The corners of her mouth twitched. Her sense of fun wanted release. It was difficult to control the impulse to respond in kind, to let her eyes flirt with his. *Remember, remember how quickly he can change,* she sternly berated herself. It was incredibly stupid of her to suddenly feel light-hearted, pleased that he hadn't given up.

"I think that's between you and God," she answered blandly. "Isn't hatred one of the seven deadly sins?"

''No. Pride, avarice, lust, anger, gluttony, envy and sloth,'' he answered, with admirable recall of that rather arcane piece of knowledge. His eyebrows slanted in comic ruefulness. ''You've definitely got me on three of them, and I've been in sackcloth and ashes all the way from Sydney, doing penance.''

Lauren was having real difficulty in keeping her mouth straight. As an exercise in self-control she did a mental juggle and came up with pride, lust and anger for the three deadly sins he confessed to. Lauren was highly unsettled by the fact she was having considerable trouble with lust herself.

Despite her serious reservations about Michael Timberlane's character, she could barely glance at him without remembering and wanting the sexual excitement and intense pleasure of his lovemaking. His mouth was sinfully sensual, the smile playing on it extremely provocative, suggesting soft and tantalising little movements.

She wrenched her eyes away from the inviting twinkle in his and glanced out the rear window, where Evan and the taxidriver were nattering away, taking their time about getting going. She wished they'd hurry up. Michael Timberlane was far too treacherously attractive for any peace of mind.

How many times had she excused inexcusable things from Wayne for the comforting illusion of closeness that physical intimacy provided? If she didn't apply the lessons learnt from painful experience, she was a fool. Sexual attraction—lust—was treacherous. One didn't spend one's whole life in bed. There had to be something good in the rest of it.

"Did Roxanne say I hated you?" Michael asked quietly.

"Yes." And she'd better keep remembering that, too.

"I've never hated anyone, Lauren."

The sweeping claim was such a downright lie, it swung her gaze to his in sizzling challenge.

"I confess I was fed up with hearing 'Lauren says' every time Roxanne wanted to score off me, but my hatred was for the way she wouldn't face up to—"

"I'm not stupid, Michael," Lauren cut in impatiently. "I know what I felt coming from you in the Golden Wing lounge."

His expression instantly changed, responding to the seriousness of the charge. He nodded gravely. "Yes, that was hatred, Lauren. The hatred of knowing the guts had been torn out of something I believed beautiful and seeing the shell of it still there, yet unable to fix it, unable to breathe life into it again."

His eyes stabbed into hers, tearing at her interpretation of his emotions. "I certainly hated that. I can't view the destruction of something rare and precious with indifference or even equanimity."

The passion emanating from him, throbbing through his voice and flashing from his eyes, clutched at her heart and shook her mind into encompassing more than it had before. Rare and precious. She had felt that, too.

"I hate a lot of things people do and say, especially when it hurts others," he went on. "And now I find I'm guilty of that myself, much as I regret it." He heaved a sigh. His eyes softened to appeal. "Hasn't there ever been a time when you wish you could undo what you've done and make it better?"

Lauren felt so churned around it was a welcome relief when their private tête-à-tête was broken by Evan and the taxidriver, finally taking their seats. Football talk flowed unabated from the front of the cab as the taxi left Tullamarine Airport and headed for the city. The good-natured banter provided a convenient cover for Lauren's retreat into herself.

Her thoughts were turbulent. The straight line she had drawn in her mind was now wavering all over the place. Michael had pleaded a strong case for himself. Everybody made mistakes. While never having set out to hurt anyone, Lauren had her own private list of things she'd do differently, given the time again. It was all too easy to jump in and make black-and-white judgments instead of waiting to weigh all sides of a situation.

Maybe she should give him another chance.

If it hadn't been for Roxanne feeding her the hate message... Had that been inspired by what Graham Parker predicted would be a dog-in-the-manger attitude? Roxanne could hardly call her second husband a sexy male animal. He was close to fifty, carried a middle-aged paunch and somehow reminded Lauren of a lolloping lick-happy Labrador. Whereas Michael had the sleek, beautiful, lethal power of a Doberman.

Her gaze strayed sideways. His hand rested loosely on his thigh. She knew the tensile strength of those muscle-moulded legs, knew the tenderness and sensual skill of his hands. There wasn't one part of his magnificent body that she didn't know intimately, the way it felt, the way it responded to her, the way it could make her feel.

She could picture it perfectly, remember the exquisite sensations… A purely wanton excitement coursed through her, tightening her muscles. If she reached out to him…

Lauren took a deep breath and clamped down on the dangerous impulse. She wasn't prepared to commit herself so wholly to Michael Timberlane again, not until she was more sure of what he was really like. She needed to see how he reacted to a number of situations before giving him her complete trust. Another chance didn't mean shutting her eyes and hoping for the best.

She looked out the side window to keep temptation at bay. The taxidriver was right about the traffic. It was crawling from one red light to the next.

"We'll be out of this at the next turn right," he announced in his genial manner. "We should have a better run to your hotel from there."

A few moments later he manoeuvred the taxi into the right-hand turning lane, and there they stopped, waiting for another light to change. The stream of cars on Lauren's side kept flowing for a while, then came to a halt, as well. She admired the stylish line of the electric blue sports car that had drawn level with the taxi. It stirred a curiosity about its owner. She glanced at the driver and gasped in shock.

Wayne!

She stared disbelievingly at his profile, trying to convince herself it must be a look-alike. There were other men with curly black hair, aquiline noses and full-lipped mouths. Wayne wouldn't waste his money on an expensive sports car. It couldn't be him. It was too much of a coincidence, seeing her ex-husband like this when he had been featuring so much in her thoughts about Michael.

As though sensing he was being stared at, the object of her inner turmoil suddenly turned his head and looked straight at her. A steel clamp squeezed her heart. It *was* Wayne! And his recognition of her was instant and frightening.

His dark eyes glittered as they always did when he won his way about something. His mouth curled with satisfaction. She was here in Melbourne, and he knew she was here. Despite the length of time they had been apart, there was no resigned acceptance of their separation, for Wayne.

Lauren silently and fiercely railed against the fickle trick of fate that had placed them both here. Two years had passed since she had broken with him. She had taken care that their paths didn't cross. Avoidance at all costs had been her strategy for a trouble-free life. Now this, of all times and all places!

Wayne leaned forward to look at the man sitting beside her in the back seat. Was Michael aware of it? Was he watching? She dared not glance at him. It would reinforce the kind of personal connection she didn't want Wayne to make. Though surely with Evan in the front seat, Wayne would realise it was a business trip and not a private outing.

She saw his jaw tighten into pugnacious mode. He glared at her, angry, jealous, possessive. His attitudes certainly hadn't changed. The sports car was probably an ego-booster, another superficial attraction to add to his pulling power with women, but however many women there had been in his life since her departure, he still resented her leaving him. A wife didn't do that, in Wayne's world. A wife did as she was told and pleased her husband.

The taxi started moving forward. Wayne jerked his attention to the cars ahead of him. They were also on the move, and since they were not in a turning lane there was nothing to slow them down. Wayne drew level again, threw her one last baleful glare, then, prompted by a horn blowing behind him, accelerated away.

Lauren wasn't really aware of the rest of the drive to the hotel. Memories of her marriage to Wayne crowded in on her. She became conscious, at one point, of her fingernails digging into her palms. Her hands were tightly clenched. She uncurled them and stretched out her fingers.

No mark remained on the third finger of her left hand. When she had walked out on Wayne, she had left the rings he had given her behind, too. They should have been symbols of belonging together, not domination.

"Are you all right, Lauren?" Michael asked softly.

She swung around to face him, instinctively defying his concern, not wanting to discuss what she was feeling and why. "Yes, of course. Why wouldn't I be?"

His eyes probed hers but met a blank wall. "You didn't eat on the flight," he remarked. "The hotel restaurant, Maxim's, has an excellent reputation. Evan and I plan to have a leisurely dinner there. If you're not too tired, we'd both like your company."

A tactically worded invitation, designed to allay any fears that he might come on to her. In the normal course of events she might have accepted. Nothing was normal now.

"Thank you, but I won't join you."

He frowned. "Because of me?"

She shook her head. "My family live in Melbourne. I'm going to visit my mother."

"Fair enough."

Lauren didn't care if it was fair or not. Michael Timberlane could wait. She didn't want any man close to her right now. She needed her mother, her sane, sensible, down-to-earth mother, who was never flustered by anything.

They arrived at the Como Hotel. It was situated right next to the Channel Ten studios and catered to the security concerns of visiting celebrities. Lauren was glad of the security measures that protected all the guests from unwanted visitors. No one could operate an elevator without a room key. Once they were booked in and on their way to their rooms, she would feel safe from Wayne.

She kept an eye on the road while the luggage was unloaded, and she got a receipt from the driver for the taxi fare. No electric blue sports car pulled up or cruised by. Her apprehension eased somewhat as they proceeded inside to the reception desk.

When she was absolutely certain Wayne hadn't tracked her to the hotel, she would ask the concierge to have a taxi waiting at the door for her and she would slip out of the hotel and go home. That took care of tonight.

Tomorrow... Well, she would cope with tomorrow as best she could when it came.

CHAPTER ELEVEN

NO WONDER Evan was overweight, Michael reflected, idly watching him heap strawberry conserve onto his third piece of toast. This followed a cooked breakfast comprising eggs, bacon, grilled tomato and hash browns, which had been preceded by a bowl of muesli heaped with dried fruit. However, it could be argued that Evan would burn up a lot of energy today with the list of interviews Lauren had lined up for him.

She hadn't come down to the restaurant for breakfast. Not yet, anyway. Michael checked his watch. Evan was to meet her in the foyer at nine-thirty. It was now eight twenty-six. Still time for her to appear. On the other hand, perhaps she preferred to eat in her room. Or was she deliberately avoiding him?

"We've plenty of time, haven't we?" Evan asked.

"Yes. I think I might have some cheese with my coffee."

Michael stood up to go to the continental breakfast smorgasbord. The glass frontage of the restaurant faced the reception area. He caught sight of Lauren hurrying down the half flight of steps from the foyer. In the few seconds it took her to race through reception to the elevators, Michael was struck by far more than the unexpectedness of seeing her come from the direction of the entrance to the hotel.

Her hair was in wild disarray, ungroomed.

Her face was devoid of makeup, pale and shiny.

There was a grim line to her mouth, unhappy, strained.

The shadows he'd noticed under her eyes were more pronounced.

She wore exactly the same clothes she had worn yesterday.

The conclusion was obvious. She had stayed out all night and was just now returning to the hotel. Which was odd. Why take a room if she intended staying overnight with her family?

The elevator doors opened, and she disappeared from Michael's view.

''What's wrong?'' Evan asked.

''Nothing.'' He shrugged and smiled. ''Thought I saw someone I knew.''

He moved off to the smorgasbord, cogitating on Lauren's actions. It must have been an impulsive decision to sleep at her mother's home. Otherwise she would have taken makeup and a change of clothes with her. She had looked tired yesterday. Tired and stressed. The blame for that probably rested with him.

Had he discussed him with her mother? If so, had she listened to advice that was positive or negative towards him? Pondering unknowns didn't help. Today would tell him where he stood with her. He thought he'd made some headway in correcting her view of him in the taxi last night, but…

He remembered her clenched hands, the nail marks on her palms, the odd action of spreading her fingers and staring at them. He wished he could have seen what was going through her mind right then. The result had been closing him out again and no chance to recover what ground he'd made.

He cut himself a slice of King Island Brie, picked up a couple of crackers and returned to the table, fighting a sudden wave of depression with gritty determination. Whatever Lauren's baggage was from her relationships with other men, it wasn't going to apply to him. Somehow he'd make her see that.

"I am replete," Evan declared, having polished off his toast. "Do you want me to make myself scarce if Lauren comes down?"

"I doubt she will."

Evan grimaced. "Tasha and I thought you and Lauren had something really special going. Roxanne sure must have done a good slander job on you."

He'd done himself more damage than his ex-wife had, but he preferred not to confess that to Evan. "My fault. I should have told Lauren about her," he said briefly.

"Tricky business," Evan sympathised. "You won't get much chance to do any good today, Michael. We don't even get time for lunch until after the pre-record session at Channel Ten. That's scheduled to finish at three this afternoon." He looked at the cheese. "You should have had a bigger breakfast."

"I can always grab something. You're doing the interviews, not me."

"Well, if you're counting on time alone with Lauren, forget it. If she's not nursemaiding me through the technological wonders of live radio, she's on her mobile phone, checking and rechecking the schedule with producers."

Michael frowned. "Has she got an insecurity complex about her work?"

Evan laughed and shook his head. "It's a real education seeing how the media work. Not much runs exactly to the minute, I can tell you. Something else comes up. Interviews get shuffled around. Lauren juggles things all day, shifting, compromising, doing deals. And keeps her temper, despite the frustration of hold-ups and changes she can't predict. That woman has the patience and persistence of a saint."

They were admirable qualities. Michael vowed to apply them in his pursuit of Lauren Magee. She liked her job. It deserved respect. It would certainly be self-defeating for him to get in the way of it.

"Thanks for the warning, Evan. I'll keep out of her hair."

Evan grinned. "Great hair."

Michael smiled back. "Great lady."

When Lauren joined them in the foyer at precisely nine-thirty, her appearance was immaculate and stunning. She had teamed a deep wheat-gold ribbed sweater with her black pants-suit, and added a jazzy silk scarf that was pure class. Subtle make-up around her eyes eliminated the shadows and accentuated their vivid blue. Her lovely mouth was a glistening red, and her hair had obviously been subjected to a vigorous brushing. While the gleaming mass of curls and waves retained an untamed look, there were no tangles in sight.

"Good morning." She gave them a bright smile. Overbright, Michael thought. "How was your dinner at Maxim's last night?"

"Superb," Evan answered. "Smoked trout, braised king prawns and a pear tart with caramel sauce. You should have been with us."

She laughed. "I'm glad you enjoyed yourself, Evan. Is Tasha all right?"

"Green with envy. She adores epicurean delights."

"How was your night?" Michael asked.

"Oh, fine! It's always nice to see the family. I miss not having them around me in Sydney." Another overbright smile, not reaching her eyes. "If you're ready, let's get going."

She wasn't really with them, Michael thought. Something else on her mind. Not him. There was not the slightest sense of either positive or negative vibrations flowing towards him. She simply acknowledged and accepted his presence as an adjunct to Evan.

She took the front seat of the taxi. "The ABC Studios at Southbank," she said to the driver. Then out came her mobile phone, and Lauren Magee was at work.

The day went precisely as Evan had outlined. At the ABC Studios he and Lauren disappeared into special telephone booths that were built to contain only two people. These provided direct live-to-air links for interviews with radio presenters in Adelaide and Hobart. Michael drank coffee in the cafeteria, which overlooked the foyer from the first floor.

Indeed, every floor overlooked the foyer. Michael was reminded of the inside of a prison with rows of walkways running around banks of cells and the connecting flights of stairs, all open to view from the ground floor. It was quite interesting architecture. He had plenty of time to study it in detail.

When Evan and Lauren reappeared, it was in a rush to catch a taxi to the studio of a popular commercial radio station where Evan was to do a half-hour talk-back session. After that, it was a quick return to the ABC for an interview with a regional presenter, followed by another for a Melbourne station. Michael could, at least, listen in to these and comment on them, sharing in what was happening.

They raced from Southbank to South Yarra to the Channel Ten studio for the prerecord of a popular morning show. Evan went straight into make-up. Lauren disappeared to confer with the producer. They gathered in what was designated as the Green Room, where Evan was fitted with a microphone and tested for sound. The call came to go to the set. Michael and Lauren were invited to watch the action from behind the bank of cameras.

By this time Evan was in top form, relaxed, happy, striking up a good rapport with his host, burbling on about his book in a highly entertaining fashion. Michael caught Lauren's eye and grinned, delighted at his friend's performance and automatically wanting to share his warm pleasure. Momentarily off guard, Lauren grinned back, her eyes dancing with his, and Michael felt his heart turn over. The special sense of intimacy between them was acute, if only briefly.

She returned her attention to the set, the grin quickly fading. Michael hoarded the moment, greatly encouraged. Whatever strain she had been under this morning seemed to have eased as the day wore on. She looked pensive, but not stressed. His laid-back attitude had definitely been the right one to adopt.

Evan's segment ended and amidst a happy flow of congratulatory comments, they retired to the Green Room where his microphone was removed. Since they had two hours free before a telephone interview with a Perth radio station, Lauren suggested, with a good-humoured twinkle in her eyes, that they pass the time in a restaurant so that Evan wouldn't die of hunger or thirst.

Below the television studio was a shopping mall, which led to a classy little restaurant facing onto Toorak Road. It was obvious that Lauren was familiar with the place, confidently choosing a table and summoning a waiter for menus and a wine list. It didn't take long for them to decide on their orders. Then they sat back, relaxed and smiling at each other.

"No call from Tasha, so I guess everything's fine with her," Lauren remarked, her eyes on Evan. "Will you be driving home to the Blue Mountains when we land in Sydney tonight?"

"Sure will. I've got my car stashed at Michael's place."

"I could give you a lift home from the airport, Lauren," Michael quickly offered.

She gave him a weighing look, which he held, careful to project no more than the warmth of friendship, yet his body tingled in a thrall of anticipation, his heart felt caught in a vice, and his mind burned with the need for her to open up to him again. *Another chance…* He willed the words at her with all the magnetic power he could muster.

"Thank you, but it's more straightforward if I take a taxi," she said, speaking a truth he could not argue against. It carried the underlying message that she was not ready to be alone with him.

"I presume Global pays for it," he said, shrugging off his disappointment.

"Yes. Part of my travel budget."

The waiter arrived with their drinks, a glass of white wine for Lauren, gin and tonics for Evan and Michael. Lauren lifted her glass in a toast.

"To one of the nicest authors I've ever had to deal with."

Evan chuckled. "Have you had any nasty ones?"

''Mmm…let's say difficult. Some expect too much. It's impossible to drum up media interest if the book subject is perceived as—'' she wriggled her fingers ''—too deep or downbeat. Sex and controversy are always welcome. So is entertainment.''

''What's been your most memorable experience with an author?'' Michael asked with interest.

She gave him a sharp look, realised he was not implying the kind of sexual encounters he had accused her of yesterday, then smiled reminiscently as she launched into a story about a group of highly eccentric artists whose work had been photographed and displayed in a glossy coffee-table book. They weren't the authors of the book, but it had been decided they would provide colourful publicity for it. Extremely colourful, as it turned out.

Michael and Evan were laughing over one recounted incident when Lauren reached for her glass of wine and froze with her hand still outstretched and empty. The amusement that had lingered on her face was wiped out instantaneously. Her eyes widened, then seemed to dilate with…fear? Shock?

Michael swivelled to see what had caused the reaction. Her gaze was fastened on a man who had apparently just entered the restaurant. He stood near the doorway as he scanned the tables on the other side of the room to where they sat. Michael did a swift assessment. Tall, well-built, expensive suit, early thirties, soap-opera handsome. Glossy black curls added a little-boy appeal.

As his face slowly swung towards them—dark, deeply socketed eyes, strong aquiline nose—Michael was niggled by a sense of recognition. Yet he didn't know the man, had certainly never met him. Perhaps an actor?

Out of the corner of his eye he saw Lauren's outstretched hand curl convulsively into a fist. Tension vibrated from her. She snatched her hand down, hiding it in her lap. Nails digging into her palm, Michael thought, and was instantly reminded of last night in the taxi. He flicked his gaze to the man, who was now approaching their table, dark eyes glinting derisive triumph at Lauren. A connection clicked in Michael's brain with explosive force.

The man in the blue sports car, peering past Lauren to see who was lucky enough to be with such a gorgeous redhead, idle curiosity, filling in the time until the traffic lights changed… That's what Michael had thought. Two cars stopped adjacent to each other, a chance thing, meaning nothing, merely a speculative bit of imagination.

Wrong!

Big wrong!

The man had the eyes of a snake, and Lauren sat like a mesmerised mouse, letting him come at her.

Every nerve in Michael's body snapped to red alert. His mind spun on all cylinders. Links formed with lightning speed. Lauren's stress, strain, distancing herself from him, withdrawing to some untouchable place…all caused by this man.

A wave of primitive aggression rolled through Michael. Lauren Magee was *his* woman, and he'd fight anyone who tried to hurt her, frighten her, threaten her, distress her in any way whatsoever. If this guy was looking for a confrontation, he'd get it. To Michael he represented one thing with absolute clarity.

The enemy.

CHAPTER TWELVE

"Having fun, Lauren?"

Wayne's silky intonation promised the worst kind of trouble. Lauren barely repressed a shiver of apprehension. Her refusal to see or speak to him last night had obviously fuelled his determination to seek her out where she wouldn't have the protection of her family. But she had Michael with her. Michael… Silly, desperate thought. She'd given him no reason to help her.

"I'm on a job, Wayne," she said, striving for an air of calm control to cover the feeling of being hunted, trapped.

"But not exactly working at the present moment," he rejoined smoothly.

"It's a business lunch. And you're intruding," Lauren stated, a touch of belligerence creeping into her voice. Why, why, why did he have to persecute her like this?

"Oh, I don't think your, uh, clients—" he swept an oily smile of appeal at Michael and Evan "—would mind if you joined me at another table for a little private conversation. I'm sure you gentlemen will agree a husband has some rights on his wife's time."

"*I* mind, Wayne," Lauren snapped, infuriated by his glib and condescending way of taking over and fright-

ened that Evan and Michael might swallow the persuasive line. "And you are no longer my husband,"
she added bitingly.

"Don't be petty, darling," he chided, again turning
to her companions and begging their indulgence. "We
have some making up to do."

"It's all been said and done," Lauren insisted
fiercely.

Wayne sighed in exasperation and shook his head
at her as though she was being childishly wilful and
difficult. "Don't let's make a public scene of it,
Lauren."

He reached down and grasped her left wrist, his fingers bruising in their intent to take and possess, his
dark eyes blazing with the promise he would make one
hell of a public scene if she didn't give in. "Just come
with me now and—"

"Let me go, Wayne," she said, seething, hating his
superior strength, hating his slick presentation of himself, refusing to play his game no matter what it cost
her in the eyes of others.

Sheer malicious spite underpinned his words as he
answered her. "You're embarrassing your clients with
your less than civil manner, Lauren."

Heat scorched up her neck and stung her cheeks. He
knew where to hurt. Her body first, her career...

"Not at all," Michael broke in, his tone light and
easy, eschewing any sense of tension whatsoever. "I'm
not the least bit embarrassed. Are you embarrassed,
Evan?"

Evan looked startled. "Well, uh…"

"Of course not." Michael grinned at him. "Soaking it all in for your next book, weren't you?"

"Oh, yes." Evan nodded earnestly. "Very interesting situation."

"Quite a masterly piece of sly harassment," Michael remarked, wagging a finger at Wayne. "You do it very well. But you picked the wrong marks with Evan and me. We have a very healthy respect for women's rights."

"Certainly do," Evan said supportively, getting into the swing of the argument.

"Now be a good chap and release Lauren's wrist," Michael added. "She did ask you to let her go. And while you clearly haven't ingested the idea of being a sensitive new age guy, let me assure you that physical force on a woman does you no credit whatsoever."

"Quite so," said Evan gravely. "No gentleman holds a lady against her will."

Lauren sat in a stupor of amazement. She hadn't expected Michael to come to her rescue. She had been an emotional mess all day, barely taking notice of him, continually keeping an eye out for Wayne, deeply oppressed by his having camped in his car outside her mother's home all night.

Her brother had sneaked her out in his car this morning, bringing her to the Como Hotel, but she had known that evasive tactic might not be enough. Wayne had only to listen to the radio, pinpoint Evan as her client and ring in to the station to start trailing her movements.

His fingers tightened around her wrist. He'd found her, all right, and he was not about to let go. He leaned a fist on the table and gave Michael a venomous glare. "This is none of your business," he hissed, aggression emanating from him in blatant intimidation.

"On the contrary. This is our business, and as Lauren pointed out, you're intruding on it," Michael retorted, completely unperturbed by Wayne's manner. "In fact, we'd all appreciate it if you'd retire gracefully. Right now."

"Yes. And take your hand off Lauren," Evan chimed in with beetling disapproval.

"Fat chance! Stay out of my way, *gentlemen*," Wayne jeered at them, then yanked Lauren out of her chair. "She's coming with me."

It happened so fast, Lauren was robbed of any initiative, either in protesting or resisting. Wayne hauled her towards the doorway to the street in such a powerful surge, her stumbling feet barely kept her upright. She was semiaware of startled patrons looking on in shock, raised voices, chairs tipping, but far more aware of the relentless grip on her wrist, the wild thumping of her heart and the panic screaming through her mind.

Everything seemed to blur. She heard a bellow of pain from Wayne. Her wrist was abruptly freed. She automatically hugged it close to her chest, nursing it protectively as she found her feet, straightened, caught her breath, tried to find her scattered wits. She was shaking uncontrollably.

A comforting arm circled her shoulders, hugging her to warm solidity. ''It's okay,'' Evan soothed as she darted a panicky glance at him. ''Best if we back off a bit and let Michael handle this.''

Michael! Her eyes belatedly focused on the formidable figure blocking Wayne's route to the door. Gone was any pose of relaxed affability. The man confronting her ex-husband projected an air of lethal power and purpose.

He stood as tall, if not taller than Wayne, and there was a sense of tightly sprung readiness in his stance, suggestive of explosive force on a hair-trigger. His face was subtly altered, all hard planes and angles, any trace of softness eradicated. The silvery eyes gleamed like sharp and polished swords, aimed in direct and deadly challenge at her erstwhile assailant and abductor.

''You broke my arm!'' Wayne accused him in bitter outrage.

Lauren flicked a startled glance at him. He was clutching an area close to his shoulder, and the arm hung limply at his side as though it had lost all strength. No wonder he had let her go, she thought, looking at his now flaccid fingers.

''Purely a paralysing blow,'' Michael answered in cool dismissal.

''Got a black belt in karate,'' Evan whispered in her ear.

''By all means get it X-rayed, but I think you'll only

suffer bruising,'' Michael went on matter-of-factly. "A just desert for what you did to Lauren's wrist, wouldn't you say?''

"Who the hell do you think you are, butting in to a private affair?'' Wayne asked, almost choking in fury.

"Well, I'm beginning to see that my role in life is looking after Lauren whenever she needs or wants looking after.'' Michael nodded pensively. "I've always had this rather primitive, protective streak in me, and Lauren certainly brings it out. Try to remember that, Wayne, because looking after Lauren has just become my number-one priority.''

They had the strangest effect, those words, acting like a sweet magic nectar filtering through Lauren. Her mind turned to a rosy mush. The need to be strong for herself and everyone else melted around the edges. Her steely sense of independence collapsed into soft, filmy femininity, and her heart suddenly felt as though it was floating in a warm sea of security.

"I should have known,'' Wayne jeered. "You've got the hots for her. That's what you're protecting.''

It jolted Lauren out of her thrall of pleasure.

"Why don't you just leave, Wayne, while you've still got a mouthful of teeth?'' Michael invited, pointedly waving to the door and stepping aside to facilitate his exit.

"I'm on my way, sucker,'' came the derisive acquiescence. He swaggered past Michael, then paused at the doorway to cast an insultingly lecherous look over Lauren. "She's a hot little number, all right. Enjoy it while you can, buddy. Tomorrow she'll be giving you the same big chill I got today."

"You're pushing it, Wayne," Michael warned in a steely tone.

"Just doing you a favour, letting you know what to expect." Wayne tossed the words at him in arrogant confidence. "It's a game she plays, turn on, turn off. Easy for her in her job, with you fly-by-night authors providing a convenient turnover."

The torpedoes of Wayne's black jealousy zeroed in on Lauren's heart and sank it. Never any trust for the person she was inside. Wayne had far less justification for painting the same picture Michael had painted of her in his frustration with her rejection. It was pure malevolence. Yet the reinforcement had to be a dead-set killer of any credibility and respect she'd earned with Michael Timberlane.

"Little mistake, Wayne. I'm not an author," he said, but his face had tightened as though the hit had struck home. "I'm more an action man. Keep it in mind."

Lauren felt sick.

"Well, she sure as hell wasn't with you last night, action man," Wayne mocked savagely. "She was in my bed. So remember that when you slide between her sheets tonight and think it's going to last."

On that wantonly destructive note Wayne made his exit.

CHAPTER THIRTEEN

FOR several moments there was a frozen tableau in the restaurant, not a sound or a movement except for the swing of the door that punctuated Wayne's departure. It was as though everyone was holding his or her breath, waiting for what might happen next.

Regardless of her shocked daze, Lauren knew what would happen next. They would all look at her to size up what Wayne had put in their minds. She felt so hopelessly besmirched she wished she could shrivel up and die. She should move, run, hide, but she was bereft of the energy to carry through any purpose. Despite still being on her feet, she was completely knocked out.

"Right!" Michael swung around with a sharp clasp of his hands, startling everyone. "That guy is a dangerous nut case. Waiter, lead us to your kitchen. I want a safe place for this much-abused lady until we're sure her attacker is not coming back."

In another blurring burst of action he scooped Lauren out of Evan's supporting hug, off her feet, in his arms and cradled against his chest. "Evan, keep watch for us," he commanded. "Clear a passage, people. Waiter?"

"This way, sir."

With bewildering speed, Lauren found herself whizzed away from the peering curiosity of patrons, carried into a busy commercial kitchen and, amidst the fluttering concern of chefs and kitchen hands, lowered carefully onto a chair that someone quickly supplied.

"Now let me look at your wrist, Lauren," Michael said with quiet authority.

It took her a moment to realise she was still nursing it. Very gently Michael pried it loose from her hold and ran tender fingers over the bruised flesh. She stared at his face, wondering if bad thoughts of her were festering in his mind behind the mask of human conern.

Action man. He was certainly that. She was intensely grateful to him for rescuing her from a horribly humiliating situation. And worse. If Wayne had succeeded in taking her with him… Her mind shied from following that train of thought.

What to do now? That was what she had to concentrate on. She tried to control the conclusive tremors that were still attacking her body with embarrassing frequency.

"Could be sprained but it's not broken," Michael assured her, gently laying her hand on her lap. "We'll get an elastic bandage on it as soon as we can, Lauren."

She nodded.

Evan came in. "One of the waiters is on watch, but I think the slimy toad has nicked off."

"I should have landed him on a hard, dry rock to bloat up and die," Michael muttered murderously.

"Oh, I think you put paid to him, Michael," Evan said with cheerful confidence. "He won't want a return bout."

"He really needs that dirty, lying mouth of his smashed in, Evan."

"Better to sue for defamation," Evan advised. "Hits him where it hurts in the pocket, and you don't get charged with assault."

The import of their words seeped through Lauren's daze of despondency. "You didn't…you didn't believe him?" she asked on a weak quaver.

Michael's face creased to caring concern as he realised the depth of her distress. "Lauren, honey, when it comes to exes wanting to dig their claws in, that guy beats Roxanne hands down. You think I'd believe *him?*"

"Oh!" Tears welled in her eyes. The shame of having believed Roxanne against him… How could he call her honey? Dear heaven! She never cried, and here she was, out of control, making an exhibition of herself, and the tears wouldn't stop. Her chest was so tight and… She had to get hold of herself. Had to…

But it was Michael who took hold of her, lifting her out of the chair and wrapping her in a tight embrace, supporting her in a cocoon of warmth and strength and tenderness as he showed his understanding in soothing words.

"You're safe now. It's over, Lauren. Just let me look after you. Okay?"

"Yes," she said, sobbing. The want, the need to just cave in and wallow in being looked after was overwhelming. Someone fussing over her, caring for her, indulging her, fulfilling all her innermost desires…

"Your handkerchief, Evan," Michael commanded.

"Here it comes, Lauren."

A wadded cloth was shoved over Michael's shoulder. Lauren snatched it gratefully and tried to mop up, but there seemed to have been a dam burst in her tear glands. There was this awful pressure in her chest.

"Better fetch Lauren's bag," Michael instructed.

"Right you are," Evan agreed and seemed to be back in a trice. "Lauren's room in the hotel is still booked," he informed them. "That's where the five o'clock call from Perth is to come through."

"Fine. I'll take her there. Fix up about the lunch we ordered, will you, Evan?"

"No problem. I'm hungry enough to eat the lot. Might take me up until five minutes to five to get through it all."

"Good man," Michael approved warmly. "Do you feel up to walking with me, Lauren? I'll carry you if your legs are wobbly."

"No. I can walk."

"Big breath, and then we'll set off."

He was treating her like a child, but somehow she

didn't mind. She dragged in a big breath and let it slowly shudder out. The pressure in her chest eased. She did more damage control with Evan's handkerchief as Michael tucked her beside him for the walk out of the restaurant.

"We'll go through the mall again. Quickest way to the hotel," he said, holding her close for secure support.

It was also in the opposite direction to the way Wayne had gone. Lauren appreciated this consideration more than the distance factor. Not that she really feared bumping into Wayne again, not with Michael with her, but she'd prefer it not to happen.

Tears welled as they made their way to the back exit of the restaurant, shepherded there by kindly staff. "Sorry I'm such a mess," she mumbled, dabbing at her eyes.

"You've been on overload," Michael said kindly. "It's not surprising you reached breaking point, Lauren."

"But I've always coped."

"First me. Then him. It was too much. Did you get any sleep last night?"

"Not a lot."

"Did he go to your mother's home after seeing you in the taxi?"

She looked up in wet-eyed astonishment. "How did you know?"

He gave her a rueful smile. "Sometimes when I put two and two together, I arrive at the right answer.

I spotted you coming in this morning. You looked… harassed.''

''He stayed parked outside Mum's house. Johnny, one of my younger brothers, had to smuggle me back to the hotel.''

So easy now to pour out the words. It was a relief to have Michael's understanding, not to have to bottle it all up inside herself and carry on as though life was perfectly normal. Though at least the mall provided a sense of normality after the traumatic scene in the restaurant. The shoppers passed them by, intent on their business, not seeing anything to capture their interest in Michael's and Lauren's slow traverse of the walkways.

''Did you ever take a restraining order out on Wayne?'' Michael softly inquired.

Again he surprised her with his comprehension of her situation. ''Yes. But it didn't do any good.''

''Hence your move from Melbourne to Sydney.''

''He wouldn't let go.''

''Possessive and abusive.''

''Yes.''

''Your family couldn't look after you?''

''My father died a few months after my wedding to Wayne. I'm the eldest in the family. Mum had enough worries, Michael.''

''And you didn't want to add to them. You've had it tough, Lauren, going it alone,'' he said with gentle sympathy.

It triggered more tears. She was turning into a regular waterworks. "Thanks for standing up for me."

"I was glad of the chance to show you I wasn't a total write-off."

She blew her nose, took a couple of deep breaths and realised they were almost through the mall. "I didn't mean to make you feel that, Michael," she said carefully. "I just had other things on my mind today."

"A lot of baggage. Which I added to. Am I forgiven for thinking badly of you?" he asked quietly.

"Well, you obviously don't believe I'm some heartless playgirl any more." She mustered up an ironic smile. "Am I forgiven for thinking badly of you?"

He gave a wry little laugh. "That was definitely my fault."

They emerged from the mall, stepping out onto the open paving in front of the hotel. The afternoon had turned grey, and Lauren remembered that rain was forecast. Pots of cyclamens in the garden boxes provided bright splashes of pinks and purples and reds, but not even their intense colours could dispel the bleak onset of a wintry evening.

The cold Melbourne wind snapped at them. Lauren shivered and huddled closer to Michael as they headed for the entrance to the hotel. Suddenly the warmth and comfort of a trusted friend and confidant took on more intimate dimensions and sensitivities.

Lauren found herself acutely conscious of hips and

thighs touching, a heated friction where their bodies bumped and rubbed, Michael's arm slanting across her rib cage, brushing against the underswell of her breasts, holding her to the hard wall of his chest.

The image of his naked body flashed into her mind, the muscular power of it exciting her, pleasuring her, driving her to exult in her femininity, pleasuring him. That one wonderful night of making love together... so very much together...as they were now...or seemed to be. Could she believe in it? Did dreams really come true?

Her heart skipped and started to swing like a hard-beating metronome between caution and desire. Remember Wayne and Roxanne, caution insisted. But they were the past, and why should she let the past shackle her forever? She had a fierce desire to fly free, leave the baggage behind. She wanted to embrace all that could be, should be. Or was that blind faith in a future that wasn't ever truly possible?

Michael was taking her up to her hotel room. Evan was not joining them there until five o'clock. She'd heard them arrange it. Had Michael been thinking...?

No, he wouldn't try to force her, wouldn't do anything she didn't want.

So what did she want?

CHAPTER FOURTEEN

MICHAEL stopped by the concierge's desk. "Miss Magee has an injured wrist. Would you please send someone out for an elastic bandage and a bottle of witch-hazel or whatever else eases bruising? We'll be in Room 404."

"Certainly, Mr. Timberlane."

"On the double, Henry."

"All speed, sir."

It reminded Lauren that Michael was a very wealthy man. "I guess you're used to the best service," she remarked as they proceeded to the elevators.

"I'm known in many places," he answered offhandedly.

"Like what?"

"I do quite a bit of sitting in various boardrooms to get things done for those who don't have the means to cover their needs." He slid her a whimsical smile. "I'm called a friend."

He might share his wealth in many places, but he was a very private man, Lauren decided, not given to splashing it around in public or showing off. It was interesting that he was focused on people in need. She wondered if that was a tradition in his family or a personal choice?

With her acquiescence, he took her room card from her bag and operated the elevator. A few minutes later she was comfortably settled in an armchair in the privacy of her hotel room and Michael was ringing for more service.

"Two of your soup of the day, a basket of French fries and a bottle of your best chardonnay. Room 404. I'll be very appreciative if you get that to us as quickly as possible."

Lauren wondered if those were the code words for a big tip. When Michael took charge, he was certainly master of the situation. Very impressive. He had not only a natural command that people responded to but also a quick eye and mind for effective and efficient organization. Lauren had no doubt he was very highly valued as a friend in all those boardrooms.

Michael Timberlane made things happen.

Lauren mused over this insight as he moved on to fixing her a cup of coffee. For most of today he had taken a passive role, but she realised now he had simply been biding his time for an appropriate opening to pursue what he wanted. It gave Lauren a very warm glow to know that he wanted her so much, fighting for her, looking after her, taking care of everything for her.

Or would he have done it for anyone in need?

Lauren suspected he would have. It was in his nature to stand up and be counted on whatever he felt strongly about. And he didn't give up, either.

He might have acted on pure principle, but his smile, as he brought her a cup of coffee, felt very specifically for her. "You have more colour in your face now."

It wasn't surprising, with some of the thoughts she'd been having. "Thank you, Michael. I don't know what I would have done without you."

The smile turned into a wicked grin. Once again it had a heart-stopping effect on her. "I aim to keep you thinking that, Lauren," he said, his eyes dancing with hers with intimate intent, "because I don't want to do without you."

She stared at him, totally besotted for several moments. *Yes,* she thought decisively, *I want to know more of this man. I want to know everything about this man.* And not on any hearsay this time. All of it would be on direct, personal, first-hand experience, with every chance he offered her.

The door buzzer demanded attention. Michael answered the summons and returned with a packet from a pharmacy. He pulled a chair close to hers and set to work on her bruised wrist.

"Why did you marry Roxanne?"

His gaze flicked up, his eyes scanning hers sharply before lowering again. "I thought we could make a go of it."

"You weren't in love?"

He finished spreading ointment over the tender

flesh and started winding on a bandage before he answered. When his reply came it was as though he was choosing his words with care, wanting to give as accurate a picture as he could.

"Roxanne made herself very attractive to me. We were both from a background of wealth, from long-standing families. There was a commonality of understanding on many grounds. I wanted to get married. I wanted a family. She pandered to my interests at the time and led me to believe she cared about the things I cared about."

"But she didn't, really."

He shook his head. "Roxanne wanted me, but she didn't love me. I thought I loved her. I wanted to love her. But as her pretences wore thinner and thinner, I couldn't." He fastened the bandage with a plastic clip, then looked directly into her eyes. No hiding. Clear, soul-piercing truth. "I never felt with her what I've felt with you, Lauren."

It was there, pulsing between them, the memory of all they'd felt that night. And it wasn't a dream. It had been real, special, unique for both of them. They could reach for it again.

The door buzzer announced the arrival of room service. It broke the intense flow of emotion between them. Michael moved to let the waiter in. A table was wheeled into the room and quickly arranged for them, the soup and French fries set out for their convenience, wine uncorked and poured into glasses, chairs placed precisely and a handsome tip paid to speed the waiter's departure.

Michael lifted a plate cover. "Pumpkin soup. Should slide down easily," he encouraged. "Have you eaten anything today?"

"Some toast this morning."

"Try. You need it."

She ate the soup, half a bread roll, a few French fries, and did feel better for it. The chardonnay was perfect for washing it all down and leaving a pleasant aftertaste.

"Had enough food?" Michael inquired.

"Yes, thank you. It was good."

He nodded. "Why did you marry Wayne…what's his name?"

"Boyer."

"Of Charles Boyer fame?"

"Same spelling. Different family."

"He looks like an actor."

"He's done some modelling. That's how I met him. He was used for a book cover. His family owns a string of dry-cleaning shops and laundrettes. He helps manage them for the most part, and that ties him to Melbourne."

"You fell in love?"

She grimaced. "Let's call it blind infatuation, with the emphasis on blind. Wayne can be very charming, very flattering, very ardent. I was a lot younger then and I fell like a ton of bricks. I didn't see what was coming."

"Which was?"

"He wanted an adoring servant. Only his needs counted."

Michael gave her an ironic smile. "Sounds a bit like Roxanne."

"Wayne had four older sisters and a mother who'd spoilt him rotten. I didn't have a chance of making him see differently. He threw tantrums and he was violent whenever he didn't get his own way."

"So I noticed."

"He doesn't like losing, Michael." She heaved a despondent sigh as the feeling of sick fear took hold again. "I don't know what I'm going to do about coming back to Melbourne again. Getting beaten this afternoon will really stir him up. If he starts pestering my family…"

"Don't worry. I'm more than a match for the slimy toad. Didn't I prove that to you this afternoon?" He rose from his chair and stepped around the table to take her uninjured hand in his, pressing gentle reassurance as his eyes burned steady conviction. "I won't let him hurt either you or your family, Lauren."

She stood up, lifting her hands to his chest as she anxiously revealed her experience. "He's so devious and malicious. And a very convincing liar when he's put on the spot. You saw that, Michael."

His eyes glistened with compassion. "It must have taken a lot of courage to set your own course and keep to it."

"More desperation than courage. Though there's

really no knowing where or how he'll hit next. There's no sure defence," she cried, the anguish of her fear and frustration echoing through her voice.

"He won't hit again. I'll look after you, Lauren."

"Michael…" She looked helplessly at him. "Even the police couldn't keep him away."

"I have more resources than the police," he said, and once again his face was transformed by the wicked grin that defied the world and rejoiced in a freedom that knew no fear or boundaries.

She shook her head, dazed by his confidence and the sheer blazing brilliance that bathed her in it. She didn't comprehend how he could stop Wayne from pursuing a vindictive vendetta, yet she felt the weight lifting from her heart, and her mind tingled with hope.

"I don't want you to get hurt," she said. A black belt in karate was all very well, but Wayne didn't play fair.

"I promise you, no-one will get hurt." He stroked her cheek in a soothing caress. His eyes compelled her to believe him. "I learnt how to look after myself a long time ago. I *can* look after you, Lauren. And I shall."

"I…I don't know what to say." A brittle laugh burst from her throat. "I'm the one who's always done the looking after. It's…"

He pressed a soft, silencing finger to her lips. "It's your turn. Let the fear go, Lauren. Trust me."

"Yes," she whispered, wanting to.

His eyes simmered into hers, his silver irises soft-

ening to a smoky grey as he tilted her chin and lowered his head. She had the chance to say no if she
didn't want his kiss. The truth was she yearned to
taste it again, was breathlessly waiting for it.

His lips brushed hers, softly, sweetly, building a
sensation that reached deep inside her, coiling itself
around her heart, sliding through her stomach in little
rivulets of pleasure, tingling down her thighs. Her
mouth opened to his enticing warmth and tenderness,
the languid caress of his tongue more thrilling than
passion. He cared about her. He truly did. And she
loved him for it.

The feeling burst from her heart and filled her response to him, her arms sliding around his neck, fingers thrusting through his hair, bringing his mouth
more thoroughly, more vibrantly to hers in an explosion of intense excitement and exultation because the
magic was there again, richer than before, more powerful, the throbbing pulse of togetherness thrumming
wildly through their bodies.

"Lauren." It was a groan of need, his lips still hot
and moist on hers as he struggled for breath, for control. "We don't have enough time," he rasped.
"Evan's call…"

It pierced the delirium of happiness swimming
through her mind. "Sorry."

"I'm sorry, too," he said gruffly, forcing himself
to pull back, his eyes stabbing an urgent plea past the
passionate daze in hers. "Please listen, darling."

Darling… How wonderful that sounded! "Yes?"

"I need the address where your mother lives."

She didn't understand why but she gave it.

"Now I won't be flying back to Sydney with you, Lauren."

"Oh?"

"I have important and urgent business here."

"I thought you came for Evan."

"Yes. But something came up last night, and—" he smiled ruefully "—Evan doesn't need my protection."

"So you have to stay." She tried to keep the disappointment out of her voice.

"Two days. No more. Then I'll be back in Sydney." His eyes pleaded for her patience with compelling intensity. "Promise me you'll be waiting. That you won't let anything turn you away from me."

That was easy to give. "I promise."

A sigh expelled with force, followed by a smile that encompassed her in a blaze of desire.

The door buzzer heralded Evan's arrival.

"I'll leave you with Evan to do the Perth call, but I'll be back to accompany you to the airport and see you safely onto your flight. Okay?"

"Yes. Thank you, Michael." Her eyes adored him.

"Thank you." Husky happiness.

One last brief kiss, a seal of their promises to each other.

Lauren watched him go to the door to admit Evan. Surely nothing could go wrong between them now.

The bond was there, the sharing she'd dreamed of, the understanding, the trust, the sense of belonging.

Yet she could not entirely banish the spectre of Wayne and his potential for evil nastiness. Michael didn't know him as she did. However strongly the cloud with the silver lining beckoned to her, promising an end to the darkness lurking in her background, she knew Wayne could not be dismissed as easily as Roxanne could be.

She could not help being afraid that Michael was underestimating Wayne's capacity to damage and destroy. Underestimating Wayne was dangerous.

CHAPTER FIFTEEN

MICHAEL lounged at ease in the stretch limousine, smiling as he imagined the scene being played out in Wayne Boyer's office. Lauren had a great family. All they had needed was a bit of direction, a bit of organisation, and the heart was certainly there to see her freed from being emotionally and physically victimised by a man who deserved no place in her life.

He almost wished he smoked. A cigar would have added an extra little punch to the image he wanted to imprint on Wayne Boyer's brain. But enough was enough. He'd bought a pinstripe suit he didn't need and other bits and pieces of flashy apparel he'd never wear again. The opal and gold cufflinks were a particularly nice touch. There had been a big spread in last Sunday's newspapers about a lawless gang of ratters raiding the opal fields in Lightning Ridge.

Wayne Boyer was a rat of the worst kind, spreading the disease of fear with his nasty marauding attacks on Lauren. Michael was only too aware of how debilitating fear was. His brother, Peter, had never really recovered from the sadistic practices of their grandmother. That Lauren had managed to keep such a strong sense of self in spite of her ex-husband's abusive tactics was a marvel to Michael.

It was going to give him a lot of satisfaction to give Wayne Boyer a lesson in fear today. Michael could say one thing about his grandmother. She'd left him with some fine examples of how to get a point across with optimum effect. He hoped Wayne would appreciate the thoroughness with which a plan could be carried through.

The door to the dry-cleaning factory opened and out they came, Wayne Boyer accompanied by two burly policemen—or at least what one could call splendid facsimiles of burly policemen. They were, in fact, two well-built amateur actors who had adopted their character roles with relish and wore their costumes particularly well.

Wayne was expostulating vigorously, but his words had no visible effect on Lauren's cousin, Joe Hamish, and his mate, Terry Johnson. They flanked Wayne as they crossed the sidewalk, hedging him in so when Joe opened the back door of the limousine, Wayne really had nowhere to go but into the car.

"What the hell is this?" he demanded. Clearly it was not a police vehicle.

"Get in, Mr. Boyer," Joe said phlegmatically. "We're taking you for a little ride, courtesy of the boss here."

"Who?" He ducked his head to see. "You!"

It was clearly a mind-stunning moment for Wayne—the recognition of the face of his assailant, unexpectedly transposed to a vastly different appearance and coming with the accoutrements of a posh limousine and the evocative title of "the boss."

Seizing the advantage of the element of surprise, Terry wasted no time in bundling the shell-shocked Wayne into the double-seated rear compartment of the limousine. He and Joe climbed in after him, shoving their guest to the end of the seat directly facing Michael. Everyone ignored his cursing and yelling. The back door was closed. Terry tapped the glass partition between them and the chauffeur. The limousine purred off down the road.

"Might as well calm down and behave, Mr. Boyer," Joe advised. "No-one can see in. The windows are tinted."

"This is an abduction," Wayne fiercely accused. "You said I was wanted down at the police station because my ex-wife had signed an official complaint against me."

"He lied," Michael drawled, "just as you lied about Lauren the other day, Wayne."

The black ferocity of Wayne's eyes reminded Michael of a wild animal that had been cornered but not cowed. "My secretary can identify these two cops. Don't think you can get away with any further assault on me."

"I have no intention of harming a hair on your head. Provided I get your cooperation."

"What do you want?" he growled.

"Oh, I thought we'd just talk for a while."

"Who are you, anyway?"

"Many people think of me as a friend, Wayne. One could say I have the reputation of being a friend to quite a lot of powerful people." Michael paused to let that thought linger. "I'm also a friend of the Magee family. And I'm very particularly a friend of your ex-wife."

Wayne snorted derisively. "You can't intimidate me."

"I was thinking more along the lines of exterminating you, Wayne."

That got through his belligerent guard. He swallowed convulsively and tried to hide the flicker of fear in his eyes. His gaze dropped to Michael's flamboyant tie, wandered to the silk handkerchief featured in the top coat pocket of the pinstripe suit and shot across to the door, where Michael's arm occupied the armrest. The opal cufflink earned some sobering study. Michael casually crossed his legs, dangling one obviously Italian shoe for perusal.

"Unfortunately, Lauren said not to hurt you," he went on in a tone of mournful indulgence. "A pity, really. Extermination is such a neatly final solution."

"To what?" Wayne demanded harshly.

"To you bothering her and her family. It has to stop, Wayne. I really won't tolerate any more of it. You upset everyone the other day."

"Tough!" he muttered scornfully.

"Well, I knew words wouldn't be enough to convince you, Wayne, so I thought I'd arrange a little demonstration. That's quite a nice sports car you drive. A Ford Probe, isn't it?''

"Yes, it is." Wary suspicion.

"Cost about fifty thousand?"

"About that."

"Fully insured?"

"Yes."

"That's good. I like to deal with a careful man."

The wind was definitely up Wayne's sails. He looked deeply worried, though true to his bullying form, he continued to bluster. "If you've damaged my car—"

"Now that's what I want to get across to you, Wayne. Damage control. What we need to work out is what price you put on things. Like doing a valuation on your life. You do value your life, don't you, Wayne?"

He looked confused.

"Then there's quality of life. You wouldn't want that messed up with busted kneecaps or other little unfortunate accidents."

"What the hell are you getting at?" Wayne burst out, no longer sure of anything.

"Ah, here we are."

The limousine pulled to a halt alongside a row of vehicles in the car park Wayne habitually used. An electric blue Ford Probe occupied a bay in the row to their right. Wayne had a good view of it.

"As I mentioned, Wayne, a demonstration tends to fix things in a person's mind," Michael said affably.

''I might add there is nothing you can do but sit and watch. These doors and windows are power-locked.''

Even as he spoke, a huge caterpillar tractor came trundling into the car park. The Magees had contacts in the earth-moving business. The big cat lined up behind the Probe, lifted its massive front-end excavating bucket and crashed it down on the glistening blue bonnet. There was a squawk of anguish from Wayne. Michael and the two policemen watched impassively as the bucket lifted and descended again, mangling some more bodywork.

''For God's sake! Stop it!'' Wayne cried.

''I want you to stop bothering Lauren and her family,'' Michael said in a tone of sweet reason.

Another thumping, metallic crunch.

''Are you mad?'' Wayne shot at him, visibly cracking up with the destruction of the car.

''The car is only a start, Wayne. I can think of lots of other things to damage,'' Michael said carelessly.

''You guys are cops!'' Wayne yelled at Terry and Joe. ''Are you going to let him get away with this?''

''We're not cops,'' Joe said with a shrug.

''I didn't want the boys coming the heavy with you, Wayne. It was a smoother operation to have your cooperation in leaving your office,'' Michael explained.

Wayne muttered a few expletives under his breath as he jerked his gaze to the electric blue wreck. ''My car...'' He choked.

''I feel the same way about Lauren,'' Michael said

earnestly. "When you hurt her the other day and said such nasty things about her…" He shook his head. "I would like to come to some agreement with you, Wayne. It's a matter of damage control, you see. I can do this to your car, trash your apartment, set fire to your laundrettes, make your life generally unpleasant…"

Wayne stared at him in horror.

"But if you stay right away from Lauren and her family and swear never to come near them again—"

"I swear. I swear," he repeated hoarsely.

"But have you really got the message, Wayne? I need conviction here." Michael glanced out the window. "Ah, the clean-up crew. I have a very tidy mind, Wayne. I like to get everything cleaned up to my satisfaction."

The big machinery moved out and a tow truck moved in, courtesy of one of Lauren's uncles. Wayne's olive skin had turned sallow. He watched the wrecked Probe being towed away with glazed eyes. A pickup truck arrived. Men in overalls alighted and swept up the broken glass and bits of metal with big industrial brooms. Lauren's brothers were very thorough.

"Well, there goes the evidence," Michael said cheerfully. "What do you say, Wayne? Are you convinced it's a good idea to leave Lauren and her family alone?"

"Yes. She's not worth it," he said dully.

"I'm relieved to hear you think that, Wayne. On

the other hand, Lauren and her well-being and happiness are worth a lot to me. Matter of fact, I paid fifty thousand dollars for the car you've just seen destroyed.''

''You? But...but it was my car!'' Wayne croaked, his eyes almost rolling in helpless shock and distress.

''No. Your car is being driven back into place right now.''

Wayne stared disbelievingly as another electric blue Probe was parked in the cleanly swept bay. ''I don't understand,'' he mumbled.

''It was a demonstration, Wayne. Lauren said I wasn't to hurt you, but I've always been an action man. It's my nature, taking action. Lauren tied my hands this time, but I did want you to see what I can do. Anytime I like.''

''You spent fifty thousand—'' He looked at Michael with the full realisation he was face to face with a ruthless fanatic. It scared him witless.

''Let's call it an initial outlay. If there's a next time I won't feel so generous.'' Michael looked inquiringly at Terry and Joe. ''What's the going rate for a good hit man, boys?''

''Eight thousand is the word,'' Joe answered.

''Yeah, eight's the top,'' Terry agreed.

''Could have hired six hit men for fifty grand,'' Michael mused. He wagged a finger at Wayne. ''You're a lucky guy. If Lauren didn't have such a soft heart...''

''Look!'' Wayne leaned forward, hands outstretched in desperate appeal. "I swear she's as free as a bird, as far as I'm concerned. I'm out of her life for good. Okay? Please?"

"Well, we'll just drive around while I think about that. Would you tap the chauffeur, please, Terry?"

Michael lolled back in his seat, watching Wayne through meanly narrowed eyes as the limousine rolled towards the exit of the car park. Beads of perspiration broke out on Wayne's skin. He looked every bit as sick as Lauren had in the restaurant kitchen. Michael was satisfied that at least some justice had been done.

"You think he means it, boys?" he asked Joe and Terry.

"He'd be a damned fool if he doesn't," Terry grunted.

"I wouldn't waste another car on him," Joe said contemptuously.

"Oh, I don't intend to, Joe. I never give repeat lessons," Michael stated decisively. "If someone's too dumb to learn—"

"I swear I've got the message," Wayne cried, unable to bear the tension of not knowing his fate.

"I guess I'm going to have to take his word for it. Lauren doesn't want me to hurt him. Tap the chauffeur to stop, Terry."

The limousine drew to a halt.

"Well, Wayne, this is goodbye." Michael opened the door on his side. "I'd go while the going's good, if I were you."

He scuttled out and ran.

Michael closed the door and grinned at his companions. "Thanks a lot, guys. I reckon we did it."

They broke into wild, rollicking laughter.

Michael leaned over and slid open the glass partition. "To the airport," he instructed. "I've got a very important date with the lady of my life."

CHAPTER SIXTEEN

Two pink lines appeared.

Lauren's heart sank. There was no refuting that evidence. The test results were quite specific. Two pink lines meant she was positively pregnant.

If only she'd stayed on the pill! Her mother had always warned her, don't trust a man to protect you from pregnancy. Although Michael had used condoms. She had even helped him with one during that long, lustful night together. She looked at her long fingernails. Maybe it was her fault.

Well, it was done now, she thought, heaving a sigh to relieve the constriction in her chest. She hadn't even considered such a possibility until yesterday, when she'd noticed a tight tenderness in her breasts. Then she remembered her mother saying it was the first sign.

Having been through nine pregnancies, her mother had considerable experience and knowledge of the condition. Even so, Lauren hadn't really believed this was an infallible sign. The test she'd bought was more a peace-of-mind measure. She now had no peace of mind at all!

So, where to go from here? she asked herself as she went through the motions of getting ready for work. Michael would be back today. He wanted her to be waiting for him. But with this news? It was so…unplanned, premature, mind-boggling.

It had to be faced, of course, but Lauren decided she needed some breathing space first. Becoming a parent was a big responsibility. Her job would certainly be affected, as well as a lot of other things. One little baby represented change on a huge scale. Lauren wasn't sure yet how she felt about it. Once she got over the shock of the idea… Well, she'd face it properly then.

She arrived at work in a state of distraction.

"Hi, Lauren!" Sue Carroll, the receptionist, gave her a cheery wave. "Got anything planned for the weekend?"

"Weekend?" she echoed, not connecting anything much together.

"It is Friday today," Sue informed her dryly.

Thank heaven for that, Lauren thought. "Yes. Big weekend," she replied. Michael…baby…

Sue prattled on about her plans until Lauren escaped into an elevator.

Graham Parker caught her on her way to her office. "The rain in Spain falls mainly on the plain," he intoned.

"What?" Lauren looked blankly at him.

"You're late. Roxanne has limped forth. Your ear is about to catch a drumming."

"Oh! Thanks, Graham."

Lauren tried to do some mental girding. Roxanne

seemed totally superfluous to the issues that were running around in her head, but Michael's ex-wife could not be discourteously dismissed. They still had to work together.

Nevertheless, since Roxanne had been off work for the past one and a half weeks, there was something definitely perverse about her returning on a Friday. Most people would have waited until after the weekend. It wasn't as though Roxanne was critically needed in her department. She liked the intellectual eclat she perceived in the image of having a job in publishing, but she wasn't exactly a workaholic.

Something had to be eating at her, and Lauren suspected that something was Michael. Roxanne couldn't bear not knowing if her telephone call had borne the fruit that would taste sweet to her. If that were the case, Lauren was about to give Roxanne a dose of sour grapes.

Her office was blessedly empty when Lauren entered it. No-one actually had any right to be there without her permission or direction. Roxanne didn't always respect these little niceties, but apparently she had this morning. Lauren had time to go through her usual routine of checking incoming faxes before the rain descended.

"May I come in?"

Lauren affected surprise. "Roxanne! How's the ankle?"

"Still rather weak." She hobbled in and collapsed

gracefully into the chair on the other side of Lauren's desk. "It was up like a balloon for days. So painful!"

"Yes. I've heard a sprain is often worse than a break. You should have kept resting it until after the weekend."

A delicate wrinkling of the nose. "I was getting so bored. Godfrey is a dear, but he fusses."

The shine wearing off the honeymoon? Lauren made no comment. She was not about to encourage Roxanne's confidences. As Graham had warned, they would fall anyway. That was as inevitable as the sun going down each day.

Lauren appraised the woman sitting opposite her, trying to see her through a man's eyes. Michael's eyes. She was shorter than Lauren but her figure was in proportion and very shapely, enhanced by the designer clothes she wore. Her pretty china-doll features were ideally framed by the long silky fall of hair that shone like spun gold.

Lauren suspected the colour was not natural, but it was certainly kept beautifully. No dry, strawlike effect from continual dying. No split ends. Glossy perfection at all times. It was hair that invited touching. For a sensualist like Michael, it would be very attractive.

Then there were the green eyes. So green Lauren wondered if Roxanne wore tinted contact lenses. But that was probably being a bit green-eyed herself. Lauren had to concede they were striking eyes. A man could very easily drown in them if they were glowing at him with doting admiration.

Roxanne Kinsey was a highly polished package who would be prized by any man who wanted an ornamental wife. Opening the package was another proposition. All the same, Lauren reminded herself it had taken a while for her to see Roxanne in her true colours. Those big green eyes could be very effective in projecting whatever Roxanne wanted to project.

"I feel really badly about you not knowing who Mikey was," she opened up, her expression eloquently awash with sympathetic concern.

"Not to worry, Roxanne. Michael and I have sorted out that little misunderstanding," Lauren said dismissively.

Roxanne frowned. "You don't mean you intend to go on seeing him?"

"Yes, I do. I happen to like the man. Very much."

Metaphorically, it knocked Roxanne's socks off. She started to her feet, remembered her fragile ankle and subsided in her chair again, green eyes narrowing. "I see," she said coldly. "I thought you'd have better sense, Lauren."

She smiled. "There's a certain zest in living dangerously." Though the consequences weren't so happily zestful at the present moment.

Roxanne managed a careless shrug. "One lives and learns."

"Yes. One does," Lauren agreed.

Roxanne looked askance at her, heaved a sad sigh

when Lauren's expression remained impassive, then produced a brilliant smile. "Anyhow, I have some wonderful news, and I wanted you to be the first in the office to know." She leaned forward confidentially, her eyes sparkling with delight as she whispered, "I'm pregnant."

It hit Lauren in the throat, making speech impossible. Her mind stuck on the words, *I am, too.* But she couldn't feel delight, not in the circumstances. She felt quite sick with uncertainties. Even sicker with Roxanne crowing her wonderful news.

"Godfrey is tickled pink," she prattled on. "He fusses over me all the time."

Michael wants a family. He said he'd look after me.

"When I had that fall last week, he was beside himself with worry until the doctor assured him there was no problem. He's so proud that I'm having his baby."

"That's nice. That's great, Roxanne." Lauren forced the words out, trying to have some generosity of spirit. It wasn't the other woman's fault she was feeling so vulnerable about the future.

Roxanne heaved a happy sigh and leaned back in her chair, settling comfortably. "Yes, it is great. I've always wanted children. I just couldn't risk having them with Mikey."

That jolted Lauren into asking, "Why not?"

Roxanne rolled her eyes. "Madness runs in the Timberlane family."

Lauren stared at her, inwardly rejecting the statement, yet uncomfortably aware she knew next to nothing about Michael's family history. "If that's the case, Roxanne, I'm amazed you married into it," she remarked as lightly as she could.

"Oh, everyone said Mikey was all right. He administers the estate and on the surface he seems fine." She lowered her voice ominously. "You don't find out about his dark side until you live with him."

Was this malicious spite? Lauren wondered. "Everyone has a dark side, Roxanne," she said sceptically.

Roxanne gave her a pitying look. "Of course, coming from Melbourne as you do, you can't possibly know the family background."

Lauren leaned back in her chair, crossed her legs and waved a casual invitation. "Go ahead and spit it out, Roxanne. You're obviously dying to."

"It's for your own good, Lauren."

"Naturally." Do-gooders always said that before grinding their own axes.

"The Timberlanes were well-known for being extremely eccentric. Most of them died young and in extraordinary or mysterious circumstances. Like Mikey's parents. They disappeared in Africa."

"The Dark Continent just swallowed them up, did it?"

"Nobody ever found out. They certainly never came back, and Mikey and Pete were only little kids then."

"Pete?"

"Mikey's younger brother. He's a wastrel, frittering away his inheritance in Monaco."

Lauren recalled Michael's mention of a brother in Monaco.

"They were left to the dubious mercies of their mad grandmother. She lived in a massive stone mansion at Hunter's Hill and she used to lock the boys in the cellar if they were naughty. It drove Pete crazy."

"Not Michael?"

"He kept a stash of books down there. She found out about it one day and made a bonfire of them to teach him he couldn't escape being punished."

"Not much love," Lauren remarked sadly. No riches at all, she thought, remembering what Michael had said.

"He withdraws into himself. You can't reach him when he does that, Lauren. No-one can. He just cuts himself off."

The tactics of a survivor, Lauren thought. She knew all about the need to remove oneself from crushing realities, the strength it took. Michael understood where she had been coming from, she suddenly realised. He obviously had a very personal acquaintance with abuse.

"As I said, the grandmother was mad," Roxanne repeated with relish. "She stayed in that old mansion and never went out. People were summoned to her. The staff nicknamed her 'the duchess'."

"Being autocratic is not necessarily mad," Lauren remarked.

"Huh! She had to pay her staff double wages to keep them. None of them would have put up with her otherwise." Roxanne leaned forward to press home her poison. "And let me tell you, Mikey is precisely the same kind of autocrat. He can chill you right through to the bone with those icy eyes." She illustrated this with a theatrical shudder.

Michael, the judge, Lauren thought, but he did try to be fair. He listened. Lauren had little quarrel with the way he had acted in the circumstances presented to him. And he had been magnificent, standing up against Wayne.

"Blood will tell in the end," Roxanne said darkly. "I'm glad I didn't have any children by him."

The reiteration of that sentiment stirred Lauren's blood. "You may very well prefer Godfrey's genes, Roxanne, but I'd pick Michael above any man I've ever met to be the father of my child."

Lauren wasn't absolutely sure of that, but Michael had stood up for her against Wayne, and she was not going to let his ex-wife's nastiness go by without standing up for him.

Roxanne's jaw dropped. She collected it again and snapped, "Haven't you been listening? The man is a monster."

Mikey the monster. Roxanne's self-serving fiction. The idea of a taint of madness in his family was not a comfortable one, but Lauren was not about to let Roxanne get away with maligning Michael any more.

"Well, it's been interesting, Roxanne, but I have a different view of Michael, and I don't want to hear him slandered by you."

"Slandered!" She looked deeply affronted.

"In fact, he could very well have a defamation case against you," Lauren went on matter-of-factly. "I don't think Godfrey would like it if you ended up in court. Michael can be very formidable once he swings into action."

Roxanne stared glassily, as though she was seeing her life pass before her eyes.

Lauren went for the kill. "With his wealth, he wouldn't have to worry about how much a barrister costs or how long the case dragged on. It's a very touchy and dangerous business, damaging a person's reputation, Roxanne, and Michael strikes me as the kind of man who could make a very bad enemy."

"I was only telling you for your own good," Roxanne snapped, recovering as best she could but unable to hide a flicker of fear in her eyes. "Before it's too late," she added defiantly.

"Thank you. But when I need your advice, I'll ask for it. Now, if you'll excuse me, I've got work to do." Lauren uncrossed her legs, dragged her chair toward her desk and gave Roxanne a dismissive smile. "Have a nice day. Oh, and congratulations about the baby."

Roxanne's pouty mouth thinned into quite an ugly

line. She flounced out without another word, fuming with frustration. As the door banged shut behind her, Lauren sent Graham Parker a telepathic warning.

Stormy weather on its way!

Her victory over dark forces, however, did not afford Lauren much pleasure. She fiercely wished she had known Michael much longer before falling pregnant to him. Not that she believed he was in any way insane. He was a survivor, like her, but backgrounds and upbringings did have a bearing on how people acted within marriages. Wayne had taught her that.

For her baby's sake, she couldn't afford to rush into any rash decisions, no matter how vulnerable she felt being unmarried and unprotected by a husband. She needed time to think. It was strange how quickly she was beginning to accept the reality of a baby, of it being a real person to care for.

Perhaps it was best not to let Michael know of her condition for a while. Pregnancy seemed to cause too many emotional pressures for clear thinking. Here she was on day one, so to speak, already worrying about a child that hadn't even begun to form.

The morning passed with aching slowness. She wondered how Michael's business in Melbourne was going. By midafternoon she was suffering a bout of intense loneliness. She decided it was a very lonely thing finding out one was pregnant when not surrounded by any loved ones who would feel good about it. She wanted to feel good about it herself, but she didn't.

She wished Michael would call her. She was staring at the telephone, willing him to, when it rang. She snatched up the receiver, giving her name in an eager rush.

"Lauren, it's Evan Daniel."

Disappointment.

"I'm a daddy."

"What?"

"Tasha had the baby this morning. It's a girl. The most beautiful little girl in the world."

Such pride and love! Tears pricked Lauren's eyes. "That's wonderful, Evan. Is Tasha okay?"

"Fine. Everything's fine. I'm with her right now in the maternity ward at Leura Hospital and she's cradling our daughter in her arms and we're both over the moon with happiness."

"Give her my love and best wishes."

"Will do. I wanted to talk to you about the Brisbane tour. I don't know whether I can do it or not. It means leaving—"

There was an altercation at his end of the line, then Tasha's voice. "He'll do it, Lauren. Evan's not thinking straight."

Lauren laughed. "I'll come and visit you this evening. We can talk about it."

It was an impulsive decision, but Lauren immediately warmed to the idea. Maybe seeing Tasha with her baby would settle her own feelings about having one. Besides, they were Michael's friends. She'd like to hear what they said about him as opposed to Roxanne's highly coloured views.

She rang Michael's apartment and got his answering phone. The message she left on it told him where she would be if he wanted to contact her when he arrived home. Going up to Leura in the Blue Mountains wasn't exactly waiting for him, but she needed activity, needed someone to talk to, needed sympathetic people who knew both of them.

Evan and Tasha would help. Maybe their baby would help. To Lauren, at this time of upheaval in her life, they suddenly represented a substitute family for the family she couldn't go home to in Melbourne.

CHAPTER SEVENTEEN

BEING three weeks premature, the baby was tiny, still a little crinkled and red-faced, but definitely beautiful, like a rosebud still unfurling. The soft little body, the sweet baby smell, the clutch of miniature fingers… Lauren's heart was caught from the moment Evan laid his daughter in her arms.

"Isn't it lovely she's got Evan's hair?" Tasha said with proud delight.

The brown fuzz was tightly curled. Lauren smiled. "She's very lucky."

"It was so good of you to come all this way to visit. Evan will do the tour, Lauren. He was just over-excited about the baby."

"I can cancel if you'd rather have him with you, Tasha."

"The book is important. We can't lose sight of that." Tasha eyed her besotted husband sternly. "He'll catch the flight to Brisbane on Sunday night and be back here Monday night. We can manage without him for one day."

Lauren grinned. Tasha had her feet more on the ground than Evan at the present moment.

"Michael rang. He's on his way up, too," Evan

said happily. "If you'd waited a bit longer you needn't have caught a train, Lauren."

"Well, she wasn't to know that," Tasha said sensibly, then gave Lauren a smile of warm pleasure. "I'm so glad you and Michael have made up your differences. He's such a special man."

"Yes. Though I don't really know much about him." She grimaced. "Roxanne gave me another earful today. None of it nice. I remembered what you said about defamation, Evan, and warned her that Michael might sue her for slander if she kept on."

"What was she saying?" Tasha asked, shocked at such nastiness.

Lauren gave them the gist of the conversation, and both of them were outraged at the slur of madness in Michael's family.

"They had too much money for their own good," Tasha declared. "It spoils people. They left their children to nannies and posh private schools and went off and did what they liked. Self-indulgence is not madness."

"And there was nothing mysterious about his parents' deaths," Evan said angrily. "They went on safari in Africa. His father was trampled by a bull elephant that charged him, and his mother succumbed to some tropical virus that killed her before they could get medical help. They lived dangerously and died doing what they wanted to do."

"What about his grandmother?" Lauren asked tentatively.

"Huh!" Evan snorted. "A right old Tartar, she was. Liked to crack the whip. But believe me, Lauren, there's a lot of people who revel in power in this world. Especially people of great wealth whom no-one can really touch. It goes to their heads. I could tell you about quite a few of them in our Australian history. No-one considered *them* mad."

"It's true, though, she did abuse Michael and Peter, Evan," Tasha said softly. "She was a cruel, unfeeling woman."

"She never got the better of Michael," Evan argued.

"No, Michael wouldn't let anyone or anything beat him," Tasha said knowingly, then sighed. "But I do feel sorry for him. He's never had the love he deserves." She looked hopefully at Lauren. "We all need love. It doesn't matter how self-sufficient we can be, nothing makes up for not being loved."

The riches of life, Lauren thought.

"Well, I know someone who's going to be showered with love." She smiled at the baby. "Have you decided on a name for her?"

While Tasha and Evan happily discussed the merits of their preferences, Lauren pondered Tasha's perception of Michael, appreciating the other woman's longer knowledge of him.

While she herself had been lonely in Sydney, she had never known the loneliness that must have been integral to all of Michael's life. His parents had deserted him. His grandmother certainly hadn't loved him. Neither had Roxanne. His brother had chosen to live on the other side of the world.

Lauren wondered about his brother and the aunt in Italy, both apparently alienated from their natural heritage and leaving the responsibility of administering the Timberlane estate to Michael. Was that why Michael was keen on having a family of his own?

She looked at the tiny scrap of humanity cradled in her arms. It embodied so many hopes and dreams for the future. She was suddenly certain that Michael would do his best to give his child—his children— all he had been deprived of himself, the love, the caring and the happiness that came with sharing. If it was within his power, he would make the hopes and dreams come true.

"Michael!" A warm cry of welcome from Tasha.

Lauren glanced up. He was in the doorway to the ward, carrying an exquisite arrangement of pink tulips, but it was the look on his face that arrested her attention. His eyes were on her and the baby, and the hopes and dreams of the inner man were poignantly written there, and in the soft smile lingering on his lips. She had seen him looking forbidding and formidable—the dark side, as Roxanne put it—but this was the face of love, and Lauren's heart leapt in response.

She was holding Tasha's baby.

When she held her own…his…

"What beautiful flowers!" Tasha said with pleasure.

He dragged his gaze from Lauren and grinned at her. "I figured Evan would supply the roses." There was, indeed, a vase of pink roses on Tasha's bedside table. "Congratulations to both of you."

He kissed Tasha's cheek, shook Evan's hand, admired their newly born daughter, refused to arbitrate over the choice of names, declaring them all lovely, while at every opportunity his eyes told Lauren how beautiful, how desirable, how special she was to him, melting the chill of loneliness she had felt all day.

Tasha's parents arrived, and Lauren gave the baby up to its grandmother. In the flood of family talk that followed, Michael drew Lauren aside, threading his fingers through hers and gripping her hand with the same strong feeling reflected in his eyes.

"I've booked a suite at the Fairmont Resort. It's only ten minutes from here. Will you come with me, Lauren?"

"Yes." No hesitation. She wanted, needed to be with him.

His smile bathed her in warmth. "Shall we leave the happy family?"

She nodded. "We're superfluous now."

But she did feel better for having come, less disturbed about where she might be heading with Michael and more secure about her judgment of him. She knew, as they took their leave, that Tasha and Evan would become her friends, too. They were good people.

Getting into Michael's car reminded her of the

sense of setting out on a new, important journey she had felt on the night of Global's launching party. This time it was stronger, sharper. It wasn't just her and Michael's intent on discovering more of each other. A child had been conceived. It added a highly critical element to their relationship.

Should she tell him now?

He settled beside her in the driver's seat, this man who had made love to her more intimately than he knew, his seed becoming part of her, inextricably entwined in a new life. Would he share that life as she wanted him to, not only as a father to their child, but as a true and loving partner to her in every way?

He felt her measuring look and cast an inquiring glance at her as he started the engine. "Is this all right with you, Lauren? If you're not sure…"

"I'm glad you came. It's fine with me, Michael," she assured him. "How did your business go in Melbourne?"

"Oh." He flashed her his wicked grin, then set the car in motion. "Ultimately rewarding, I think. Well worth doing."

"What boards do you sit on?" she asked, wanting something more concrete from him.

"Most of them have to do with funding various charities," he said offhandedly.

"Like what?" she persisted.

"Shelters for street kids. Homeless children. The association for crippled children. Rehabilitation programs. The general aim is to give young people a better chance at life.''

"That's certainly worth doing,'' Lauren said with warm approval.

"It's good when you see the difference that hope can make. Some of them are handed such a raw deal, yet the human spirit is amazingly resilient.''

It seemed very apt to Lauren that Michael would actively encourage the will to survive against any odds. More than survive. To move forward and forge a brighter future.

"Has the Timberlane family always contributed to charities for the needy?'' she asked curiously.

"All charities are for the needy, Lauren,'' he answered seriously. "These are my special interests. The Timberlanes have always been patrons of the arts, and I keep that up, as well. I'm a friend of the opera and the ballet and so on.''

A friend. A friend to many people in many places.

"The arts may not provide food for starving kids, but they do nourish the soul and broaden the mind,'' he went on. "The tapestry of life would not be as rich without them.''

"That's true,'' she agreed, wondering what had been his favourite books during the dark times of his childhood.

"Roxanne didn't favour what she called my slum charities,'' he remarked sardonically.

"No social eclat.''

"Mmm. What do you think?''

"Whenever you want to drum up media interest to get something accomplished for those kids, I'm your woman."

His smile held private satisfaction, as though she had confirmed his expectations of her. Lauren smiled, too. Michael had confirmed her reading of his character. He followed in no-one's footsteps. He made his own decisions and acted on them.

They arrived at the Fairmont Resort, which overlooked the Jamieson Valley. The reception area was very modern—polished wood floor, leather lounges, high ceilings, staircases leading down to a bar where a huge slate fireplace supplied a welcoming log fire. The evening had turned bitterly cold, and Lauren eyed this source of heat with considerable favour as Michael went through the business of checking in.

Her mobile telephone beeped and she quickly removed it from her handbag to answer the call. Her mother's voice raised a tingle of alarm. Wayne was making more trouble—that was the thought that flew to her mind.

"What's the problem, Mum?" she instantly asked.

"No problem, dear. Quite the contrary. I just wanted to let you know how very impressed I am with your man of action."

"Who?" Lauren was completely bewildered.

Laughter, happy, carefree laughter. "Michael Timberlane. He's absolutely marvellous, Lauren. I'm so delighted you've found someone like him."

"You've met Michael?" Lauren recalled he'd

asked for her mother's address, but she'd had so much else weighing on her mind since her return from Melbourne, she hadn't wondered about it.

"Of course, dear. Hasn't he told you what he did?"

"No. What did he do?" she asked warily.

More laughter. "I'll put Johnny on. He can tell it better."

"Hi, Lauren. We're all celebrating down here," her brother crowed excitedly. "You've got a great guy in Michael Timberlane."

"Thank you, Johnny, but I'd like to know why you think that," Lauren said impatiently.

The account of Michael's "business" in Melbourne left her flabbergasted. Roping in her family to pull such an outrageous confidence trick on Wayne was mind-boggling enough, but his personal outlay in stamping home his point to her ex-husband put her value to Michael on an astronomical level.

Fifty thousand dollars for the car that had been written off, the cost of the limousine, the "boss" outfit, the other vehicles, time of men involved... It was so impossibly extravagant, so...caring. Her heart turned over. This then, was what he meant by looking after her.

"So now you're free of that creep, Lauren. You don't have to worry about Wayne any more," her brother finished.

"Thanks, Johnny," she said faintly. "And thank everyone else for me, too. Got to go now. Michael's coming for me."

He'd turned away from the reception desk and was walking towards her, an eager spring in his step, his face alight with anticipation, a man of purpose, a man of action, a man who cared so much for her.

Lauren knew in that moment there could be no holding back from him. He had earned her trust, her respect, her loyalty and her love. The words *too soon* no longer had any meaning. He had given her the gift of freedom from her past. She hoped she had the means in her power to give him the gift of freedom from his past.

CHAPTER EIGHTEEN

"WHAT would you like to do first?" Michael asked, leaving the choice to Lauren.

The warm, relaxing atmosphere of the bar and the open fire was forgotten. She held out her hand to him. "Let's go to our suite."

The communication of urgency was silent and swift. Michael didn't question. The need to be alone together was deep and mutual.

Lauren was intensely aware of his hand enfolding hers as they walked down a long corridor. She didn't notice the decor they passed. The focus of her mind was entirely inward, playing through all the dimensions and permutations of one thought. Michael Timberlane might not be his brother's keeper, but she wanted him to be hers.

He unlocked a door and led her into the welcome privacy of their suite, pausing only to operate the lighting system and airconditioning. He drew her into his embrace, and she went eagerly, wanting to join with him again, yearning for the all-encompassing oneness that shut the rest of the world out and wrapped them in an intimacy that belonged only to them.

His mouth was soft and hungry on hers, and while

she knew there was no time limitation tonight, the flow of desire was so powerful, she urged him into passion, straining closer, revelling in the explosion of sensation as their mouths tangled in fierce greed for each other.

Still it wasn't enough. The memory of how it had been on that one night of ultimate magic raged through Lauren, demanding more of the same. Her hands plucked at his jacket. He tore it off. She could feel the hectic beating of his heart, the quiver of his flesh under her touch, the questing strength of his arousal, and she knew his desire was as strong as hers.

Yes, her mind sang exultantly as he lifted her long blue sweater and swept it from her arms. Yes, yes, came the feverish refrain as he pushed her skirt over her hips and she wiggled it down to her feet to kick it away, another unwanted barrier gone. She was attacking his shirt buttons when it suddenly occurred to her, with riveting clarity, that this lustful rush was open to terribly destructive interpretations.

Her fingers faltered, sensible sanity warring with teeming temptations. They were half-undressed already. Action was more eloquent than words. Naked truth was best. The radiation of his body heat was an irresistible magnet. Being naked had to be right. Nothing hidden.

"Don't stop," he growled, fanning her ear with erotic warmth as his thumbs hooked into her tights and his fingers danced an enticingly sensual rhythm beneath her hip bones.

Impossible to stop now. But she couldn't completely ignore the warning signals pulsing through her fevered brain. She didn't want Michael to get the wrong idea. Only naked truth. "This isn't gratitude," she declared fiercely, tearing at his buttons with driven haste, getting rid of his shirt.

"Nothing like it," he agreed, scooping down her tights and hoisting her up to remove them.

Breathtaking speed. Expert efficiency. Lauren loved it. She hung around his shoulders, panting with excitement. Such manly, broad shoulders, strong enough to carry off anything he set his mind to. Did he realise what she meant about gratitude? Better make it clearer.

"I know what you did about Wayne," she said quickly, adoring him for taking such a daring and dashing initiative, showering his hair and ears with hot, appreciative kisses.

"Don't think about him any more," Michael advised, easing her away from him momentarily so he could whisk off her camisole and bra.

Free to hug him, the delicious delight of squashing her breasts against his beautifully muscled chest, skin against skin. His trousers frustratingly in the way. Other things still to be acknowledged and disposed of.

"You spent a lot of money frightening Wayne off," she reminded him, breathlessly matching him in efficiency at helping to relieve him of his lower garments.

"Made me feel good." His shoes and socks went flying.

Lauren had a vague feeling he hadn't got the point. There were far more urgent points of compelling interest grabbing their attention, and control was slipping away from both of them. Urgent needs frayed the last threads of coherency in her mind. It was a sheer act of will for her to focus on anything other than how utterly magnificent he was.

"I'm not rewarding you, Michael. I want you," she insisted, determined that he understand her position and unable to resist touching him to reinforce her claim.

"And that's the greatest feeling in the world," he assured her, swinging her to the bed.

Flesh against flesh, hot and sleek and sensual. Lauren was hopelessly distracted, luxuriating in the feel of his lean, lithe physique, so powerfully constructed and excitingly responsive to her touch. Deep, drowning kisses, arousal swift and sweet.

"Michael…" His name exploding from her lips, a frantic need to communicate before she lost herself in him, lost the chance to set everything straight between them. "I'm not trying to trap you."

"You think I don't know that?" A wild, primitive glow of triumph in his eyes.

"Roxanne…"

"Malicious spite. Don't listen to her," he mumbled, carelessly dismissive of a past that held no power to reach him in the face of what he had now.

He burned a trail of kisses down her throat, lower, grazing the swell of her tight, tingling breasts. Her body arched instinctively, craving the pleasure of his mouth, the moist heat, the tantalising caress of his tongue, the rhythmic sucking that inundated her with waves of intense sensation.

But at the last moment she couldn't let him… Couldn't, because the image of a baby burst into her mind and she had to tell him. Her hands clutched his head, forcibly lifting it, making him meet her eyes.

She saw the passion glaze clear to a sharp questioning as he realised something had to be badly wrong for her to stop him. He dragged in deep lungfuls of air, struggling to clamp down on his raging impulses, recognising there was a need that had to be answered before he could go on.

"What is it, Lauren?" His voice was hoarse, straining to respond, to give whatever she required of him.

She had his attention. He was listening. They were naked together, making love. It had to be all right. Yet a frightening sense of vulnerability thickened her throat and scrambled her mind. "You… I… We… It was an accident, Michael."

"It's all right," he soothed, quickly repositioning himself over her and tenderly brushing her hair away from her face. "Tell me what's worrying you."

It was so big, so important. She choked on it. "Roxanne said she wouldn't have a baby with you."

He looked perplexed. She wasn't making sense. Yet, seeing her distress, he tried to answer her.

"The truth is she couldn't, Lauren."

"Couldn't?"

He didn't understand what relevance this had, but again he responded, forcing himself to be patient, to wait until she could give herself to him again. "She's infertile. Quite happily, so don't feel sorry for her. It suits Roxanne just fine. Pregnancy would ruin her precious figure," he added sardonically.

"But…" Incredulity forced her to speak. "She told me she's pregnant to Godfrey."

He shook his head. No flicker of doubt. "I've seen her medical record, Lauren. Roxanne cannot conceive a child. Maybe she's now lying to Godfrey as she once lied to me about wanting to have children."

Or lying to Lauren to put her off Michael. Lying malevolently about madness in his family. The sheer viciousness of Roxanne's spite sickened Lauren. Being married to her must have been as soul-destroying for Michael as her marriage had been to Wayne.

The realisation gave her the courage to say what had to be said. "When we made love before…"

His eyes simmered into hers. "It was perfect. The best night of my life, Lauren. I'm sorry there's been so many other forces coming between us, but I promise you I'll sort them all out."

"I don't know how it happened, Michael."

"It happened because we're right for each other," he insisted with husky fervour. His gaze moved to her mouth and his head began to lower, intent on establishing the rightness again.

"No, I mean..." She took a deep breath and spoke the truth in a rush. "I did a pregnancy test this morning and it was positive."

Shock. Utter stillness as he absorbed the connotations of what she was telling him, his eyes focusing more and more intensely on hers as he sought to read her mind and gauge her feelings. His face reflected a churning of many emotions, a soft tenderness, a jaw-clenching determination, a grimace of regret.

"I should have been with you," he finally said, and she knew intuitively that he felt he'd failed to look after her when she needed him at her side.

"You weren't to know," she softly assured him.

He stroked her cheek with gentle fingertips. "Are you unhappy about it, Lauren?"

His concentration on her stirred uncertainty about his response to having fatherhood thrust upon him and the commitment it involved if they were to share a future. "That depends on you, Michael," she answered simply and directly. "What do you want?"

An irrepressible smile broke across his face. "To marry you this minute and shout to the world that we're going to have a baby."

She looked at him in startled bemusement. "Roxanne hasn't put you off marriage?"

"That wasn't marriage. It was a travesty of what a marriage should be." His eyes blazed with conviction as he added, "What we share is the real thing. You feel that too, Lauren."

"Yes. Yes, I do," she acknowledged, awed that he was so certain.

His grin was a flash of dazzling happiness. "Then it's settled. We get married and work everything out together. Partners and parents."

"Not so fast. I think we should work everything out *before* we get married." But his happiness was infectious, and Lauren couldn't be stern or sensible when her heart was bubbling with joy. He wanted them both, her and the baby, no hesitation at all about a lifelong commitment. She wound her arms around his neck and stretched her body provocatively. "Though I like the togetherness part," she added invitingly.

Wicked delight danced into his eyes. The critical talking was done, and the loving could go on…and on, a long celebration of togetherness that climbed to a crescendo of exquisite ecstasy, binding them blissfully to the fulfilment of their dreams.

CHAPTER NINETEEN

MICHAEL finished negotiating the purchase arrangements with the real estate agent and went in search of Lauren, who had wandered off to take another look at the garden. It gave him a pleasurable sense of achievement to have found the kind of family home that appealed to her. Above all, he wanted her to feel happy in it.

She shouldn't be out in this heat, he thought, feeling the full blaze of the midafternoon February sun as he strode down the path to the landscaped harbour frontage. The baby was due any day now. Lauren should be resting.

His concern eased when he spotted her standing under the shade of a tree. She didn't see him coming. She seemed unaware of anything around her, absorbed in some world of her own. He stopped, reluctant to break her private enthralment, the stillness that captured a beauty so special it caught at his heart. He wanted to drink her in, to record this picture of her in his memory forever.

Her head was slightly lowered, looking down, her lids half-closed, long lashes shading her eyes. Her expression was pensive, a hint of a smile softly curving her lips. The wild mass of her burnished curls was tied from her face, fastened by a leather string at the nape of her neck, keeping the flow of it restricted to a thick tumble down her back.

The loose sundress she wore was mainly white with a pretty print of tiny red carnations and green leaves. The neckline was low, dipping to the swell of her breasts. Her arms were bare, slender, graceful. One hand held a large straw hat, its brim decorated with a long spray of red carnations.

A breeze from the water moulded the fabric of her dress to her belly, revealing how big she was with child. To Michael she looked breathtakingly beautiful, aglow with inner contentment, soft and serene and infinitely seductive—his wife, waiting for the birth of their baby.

He approached quietly, but she sensed him near and turned to smile at him as he moved behind her to slide his arms around her waist and gently hold the weight she carried. Her head tilted onto his shoulder, a long sigh eloquently expressing her pleasure in the embrace.

"All done?" she asked.

"It will probably take six weeks before it's completely settled, but don't worry. I'll take care of everything."

"I know. You always do."

"I love you," he murmured, nuzzling her ear.

"Mmm...I'm going to need a lot more loving, Michael. I think I had my third contraction about fifteen minutes ago."

Excitement shot through him. "You mean…"

She laughed and turned to slide her hands around his neck, her cornflower blue eyes lit with the same excitement. "Can you handle taking your pregnant wife to hospital?"

"For you I can handle anything," he promised huskily.

Twelve long, nerve-tearing, emotion-laden hours later, Michael had an excruciating awareness that Lauren handled some things better than he did, but he staunchly stood by, pouring out intense waves of love to make up for the pain.

Then, like a miracle, the ordeal was over, and a nurse laid a squalling infant in his arms, and it was his son, his and Lauren's son, a perfect piece of magic that mended everything because Lauren looked at him with tears of joy in her eyes and a smile that made his heart fill up again and overflow with so many emotions he knew he could never forget this moment as long as he lived… Lauren, making this happen for him.

Mary Magee, Lauren's mother, flew to Sydney the next day, bringing with her the well wishes of the family and showering Michael with her pleasure in her new grandchild. So different from his grandmother, he thought, rejoicing in the difference and loving Lauren all the more for drawing him into belonging to a real family.

Tasha and Evan visited, warmly congratulating

them. Evan's book had been a best-seller, and he had written a sequel, which Global was to publish for the coming Christmas market. Lauren had pushed for this time slot, and while she now had a full-time assistant to do the legwork of her publicity schedules, she had promised Evan she would personally handle all the media arrangements for him and his new book.

It kept running through Michael's mind—Lauren made things happen. Good things. Wonderful things. Incredible things.

To his utter amazement, Peter took it into his head to fly home to Australia for the first time in years and suddenly turned into a doting uncle—his brother, who had determinedly turned his back on anything related to the family he had been born into.

"I'm going to keep on checking that you bring him up right," Peter warned. "We didn't have much of an example, Michael."

"Lauren did," he answered happily and proudly, though privately pleased that Peter now had someone he could let himself care for. Another miracle.

Peter grinned at Lauren. "I can see how successful she's been at looking after you, big brother. You're a very lucky man. Happiness becomes you."

Looking after him. The insight burst through Michael's mind. It was so true. Lauren filled his heart, fed his soul, gave him the looking after he'd never known before he had met her. She made so many differences to his life.

On top of Peter's unexpected descent on them came

Aunt Rose from Italy. Having viewed the new generation, she declared him a Timberlane through and through, the spitting image of one of Michael's great-uncles who'd captained a ship that had been lost at sea. She commanded Michael to bring Lauren to Capri in the near future, because she knew just the artist who would do her justice and she ought to be painted at the height of her beauty.

Magic, Michael decided, the special magic of a woman who loved openly and honestly, the woman who had walked into his life one dark night to give him the light of her love, making his life glow with a new and happy purpose—looking after Lauren and the family they made together.

He searched for words to express what she had done for him, but despite all the words he had read in a multitude of books and manuscripts, he could not find any that satisfied him. In the end he simply held her as she nursed their baby son and spoke from the fullness of his heart.

"Thank you, Lauren."

"For him?" she asked.

"Yes. But mostly for you."

She smiled at him, her eyes the blue of summer skies, bathing him with a warmth that reached deeply into his soul. "I love you, Michael."

And that, of course, was the answer to everything. She loved him.

Aunt Rose from half-full houses and the teacup

... the nature larger ... to Office ... with ...

... She ... a length ... and ... to

Capri in the their young. However she wanted was the

artist who would do her justice, and she ought to be

painted at the height of her beauty.

Magic, Michael decided, the special magic of a

woman who loved openly and honestly, the woman

who had waited once his life and that up there, give

him the faith of her love and an Rembrandt low with

a new and happy prospect. Looking after the rest and

the family they made together.

He searched for words to express what she had

done for him, but despite all the world be and read

in a multitude of books and monuments, he could not

find any that satisfied him. In the end he simply held

her as she nursed their baby son and gazed from the

fullness of his heart.

"Thank you," I said.

"To time," she asked.

"Yes. The moody for you."

She smiled at him, her eyes the blue of summer

skies, beaming him with a warmth that reached deeply

into his soul. "I love you, Michael."

And that, of course, was the answer to everything.

She loved him.

Although born in England, **Sandra Field** has lived most of her life in Canada; she says the silence and emptiness of the north speaks to her particularly. While she enjoys travelling, and passing on her sense of a new place, she often chooses to write about the city which is now her home. Sandra says, 'I write out of my experience; I have learned that love with its joys and its pains is all-important. I hope this knowledge enriches my writing, and touches a chord in you, the reader.'

Look out for Sandra Field's next book, coming soon in Modern Romance™!

AFTER HOURS
by
Sandra Field

CHAPTER ONE

SHE was losing it. Going bonkers.

Marcia Barnes stood in the living room of her condo, gazing out the window at the Rideau Canal; along the bicycle path that followed the curves of the canal a couple of intrepid cyclers zipped along, undeterred by the rain. It was a peaceful scene. Trees that had just burst into leaf, tulips in geometric beds, tidy arrays of well-kept houses. Everything neat and in perfect order.

Not like her.

She pulled a hideous face in the plate glass window. However, if this had been an attempt to quell the anxiety that had been with her ever since the meeting that afternoon at the medical research institute where she worked as an immunologist, it failed miserably. At the meeting the director, in a voice as smooth as cream, had spoken of budgetary restraints that might lead to cutbacks in staff. Cutbacks that could go as high as fifty percent. Although Marcia had worked there for seven years, she by no means had seniority.

Her work was her life. Had been as long as she could remember. She'd be lost without it.

She took a couple of deep breaths, trying to calm herself. Thank goodness she'd had the sense to refuse Lucy and Troy's invitation to dinner. Bad enough that she'd agreed to go to the gallery where their friend Quentin what's-his-name's show was opening.

Quentin. The name conjured up Harris tweed jackets and a pipe. An uppercrust British accent. Landscapes modeled after Constable's, with puffy white clouds and placid brown cows.

The last thing she felt right now was placid—she who everyone thought was so into control. Rather, she felt as though her life, so carefully constructed and so rigidly maintained, was falling into pieces around her.

She went into the kitchen and located her invitation to the gallery—the most exclusive gallery in town. Not that she cared. She didn't want to get dressed up and go out again. She didn't want to meet Quentin Ramsey, whose show, called *Multiple Personalities*, was being touted in such glowing terms. Nor did she want to see her sister Lucy and her brother-in-law Troy, who had arrived in Ottawa yesterday just to be at the opening.

What she wanted to do was fill her bathtub to the rim with steaming hot water and big globs of bubble bath, turn on the most soothing music she possessed and forget all about the outside world. After that she'd go to bed. How else to end a day from hell?

She sighed. Lucy was already puzzled by her refusal to have dinner with them. Although Lucy and Troy lived in Vancouver, they were spending the next two months in Ottawa because Troy was teaching pediatric residencies in two of the city hospitals. They'd brought the baby with them. If Marcia didn't turn up at the art gallery, Lucy would think something was wrong.

Nothing's wrong, Marcia thought wildly, rubbing at her forehead. There's a good chance I'm going to lose my job, the woman I've always been has deserted me and I don't have a clue who else to be, and I don't want to see my own sister. I don't even want to be around her. What kind of person does that make me?

Tall, beautiful Lucy, with her mop of untidy curls and her full figure and her rich, uninhibited laughter was the very antithesis of her elder sister Marcia. Or her younger sister Catherine. Or their mother Evelyn, come to that.

Do I envy her? Is that what it is?

Was envy one of the seven deadly sins? If it wasn't, it should be.

The old-fashioned grandfather clock, which had indeed belonged to Marcia's grandfather, a renowned neurosurgeon, chimed the half hour. I'm going to be late... Oh, well, that means I'll miss the speeches at the beginning and I'll get to meet Lucy and Troy in the middle of a whole lot of people. No chance for intimacy. Sounds good.

Marcia went into the bedroom, which faced west and was filled with the fading light of evening. Raindrops were beating against the windowpane in a miniature tattoo. Firmly closing her mind to the prospect of a hot bath, Marcia rummaged through her closet. Lucy always had been too intuitive for comfort. So the persona of the Marcia she had always been was going to be firmly in place. Cool, competent Marcia, in control of her own life. Unemotional, detached Marcia, who never made demands.

All her movements neat and efficient, she stripped off her work clothes, had a quick shower and dressed in a navy blue linen suit whose tailored elegance was worth every penny she had paid for it. Silky navy hose, Italian leather pumps and discreet gold jewelry came next. Expertly she applied her make-up. Then she brushed her sleek dark hair, in its expensive cut that curved just below her ears, and checked her appearance in the full-length mirror in her bedroom.

She didn't look thirty-three.

Not that it really mattered how old she looked.

Hastily she jammed her big horn-rimmed glasses on her nose. She could have worn her contacts. But her glasses gave her something to hide behind—and to meet Lucy she needed all the help she could get. Grabbing her shiny forest-green raincoat and still-damp umbrella from the hall closet, she left her condo and took the elevator to the basement.

She'd go straight to the gallery, meet the famous Quentin Ramsey, make appreciative noises about every one of his multiple personalities and invite Lucy and Troy to dinner on Sunday along with the rest of the family. And then she'd come home, duty done.

Multiple Personalities, she thought crossly, backing out of her parking lot. What kind of a name was that for a bunch of paintings? Too clever by half. Too cutesy. Altogether too self-conscious. He might be Lucy and Troy's friend, but that didn't mean that she, Marcia, had to like him.

Scowling, she pressed the remote control to open the garage door, and drove out into the rainswept evening.

Quentin, too, had checked his appearance in the mirror before he'd left for the art gallery. The amount of money he'd had to spend to get a decent suit that he planned to wear no more than half a dozen times a year had astounded him. He looked like an ad in a glossy men's magazine, he thought irritably, hitching at the knot in his silk tie: ''The Successful Artist of the 90s. Man-about-town Quentin Ramsey attending the opening of his highly successful show *Multiple Personalities*.''

What in hell had possessed him to come up with that title?

He ran a comb through his thick black curls, which instantly went right back to their usual state of disarray. He grinned at himself, feeling somewhat more cheerful. At least his hair refused to do the correct thing. And he'd always hated openings. Hated them with a passion.

He painted to communicate—no doubt about that. He didn't want his works stashed away in a studio with their faces to a wall. But he couldn't stand to hear people discussing them, stereotyping them, analyzing all their vitality out of existence with words like "deconstructionism" and "postmodern abstractionism". At least the critics had had to come up with some new labels for this show, he thought, grinning again. Time he shook them up a bit.

Someone would be bound to tell him that his new style was a cop-out in the interests of commercialism. And someone else would be sure to praise his raw honesty. For some reason his kind of honesty was nearly always called raw.

Speaking of which, he'd forgotten to eat anything.

Quentin went to the minibar and pilfered its entire stock of peanuts and pretzels. Chewing absently, he realized how much he was looking forward to seeing Lucy and Troy. He'd turned down their invitation to dinner because he had to be at the gallery early. But, if he had his way, he'd end up the evening at the apartment they'd rented and he'd take off his tie and his shiny leather shoes that were already pinching his feet, and toss back a beer or two. And he'd be sure to admire the new baby. He knew rather more than most people what that baby meant to them.

And as soon as he could he'd get out of Ottawa. Too tidy a city for him. Too prettified. He wanted pine trees and running water and maybe a mountain or two.

Not a hotel room—no matter how luxurious.

He opened the second bag of pretzels. What he really needed to do was take a break from painting and build another house. The bite of saw into lumber, the sweet smell of wood chips, the satisfaction of seeing a roofline cut into the sky—they all anchored him to a reality very different from that of paint on canvas. It was a reality he was beginning to crave.

There was nothing new about this. In his travels around the world Quentin had always alternated periods of intense artistic activity with the more mundane and comforting reality of house construction. What was new was that the house he wanted to build this time was a house for himself. His own walls. His own roof.

He glanced at his watch and gave an exclamation of dismay. Grabbing his raincoat, he ran for the elevator, and in the lobby of the hotel hailed a cab. But as he was driven through the gleaming wet streets, still chewing on the pretzels, his thoughts traveled with him. He wanted to settle down. He'd been a nomad ever since he'd left his parents' yard at the age of three to follow the milk truck down the road, but now he wanted to have a place that he could call home.

It had been a long time since that little boy had stumbled along the dirt ruts, hollering at the milkman to wait for him. He was thirty-six now. And while he wanted a home, there was more to it than that. He wanted a woman to share that home. To share his home. His bed. His life. But she had to be the right woman.

He gazed vaguely at the beds of tulips that edged the road, neat blocks of solid color that moved him not at all. He'd been considerably older than three—eleven, perhaps—when he'd come to the conclusion that he'd know the woman he was meant to marry from the first moment he saw her. He knew perfectly well where that conviction had come from. His parents had had—he now realized, as an adult—the kind of marriage that happens only rarely. A marriage alive with love, laughter and passion, with fierce conflicts and an honesty that could indeed have been called raw.

He hadn't been able to verbalize this at age eleven, but he had intuited that there was something very special between the man and woman who were his parents. One of the often-told stories of his childhood had been how they had fallen in love at first sight, recognizing each other instantly as the partner each had been waiting for.

At the age of twenty-five, impatient, he'd ignored that certainty and married Helen. And within six weeks had known that he'd done the wrong thing. He'd hung in to the very best of his ability, and when she'd left him for a bank president twice her age had heaved a sigh of relief and vowed never to repeat that particular mistake.

Quentin was not a vain man, and it never ceased to surprise him that women flocked to him like blue jays to a feeder on a cold winter's day. Tall women, short women, beautiful women, sexy women. But not one of them so far had touched his soul.

What if he never found this mythical woman? Was he a fool to believe in the romantic dream of an eleven-year-old?

Maybe if he built the house first she'd somehow follow, as naturally as sunrise was bound to follow sunset.

Or maybe he was a fool even to think of settling down. He'd always rather prided himself on being a free spirit, going where he pleased when he pleased and staying as long as he pleased. If he got married, he wouldn't be able to do that.

The right woman...did she even exist?

He tried to wrench his mind away from thoughts that were, he'd sometimes concluded, both non-productive and infantile. The taxi swished through a puddle and drew up outside the gallery. Pots of scarlet tulips decorated the sidewalk, standing stiff and tall in the rain, like valiant soldiers on watch. I'm lonely, Quentin thought with a flash of insight. Despite my success, despite the incredible freedom of the way I live, I'm lonely.

"Ten seventy-five, sir," said the cabbie.

With a jerk Quentin came back to the present. He fumbled for the fare, added a tip, and ran for the gallery door. He wasn't all that free. Because he'd rather be walking the wet streets tonight than going to his own opening.

The owner of the gallery was a woman in her fifties, wife of a senior government official and dauntingly efficient; Quentin always wanted to call her Mrs. Harrington-Smythe rather than Emily—a name that did not suit her in the slightest. As he hung up his raincoat she gave his suit a quick appraisal and nodded her approval.

Wishing he'd left the price tag pinned to the cuff, Quentin allowed himself to be whisked on a tour of the gallery. Her placement of the paintings was all he could have asked; he only wished that they didn't make him feel as though he was about to undress in public. Emily gave him a copy of the catalog and ran through a list of the most prominent ministers, several deputy ministers and a sprinkling of diplomats.

Not bad for a kid from a little village in New Brunswick, thought Quentin, and did his best to memorize the names. Then the doorbell rang and he steeled himself to get through the next hours without abandoning the good manners his mother had worked very hard to instill in him.

Three-quarters of an hour later the place was humming. Eleven paintings had sold, the bartenders had been run off their feet and Quentin had been extremely civil to the first of the cabinet ministers—who didn't approve of anything painted after 1900 and wasn't backward in expressing his views. Then, from behind him, Quentin heard a woman call his name. He turned, gathered Lucy into his arms and hugged her hard. "Wonderful to see you!"

She said softly, "I can't believe you were being so polite—is this the Quentin I know?"

"I'm on my best behavior. You look gorgeous, Lucy—that's quite a dress."

Its purple folds made her mahogany curls glisten, and its *décolletage* verged on the indiscreet. "I thought you'd like it," she said complacently. "Troy picked it out for me."

Troy clapped Quentin on the shoulder. "Good to see

you. When this affair is over, we want you to come back
to the apartment so we can catch up on all the news.''

''Done,'' said Quentin. ''As long as you've got some
beer.''

''Bought a twelve-pack this afternoon.''

Troy was two or three inches taller than Quentin's five-
feet eleven, blond where Quentin was dark, and a medical
doctor rather than an artist; but from the time they had met
on Shag Island off the coast of Nova Scotia the two men
had liked one another. And when Quentin pictured the
home he was going to build for himself it was always situated somewhere on the west coast within reach of Vancouver.

Emily was fast approaching, with a man in tow who
looked like cabinet minister number two. Quentin raised
his brow at Lucy. ''Duty calls. Talk to you later.''

''We'll give you our address before we leave.' Tucking
her arm into Troy's, she headed for the works in acrylic
that were such a break from the abstracts he had been doing
on the island.

The second cabinet minister asked several penetrating
questions and listened with genuine interest to Quentin's
replies. Then Quentin suffered through a very rich widow
with fake eyelashes who simply didn't understand the first
thing about art, and an importer of foreign cars who understood only too well and insisted on inflicting his theories
on the artist. Quentin finally got rid of him and headed for
the bar. The pretzels had made him thirsty.

He had just taken a gulp of what was a quite decent
Cabernet, hoping it would inspire him to plunge back into
the mêlée, when the door was pushed open once again. Idly
he watched as a woman walked into the foyer. She closed
her umbrella, shook water from it and straightened, the light
falling on her face and the smooth swing of her hair. Dark
hair that shone like polished wood.

Oh, Lord, thought Quentin. It's happened. At a gallery opening, of all places. That's her. The woman I've been waiting for.

He plunked his glass on the counter and pushed past several people who all wanted to speak to him, deaf to their remarks. The woman was hanging her dark green raincoat on the rack by the door, all her movements economical and precise. She's not my type, he thought blankly. Look at that suit. And those godawful glasses. What in heaven's name's going on here?

He was still ten feet away from her. She turned, taking the glasses from her nose and rubbing the rain from them with a tissue from her pocket, her face composed as she surveyed the crowded room. She might not be his type, but she was utterly, beguilingly beautiful.

His heart was banging in his chest like the ring of a hammer on boards. Feeling as clumsy as an adolescent, Quentin closed the distance between them and croaked, "I don't believe we've met."

She was no more than five feet five and delicately made, so that he felt large and clumsy. Her irises were the deep velvety purple of pansies and her lashes dark and thick; her bone structure was exquisite and her make-up flawless. Last of all, he saw how very soft and kissable was her mouth, and he felt his heart give another uncomfortable thud in his chest. She said in faint puzzlement, "Are you the gallery owner? I thought—"

"I'm the artist."

Her lashes flickered over unmistakable hostility. "Quentin Ramsey?"

He nodded. "And you?"

"Surely you don't meet everyone at the door?"

"You're the first."

"And to what," Marcia said silkily, "do I owe that honor?"

"Stop talking like a nineteenth-century novel. It doesn't suit you."

So much for the aristocratic British accent, thought Marcia. Not to mention the British good manners. "How can you possibly have any idea what suits me—I could be a professor of Victorian literature for all you know. Are you always so rude to potential customers?"

But Quentin was frowning, struggling to anchor a memory. "I've seen you somewhere. I'm sure I have."

"That's one of the oldest lines in the book."

"You cheapen both of us by that kind of remark."

"Oh, pardon me," she said. "In my experience, men—"

"I *have* seen you before."

"You're quite wrong—I've never met you." Because I would have remembered you, thought Marcia, trying to calm down. For the blue of your eyes, if nothing else. The deepest blue I've ever seen. Deep enough to lose myself.

"What's your name?"

She took a deep breath. Her imaginary portrait of Quentin Ramsey couldn't have been more inaccurate. This was definitely no tweed-jacketed Englishman who painted pretty landscapes under the influence of a great master. This man was a rugged individualist if ever she'd met one. Rugged, indeed; he looked as though he'd be more at home with a chainsaw than a paintbrush. She said coolly, "Dr. Marcia Barnes."

"*What*? You're Lucy's sister?"

He looked as shocked as though she'd just thrown a glass of wine in his face. She said, wondering why she should feel so angry, "We're very different, Lucy and I."

"No kidding. But that's why I thought I'd met you—Lucy has a photo of you in her living room." Fighting down a tumble of emotions that had an acute disappointment chief among them, Quentin said, 'You're the immunologist.'

"Yes."

Glaring at her, he demanded, "Why haven't you bothered visiting them since the baby was born?"

"I did! Last November."

"Sure—you managed to stay for two whole hours on your way to a medical conference. I said *visit*."

"It's really none of your—"

"When a conference is more important to you than your own family, you're in a bad way. Lucy's told me about you. 'Workaholic' is one way to describe you."

With studied charm Emily Harrington-Smythe said, "Quentin, may I borrow you for a few minutes? Mr. Brace has a couple of questions for you before he purchases the largest of the acrylics." She directed a polite smile at Marcia. "If you'll excuse us, please?"

"With pleasure," Marcia said crisply.

Determined to have the last word, Quentin announced, "Your sister and brother-in-law are in the other room. If you can spare the time, that is."

Seething, Marcia watched him cross the room and plunge into the crowd. His black hair was too long, curling at his nape, but at least those penetrating blue eyes were no longer pinning her to the wall. Just who did he think he was, daring to criticize her within moments of meeting her?

Deftly she secured a glass of wine at the bar. Lucy must have complained to him about that visit. It had been short, no question. But she'd just attended a conference on AIDS and had been on her way to another on immunodeficiency syndrome, and an afternoon had been all she could spare.

Even less anxious to meet her sister now, Marcia began to circle the room, turning her attention to the paintings. Within moments any thoughts of Lucy were banished from her mind. The works on this wall were all abstracts—some monochromatic, some boldly hued—and their emotional intensity tapped instantly into all the emptiness and confusion that she was beginning to realize she had been carrying around for quite a long time. The threat of losing her job had made them worse. But it hadn't given birth to them.

Eventually she found herself in front of a work titled *Composition Number 8*, whose vibrant spirals of color pulled her into their very depths. Her throat closed with pain. She'd never experienced what the immediacy of those colors symbolized: the joy, the passion, the fervent commitment—moment by moment—to the business of being alive. Never. And now maybe it was too late. Panic-stricken, she thought, I can't cry here. Not in a roomful of strangers.

I never cry.

"Are you all right?"

She would have known the voice anywhere. Trying to swallow the lump that was lodged tight against her voice box, Marcia muttered, "Go away."

A tear was hanging on her lashes. The sight of it piercing him to the heart, Quentin said flatly, "I'm sorry I was so rude to you. You're right. What's between you and Lucy is none of my business."

Orange, yellow, a flare of scarlet; the colors shimmered in Marcia's gaze, swirling together like the glowing heart of a fire that would burn her to a crisp were she to approach it. With an incoherent exclamation Quentin seized her by the arm, urged her toward a door near the corner of the room and opened it, pushing her inside. He snapped the door shut and said, "Now you can cry your eyes out—no one will see you here."

You will, she thought, and tugged her arm free. "I'm not crying. I never cry!"

"Then you must be allergic to paint. Your eyes are watering and your nose is running. Here."

He was holding out an immaculate white handkerchief. Marcia said the first thing that came into her head. "You don't look like the kind of man who'd go in for white handkerchiefs.''

If she'd been looking at him rather than at the handkerchief, she would have seen his eyes narrow. "What kind of man do I look like?"

Blinking back tears that she still didn't want to acknowledge, Marcia glanced up. "When I was a little girl I used to play with paper dolls. You know the kind I mean? Cardboard cutouts that you put different outfits on with little paper tabs. Your suit looks like that—as though it's been stuck on you. With no regard for the kind of man you are. You should be wearing a sweatshirt and jeans. Not a pure wool suit and a Gucci tie.''

"I'll have you know I spent a small fortune on this suit."

She said recklessly, "And begrudged every cent of it."

He threw back his head and laughed. "How true!"

Marcia's jaw dropped. His throat was strongly muscled and his teeth were perfect. Even his hair seemed to crackle with energy. This was the man who had created that painting—all those vivid colors suffused with a life force beyond her imagining. She took a step backward, suddenly more frightened than she'd been when the director had announced the cutbacks. More frightened than she could ever remember being. "The suit fits you perfectly," she said lamely. "I didn't mean to be rude."

It did fit him perfectly. But it still gave the impression of shoulder muscles straining at the seams, of a physique all the more impressive for being so impeccably garbed. She took another step back. "You're not at all what I expected."

"Nor were the paintings," Quentin said shrewdly.

She didn't want to talk about the paintings. She took a tissue and a mirror from her purse, dabbed her nose, checked her mascara and said, "We should go back—you'll be missed.''

He wasn't going to let her go that easily. "Why did that particular painting make you cry?"

Because it's what I've been missing all my life. Because it filled me with a bitter regret. Because it was as though you knew me better than I know myself. She said aloud, fighting for composure, "If you and Lucy have talked about me, you know I'm a very private person. My reaction is my own affair. Not yours."

Certainly Lucy had talked about Marcia. Not a lot, but enough for Quentin to realize that although Lucy loved her sister, she didn't feel close to her. He had gained a picture of a woman utterly absorbed in her work to the exclusion of her family and of intimacy. A cold woman who would do the right thing out of principle, not out of love, refusing to involve herself in all the joys and tragedies of everyday life.

And this was the woman he'd been waiting to meet for the last ten years? Or—more accurately—the last twenty-five? His intuition was giving him that message. Loud and clear. But maybe it was wrong.

He'd made a mistake when he'd ignored his intuition to marry Helen. Could he be making another—if different—mistake now? Had he willed Marcia into existence just because of his own needs? Because he was lonely?

"Why are you staring at me like that?" Marcia said fretfully.

Quentin made an effort to pull himself together. "The woman Lucy described to me wasn't the kind of woman who'd start to cry because some guy streaked paint on a piece of canvas."

Marcia wasn't sure what made her angrier—that Lucy had talked about her to Quentin or that his words were so accurate. "Oh, wasn't she? What—?"

A peremptory rap came on the door. Much relieved, Marcia said, "Your public awaits you. You'd better go, Mr. Ramsey."

"Quentin. Are you going to Lucy and Troy's place when this shindig is over?"

"I am not."

The door opened and Emily Harrington-Smythe poked her head in. "Quentin? I really need you out here."

"I'll be right there." He reached out and took the glasses from Marcia's nose. "You have truly beautiful eyes. Who are you hiding from?"

"From people as aggressive as you."

She grabbed for the glasses. Laughter glinting in his own eyes, he evaded her. "You can have them back if you promise to have lunch with me tomorrow."

"I'm sure any number of women in this gallery would be delighted to have lunch with you—but I'm not one of them."

"I'll wear my jeans."

His smile was very hard to resist. Marcia resisted it with all her will power. "My glasses, please."

"I'll get your phone number from Lucy."

"My telephone displays the number of the person calling me. If I think it's you, I won't answer."

"It'll take more than modern technology to defeat me, Dr. Marcia Barnes. Because you still haven't told me why my painting made you cry." He passed her the glasses and dropped a kiss on the tip of her nose. "See you around."

He strode out of the room. For the space of five minutes he hadn't felt the least bit lonely. Taking Emily by the arm, he said urgently, "*Composition Number 8* in the catalog— I want you to put a 'Not for Sale' sign on it."

Emily said bluntly, "I can't do that. Not when it's listed."

"Then mark it 'Sold'."

"It's not," Emily said with indisputable logic.

"It is. I'm buying it."

"Quentin, what's wrong with you? I've never seen you behave so erratically at an opening."

"I'm buying *Number 8*," he repeated patiently. "There's nothing particularly erratic about that."

"You can't buy your own painting! Anyway, Mr. Sorensen has his eye on it, and he wields a lot of influence in this city."

"Too bad. Mr. Sorensen isn't getting it. I am."

"But—"

"Do it, Emily," Quentin said with a pleasant smile. "If you want another Quentin Ramsey show next year."

His shows were enormously successful financially. "Very well," Emily said huffily. "But I'll have to charge you the full commission."

"After tonight I'm sure I can afford it," he said. "That looks like the last of the cabinet ministers. I'll go and do my bit."

Trying to push out of his mind the image of a woman's long-lashed violet eyes swimming in tears, wondering how she'd react when he presented her with an extremely expensive painting, he made his way toward the man in the gray pin-striped suit.

CHAPTER TWO

MARCIA stayed behind in the room that she now decided must be the gallery owner's office, struggling to subdue a mixture of rage at Quentin's effrontery and a truant amusement at his persistence. Mr. Quentin Ramsey, she'd be willing to bet, wasn't used to women who said no. Not that she'd been playing games with him. She was in enough trouble at work, without adding a man who asked questions she didn't want to answer, who had blue eyes that seemed to burn their way into her very soul and who was—she could admit it now that she was alone—sexual dynamite.

It wasn't just his body, its hard planes ill-concealed by his tailored suit. His fingers were long and sensitive, the backs of his hands taut with sinews, and his face with its strong bones had character more than standard good looks—a character hinting at the complexities of the man within. It was an inhabited face, she thought slowly, the face of a man who'd tasted deeply of life, experiencing its dark side as well as its light.

She'd noticed an awful lot in a very few minutes. Too much for her own peace of mind. Altogether too much.

Every instinct she possessed urged her to head straight for the coat rack and leave. But if she did so Lucy and Troy would have a fit. She squared her shoulders and marched back into the gallery, purposely not looking at the painting so unimaginatively called *Composition Number 8*.

She picked out Quentin immediately; he was talking to a man in a pin-striped suit with every evidence of courteous attention. But then his eyes swiveled to meet hers, as though he'd sensed her standing there watching him. He winked at her. Marcia tilted her chin, turned her back and headed for the far gallery.

Lucy and Troy were gazing at a small work in one corner. Troy had his arm draped around Lucy's shoulders while Lucy's body language said more clearly than words that the man holding her was the man she adored. Again hot tears flooded Marcia's eyes. I've got to stop this, she thought frantically. Right now. I've avoided marriage and commitment like the plague. So why does the sight of my sister's happiness make me feel like a failure? Smarten up, Marcia!

She made a gallant effort to gather the shreds of the control for which she was so famous. Then, her lips set, her chin high, she said casually, "Hi, Lucy…Troy."

Lucy whirled, ducking out of the circle of Troy's arm. "Marcia—I'm so pleased to see you!"

Marcia had never encouraged hugging. Lucy contented herself with kissing her sister on the cheek and Troy brushed his lips in the vicinity of her other cheek. Then Lucy stood back, scrutinizing her sister. "You look tired," she said. "Are you all right?"

Exactly the question Quentin had asked. "I'm fine—I've been exceptionally busy at work. What do you think of the show?"

"There are four silkscreen prints on the other wall that I lust after. And I think the acrylics are brilliant—such a departure." Lucy put her head to one side. "This one, for instance—it's a jewel."

In exquisite detail Quentin had painted three little girls running through a meadow full of wildflowers; it was a tribute to his talent that the work was entirely without sentimentality. "They look like us," Marcia blurted.

"Oh…I hadn't thought of that. You and I and Cat, you

mean. You're right—two brunettes and a redhead!" Lucy laughed. "Maybe he saw the photo I have of the three of us on the piano."

"Would you like to have it?" Troy asked, his slate-gray eyes resting affectionately on his wife.

"*I* would," Marcia heard herself say.

Lucy was gazing at her speculatively and Troy's eyebrows had shot halfway up his forehead. Aghast, Marcia sputtered, "I didn't really mean that—I don't want it, of course I don't. You get it, Lucy."

"Have you met Quentin?" Lucy asked.

"Yes. Very briefly. Please, Lucy, forget I ever said I wanted it. Buy her the painting, Troy."

"I'll get it for you, sis," Troy said. "I didn't give you anything for your last birthday."

"But we never give each other expensive presents!"

"This will be the exception that proves the rule… I'll be right back."

And Marcia, for the third time that evening, found her eyes brimming with tears. Lucy drew her further into the corner, shielding her from the other guests. "You're not yourself—what's wrong?"

"Nothing. Everything. *I* don't know."

"Have lunch with me tomorrow."

"I can't. I've got to go into work."

"Darn your work, Marcie!"

Lucy only used Marcia's childhood name when she was upset. Marcia said, "I'm going to phone Mother in the morning—could you and Troy come for dinner on Sunday? Catherine's free."

"Love to," Lucy said promptly.

"Come around six, then… I do wish Troy wasn't buying me that painting."

"Too bad we can't take it home right away. It'd look perfect in your bedroom."

A painting of Quentin Ramsey's in her bedroom? No way, thought Marcia, and from the corner of her eye saw Emily Harrington-Smythe parting the crowd with Troy in her wake. "An excellent choice," Emily said, sticking a little red circle beside the painting. "Congratulations, Dr. Donovan."

"Happy birthday, Marcia," Troy said, with a lazy grin at his sister-in-law.

The painting was hers. Whether she wanted it or not. Standing on tiptoes, Marcia kissed Troy on the chin and said limpidly, "Thank you, Troy, that was sweet of you."

"Let's go and find Quentin and tell him what we've done," he rejoined.

In sheer panic Marcia said, "I've really got to go—I was in the lab at six this morning. But I'll see you both on Sunday." Giving them a quick smile, she almost ran from the room.

Quentin was standing in the far corner of the gallery with three very attractive women—two of them blondes, the other a voluptuous creature with glorious black curls. He was laughing at something one of them had said. Marcia pulled on her coat, picked up her umbrella and scurried out into the rain.

Marcia's mother, Dr. Evelyn Barnes, was a forensic pathologist, a poised and gracious hostess and a demon golfer. But when Marcia phoned her from work the next morning, Evelyn sounded unusually flustered.

"Dinner? On Sunday? With the family? Let me get my book… I—Marcia, could I bring someone with me? A friend?"

"Of course. Is Lillian in town?"

Lillian was her mother's best friend, who had moved to Toronto only a month ago. "No—no, it's not Lillian. It's a man."

Evelyn always had an escort to the concerts and dinner parties she frequented, but never allowed these undoubtedly very fine men to mingle with her family. "You're being a dark horse, Mother. What's his name?"

"Henry Woods. He's a broker. I—I'd like you to meet him."

Trying very hard to hit a balance between unmannerly curiosity and diplomatic uninterest, Marcia said soothingly, "That's just fine. Six o'clock?"

"Lovely. We'll see you then." Evelyn, who usually liked to catch up on all the family news, smartly cut the connection.

More slowly, Marcia put the receiver down. If she didn't know better, she'd say her mother was in love. Her cool, unemotional mother in love?

It didn't look as though her dinner party would be dull.

At five to six on Sunday Marcia was putting the finishing touches to her make-up. The same perverse instinct that had caused her to claim the painting of the three little girls had induced her to ignore the elegant but rather dull outfits that made up the bulk of her wardrobe, as well as her horn-rimmed glasses. She was wearing black stirrup pants with a long black sweater emblazoned with the golden face of a lion; her pumps were black with gold buckles. Despite the addition of the mysterious Mr. Woods, this was only a family dinner, she thought defiantly, adding scarlet lipstick and big gold earrings that dangled against her neck. Besides, it had rained all weekend.

The security buzzer sounded and Lucy's voice came over the intercom. A few moments later there was a tap on the door. Before Marcia could say anything, Lucy handed her sister the baby so she could take off her coat and said ingenuously, "We brought Quentin along. I hope you don't mind? The cocktail party he was supposed to go to was canceled because the hostess had the flu."

Christopher Stephen Donovan grabbed at Marcia's earrings and drooled down the shoulder of her sweater. Quentin's eyes were even bluer than she remembered them. Marcia backed up so that they could come in and mumbled untruthfully, "No, that's fine. No problem at all."

Lucy handed Troy her coat and swiped at Lucy's shoulder with a tissue. "He's teething again—I keep telling Troy someone should invent a better method for the acquiring of teeth. Here, I'll take him now."

But Christopher had locked his arms around Marcia's neck and burrowed his face into her shoulder. He smelled sweetly of baby powder and warm skin, his weight solid against her body. Her arms tightened around him as she rested her cheek on his wispy hair. Oh God, she thought helplessly, here I go again. I want to weep my eyes out. I'm cracking up. I've never wanted children. Not once in my thirty-three years.

Quentin, meanwhile, had been hanging up his coat and combing the raindrops from his hair—more to give himself time to collect his wits than from any urge for neatness. His first glimpse of Marcia in all that black and gold had sent a jolt through his system as though he'd grabbed a live wire; he'd simultaneously wanted to look his fill and throw her down on the carpet and kiss her senseless. Then Lucy had given her the baby, and, as though the carpet had moved beneath his feet, he'd seen her holding his child, their child, the fruit of their love.

You're nuts, he told himself astringently. She hasn't even agreed to have lunch with you and you're already into fatherhood? He said, "Marcia, I brought you these. They were selling them at the market."

Marcia looked up. He was clutching a large, inartistic bouquet of mixed flowers—oranges clashing with pinks, purple next to magenta. His gaze locked with hers and she found herself quite unable to look away. "Thank you," she said breathlessly. "Lucy can show you where to find a vase."

"Left my suit back at the hotel," he added.

He looked extremely handsome in soft-fitting gray cords and a dark blue sweater. "I see," Marcia said inanely.

Quentin handed the bouquet to Lucy and stepped closer to Marcia. "He's going to pull your hair out by the roots… Let go, Chris." Then she felt the warmth of a man's fingers against her nape and felt his breath stir her hair. Every nerve in her body sprang to jangling life. Her shoulders rigid, her breathing caught in her throat, she heard Chris mumble a protest; his little fist tightened on her hair and she winced.

"Easy, Chris…there we go."

With infinite gentleness Quentin had loosened the baby's hold. As he eased the child out of her arms his forearm brushed her breast. The shock ran through her body; he must have felt it. She flashed a desperate glance around and saw that Troy and Lucy were watching her with considerable interest. I will not blush. I will not, she told herself. She said in a strangled voice, "I've got to keep an eye on the dinner. I'll be right back."

Troy started setting up their portable playpen, Quentin swung baby Chris high over his head so that he gurgled with laughter, and Lucy followed Marcia into the kitchen. "Is Mother coming? Yummy—something smells delicious."

Glad to talk about anything other than Quentin, Marcia

said, "She's bringing a man," and relayed the gist of the phone call. Before she'd finished Catherine arrived and sauntered into the kitchen, and she had to go through her story again.

Dr. Catherine Barnes was petite like Marcia, elegant like their mother, and did research in pancreatic cancer. "I'm on holiday for three whole weeks," she crowed. "I'm looking after Lydia's dogs next week, so I'll get lots of exercise and fresh air. You look like you could do with some sun, Marcia, you're much too pale."

Cat was a fitness freak who could always be counted on to say it like it was. "Thanks," Marcia said drily. "But it does happen to have been raining for the last four days— or hadn't you noticed? Would you pass around the crab dip, Cat? And I'll get Troy to pour drinks."

Lucy had jammed the flowers in Marcia's largest vase. "Where'll I put them?"

Quentin was standing in the kitchen doorway, minus Chris. "I'll put them in the middle of the table," he said.

Marcia had placed an attractive arrangement of silk flowers that matched her china as a centerpiece. She watched Quentin plunk it on the sideboard and put the motley bouquet in its place. He was exactly the kind of man she disliked—making decisions without consulting her, taking over as though he owned the place. As he came back in the kitchen she said frostily, "The only thing missing from that bouquet is skunk cabbage."

"Better luck next time."

"Next time? You don't look the type to enjoy city life. I can't imagine you're going to stay in Ottawa for long."

"I wasn't going to—but I've changed my plans," he said. "A friend of mine who's away owns a place in the Gatineau Hills, so I'm going to stay there for a while. You and I still have to have lunch—or had you forgotten?"

"You're very sure of yourself, Mr. Ramsey."

"Confidence gets results, Dr. Barnes."

"Up until now confidence might have gotten you results," she said sweetly.

"Are you suggesting I should change tactics?"

"I'm suggesting you abandon the project."

"I don't think so. You're an interesting challenge."

Her nostrils flared. "Now you're being insulting."

He stepped closer and said softly, "You liked it when I touched you."

Gritting her teeth, Marcia thought about icebergs and glaciers and Scotch on the rocks, and her cheeks stayed only as pink as the heat of the stove warranted. "You took me by surprise, that's all. A man of your experience should be more adept at distinguishing between a woman who's startled and a woman who's ready to fall at your feet."

Quentin was by now thoroughly enjoying himself. "Dear me…a woman has never once thrown herself at my feet. Does that make me a failure as a man? Although it does sound rather a deranged thing to— Oh, thanks, Troy. I'll have a beer."

Had Troy been listening? Appalled, Marcia said stiffly, "You'll have to excuse me… Oh, there's the buzzer—that must be Mother."

Evelyn Barnes looked very attractive in her rose-pink dress with her gray hair softly curling round her ears. Her usual escorts were tall, patrician-featured men, who considered themselves essential to the running of the country; Henry Woods was short, stout, bald and unassuming, with a pair of the kindest brown eyes Marcia had ever seen. She warmed to him immediately. She made introductions all around, Troy passed the drinks, and Marcia set a place for Quentin at the table, seating him where the flowers would screen him from her view.

Two and a half hours later Marcia was plugging in the coffee-machine in the kitchen. She was pleased with the success of her dinner party. Quentin and Henry had proved to be witty and entertaining, Cat had thrown off her normal reserve and the baby had filled any gaps in the conversation. As for herself, she'd managed to avoid anything but minimal contact with Quentin. He couldn't move out to the Gatineau Hills fast enough for her.

She reached in the refrigerator for the cream. But the container was almost empty and she'd forgotten to buy a new one. She went back in the living room. Troy and Quentin were getting out the chess pieces while Evelyn was giving Chris his bottle. "I'll have to run to the corner store— I'm out of cream," Marcia said. "Won't be a minute."

Quentin got to his feet. "I'll come with you. I need to walk off some of that excellent dinner."

She couldn't very well tell him to get lost. Evelyn wouldn't approve of that. So Marcia got her purse, pulled on shiny black boots and her raincoat and went out into the hall with him. His belted trenchcoat gave him the air of a particularly rakish spy.

"Let's take the stairs," Quentin said. "I shouldn't have had a second helping of that chocolate dessert—deadly."

"It was only Belgian chocolate, whipping cream and butter," Marcia said, wide-eyed. "Oh, and six eggs too."

"It should be against medical ethics to make caffeine and cholesterol taste so good."

"It's Cat's favorite dessert. That article she told us about was interesting, wasn't it?"

But Quentin hadn't braved the rain to talk about Cat. As they went outside he opened Marcia's umbrella, held it over their heads and pulled her close to his side, tucking her arm in his. "There," he said. "Alone at last."

His strong-boned face was only inches from hers; his

gaze was intent. She said coolly, "This is a big city—we're scarcely alone."

"Don't split hairs, Marcia. There are just two people under this umbrella—tell the truth for once."

"All right, so we're alone. So what?"

"Why did my painting make you cry?"

"Quentin, I have guests who are waiting for their coffee—come along!"

"You're bright, you're competent, you're a dab hand with Belgian chocolate—and you're scared to death of your own emotions. That's quite a combination."

Besides a rum and cola before dinner, Marcia had had two glasses of red wine with dinner. She said, pulling her arm free as she turned to face him and wishing that the umbrella didn't cloister them quite so intimately, "You want the truth? I'll give you the truth. You're wasting your time, Quentin. I'm thirty-three years old—not fifteen. If I'm scared of emotion I presumably have adequate reasons, and if I'm as bright as you say I am they must be good reasons. I'm also much too old to be spilling out my life story to every man that comes along."

Quentin didn't like being bracketed with a procession of other men. He wanted to be different. He wanted to shake her up. As raindrops spattered on the umbrella he stroked the smooth fall of her hair with his free hand and said huskily, "You look like an Egyptian goddess in that outfit you're wearing."

Hot color flared in her cheeks. "I wouldn't have worn it if I'd known you were coming," she said, then could have bitten off her tongue.

He pounced. "You don't want me seeing the real you?"

"I don't know who the real me is anymore!" Marcia exclaimed, then rolled her eyes in self-disgust. "Telling the truth seems to be addictive. Quentin, it's pouring rain. Let's go.''

''Maybe I call you to truth,'' he said quietly. Then he clasped her by the chin, lowered his head and kissed her full on the lips. Her lips weren't cold; they were so soft and desirable that he lost all track of time and place in the sheer pleasure of the moment. When she suddenly jerked her chin free, it came as a physical shock.

''You mustn't do that,' she gabbled. ''You scarcely know me. You can't just go kissing me as if we're lovers in a Hollywood movie—and now you've got lipstick all over your mouth.''

She sounded anything but unemotional, and her first, instinctive yielding had set his head swimming. Quentin fished in his pocket, producing another handkerchief. ''You'd better wipe it off,'' he said.

''So that's why you carry a handkerchief—I should have known,'' she said nastily, and scrubbed at his lips with painful vigor.

He was suddenly angry out of all proportion. Pulling his head back, he said, ''Let me tell you something—my dad was a lumberjack in a little village in New Brunswick that I'm sure you've never heard of—Holton, in the Kennebecasis Valley—and my mom cleaned the houses of the rich folk. A white handkerchief was the mark of a gentleman to her, and when I won a provincial art competition at the age of twelve she gave me six boxes of handkerchiefs. I may not qualify as a gentleman but I loved my mother, and that's why I always carry a white handkerchief.''

Marcia stood very still. Water was dripping from the prongs of the umbrella and her feet were getting cold. She said, ''I'm sorry—I shouldn't have said that.''

She was looking straight at him, and her apology was

obviously sincere. "Okay. But you really get under my skin, Marcia Barnes."

"That's mutual," she snorted, and wiped the last of the lipstick from the corner of his mouth. His nose was slightly crooked and there was a dent in his chin; his brows and lashes were as black as his hair. As for his mouth… She shivered in a way that had nothing to do with the cold. She had never been kissed like that in her life. Brief, beautiful and bewildering, she thought, tugging at his sleeve and starting off down the sidewalk, even through his coat she could feel the hard muscles of his arm.

They walked in silence for several minutes. Then Quentin said abruptly, "Have dinner with me tomorrow night."

"I can't."

"Tuesday, then."

"You'll be in the Gatineau Hills."

"I have a car. It's less than an hour's drive."

"The store where I can get the cream is in the bottom floor of that apartment block—I won't be a minute," Marcia gasped, then darted from under the umbrella and ran inside.

The harsh fluorescent lighting and the aisles packed with food restored her to some kind of sanity. One kiss and I would indeed have fallen at his feet, she realized grimly, taking the container of cream out of the refrigerator and marching to the checkout. But just because my hormones are doing a dance like daffodils in springtime doesn't mean I have to have dinner with the man. In fact, it's precisely why I shouldn't have dinner with him. I'm in enough of a muddle without adding a wild card like Quentin Ramsey to the pack.

She paid for the cream and went outside. Quentin was waiting for her, a tall, blue-eyed stranger standing under a streetlamp. He did call her to truth, she thought unhappily.

To truth and to emotion—a devastating combination for a woman used to hiding herself from both. How was she going to convince him that she didn't want to date him? Normally she had no trouble getting rid of men who forced their attentions on her.

As she cudgeled her brains, he forestalled her. "If you're too busy at work to have dinner through the week, I can wait until next weekend."

Marcia bit her lip and started to walk back the way they'd come. "Quentin, I don't want to see you again. I'm sorry if that sounds harsh, but that's the way it is."

"Why not?"

She said childishly, "Because. Just because! Okay?"

"No, dammit, it's not okay! I know you're attracted to me, and I'm willing to bet you don't lose your cool with anyone else the way you have with me. My painting made you cry, your whole body responds when I touch you, and the more I see of you the more I figure Lucy doesn't have a clue what makes you tick." He drew a harsh breath. "Plus she told me how much you wanted the painting of the three little girls—the one Troy bought for you."

Spacing her words, Marcia seethed, "I can want a painting. That doesn't mean I have to have dinner with the artist. You're not a stupid man and that's not a very complicated message. So why aren't you getting it?"

"Because I don't want to," he said tightly. Although his features were inscrutable, Quentin was beginning to feel scared; any time he'd visualized finding the perfect woman she'd been as delighted to discover him as he her.

If Marcia had used her common sense she would have changed the subject. "I don't understand you—why are you pushing me so hard?" she cried.

"If I told you, you'd laugh in my face."

"Then please just drop it, Quentin."

"I can't!" He took a deep breath, trying to think. "I'm going to be seeing a fair bit of Troy and Lucy over the summer, so I'm bound to see you again. Unless you avoid them for the next two months, of course."

"I'll make sure when I go and see them that you're not included," she snapped.

"So you're not indifferent to me... If you were, you wouldn't care if I was there or not."

"I don't like being harassed."

His steps slowed. "That's an ugly word."

"Then don't do it."

Her jaw was set mutinously. The pale sweep of her cheekbones made him ache somewhere deep inside. He said desperately, "Marcia, I don't think I've ever begged a woman to spend time with me...I guess I've never had to. So if I'm not doing this well it's because I haven't had any practise. I'm begging you now. You're important to me in ways I don't understand but that I know to be real. Give me a chance—that's all I ask."

To her infinite relief she saw they'd reached the driveway to her building. It took all her courage to look up at him, and the torment in his face almost weakened her resolve. "There's no point—please believe me." She tried to smile. "I'm sorry."

She was right, she knew she was; she was being sensible and rational. She had never thought of herself as an overly adept judge of male character, but she was certain that any relationship with Quentin wouldn't be shallow. Better to end whatever was between them now rather than later.

So why was she filled with the same bitter regret that his painting had called up in her? And why did she feel as though she'd just trampled on a whole field of daffodils?

She stalked into the building and up the stairs, and before she unlocked her door forced a bright smile on her face.

The next two hours were purgatory. But finally Evelyn and Henry stood up and everyone else followed their lead.

Quentin pushed back his chair, trying to stretch the tension from his shoulders. Troy had trounced him royally at chess because his mind had been anywhere but on the game. His thoughts had been going round and round in circles that had ended up exactly nowhere. He should have kept his cool with Marcia. Kept things light and on the surface. Instead he'd kissed her before she was ready, and badgered her as if his sole intention had been to push her away.

For a man she'd said wasn't stupid, he'd sure blown it. Nor did he have any idea what he was going to do next. According to Marcia, there wasn't any next.

He was the last one to go out the door. Marcia shrank away from him, and he saw that there were faint blue shadows under her eyes. Filled with a passionate compunction, and another emotion that he wasn't quite ready to label fear, he said roughly, "If you change your mind, get in touch with me. You can always reach me through Lucy and Troy."

"Yes...yes, of course," she said, already starting to close the door.

She couldn't wait to be rid of him—that was the message. Quentin headed for the elevator where the rest of them were waiting, somehow made appropriate small talk until Troy dropped him off at the hotel and then headed for the bar. There were times in life when only a double rum would do.

CHAPTER THREE

THE following Sunday Marcia had lunch with Lucy. When they were settled in an alcove in the salad bar that was Lucy's favorite and they'd made their choices from the menu, Lucy took a sip of her wine and said with sisterly frankness, "You don't look so hot, Marcia."

Marcia knew that she didn't, and she knew why. Opting for part of the truth, because she certainly wasn't going to talk about Quentin, she said, "Last Tuesday I was called into the director's office and informed that due to budget restraints the junior staff are being required to take a week's holiday without pay. As soon as possible. So as of Friday afternoon I've been on vacation."

Lucy went right to the heart of the matter. "What does that do to your research?"

"The particular drugs I've been working with aren't available either—all of a sudden they're too expensive. So almost three months' work could go down the drain." Marcia grimaced in frustration. "It's driving me crazy."

"How secure is your job?" Lucy asked bluntly.

Marcia twirled the stem of her glass, not looking at her sister. "I might lose it," she said, and heard the telltale quiver in her voice.

Lucy reached a hand across the tablecloth. "Oh, Marcie…"

Marcia bit her lip. "It's crazy—there are lots of people much worse off than I am. But I really love my job." She took a big swallow of her wine. "They're supposed to make an announcement within two or three weeks."

38

Lucy said gently, "Your whole life revolves around your research."

"Stop it, Lucy, or I'll be blubbering all over you," Marcia said with a watery grin. "Have some bread."

"'Blubbering', as you put it, can be a perfectly fine response."

"Not in a crowded restaurant."

Lucy slathered butter on a slab of crunchy French bread. "I suppose you're right. So what will you do with yourself all week?"

"I'm not sure yet." Not for anything would she reveal to her sister that the thought of seven more days with absolutely nothing to do filled her with panic.

"I've got an idea! You can go to Quentin's cottage in the Gatineau Hills."

"Don't be silly," Marcia said sharply, her nerves shrilling like a burglar alarm at the sound of his name.

"He won't be there—it's perfect. He left for New York today. One of his works got vandalized in a gallery in SoHo, and he felt he had to go and see the damage himself. He said he wouldn't be back until Friday or Saturday."

She could get out of her condo and away from the city. "I never was much for the great outdoors," Marcia prevaricated.

"Troy and Chris and I were there all day yesterday— it's a beautiful spot on a lake, with lovely woods and wildflowers. And the cottage is luxurious. Not what you'd call roughing it."

"I couldn't do that without asking him, Lucy. And it's too late if he's already left."

"I'll take full responsibility—you see, he was hoping we'd stay there. But Troy gets his lunch hours free and a couple of afternoons through the week, and I like to spend all the time I can with him. So I'm sure it'd be fine with Quentin if you stayed at the cottage.''

Marcia was sensitive enough to pick up what Lucy wasn't saying. Lucy and Troy's first child had died at the age of seven months—a tragedy that had ripped apart the fabric of their marriage; they had lived separately for over a year. Now that they were back together Lucy hated to be away from Troy, and, she had once confided to Marcia, she felt safer when Troy was near for Chris as well.

Marcia said spontaneously, ''Chris is a sweetheart, Lucy.''

A film of tears covered Lucy's gray-blue eyes. ''Yes, he is—we're very lucky. Now that he's older than seven months, I feel so much more relaxed too—silly, isn't it?'' She helped herself to another slice of bread. ''Do you ever think you might want children?''

''What kind of a question's that?'' Marcia said lightly.

''You looked very sweet holding Chris—even though he was dribbling all over you.''

''I've never been a mother but I'm sure there's more to it than standing around looking sweet. How are Troy's courses going?''

''Fine. You didn't answer the question.''

''I'm not going to. Because I don't know the answer.''

Lucy stared at her thoughtfully. ''You didn't hit it off with Quentin, did you?''

Marcia scowled. ''Did you invite me out for lunch just so you could subject me to an inquisition?''

''Yes,'' said Lucy, with one of her insouciant grins.

The waitress gave Marcia her Greek salad and Lucy her seafood salad. ''Can I get you anything else, ladies?''

''That's fine, thanks,'' Marcia said, and picked up her fork.

She was worried sick about her job—that was an undeniable fact. But there was another reason that she looked far from her best. And that reason was Quentin. She'd only met the man twice, but somehow he'd insinuated his way into her life, so that his rugged face came between her and the computer screen and his loose-limbed stride accompanied her down the corridors of the institute. At work, where she was so disciplined, she'd more or less managed to keep him in order. But at home in her condo it was another story.

She hadn't slept well all week. But when she did sleep she dreamed about Quentin, night after night. Sometimes they were dreams so erotic that she woke blushing, her whole body on fire with needs that even in the darkness she could scarcely bring herself to acknowledge as her own. But at other times she woke from nightmares—horrible nightmares that left her heart pounding with terror and her palms wet.

They were always the same: she was drowning in the sea, being pulled down and down into the deep blue depths of a bottomless and merciless ocean, and when she suddenly saw Quentin's face through the swirling currents and tried to signal to him to rescue her he was always out of reach, his black hair waving like seaweed, his smile full of mockery.

"I really don't want to talk about Quentin, Lucy," she said shortly.

Lucy, known for being impulsive, chewed on a mouthful of shrimp and said nothing. Marcia picked at her black olives and decided they'd used too much olive oil. She said at random, "What did you think of Mother's friend Henry?"

"I thought he was a sweetheart. Do you think she'll marry him?"

"Mother? Get married again? No!"

"She must get lonely sometimes. Troy and I live in Vancouver, and you and Cat are both very busy women."

"Workaholics, you mean," Marcia said drily. It was the word Quentin had used.

"I'm trying to be polite," Lucy chuckled. "Oh, Marcia, it's so neat that Troy and I are having a couple of months in Ottawa! I love Vancouver, and I don't have to tell you how much I love Troy and Chris—but I do miss my family."

It was the perfect opportunity for Marcia to say that she missed Lucy. But was it true? Or did Lucy, with her tumbled curls and her untidy emotions, simply stir Marcia up in ways she both resented and feared? "Families are complicated," she said obliquely.

"Mmm, that's true enough… You know, it's funny, but I really thought you and Quentin would like each other."

"Lay off, Lucy."

"When we saw him yesterday he looked as awful as you do. And he didn't want to talk about you any more than you want to talk about him."

"Then maybe you should take the hint."

"But he was such a good friend to me on Shag Island—I met him there, remember, when Troy and I were separated." Lucy speared another shrimp. "He was like the brother we never had."

Marcia could not possibly picture Quentin as her brother. She said flatly, "He's too intense for me—he came on too strong. I'm sorry I spoiled your fantasy, but there it is. Now, can we please talk about something—or someone—else?"

Lucy sighed. "Troy's always telling me I'm a hopeless romantic. Okay, okay—I'll drop it. But I will give you the key to the cottage and the directions. You should take your own food—Quentin's not what you'd call a model housekeeper. And, providing you leave there by Friday morning, there's no danger of you running into him. More's the pity.''

Marcia glared at her. Lucy went on hurriedly, ''Next Saturday why don't you come for dinner with Troy and me and we'll go to a movie? Cat's offered to babysit.'' She gave a shamefaced smile. ''I'm still not comfortable leaving Chris with a sitter who doesn't have an MD after her name. Silly, isn't it?''

''I think it's very understandable,'' Marcia said, sharing the last of the carafe of wine between them. ''What movie do you want to see?''

As Lucy began discussing the merit of various new releases Marcia found herself remembering the year that Lucy had lived in Ottawa and then on Shag Island, and Troy had lived in Vancouver; their unhappiness had been a measure of the depth of their love—she hadn't been so wrapped up in her own concerns that she hadn't understood that. She had been helpless to fix what was wrong, and that, too, had been a new experience. She liked to feel in control of events.

Maybe, she thought slowly, that was the year when she'd begun to sense the sterility of her own life; the tragedy that had struck Lucy and Troy had been the origin of a confusion and a lack of focus that was both new to her and horribly unsettling.

And that made Quentin fifty times worse.

''There's that new historical movie too,'' she said. ''One of the technicians at work saw it and really liked it.''

For the rest of their lunch they talked about anything but family and men, although Marcia did find herself clutching the key to the cottage and a map sketched on a paper placemat when she went back to her car. And why not? she thought rebelliously. If she spent all next week in her condo, she'd be talking to the plants. A few days beside a lake with lots of books and no people would be just fine.

But she'd leave there Thursday evening, to make sure that she didn't meet up with Quentin.

Marcia got away on Monday morning, her little gray car loaded with food, clothes, books and a portable TV. She drove along the eastern shore of the Gatineau River, humming to herself. How long since she'd done something like this? Too long. Her vacations tended to be carefully planned affairs with equally carefully chosen friends, not last-minute escapades all by herself.

She was going to read all the novels she'd bought in the last year that had been stashed on her shelves because she hadn't had time to get at them. She'd experiment with some new pasta recipes. She'd watch the shows she always missed on TV because something needed doing at the lab. She was going to have a great time.

Marcia got lost twice trying to follow the penciled squiggles on her sister's map; Lucy wasn't blessed with a sense of direction. But finally the little side road she had been following forked in two just as it was supposed to. When she took the right fork within three hundred yards she saw a wooden gate with a plaque attached to the post. "Richardson" it said. That was the name of Quentin's friends, the ones who owned the cottage.

Marcia got out, opened the gate, drove through and closed it behind her. Her car bumped down a lane overhung with newly leafed beech trees and red-tasseled maples. Then she emerged into a clearing and braked.

Through the lacy fretwork of the trees the lake sparkled and danced. A carpet of white trilliums patterned the forest floor. And the cottage—the cottage was beautiful.

It was a house more than a cottage, a cedar house with

a wood-shingled roof and a broad stone chimney; it merged with its surroundings perfectly. Smiling fatuously, Marcia drove to the circle of gravel at the end of the driveway and parked her car.

Over the deep silence of the woods she could hear the ripple of the lake on the shore and a chorus of birdsong. The front of the house, which faced the lake, was made of panels of glass set in thick beams reaching to the peak of the roof. The tree trunks and the blue of the sky were reflected in the glass.

Like a woman in a dream she walked up the stone path to the front door. The key turned smoothly in the lock. She stepped inside and gave a gasp of dismay.

What had Lucy said? Something about Quentin not being a model housekeeper?

That, thought Marcia, was the understatement of the year.

Clothes were flung over the furniture, books, newspapers and dirty dishes were strewn on the tables and the floor and an easel and a clutter of painting equipment decorated the corner with the most light. She wrinkled her nose. Over the smell of turpentine and linseed oil was a nastier smell. From the kitchen. Bracing herself, she stepped over an untidy heap of art magazines and discovered on the counter the remains of Quentin's supper: a wilting Caesar salad over which three houseflies were circling. The anchovies were the source of the odor.

He might be a great artist. He was also a slob. By the look of it she wasn't going to get to her novels today; she was quite sure that she couldn't live with this mess.

Marcia went outside again, brought in all her stuff, then changed into a pair of shorts and a T-shirt and got to work.

The contents of the refrigerator revealed that Quentin liked foreign beer, Gruyère cheese and steak, but his taste

in books was eclectic; several of them she herself was interested in reading. His clothes ran to the frankly shabby—
a long way from the expensive suit he had worn at the opening.

In the back porch she found a pair of jeans and a shirt that were liberally daubed with mud; she dumped them in the washing machine in the basement, then, astounded that it was already midafternoon, made herself a cup of tea and a sandwich.

She'd run the vacuum over the floor when she'd finished, and shake the woven rugs outdoors. Then the downstairs would be done.

Because she was sitting down, she took the time to look around her. The house was constructed on an open plan, with thick beams supporting the high ceilings. Sunlight patterned the polished hardwoods floors and from every window Marcia could see trees and water and sky. Now that it was tidier, she could allow the spirit of the house to move her. A generous spirit, she thought. User-friendly.

One of Quentin's abstracts hung over the stone fireplace, its misty greens and blues pulling the outdoors within. She wasn't just tidying the house because mess offended her, she admitted to herself as she crunched on a raw carrot stick. She was tidying it to remove as many traces of Quentin as she could. Folding his clothes, washing dishes he had used, going through the pockets of his jeans before she put them in the washer—those had seemed very intimate acts. She knew a lot more about him than she had three hours ago. More than she wanted to know.

One thing was sure. If there were genes for cleanliness and neatness, Quentin certainly hadn't inherited his mother's.

The only things she hadn't tidied were Quentin's art supplies; somehow they seemed sacrosanct. Nor had she spent a lot of time looking at the painting on the easel, whose seething mass of sage-green coils, for all their interconnections, emitted a profound sense of disconnection. It was a disturbing painting. That it might have something to do with the way Quentin felt about her was more than she could deal with.

Half an hour later she finished the downstairs. With considerable satisfaction she looked around. Books and magazines shelved, a couple of her own books on the teak coffee-table and not a whiff of anchovy. Determinedly she headed up the stairs. But she found herself hesitating in the doorway of the master bedroom, and it was with palpable reluctance that she entered.

The first thing she saw was the unmade bed. Her mouth dry, she let her eyes flicker round the room—a beautifully proportioned room with nooks filled with cushions and skylights in the angled ceiling. The walls were a soft off-white between cedar-stained beams.

The painting over the bed made her smile, reminding her of the one Troy had bought for her. A small boy was fishing in a river, the peace of the scene enfolding her almost physically. But as she went to strip the bed a second painting struck her like an ambush: an abstract that was like a cry of pain. She backed away from it, remembering the torment in Quentin's face the last time she had seen him.

She'd done the right thing. She *had*.

Her jaw set, ignoring the indentation in the pillow where Quentin's head had lain, she yanked the sheets from the bed and added them to the pile of washing. There was no sign of any pajamas.

Maybe he slept naked.

Oh, stop it, Marcia! You've done nothing but think about Quentin ever since you arrived. How he sleeps—with whom he sleeps—is nothing to do with you. You rejected him, right?

Had Lucy suggested the stay here knowing that Marcia wouldn't be able to escape the presence of a man whose magnetism and talent infused every room of the house?

I could go home, Marcia thought, taking clean sheets out of the linen cupboard. But I don't want to. For one thing, that would be admitting defeat. Quentin would have won were she to get in her car and drive back to her condo.

Once she'd finished cleaning up she'd forget about him. She could always hide the paintings under the bed while she was here.

The other reason she didn't want to go home was a dim intuition that she needed a few days away from all her normal concerns. From her condo and her job and her family. Maybe then she'd be able to figure out what was going on. Why she loved and envied Lucy. Why she worked all the time.

Why a blue-eyed man was haunting her dreams.

CHAPTER FOUR

WHEN she went for a walk before supper Marcia discovered a screened-in gazebo by the edge of the lake, with a hammock strung from its beams. For a whole hour she lay in it, her book open on her chest, the ripple of the water lulling her into a kind of peace she rarely allowed herself to experience. She then went back to the house, turned on some music and made spinach linguine with a clam sauce followed by a fruit salad. She topped off this exceedingly healthy meal with a chocolate-coated marzipan bar from her favorite German bakery. Then she got up to change the tape.

The sun was setting behind the trees, whose shadows lay like bars across the grass. The birds were no longer singing. When she pushed the eject button on the tape player, the noise was shockingly loud.

She felt a shiver of unease. There was not another house in sight, and it had never occurred to her to drive further along the road to see where her nearest neighbors lived. She went into the kitchen and checked that the back door was locked, pulling the blind down over the window. Then she closed and bolted all the downstairs windows. She washed and dried the dishes. She put on more music and opened her novel.

It was a slick and cleverly written book that totally failed to hold her interest. She made a batch of fudge bars and washed more dishes, and then wished that she hadn't cleaned the house so thoroughly earlier in the day so she could do it now, or that she'd brought some of her notes from the lab to work on. It was completely dark outside, in a way the city never was dark. To prove something to herself, Marcia went out on the stone step. The sky was spangled with stars, cold pinpricks of light that spoke of immense distance and her own insignificance. Of her own loneliness.

Everyone gets lonely, she thought irritably, and went back indoors, where she picked out a different book and forced herself to read until ten-thirty. Then she had a shower, put on silk mandarin pajamas and went into the bedroom.

Not stopping to think, she took down the abstract painting, wrapped it in her other pair of silk pajamas and tucked it between the bureau and the wall. Standing on the mattress, she opened the skylight, because the sun had warmed the room and she was sure it wasn't going to rain. Finally she flipped off the bedside lamp and lay down on the bed. The bed Quentin had slept in only two nights ago.

She wasn't going to think about Quentin. She was going to sleep.

Which, almost instantly, she did.

Marcia woke to pitch darkness. Rubbing her eyes, she pulled the blankets to her chin because she was cold. The red numbers on the digital clock informed her that it was ten to one. And then she heard the sound that must have woken her, and sat bolt-upright.

The slam of a car door. Outside the house.

She'd been right to be afraid of her isolation, and criminally foolish not to have looked up her nearest neighbors. Who was it? A burglar? A vandal? One thing was sure: she wasn't going to stay around to find out.

Moving as quietly as she could, Marcia opened the skylight as far as it would go. Then she bent her knees and pushed off from the bed with as much of a leap as she could manage, hitching herself over the lower edge of the window. The wooden rim dug into her ribs. With a strength born of fear she wriggled through the opening and rolled over onto the roof. Then she lay very still, her thighs and belly pressed into the slats, her ears straining to hear what was happening.

A light flipped on downstairs, throwing gold rectangles on the grass. The darkness had been protection of a kind and Marcia closed her eyes tight shut, understanding perfectly well why ostriches hid their heads in the sand. Then every muscle tensed and her eyes flew open again as below her someone walked into the bedroom. More light, flooding out onto the roof, making her feel exposed and helpless. She held her breath. To her relief she heard a diminishing thud of footsteps on the stairs, followed by silence.

Marcia dug her toes into the roof to keep from sliding downwards, wondering how long she'd be able to maintain her position. Gravity, she thought with a ridiculous urge to giggle, was already beginning to win out. She shouldn't have eaten that last fudge bar.

From somewhere downstairs a voice called her name. A man's voice. "Marcia! Where in God's name are you? It's me, Quentin. You don't need to be afraid…Marcia?"

Quentin. Here at the cottage. Not an unknown burglar. Her pent-up breath swooshed out of her lungs and her hold relaxed. With a yelp of terror she felt herself slide downward. Grabbing for the edge of the skylight, Marcia held on tight.

She heard feet taking the stairs two at a time. Then the floorboards creaked in the bedroom. "Marcia? Where—?" A face thrust itself in the gap between the window and the roof and a pair of very blue eyes looked right at her. "God almighty, woman,'' Quentin said, ''you scared the living daylights out of me.''

''*I* scared *you*?'' she croaked. ''What do you think you did to me?''

''What in hell are you doing out on the roof?''

He looked solid and real and reassuringly familiar. Light-headed with relief, Marcia said, ''Star-gazing? Owl-watching? What do you think I'm doing on the roof? I'm hiding from the burglar-cum-rapist-cum-murderer who was about to burst into my bedroom.''

''It's not your bedroom. It's mine.''

''Don't be so picky about the details,'' she said fractiously.

The turmoil of fear in Quentin's chest began to subside, to be replaced by an equally tumultuous joy. Marcia was here. Here at the cottage. He had no idea why and he didn't really care. Enough that he was with her. Her eyes were black as the sky and her hair framed cheekbones that he itched to draw and lips that he longed to kiss. He said, his eyes glinting, ''You look beauteous as the night—I think I should serenade you.''

Marcia's arms were aching. But she seemed to have left behind her sensible, workaday self when she'd scrambled up on the roof. ''I've never been serenaded on a rooftop before.''

The emotion he felt was unquestionably jealousy. ''And where *have* you been serenaded, Marcia Barnes?''

She wrinkled her nose. ''I was serenaded on a very dirty canal in Venice by a gondolier who charged plenty for the privilege. That's not very romantic, is it?''

''Surely I can better that,'' said Quentin. ''Are the men in Ottawa such wimps that they run for cover when you look down your pretty little nose at them?''

''Men are rats,'' Marcia said vigorously.

"And how many men are you basing that conclusion on?" Quentin demanded, his imagination presenting him with a line-up of men stretching from the Byward Market all the way to the Houses of Parliament.

"Quentin, I am not going to discuss my love-life when I'm hanging by the fingernails over a fifteen-foot drop."

"You've got a point. Here, grab hold of me and we'll get you back into the room."

She wrapped her fingers around his wrist and tried to push herself back through the gap. A shingle scraped her anklebone, and her left elbow and the window frame connected with bruising force. Then somehow she was sliding through the window, faster and faster, her face jammed into Quentin's chest. He staggered backward and the two of them landed in a tangled heap on the bed.

Marcia was mostly underneath. He was wearing a cotton shirt through which she could feel the curve of his collarbone and the warmth of his skin; his shoulder was crushing her breast and his thighs had her pinned to the mattress. He was heavy. But not so heavy that she wanted him to move.

Then he did move, levering himself up on one elbow. "Are you all right?" he said urgently.

There was a fan of tiny lines at each corner of his eyes. His hair had tumbled over his forehead. It's a good thing my arms aren't free, thought Marcia in mingled panic and desire. Because if they were, I'd be pulling you down to kiss me, Quentin Ramsey, and to heck with the consequences.

Perhaps her impulse had shown in her face. He said roughly, "If someone'd told me when I got up this morning that I'd end up the day in bed with you, Marcia, I'd have told them they were clean out of their mind."

"We're not in—"

"Oh, yes, we are." He adjusted his wrist to make her more comfortable, letting his gaze run over her flushed cheeks, the jut of her breasts under the pale gray silk, the fragile bones of her wrist. "I think we should take advantage of it, don't you?"

He was lowering his head to kiss her, and any protest she might have made died. Mesmerized, she closed her eyes, and felt the first warm pressure of his mouth on hers. Warm, unexpectedly gentle, and with a leisurely sensuality that made her head swim. He brushed her lips with his as lightly as the touch of a feather; he nibbled on her lower lip and stroked her cheek, sliding his mouth over her cheekbone to her ear, pushing back her hair with his fingers. And all the while she was achingly aware of the weight and heat of his body hard against her.

With a tentative shyness that told a great deal about her, Marcia reached up her hands to touch his face. As she buried them in his wiry black curls, digging into his scalp, he murmured with pleasure. The nape of his neck was taut, blending into the muscled breadth of his shoulders.

His shirt felt unnatural, like a barrier, and perhaps it was this that brought Marcia to an awareness of the melting heat of her own limbs and the ache of desire deep in her belly. She moved beneath him, and with a shock that raced through her frame felt the hardness of his erection between her legs. Not for the world could she have prevented her indrawn breath, her small, involuntary sound of yearning.

"Marcia…" he whispered, and found her mouth again, deepening his kiss, parting her lips to the thrust of his tongue.

It was her dream, she thought in confusion. She was drowning in the blue depths of a man's eyes. A man who was virtually a stranger to her. She twisted her head free and gasped, "Quentin, please…we mustn't."

His body was nothing but need, a fierce, impelling need to empty himself within this woman who was his completion in ways he didn't even understand. Blindly he sought for her lips again. But she pushed him away, her face distraught and her eyes full of frantic pleading. Like a man emerging from a dream, Quentin said hoarsely, "Did I hurt you? I didn't mean—"

"No. No, you didn't. But we've got to stop."

He stroked her hair back from her face, his fingers trembling very slightly. "Why?" he asked. "Nothing I've ever done in my entire life has felt more right than being here with you."

Marcia gaped up at him. "How can you say that? You don't even know me."

"I think I've always known you."

If any other man had said that to her, she would have laughed in his face. But somehow she knew that Quentin wasn't joking. "I'll say one thing to you," she said warmly, "your approach is unique."

His gaze inimical, he rasped, "You figure I'm stringing you a line so we'll really end up in bed?"

"If this is just the dress rehearsal, the performance must be beyond belief," Marcia said recklessly, and with a surge of exhilaration knew she had spoken the exact truth.

"Oh, it will be...trust me," he said, moving his hand very lightly across the patterned silk of her top until it lay on her breast, his palm cupping the small, firm swell of her flesh. He felt her shiver with pleasure, her nipple tightening, and said with fierce impatience, "Let's make love, Marcia. Now. Maybe that's the way you and I should get to know one another—with our bodies. Leaving out all the social chitchat because we know what matters."

He teased her nipple in his fingers, watching her eyes darken with desire. "The two of us in bed together. That's

what matters,'' he went on with passionate intensity.
''Pleasing each other. Loving each other. We can catch up
on the other stuff later; we'll have all kinds of time for that.
But right now I want you so badly I can't think straight.''

Against her ribcage she could feel the heavy pounding
of his heart; at the open neck of his shirt, like an echo, was
the rapid beat of his pulse. Knowing his honesty deserved
a matching honesty from her, Marcia said, ''I'm too scared,
Quentin.''

''I wouldn't hurt you for the world.''

''It's myself I'm scared of, not you. I never behave like
this—never!''

He brought her hand to his mouth, sucking very gently
on each of her fingertips in turn. ''How don't you behave?
Show me.''

His mouth was slick and wet on her skin, making nonsense of shyness or resistance. Impulsively Marcia did exactly what she wanted to do. She circled her hips beneath
him, slowly and suggestively, rubbing against the hardness
that was the outward mark of his hunger. Then she pulled
his head down, kissing him with a wanton passion she
hadn't known she was capable of. He groaned her name
deep in his throat and rolled over, his hand roaming the
long curve of her spine as he pulled her on top of him. Her
ankle struck his shin; she flinched with pain.

''What's wrong?'' Quentin sat up, his arm around her.
''Your ankle—Marcia, you're bleeding.''

''I must have done it on the roof,'' she mumbled. ''The
shingles are made of wood and the edges are sharp.''

She didn't want to talk about roofs and shingles. She
wanted to be at the center of a desire so all-consuming that
she didn't have to think, didn't have to be cautious and
controlling and careful. A desire that obliterated the Marcia

she'd always been. She reached out her hand to take him by the shoulder.

But Quentin didn't even see her small gesture. He slid off the bed. "Stay put—I'll be right back."

Marcia's hand fell back on the bed and she stayed where she was, mostly because she didn't think she could stand up. The air coming through the skylight was cool; chills rippled across her skin. She felt—she sought for the word to express the yawning emptiness within her—bereft. That was it. Bereft.

Quentin came back in the room, carrying a towel, a small bowl of water and a first-aid kit. "I hope you didn't get any splinters in it."

She glanced down. "I don't think so. Don't fuss, Quentin, it's really nothing."

"I know you're the doctor—but let me do this, all right?"

"All right," said Marcia, with a meekness that would have astonished Lucy. She had bled on the sheets. Another load for the washer.

Quentin lifted her foot and put the towel under it, then carefully began to wash the blood from the two-inch scrape. He could easily have circled her ankle in his fingers; her skin was smooth, the veins blue in the high arch of her foot. He dabbed away at the flecks of dirt at the edges of the scrape, trying to concentrate on his task. Then he spread on an antibiotic cream, added a gauze pad and bandage, and taped it in place.

Despite himself, his hand lingered, tracing the slender bones on top of her foot. Although her pajamas had a high collar, long sleeves and slim trousers that came to mid-calf, the silk fabric tended to cling, revealing as well as concealing; he remembered how her breast had nestled in his hand like a bird and said overloudly, "The prognosis is good. The patient will survive."

But Marcia didn't laugh. Instead he saw that tears were shimmering in her eyes. Swiftly he rested his hand on her knee. "Did I hurt you?"

She shook her head. "I—I guess I'm not used to being looked after, that's all."

"You don't let people look after you."

Her chin tilted in a way he was beginning to recognize. "I like being independent."

"Ain't that the truth?"

"There's nothing wrong with being independent! I like making my own decisions and having my own money and—"

"Marcia, we are not going to argue about independence at two o'clock in the morning. Lie down and I'll get you an extra blanket. You look cold."

She was cold, inside as well as out. "But this is your room," she faltered.

"I'll sleep in the spare room." He took a fleecy blanket out of the closet. She was still sitting up in the middle of the bed, clutching the sheets to her chin, her eyes huge; he had no idea what she was thinking. He was a damned fool to be giving her a blanket when there were other, much more enjoyable ways of keeping her warm, but while her kisses had nearly driven him out of his mind, some deep instinct was warning him not to push his luck. To have found her here at the cottage was a miracle. Don't rush her, Quentin, he told himself. She'll still be here in the morning. And she's worth waiting for.

She's the one you've been waiting for all your life.

"Lie down," he said, "you look tired out."

Didn't he want her any more? Was that what he was

saying? Obediently Marcia lay down, watching him draw
the covers over her. "Goodnight," she whispered.

Briefly his lips were warm on her cheek. "Sleep well,"
he said. Then he padded out of the room, switching out the
light and leaving her alone in the darkness.

I don't know who I am any more, thought Marcia. I
would have made love with a man I don't even know. A
man who terrifies the life out of me. I wanted to tear the
clothes from his body. Me, Marcia Barnes. What's happening to me? I've got to get out of here before I do something
I'll regret.

She closed her eyes, snuggling into the warmth of the
blankets, already planning how she would leave before
breakfast. She was mentally removing her food from the
refrigerator when, as if a thick, black blanket had been
thrown over all the others, she fell fast asleep.

CHAPTER FIVE

MARCIA woke to hear a robin caroling lustily in the trees over her head. The sky was a brilliant blue. The clock beside the bed said ten-thirty.

She'd meant to wake up early. So she could sneak out before Quentin woke up.

As she stretched, feeling various aches and pains make themselves known from her precipitate ascent to the roof and just as precipitate descent from it, her thoughts marched on. She'd felt safe falling asleep in the middle of the night, knowing that Quentin was sharing the house with her; she didn't like being all alone in the woods, she'd found that out yesterday evening. She still felt safe this morning. How could she feel safe and unsafe with one and the same man? It didn't make sense.

The trilliums in the woods were beautiful. And in the gazebo she'd actually managed to relax for a whole hour. A new record, she thought ruefully. No wonder part of me doesn't want to leave here this morning. After all, if Quentin hadn't arrived in the middle of the night I wouldn't have woken up. I'd have been all right here on my own. Not totally comfortable. But all right.

I don't want to spend the rest of the week in my condo.

Damn him anyway! Why hadn't he stayed in New York?

If only he'd stayed in New York, she would still have been ignorant of the new Marcia who had emerged last night in this very bed. As she remembered the way she'd writhed beneath him, kissing him with such abandon, shame warmed her cheeks. How *could* she have behaved like that? It was totally out of character. The sooner she got home and forgot about that new Marcia, the better.

She got out of bed, limping a little on her sore ankle, and dressed in a long-sleeved shirt that hid her bruised elbow and cotton trousers that covered Quentin's bandage; she shoved her glasses on her nose, then she folded and packed her clothes into her suitcase and headed for the bathroom. Ten minutes later, her make-up impeccable, her hair smoothly shining, she went downstairs carrying her bag.

Quentin was nowhere to be seen. Quickly she opened the refrigerator and repacked her cooler, then bundled the other food she'd brought into plastic bags. She was gathering her books when through the big windows she caught sight of something moving in the woods. She straightened, holding the books, her throat suddenly dry.

Quentin had been swimming in the lake. He was striding toward the house, a towel flung over one shoulder, his swim trunks sitting low on his hips. Patterns of sun and shadow moved over the muscled planes of his body. He had a beautiful body, she thought unwillingly, deep-chested, lean-hipped, consummately male. But more than that he looked happy, as happy and carefree as a boy, and as much a part of his surroundings as the house was.

It was a good thing she was going. Quentin Ramsey spelled trouble with a capital T.

He came in the door and grinned at her. "Pour me a cup of coffee, woman. The water's freezing and—" His eyes narrowed as he suddenly saw her belongings neatly arrayed on the floor. "What the devil are you doing?"

Drops of water were trickling down his shoulders to be caught in the dark hair on his chest. Marcia dragged her eyes away and said with as much dignity as she could muster, "I'm leaving."

"*Leaving*? What for?"

"The reason's very simple—you came back from New York."

He planted himself in front of the door and began scrubbing at his chest with the towel. "I couldn't stand it there," he said. "Hot, dirty, and too many people. I did what needed to be done at the gallery and caught the night flight home. Tell me the real reason why you can't stay."

She clamped down on her temper. "I've already told you—because you're here."

"What's so awful about me?"

What's awful is the way I behave around you... But Marcia said, spacing her words as if she were explaining something to a small and not overly bright child, "I came here on the understanding that you'd be away until Friday. You came back. I, therefore, am leaving."

"This is Tuesday. Why aren't you at work?"

"Budget cuts," she snapped. "Unpaid leave."

"Well, hurray for the government. Best thing they've done for me all year. Don't you like the house?"

"I love the house."

"The woods, the lake—not to your taste?"

"Quentin, quit playing games! We both know what could have happened last night. I—"

"What if it had? Would that have been so terrible?"

"Of course it would. I'm not into casual sex."

"Neither am I," he said softly.

Marcia flushed scarlet. Breathing hard, she seethed, "Then I would have thought you'd be pushing me out the door."

"The way I feel about you is not casual," Quentin said. "Haven't you gotten that message yet?"

"The only message I've been getting is that all your other females have been willing."

''For Pete's sake—you make it sound as though I keep a harem!''

''I saw how those women clustered round you at the gallery—and you weren't exactly discouraging them.''

''Jealous, Marcia?''

''Of course not.''

''I don't believe you.''

''Are you calling me a liar?'' she snapped.

''Let me set the record straight. One, I'm not Don Juan. Two, I've already told you you're special to me in ways I don't understand. Three, if we'd made love last night I'd have done my best to give you pleasure, to make you feel desirable and wanted and fulfilled. Because that way I—''

With unconscious drama Marcia covered her ears with her hands. ''Stop!'' she choked. ''I scarcely know you. How can I possibly go to bed with you?''

''How about because you want to?''

She dropped her hands, recalled in graphic detail how she had kissed him, and to her horror burst into tears. Weeping as though her heart would break, she fell backward onto the chesterfield and shoved her head into the crook of her elbow.

Appalled, Quentin let the towel fall to the floor and knelt beside her, raising her head to remove her glasses then pressing her face into his bare shoulder. His body was shuddering with the intensity of her feelings, and in between noisy sobs that seemed to tear their way out of her chest he heard her wail, ''I never cry. N-never. I hate c-crying.''

''Never'' seemed to be Marcia's favorite word. Quentin murmured nonsensical words of comfort into her ear and wondered if he'd ever felt this way about a woman before. He was pretty sure that he hadn't, because he couldn't imagine forgetting it if he had. Tenderness, exasperation, the longing to console, all mixed together with a healthy

dose of good old-fashioned lust. Her hair smelled sweet.
The narrowness of her shoulders both excited and frightened him, filling him with the need to protect her. Lust he
knew. But tenderness? Protection?

Love?

He found himself shying away from the word. To love
a woman would change his life drastically—particularly if
the woman in question wasn't into being loved. *Was* Marcia
the right woman? How could he answer that? It would take,
he realized for the first time, two people to answer that
question. He'd never realized that before.

Not liking the direction his thoughts were taking, he said,
"Guess what, Marcia? I don't have a handkerchief."

His voice seemed to come from a long way away; she
felt as though she'd been run over by a truck. Her breath
heaving in her throat, Marcia mumbled, "I've got a tissue
in my pocket."

Where Quentin's shoulder had been wet with lakewater,
it was now wet with tears. She sat up, avoiding his eyes,
and blew her nose with gusto. Then she hiccuped, "I hate
women who c-cry. It's so feminine. Such an underhanded
way t-to win an argument."

"Who said you'd won?"

She glowered at him, her nose and eyes pink, her lashes
sticking together in little clumps that filled him with an
even deeper tenderness than before. "Quentin, I'm leaving."

"Over my dead body, sweetie."

With a flash of humor that heartened him immensely,
she retorted, "The woman I've always been may be falling
apart around me, but I d-don't really think I'm cut out to
be a murderess."

"Good." He grinned at her, sitting down on the chesterfield beside her. "You're staying. Right here where you belong."

"Oh, yeah? That's what you think." Which was, she thought with another reprehensible quiver of amusement, a reply worthy of the playground, not of a woman who could put half a dozen letters after her name.

"The Richardsons are away all month, and I'm keeping an eye on the house for them—so I can invite whoever I want to stay here. You're it."

"Keeping an eye on the house? Huh. The place was a pigsty." Marcia scrubbed at her wet cheeks with the back of her hand and put her glasses back on. "Actually, that's an insult to pigs."

"When I first walked in last night I thought I was in the wrong house," Quentin admitted meekly. "All that tidiness. It's because I was working on a painting, Marcia—I'm always messy when I paint. The rest of the time I'm really quite civilized."

Of all the adjectives she might have applied to Quentin, "civilized" wouldn't have topped the list. Frowning, she tried to behave like a sensible, rational adult. "I don't understand why you want me to stay."

"I'll tell you why if you'll tell me why you were crying."

"That's private!"

"You've been private all your life," Quentin said ruthlessly, "and it's not working, is it?"

"I hate it when you talk about me to Lucy."

"Anything you tell me stops right here."

The odd thing was that she believed him instantly. And after all, hadn't she come here to try and figure herself out? "All right," Marcia said ungraciously.

Quentin hadn't expected her to surrender quite so easily. Choosing his words, he said, "When I arrived here last night and found a strange car in the driveway and the living room looking like a photo in a glossy magazine, I didn't know what was going on. Then I picked up a book on the table and saw your name in it. I wasn't just happy, Marcia—too mild a word by far. Joy. That's what I felt. Joy… And explain that to me if you can.''

He ran his fingers through his wet hair. ''I'd already been through the house and I knew it was empty. So where were you? In the space of two seconds I had you dead, lost, raped, murdered, drowned—you name it. When I found you on the roof I wanted to hold onto you and never let you go.''

He got up, prowling restlessly round the room. ''You're important to me—I've told you that before and last night only confirmed it.'' Scowling at the easel, he added, ''You must have looked at that…it's how I've been feeling ever since the dinner at your place, when you told me you didn't want to see me again. Stay, Marcia—please.''

So her suspicion that the painting was related to her had been quite correct. ''You sure say it how it is,'' she said quietly.

''I can't be bothered with all the shenanigans people go through. Take a look at a wildflower sometime—or a lake in the sunlight. What's manipulation got to do with that?''

Marcia remembered the dappled sunlight on the carpet of trilliums and knew that he was right. Unable to think of anything to say, she stared down at her fingers, which were nervously twining and intertwining in her lap.

Quentin wiped the towel over the back of his neck, where water was still dribbling from his hair. Kissing her would convince her of the strength of his feelings, but he was almost sure she'd belt him if he were to try that particular argument. ''I want you to stay for your sake as well as mine,'' he said.

With none of her usual grace Marcia got to her feet, putting the chesterfield like a barrier between her and the man pacing up and down the hardwood floor. He'd finished. It was her turn now. But what was she going to say?

"I've always been in control of my life and my emotions—of everything," she faltered. "But lately... I don't know what's happening—and it's not just you. I *never* cry. Three times in a row in that damned gallery I could have bawled my eyes out." She dug her nails into the padded fabric and added in a rush, "I really hate this—I hate talking about myself."

Smothering the urge to take her in his arms, Quentin said gently, "You're doing just fine."

"Sex," she blurted. "That's why I cried."

His whole body tensed. "What do you mean?"

She gulped, "I'm ashamed to even think how I behaved last night."

"Marcia—"

"I suppose it's understandable if I analyze it. I was frightened when I heard someone in the house, then I spent a very uncomfortable few minutes on the roof and then you literally fell on me. Little wonder I behaved so abnormally."

His voice was as sharp as a knife-blade. "Do you really believe that?"

"I'm not sexy like Lucy," she said desperately.

Feeling his way, Quentin replied, "Of course you're not. You're sexy like Marcia."

"But you'd much rather I was like Lucy."

He hesitated fractionally, remembering his first sight of Marcia, so perfectly groomed in her severe tailored suit, her glasses warding off the world—just as they were now. His disappointment had been acute; he remembered that too.

Marcia paled. "You're in love with Lucy."

"For God's sake—"

"You'd have to be! I know you spent a lot of time with her on the island that summer she and Troy were separated, and she's so beautiful, and all her emotions spill all over the place—you'd have to be a chunk of rock not to fall in love with her."

"Marcia," Quentin said forcefully, "I never was the slightest bit in love with Lucy."

"She's got a gorgeous figure," Marcia wailed, "I can see— What did you say?"

"I never for one instant was in love with Lucy. When she turned up on Shag Island looking as miserable as a stray cat she was like the sister I never had. I couldn't have been happier when she and Troy got back together, and since then they've become two of my closest friends."

"Oh," said Marcia.

Wondering if he was burning all his bridges behind him, Quentin said, "Lucy's beautiful; sure she is. But she never once touched my soul. And I certainly never wanted to take her to bed. Not like you."

"But—"

He sat down on the arm of the nearest chair, smiling at her. "Your pajamas—let alone what you're wearing now—could have been worn by any self-respecting nun, and I was still half crazy with desire. I hate to think what'll happen when I see you in a pair of shorts."

She said in a small voice, "I've envied Lucy for years— I'm just beginning to realize that. She was always in love with someone, she always did what she wanted, even when the rest of the family didn't approve, and she was the only one of us who didn't become a doctor—she seemed so free."

"Lucy's one of the lucky ones, who was born knowing

what she wanted, and had the confidence to go after it. It's just taken you longer, that's all.'' He put all the force of his personality behind his words. ''You did nothing to be ashamed of last night, Marcia. That woman is the woman you're meant to be.''

''I'm not in love with you,'' she flashed.

He didn't like her saying that. Didn't like it at all. He said shortly, ''It's too soon to talk about love.''

''But you want to make love with me. Or so you say.''

Her knuckles were white where she was gripping the back of the chesterfield. She was like a wild creature, Quentin thought, who was trapped in a corner and lashing out at anyone who came too close. ''If you'll stay for a few days, I won't so much as touch you,'' he said. ''I swear I won't.''

And how in heaven's name was he going to manage that?

Some of the tension left her shoulders. ''Not even if I wear my shorts?'' she said with a tiny smile.

''Right,'' he said ironically. ''Will you stay?''

A question made up of three small words on which her whole life seemed to depend. ''Yes...I guess so.''

He felt suddenly exhausted, as though he'd swum the whole length of the lake. ''Good,'' he said. ''Why don't you unpack and I'll make you some breakfast?''

''We should change bedrooms.''

He raised his brow. ''You'd better stay in that room—I wouldn't want to deprive you of your escape route. I'll go up and get dressed...back in a minute.''

So Marcia spent the next ten minutes putting her food back in the cupboards and the refrigerator and wondering if she was being a total idiot to stay in the same house with Quentin.

Two days later Marcia was no nearer a conclusion. Quentin was keeping scrupulously to his bargain—so scrupulously that she wondered sometimes if she'd dreamed him saying how much he wanted her. She'd worn her shorts yesterday, and so far as she could tell he hadn't given her legs—which she'd always thought rather shapely—so much as a passing glance. He was giving her lots of space—swimming at least twice a day in water so cold it made her shudder, and disappearing on long walks through the woods; he appeared to have abandoned his painting.

At mealtimes he barbecued steak and chicken while she made pasta and salads, and they each made conversation that left her feeling utterly frustrated in a way she couldn't pinpoint. The most significant thing she'd learned about him was that eating shrimp made him violently ill. It didn't seem like much for two whole days. Not from a man who kept saying she was important to him.

It was as though the real man had gone somewhere else, leaving a pleasant, considerate, distant stranger.

She tried her best to relax. She took books to the gazebo and lay in the hammock and all the time she was wondering what Quentin was doing. When he settled down with a book in the house she'd meander along the lakeshore by herself, her nerves on edge in a way she deplored but couldn't prevent. Wondering if busyness could be the antidote, she vacuumed, made cookies, raked the lawn and weeded around the shrubs. She went to bed early and got up late.

Nothing helped. Every moment of the day, or so it seemed to her, she was achingly aware of the man who was sharing the house with her. He was keeping to his promise. Why, then, was she so angry with him?

On Thursday afternoon Quentin was hunched over some drawings at the dining room table, and something in the line of his back told Marcia not to disturb him. She went outside, slathering fly dope on her arms and legs, and set off down the shore. In a little cove ten minutes from the house she sat down on a rock, staring glumly at the water. The only thing she'd accomplished this week was not missing the lab. She'd been too busy missing Quentin.

How could she miss someone she was virtually living with?

Through a gap in the rocks a muskrat headed purposefully for the grasses along the shore. Marcia sat as still as a rock herself, watching in fascination as it nibbled at the fresh shoots, its wet fur gleaming in the sun. Then a second animal appeared round the corner, heading for the same cluster of rushes; the first one chattered and gibbered at it in clear displeasure, then plunged after it, its long tail whipping like a snake in the water. Both of them vanished from the cove. Little ripples spread across the water and splashed against the rocks.

Grinning to herself, Marcia stood up and hurried back to the house. Quentin was bent over the table. She said, "Guess what? I saw two muskrats."

"Yeah?" he said, not looking up.

She marched across the room and stood right in front of him. "Quentin, I'm speaking to you."

"Just a sec."

In a glorious flood of energy Marcia lost her temper. "I can't imagine why you were so insistent I stay here," she blazed. "You pay me less attention than if I were a slab of sirloin steak, and if this is how you behave when someone touches your soul, I'd sure hate to be around you if you were indifferent to me."

He pushed back his chair. "What the hell's gotten into you?"

"I absolutely loathe being treated like a stick of furniture!"

Her hands were on her hips, her shorts were several inches briefer than the ones she'd worn yesterday, and her violet eyes were flashing like amethysts. "That was the deal we made," Quentin snarled. "That I wouldn't touch you."

Her nostrils flared. "I didn't think we made a deal that you'd totally ignore my existence."

"It's pretty hard to do that when every time I turn around you're dusting and cleaning and tidying up."

"If you weren't so messy, I wouldn't have to!"

"You know what your problem is? You don't know the meaning of the word vacation!"

He knew exactly where to put the knife so it would hurt most. "I wish you'd never come back from New York," she said viciously.

"Not half as much as I do."

Marcia's temper vanished as precipitously as it had arisen. A cold knot of fear in the pit of her stomach, she gasped, "Is that true?"

Quentin thrust his hands in his pockets. "No."

Trying very hard to mask her relief, she said petulantly, "You're a fine one to talk about vacations. Look at you— you never stop painting and drawing." Frowning in puzzlement, she stared at the strewn papers. "That looks like a house plan." She looked closer. "A house like this."

"That's precisely what it is," he said impatiently.

"If you want one like it, couldn't you get a copy of the plans from the builder?"

"Marcia, I was the builder."

She gaped at him. "You mean, you built this house?"

"I thought you knew that—didn't Lucy tell you?"

"She did not." She looked around at the angled ceilings and the shadowed beams with new eyes. "Did you design it as well?'' When he nodded she said warmly, ''It's a beautiful house. Where did you learn how to do that?''

Her whole face was alight with interest. Keeping his hands firmly in his pockets, Quentin said, ''From my dad. I started drawing things as soon as I was old enough to hold a crayon, and it must have been clear to him that I was going to be an artist—especially after I did drawings of our seven chickens all over the kitchen wallpaper when I was five. He never discouraged me. In fact, he kind of liked it when I did sketches of the lumber crew that he could show off to his buddies. But the idea that I might earn my living as an artist—he didn't think too much of that. So he made sure I learned everything he knew about carpentry, so I'd have something real I could depend on.''

There was a half-smile on his face and his eyes were soft; Quentin had loved his father, that much was obvious. Her own father had died when she was five, a long-ago pain Marcia had done her best to repress. ''Did he build houses too?'' she asked.

''Sheds and repairs to the camp, that's all. But the people my mother worked for had a timber-frame house built for them by some contractors from the States, and that's when I fell in love with that kind of construction. All the posts and beams exposed, and the wonderful sense of space.''

''Quentin,'' Marcia said, ''this is the first real conversation we've had in three days.''

His smile was wry. ''Yeah... I overestimated my ability to keep my hands off you.''

''I thought you didn't want me anymore.''

His laugh was unamused. ''Oh, sure.''

She said rapidly, before she could lose her nerve, ''The reason I told you men were rats was because the only two men I've ever slept with both lied to me. Big time. And then you came along. First you said all that stuff about how

I touched your soul and how I was so desirable and sexy—
and then we made the deal that you wouldn't touch me and
you stopped saying it. I figured it was a line you'd been
feeding me to get me into bed. A line that hadn't worked,
so you'd dropped it." She paused for breath. "You'd lied
to me, in other words."

His eyes narrow. "Are you serious?"

"You know how I hate talking about myself. Of course
I'm serious."

There was only one way he knew of to reassure her. In
two quick strides Quentin closed the gap between them. He
put his arms around Marcia and bent his head to kiss her,
using all his considerable powers of imagination to show
her with his mouth and his body how very much he wanted
her. Almost immediately, intoxicated by the smooth curves
of her bare arms, the swell of her hips and her flame-like
response, he stopped thinking altogether.

Moments later they fell apart, staring at each other almost as if it was the first time they'd met. Quentin's chest
was heaving as though he'd run all the way to the highway
and back; Marcia's knees felt as insubstantial as the reeds
that the muskrat had been eating. The muskrat that had
started all this.

Quentin said jaggedly, "Let's take the car and go to the
local store and get a couple of ice cream cones. Because if
we don't, I'll be throwing you over my shoulder and making for the nearest bed."

"I only like vanilla," she whispered.

"Fussy, eh?"

"Very," she said, and smiled at him.

His heart turned over in his chest, for it was a smile from
which she held nothing back, like a flower opening to the
sun. "Marcia," he said huskily, "I—dammit, I don't even

know what I want to say. I promise I won't lie to you—ever.''

She thought of the painting of the three little girls running through the field, and for a moment she let her eyes wander around the generous and beautiful room in which she was standing. Swallowing hard, because she knew that she was taking a huge step, she said gravely, ''I believe you.''

''Trust...it's a big one, isn't it?''

''One of the biggest.''

His smile crackling with energy, Quentin added, ''If the local store doesn't have vanilla, we'll drive until we find one that does. Let's go.''

He held out his hand. With a sense that she was doing something momentous Marcia took it, feeling his palm warm against hers. Together they went outside.

CHAPTER SIX

As HER footsteps crunched in the gravel driveway Marcia said, "We could take my car."

Quentin gave her battered gray vehicle a disparaging glance. "I thought doctors made lots of money."

Beside his bright yellow sports model, her car did look shabbier than usual. "Cars aren't important to me. I drive them until they fall apart and then I buy a new one."

"So what do you spend your money on?" he asked lightly.

She climbed into the passenger seat of his car, inhaling the scent of leather and admiring all the dials and gadgets. "Oh, the usual stuff," she said evasively. "Food, clothes, the mortgage."

"And that's it? No stocks and bonds? No rental properties?"

With a flash of spirit she said, "You're being very nosy."

"Aren't I just? Money has a lot of power in our society, so I'm always curious how people spend it."

Reaching into her handbag for her dark glasses, Marcia muttered, "Five years ago I went to India. I help support a village hospital in the north—near Delhi."

Quentin's hand froze on the clutch. "Ever since I went to Peru four years ago I've been supporting an orphanage there... The more I see of you, the more I realize that the very smooth front you present to the world is just that—a façade. Tell me about this hospital."

Not even Lucy and Troy knew about it. Slowly at first,

but then with gathering enthusiasm, Marcia described the eye clinic and the preventive medicine unit—two of her pet projects. When she'd finished Quentin said soberly, "You're a good person, Marcia."

Feeling intensely shy, almost as though she'd taken off all her clothes in front of him, she said, "By the same token, so are you."

"A mutual admiration society?" He grinned at her and reversed in the driveway. "On a less lofty moral plane, you can now tell me about these two men. Whom I'm already prepared to thoroughly dislike."

"Do I have to?" she said, grimacing.

"Yep. And take your time. I want all the gory details. Start with number one. Name, age and occupation."

"It's going to be a triple ice cream cone," she said darkly. "With peanuts. Okay, okay, I'll start. Paul Epson. Third-year medical student. Twenty-one. I was eighteen, in my first year and away from home for the first time in my life. We fell in love and for six months I believed in every romantic cliché in the book.

"Then Paul started being less available and kind of distant...but I didn't really worry. He explained that his finals were getting close and he was under a lot of pressure. And I was buried under a mountain of work too. The whole thing fell apart when I met him at the frat house with another woman with whom he was quite clearly on intimate terms. He'd fallen out of love with me and into love with her, and the only thing he'd neglected to do was tell me."

Quentin said a word that made her blink. With more restraint he added, "Louse. Rat-fink. Yellow-bellied coward. Want me to go on?"

Marcia rather liked his response. "I was devastated. I wrote my finals in a daze, then I got the flu and couldn't shake it. I was working in a biochemistry lab for the summer, and I'd drag myself to work then go home and sleep for hours at a time, and get up just as tired as when I'd gone to bed—it was awful.''

"What did your mother and Lucy think?''

"They didn't know anything about it! Mother wouldn't have approved of me sleeping with Paul and Lucy was always so busy.'' She cleared her throat, enjoying the breeze tugging at her hair as they drove along the country road. "Paul kind of discouraged me from trying again. And anyway, I was determined to make good marks and specialize. So I was twenty-five when I met man number two.

"Lester. Thirty-one, nephrologist, lived in Toronto. Very good-looking but kind of quiet and shy—or so I thought. We liked each other and we'd get together anytime I was in Toronto. Eventually he told me he was married but couldn't divorce his wife. She was in a mental institution— it was a very sad case, and I respected him for sticking with her. A few weeks later we became lovers.''

She added with sudden fierceness, "It suited me, Quentin. Intimacy without involvement. Low-key. Discreet. And I've always been very wrapped up in my work—I didn't want a relationship that distracted me too much. We went on like that for four years. And then I went unexpectedly to a conference that he was attending. Guess what? He was there with his wife, who was no more a mental case than I am. A very wealthy wife. Whom of course he wouldn't divorce.''

This time Quentin's epithet was unprintable. Marcia wrinkled her nose at him. "Thank you—but, you know, it served me right. He *was* a married man and I shouldn't have gotten involved with him. But how could he have deceived me so systematically for so long?'' She sighed. "I came to the conclusion that I may be a very clever woman in the lab, but in the world of men I'm lacking the right radar.''

Quentin was beginning to understand why she'd been keeping him at a distance. ''Both of them went deep?'' he ventured.

''Well, yes. I don't trust often, but when I do, it's total.''

''I don't know how to convince you I'm different from them,'' he said slowly, braking and putting on the signal light. ''Here's the store—maybe chocolate chip ice cream will help me think… Hey, what's going on?''

A woman was crouched near the wooden steps beside a little boy who was screaming at the top of his lungs—sharp screams of real pain. As Quentin parked the car Marcia leapt out and ran towards them. ''I'm a doctor,'' she said, kneeling in the dirt driveway. ''What happened?''

The mother, very young with copper curls, said frantically, ''He fell off the steps.''

Marcia smiled reassuringly at the boy and carefully probed his ankle. ''He's sprained it—torn the ligament, by the feel of it.'' She looked over her shoulder. ''Quentin, could you see if they have any ice in the store? It's okay, little guy, something cold will stop it hurting so much. What's your name?''

''Jason,'' said his mother. ''He ran out ahead of me, and I tried to catch him but he fell before I could.''

Quentin came down the steps, passing Marcia some ice cubes wrapped in his handkerchief. She put it round the swollen flesh. ''There, Jason, that should help. Just give it a minute to kick in. You'll have to stay put for the next few days, I'm afraid.'' She smiled at his mother. ''You'll probably want to call your regular doctor—you might need some painkillers for the rest of the day and tonight. But I really don't think anything's broken. Do you have a car?''

''Right over there.''

Quentin said, "Here, I'll carry him."

Jason, who looked to be about four, had stopped screaming. "My popsicle's all dirty," he snuffled.

A bright red ice lolly was melting into the dirt; it was definitely not retrievable. Marcia said, "I'll go in and get you another one right now while my friend Quentin carries you to the car."

As she turned away she carried with her the image of Quentin gathering the little boy into his arms, his dark head bent, his big hands very gentle. One reason I envy Lucy is because she has Chris, she thought, with the jolt that an uncomfortable truth can bring with it. No wonder I've been avoiding her. All these years I've been fooling myself that I don't want children.

Did Quentin want them?

She hurried into the store and headed for the freezer. You're getting ahead of yourself, Marcia Barnes. You're terrified of going to bed with the man, and you're already thinking about children?

When she came back out Jason was strapped into the back seat of the car with his foot up. He accepted the popsicle with a wobbly grin, his mother thanked Marcia profusely and Marcia waved as they drove away. Quentin said thoughtfully, "You're good with kids."

"Ice cream, Quentin—we've earned it."

"I wouldn't mind having a couple of my own. Someday. What about you?" He added, "You're cute when you blush and even cuter when you're tongue-tied."

"It's a wonder to me that none of the women in your past has ever throttled you," Marcia said roundly, and realized that indirectly she was fishing for information.

"There haven't been that many, Marcia. I got married when I was twenty-five and Helen had divorced me by the time I was twenty-seven. For a very correct bank president twice her age with three times my salary. Living with an artist—so she told me—is only romantic when you're not doing it.''

Marcia had never liked the name Helen. But to be jealous of a woman she'd never met was ridiculous. ''She hurt you.''

''We hurt each other. I should have listened to my intuition. When we were walking down the aisle together it was busy telling me I'd married the wrong woman because I'd been too impatient to wait for the right one.'' He raked his fingers through his hair. ''Let's get that ice cream.''

He'd been about to say something more, she would have sworn. She led the way up the steps and into the cool, cluttered interior of a store that sold everything from canned soup to garden shovels, stopping in front of the freezer with its cardboard containers of ice cream and aware through every nerve of Quentin coming up behind her. He drew her back against his body, wrapping his arms around her waist. ''Vanilla and chocolate chip,'' he said. ''We're in luck.''

She leaned against him, loving the strength of his lean frame, curving her own arms over his and covering his hands with hers. He rubbed his cheek against her hair. ''Have I told you yet today that you're gorgeous?''

She could feel the laughter in his chest. Leaning her weight on him, she closed her eyes in surrender, the words coming from somewhere deep within her. ''Right this minute I feel superlatively happy.''

His arms tightened their hold. ''Oh, God, Marcia,'' he said helplessly, ''you take my breath away. I'm different from Paul and Lester, I swear I am.'' He nuzzled his face into her neck, her soft skin and the sweet scent of her hair flooding his senses; against his arm he could feel her heartbeat quicken. ''I am also,'' he added, ''quite prepared to make love to you on top of the freezer.''

''I know you are,'' she said wickedly. After a quick glance around to check that they were unobserved, she moved her hips from side to side with lazy sensuality.

''Stop it!'' he said in a strangled voice.

''You started it,'' she replied with unarguable logic.

''We'd better buy a bushel of ice cream,'' he said, and released her.

She turned to face him, her eyes dancing. ''I like you a lot better now than when you were being all tight-lipped and inscrutable.''

''You think I did all that swimming in the lake for fun?'' he rejoined, and watched her eyes widen and her cheeks grow pink.

''C'n I help you?''

The store's proprietor was a gnarled old man with eyes the shiny brown of chestnuts. ''Two double cones, please,'' Marcia said, edging in front of Quentin. ''One vanilla and one chocolate chip.''

Quentin paid and they wandered outside, sitting at the picnic table near the river. Ice cream had never tasted so good, thought Marcia, entranced by the fresh green of the alders and by the reflections on the water, where blue shards of sky slid between moss-coated rocks. Everything seemed immediate, newly created. Was this how Quentin saw the world all the time? Was this how she could see it if she gave herself the time?

When he'd finished his cone, Quentin went back in the store and came out with a monstrous watermelon tucked under his arm. ''I love it,'' he said defensively. ''We could have a contest to see who can spit the seeds the furthest.''

''And what's the prize?'' she teased.

''A forfeit for the loser.''

"I will not swim in the lake."

He leaned over and wiped a smear of ice cream from her lips. "That wasn't what I had in mind."

His blue eyes were intent on her face; he leaned closer and kissed her parted lips, the lightning flick of his tongue making her pulses race. "This contest could be dangerous," she said weakly. "For the winner and the loser."

"Let's go home," he said abruptly.

Home. A small word that struck her to her heart. "Where is your home, Quentin?" she asked. "Or do you still live in New Brunswick?"

It's wherever you are, he thought. "I haven't had a proper home for years," he said. "I've wandered all over the place—Asia, Africa, South America…although nearly every summer I go to Shag Island. I rent a little shack there. I've been wondering if the next house I build won't be my own. Somewhere on the west coast."

She, Marcia, worked in Ottawa. She said politely, "I'm sure it'll be lovely. Shall we go?"

Within ten minutes she was unlocking the front door of the house by the lake. She walked inside and it was as though the walls and the beams enclosed her, much as Quentin had enclosed her in his embrace. With no idea where the words came from she said, "What you do is so tangible. Paintings. Houses. You can see something for your work, touch it, look at it again and again, even live in it. Nothing I do is like that."

"Jason's mother wouldn't agree."

"Quentin, I spend my days in front of computer screens and gas chromatography units. I produce highly technical papers that only other immunologists will read. Oh, I know the research eventually reaches the public and makes a difference to people's health. But it's so indirect…and I don't know why the heck I'm saying this. I love my job. I always have. It's all I ever—''

She broke off as the telephone rang in the kitchen. Lifting his brows in surprise, Quentin went to answer it. ''Hello… Hi, Lucy, how are you…? No, I came back early… She's still here, do you want to talk to her?'' He held out the receiver. ''It's Lucy.''

Marcia didn't want her sister knowing that she and Quentin had been together for the last three days. ''Hello, Lucy,'' she said coolly.

''I won't keep you. I just wanted to check up that you were doing all right out there—I hadn't realized Quentin had come back early. That's neat. He's a pretty special guy, isn't he?''

''No, it hasn't rained here at all,'' Marcia said smoothly. ''What's the weather been like in the city?''

''I can take a hint,'' Lucy grumbled. ''But he was the best friend to me that anyone could have been that summer on Shag Island, and don't you forget it. By the way, Cat left a message on my machine asking for your number out there, so I left it on her machine. How did we ever organize our lives before answering machines? So she'll probably be calling you too. When are you coming back to Ottawa?''

''I don't know yet.''

''Stay all weekend. Troy and I can always go to the movies by ourselves on Saturday night. Glad you're having a good time, Marcie. Bye.''

Marcia put down the receiver. Lucy, if she had her way, would have Marcia and Quentin married off in no time. As she was standing there frowning down at the telephone it rang again. With a strange sense of fatalism, she picked up the receiver. ''Hello?''

''Cat here, Marcia. I'm in a bind and Lucy told me on Monday you had a week off. Could you come into town and stay at my place to look after Lydia's dogs until Sunday night?''

Catherine rarely wasted time on pleasantries but she rarely asked for favors either. ''What's going on?'' Marcia temporized.

''I've been given a flight to New York and back with a hotel reservation and three theater tickets included—my friend Lois was supposed to go and she's just had her appendix out. Too bad for her, but great for me. But I can only go if someone'll look after the dogs.''

''When would I have to come?''

''Tonight.''

She'd have to leave here right away. Leave Quentin. Which would be a very sensible thing to do. She was getting in deeper by the minute where that man was concerned, and a little breathing space wouldn't hurt at all. Trying to ignore all the contradictory emotions that the prospect of leaving Quentin caused her, Marcia said, ''Sure, I'll do that.''

''You're an angel,'' Cat said fervently. ''Mother has my spare key—you could get it from her. I'll leave a note about the dogs. The big one's called Tansy, and I swear she was born without most of her brain cells—too highly bred, if you ask me. But Artie's really sweet. Thanks, Marcia. I'll be back Sunday around four.''

''Have a good time,'' Marcia said, but she spoke into a hum on the wire; Cat had already cut the connection.

She replaced the receiver in its cradle and turned to face Quentin. His eyes were watchful. ''What's up?'' he said.

''Cat wants me to stay at her place until Sunday, to look after a friend's dogs. I'll have to leave right away.''

From Marcia's brief contribution to the conversation, he had guessed something of the kind. Tamping down anger, he said, ''You can hire people to do stuff like that.''

"It's a last-minute thing. And anyway, Cat hardly ever asks me to do anything for her—she invented the word independent."

"I don't want you to go."

Marcia said carefully, "I think it's a good idea if I go, Quentin. We both need to cool—"

"Speak for yourself."

"All right, then," she said in a clipped voice, "I need time away from you. You're too intense. Too much has happened too fast. I need to get away and think about it all."

"You've been thinking instead of feeling all your life. The last thing you need to do right now is think."

"So I can't tell you what to do, but you can tell me? Thanks a lot."

She looked as though she'd like to throw the phone at him. Quentin swallowed hard and said in a more conciliatory tone, "Look, I'm doing a lousy job here. Can we start again? Why don't I come with you to Catherine's? I could help you with the dogs."

It was one thing to share a house with him in the country, another thing in the city with her family all around. "No thanks," she said. "I really need some time by myself."

"That's the old Marcia speaking. Not the real woman."

"Quit diagnosing me!"

"You're running away from everything that's happened since you came here. Keeping busy so you won't have to come face to face with yourself. Let alone with me."

"We're opposites!" she cried. "I'm tidy; you're messy. I'm a scientist; you're an artist. I'm from the city and you're from the country. I like pasta and you like steak. Don't you see? We're too different."

"How about this version?" he rapped. "You support a hospital and I support an orphanage. I love my job and you

love yours. I want to go to bed with you and you want to
go to bed with me. We're not so very different, not in the
ways that count.''

"I don't want to go—''

"You didn't like it when Paul and Lester lied to you. So
don't lie to me.''

He had an answer for everything. Angrier than she'd ever
been in her life, Marcia said tightly, "As soon as I get
packed I'm going into town. I really wish we didn't fight
so much.''

"You live alone and so do I, and we're both used to
making our own decisions. That's one reason we're fighting
and it's one more thing we have in common,'' he said with
a wolfish grin.

"One more reason we should stop seeing each other.''
She hadn't known she was going to say that; her stomach
clenched as if cold fingers had wrapped themselves around
it.

"Let me tell you something else! You can hide my paintings if you like—I noticed one was missing from the bedroom. It had too much emotion in it, didn't it? It was too
real. But don't think you can dispose of me so easily. Because I'm not just fighting for me, I'm fighting for you as
well.'

"Nobody asked you to do that!''

"I'm beginning to think that Paul and Lester deserve my
sympathy,'' Quentin grated. "You do what you like. I'm
going out back to stack some wood.''

The only good thing about all this, thought Marcia with
icy clarity, was that she was much too angry even to think
of crying. She stomped upstairs and packed in record time,
hung the abstract back on the bedroom wall and poked her
tongue out at it—an immature gesture that gave her considerable satisfaction—then shoved her books into her plas-

tic cooler. He could keep the food. It would make a change from steak.

She lugged everything outside and loaded the trunk and the back seat of her car. From behind the house she could hear the steady thunk of log against log. She should say goodbye. She didn't want to say goodbye. She got in her car and turned the key.

CHAPTER SEVEN

THE ignition gave a faint click, but nothing happened. Marcia tried again. The motor didn't even turn over. Tight-jawed, she sat still for a minute or two, with some vague notion that she might have flooded the engine. Although how could she have if the motor hadn't turned over? She pushed the accelerator to the floor a couple of times, put the clutch in neutral and turned the key again. Still nothing.

"You would have to let me down now, wouldn't you?" she seethed, glaring at the gas gauge as though it were a face. "You couldn't have waited until I was in the city, with a nice garage down the street. Oh, no. *Now* what am I going to do?"

"Trouble, Marcia?" Quentin asked blandly.

She didn't even look up. "My car won't go," she said with noticeable restraint.

"Maybe if you got out and kicked it?"

"It'd probably fall apart if I did that. Although it would make *me* feel a whole lot better."

"Looks as though I'll have to drive you into town," he said.

She made the mistake of looking up. Wood chips were clinging to his T-shirt, which was clinging to his chest. His hands and his jeans were dirty and his eyes were laughing at her. Determined not to let the corners of her mouth curve upwards in response, she said crossly, "You've got bits of wood in your hair."

"I need a good woman to look after me."

"Someone to darn your socks and iron your shirts? You're in the wrong century."

"Someone to warm my bed on cold winter nights," he said. "Is your trunk locked? I'll transfer your stuff to my car."

What choice did she have?

Marcia got out of her car, rolled up the window and reached in the back seat for the cooler. Ten minutes later, with Quentin now in clean jeans and an open-necked shirt, they turned onto the highway. They traveled in silence for a few miles, then Marcia said stiffly, "Thank you for driving me in. I appreciate it."

"So you should—considering it's against my own best interests."

Marcia had had time to cool down. Very briefly she rested her hand on Quentin's knee. "I'm sorry I was so bitchy. It's not like me to keep losing my temper all the time. But seriously, Quentin—everything's happening too fast. I do need some time to myself."

"Can I phone you on the weekend?"

"I—I guess so."

With suppressed violence he said, "Just don't shut me out—that scares the hell out of me."

"I just wish you weren't so intense!"

"I'm the way I am," he retorted. "All your detachment and control, it's not working for you anymore. I'd bet my last dollar it's your own intensity you're so afraid of—and if I'm wrong, you can laugh all the way back to your city condo."

Marcia had no answer for him. She locked her fingers together in her lap and stared out the window; she didn't speak again until she had to give him directions to her mother's house. He pulled up behind a sleek black Mercedes and said briefly, "I'll wait out here."

She'd been afraid he'd want to go in with her. She ran up the walk and rang the doorbell. When no one came, impatiently she pressed it again. She was about to ring for the third time when Evelyn Barnes opened the door just a fraction.

"Marcia!" she exclaimed. "What—? Oh, my goodness, the key. I'd forgotten all about it." She shot a hunted glance over her shoulder. "What on earth did I—? You'd better come in."

She was wearing a long silk robe, exquisitely embroidered, her cheeks were flushed and her invitation had lacked any real welcome. "Sorry, Mother," Marcia said. "Perhaps I should have phoned. Are you getting ready to go out?"

Evelyn blushed, her cheeks a deep, rosy pink. "No—no, I'm not. Not really," she said incoherently, her eyes looking anywhere but at her daughter.

"Is there anything wrong?" Marcia said sharply, reaching out a hand to touch her mother's wrist.

Evelyn stepped back. "No! I'm just… Now where did I put that key? It's around here somewhere."

Evelyn was usually the most self-possessed of women. Puzzled and obscurely hurt, Marcia stayed in the hall. From where she was standing she could see into the living room. With a tiny shock she saw a man's jacket thrown over one of the chairs and a glorious bunch of tulips on the coffee-table in her mother's favorite crystal vase. Henry, she thought blankly. Henry's here. That's why Mother's so upset. That black Mercedes must be his.

He's upstairs. Upstairs in my mother's bed.

That's why it took her so long to answer the door. And why she's wearing a robe.

Her one desire to leave, Marcia tried to still the tangle of emotions in her breast and waited in an agony of impatience. Finally Evelyn hurried back into the hall. "I'd left it in the kitchen," she said, dropping the key into her daughter's palm. "Sorry I kept you waiting—I expect you're in a hurry to get to Cat's."

It was less than a subtle hint from a woman known for her hospitality. But Marcia had no wish to linger. She muttered, "Thanks…take care," and ran down the steps.

But Quentin was—of course—still waiting for her. Quentin, with his artist's eye that didn't miss a trick. She schooled her face to the detachment he was always accusing her of, and more sedately walked toward him. Climbing into the car, she said, "Keep going down this street to the second set of lights, then turn left," and took her time adjusting her seat belt.

"Anything the matter? You didn't stay long."

"She was getting ready to go out," Marcia said, despairing herself for the lie but knowing that she couldn't possibly tell him the truth. My mother was in bed with her lover. How would that sound? The fact that it was broad daylight made it all the worse.

What a prude she was.

If Quentin knew the truth, he'd tell her that it was her own sexuality she was afraid of, not her mother's. He'd be wrong, Marcia thought vehemently, absolutely wrong. But oh, God, how she longed to be by herself. She'd never realized how exhausting emotion could be. Terror, passion, happiness, rage, jealousy, shock…she'd experienced them all in the space of a few short days and she needed a break. She'd rent a mindless video tonight and she'd forget the whole lot of them: her mother, Henry, Lucy and Quentin. Most of all Quentin.

"Left again at the intersection," she said hastily.

Cat's house was on a quiet, tree-lined street, and was in immaculate condition. As Marcia walked up the front path she could already hear barking from inside: a bass and a soprano, she though drily, wondering if the neighbors had complained about the noise yet. She unlocked the door and pushed her suitcase in ahead of her. A big brown and white dog, its eyes peering through a thick fringe, ran at her joyously and planted its front feet on her chest, its pink tongue aimed for her nose. She ducked and said authoritatively, ''Down!''

The dog licked her chin and shifted its paws to her shoulders. ''You,'' said Marcia, ''must be Tansy.'' She dropped her suitcase and put the paws back on the floor. Tansy grabbed at the handle of her suitcase and tried to drag it into the kitchen, growling ferociously.

''Are you sure you don't want me to stay?'' Quentin drawled.

She looked around. He was carrying the cooler and her jacket; he looked large and solid and capable. I'm going to miss you, she thought unhappily. ''I have a better idea,'' she said. ''You can take Tansy back to the cottage with—''

The suitcase collided with a small table in the hall. As the table tottered Marcia grabbed for the pottery vase that was sitting on top of it. The table crashed to the floor, Tansy gave a yelp of terror and scrambled under the kitchen table, and Artie, a rather elderly Scottie, growled his displeasure. His was the bass voice. Marcia put the vase down on the floor and said, ''My sentiments exactly, Artie.''

Artie wagged his stub of a tail and waddled up to sniff her outstretched hand. Quentin put her belongings down on the pale blue carpet and made his way into the kitchen. Tansy made a rush for his ankles. ''Stay,'' Quentin ordered. To Marcia's extreme annoyance Tansy stopped dead in her tracks and gazed adoringly into Quentin's eyes.

''You do have a way with females,'' Marcia remarked.

''So why doesn't it work with you?'' He fished a scrap

of paper out of his pocket and read out Cat's number from the telephone on the wall, copying it on the paper. Nothing underhanded about Quentin, Marcia thought shrewishly. I wonder how soon after he leaves here he'll start phoning.

The hall clock chimed the hour. Faintly surprised that it was so late, Marcia sat down hard on the nearest kitchen chair. "I should invite you for supper," she said. "Especially since you drove me all the way into town. I know I should."

"But you're not going to." To his own surprise as much as Marcia's, Quentin suddenly banged his fist on the table. Artie gave a startled yelp and Tansy made another theatrical dive for the table. Quentin said furiously, "I'm pushing you too hard, I know I am—I can't seem to help myself. But when I leave you like this I'm scared I'll never see you again, and that's the plain and unadorned truth. Have dinner with me on Saturday."

She gripped the edges of the chair and said steadily, "Quentin, I don't want to see you on the weekend. I need time out. A rest. An intermission. A break. Call it what you like."

"On Monday you go back to work. And we both know what that means."

The lab seemed like another world, remote and insignificant. "Then maybe next weekend," Marcia said.

"Maybe—is that the best you can do?"

Her own temper rose to meet his. "Yes."

"Fine. If I'm still around, I'll give you a call. If not, I'll send you a postcard. From Peru. Or Australia. Or the North Pole." He hauled her to her feet, planted a kiss of mingled rage and desire somewhere in the vicinity of her mouth, and marched out of the room. The front door slammed. Marcia sat down again and Tansy raised her aristocratic nose to the ceiling and let out a howl worthy of a coyote.

"I'm not going to cry," said Marcia. "I absolutely refuse to."

Nor, by a superhuman effort, did she.

He wouldn't go to Peru...would he?

That evening Marcia drank cup after cup of herbal tea and
indulged in some long-overdue reflection. By nine o'clock
she'd worked out that her mother had been afraid to tell
her eldest daughter the truth about Henry. She's scared of
me, thought Marcia in dismay. Scared to be real with me.
Because I've been sending out messages for years not to
bother me, please, that I'm busy with more important matters than family and intimacy... I haven't been a very good
daughter.

Not giving herself time to think, because if she did she
might rationalize her way out of it, she picked up the phone
and dialed her mother's number. "Evelyn Barnes," her
mother said briskly.

"Mother, it's Marcia." She licked her lips, horribly nervous, and said idiotically, "How are you?" Then in a rush
she went on, "I didn't call you to ask that. I wanted to tell
you that I figured out Henry was there and I—"

"I should have told you. But somehow I couldn't."

"Mother, it's fine with me—truly it is. I want you to be
happy. That's all."

There was a long silence during which Marcia listened
to the racing of her heart and felt her palm clutch the receiver. Yet she knew she had spoken the simple truth. Evelyn said slowly, "Why, Marcia...that's very sweet of you."

"Henry seems like a really nice man; I'm so glad for
you. I'm only sorry I've kept you at such a distance all
these years that you didn't feel comfortable telling me
about it."

Evelyn gave a sudden throaty chuckle. "Well, you know,

it's very new to me too. At my age, to fall in love! Some
days I feel like a sixteen-year-old, Marcia. It's so wonderful.'' She hesitated. ''So if we were to announce our engagement, you wouldn't mind?''

''Mind?'' Marcia said warmly. ''I'd be delighted. We'll
throw a big party to welcome Henry into the family.''

''Oh, Marcie, I'm so glad you phoned,'' Evelyn gulped.
''Here I am weeping and it's only because I'm happy. I
was afraid you wouldn't approve, I guess. That you'd think
I was too old… We thought we'd get married before Lucy
and Troy go back to Vancouver—do you think that's a
good idea? Originally I was planning a very quiet ceremony
with just a couple of witnesses, but Henry says he's so
proud of me he wants all our friends and relatives to take
part.''

''Henry's absolutely right,'' Marcia announced. ''I'll
help you with the planning—I'd love to do that.'' She
would, she thought in amazement. It would be fun.

''We'll let you know the date as soon as we've settled
on it. Marcie dear, thanks so much.''

Marcia cleared her throat. ''A big hello to Henry. And
my love to you, Mother.''

''Thanks, darling. I love you too. Bye for now.''

I'm crying again, thought Marcia, and blew her nose.
Making changes is hard work. But worth it. Definitely
worth it.

On Friday, in between more bouts of concentrated thinking,
Marcia walked the dogs—a perilous proceeding as Tansy
had no road sense and was possessed by the need to greet
personally every man, woman, child, cat and dog that she
came across. She was also, Marcia discovered, disconcertingly strong.

Marcia tried taking the dogs four times that day, hoping

to wear Tansy out. But Tansy's energy bordered on the manic, and Artie with his short legs and Marcia with her longer ones were the ones who ended up worn out.

In the morning she arranged to have her car towed to the garage. In the evening she went shopping. Her wardrobe, she decided, reflected her personality. Safe, conservative and dull. In the Sparks Street Mall she found a swirling gored skirt and a cowl-necked top in a gorgeous shade of raspberry-red, and in a trendy boutique she bought a white silk shirt and a pair of very flattering designer jeans, along with a Mexican silver belt and some turquoise jewelry.

She then decided that if she was going to look different outwardly she should also be more adventurous from the skin out, and spent three-quarters of an hour and rather a lot of money in a lingerie shop. She'd had no idea bras and panties were so pretty—flowered, lacy, all the colors of the rainbow. It was a long time since she'd browsed like this, she concluded. Too long.

Loaded up with her packages, she went home and phoned Lucy to tell her that she was free to babysit for them Saturday evening. ''Come for supper,'' Lucy said. ''On Saturdays we usually order out—no fuss, no muss. How's Quentin?''

''Fine, I guess.''

''You guess,'' Lucy snorted. ''If I'd known Cat wanted you back in town, I wouldn't have given her your number. Tell you what, why don't I see if Mother and Henry will babysit? Then you and Quentin could come to the movie with us.''

''No,'' said Marcia.

''Marcie, one of these days you're going to wake up and find out that life has passed you by,'' Lucy flared. ''Regret makes a cold bedfellow. I discovered that when Troy and

I were separated. I'll see you tomorrow. Bye.'' She banged the receiver down in Marcia's ear.

Quentin had slammed the door and now Lucy was slamming down the telephone. It would be nice, Marcia thought, if other people weren't quite so sure that they knew what was good for her.

But if Lucy had suggested inviting Quentin to the movies, then presumably he hadn't gone to Peru.

Not yet, anyway.

She brewed another pot of herbal tea and sat in the tiny patch of sunlight on Cat's deck. Artie flopped at her feet and Tansy tore round the yard looking for a gap in the fence, barked at the maple tree and tried to climb in Marcia's lap. Finally she, too, subsided on the plank floor.

Shutting her mind to the conversation with Lucy, Marcia thought about Jason and Jason's mother, and about the muskrat, and about how long it had been since she'd walked through a field of wildflowers, or even sat on a deck in the sun. She thought about the hospital in India, so very worthwhile and so very far away. Too far for emotional involvement. She thought about her mother and Henry, who would be her stepfather in just a couple of months. The only person she didn't think about was Quentin.

She didn't want to think about Quentin.

That night she dreamed again. The same nightmare where she was drowning in the swirling currents of a deep blue sea. She sat up in bed, trying to quell the racing of her heart. I'm in terror of Quentin and of all he represents, she thought with the clarity of extreme fear. That's why I don't want to think about him. If I let him into my life, really let him in, I'm afraid I'll disappear, that I'll lose myself.

According to Quentin—and to Lucy—she'd find herself. Could that be true? And what if she made love with him…what then? She'd never be able to go back to the way she was.

What if he were here now, beside her in the bed, in the opaque darkness of a city night? What would happen?

Her body sprang to life and her imagination began to gallop down pathways scarcely known to her. In utter exasperation Marcia went downstairs, made herself a peanut butter sandwich and watched a very silly movie on TV; at seven in the morning she woke up on the chesterfield with a crick in her neck and the television still bleating.

She snapped it off. Men, she thought vengefully. Or rather, one particular man. A man who built wonderful houses that let the sunshine in, who painted people's emotions, who kissed her as if there was no tomorrow. Quentin knew what he wanted.

He wanted her, Marcia. He'd made no secret of that.

Although he hadn't phoned her once since she'd come to Cat's.

Tansy whined horribly at the basement door and Artie gave the muted woof that meant he needed to go out. Cautiously Marcia moved her head from side to side, stretching her neck muscles. She was going to buy herself a new car that very morning. Which was undoubtedly a classic case of avoidance. Her mouth set, she headed for the basement door, bracing herself for Tansy's hysterical onslaught.

Her little gray car looked very dilapidated parked next to all the gleaming new models at the dealer's. But Marcia was feeling militant, and when she and the salesman parted company at noon, she felt she'd gotten a bargain. She drove out of the lot the proud owner of a bright red car no bigger than her old one but decidedly more noticeable. After she'd parked it in Cat's driveway and walked around it a couple of times, patting its sleek sides and admiring her reflection in the shiny chrome, she took the dogs for another walk.

Later that afternoon she drove her car to the apartment Troy and Lucy were renting for the summer; the paint on the car clashed with her raspberry-red outfit, which she'd decided to wear even though it was quite unsuitable for babysitting. It symbolized something. Something she wasn't yet ready to put into words.

"Wow!" said Lucy as she let her sister in the door. "Jazzy outfit. You're the best-dressed sitter in Ottawa… We've just ordered pizza—I hope you're hungry."

By the time they'd eaten pizza with the works, Lucy had also fed Chris his supper. In between mouthfuls he kept pushing his fingers into his mouth, whimpering. "He's teething again," Lucy said unhappily as Troy lifted him out of his high chair. "Troy, are you sure we should go? I hate leaving him like this."

Chris was snuffling into his father's shoulder. Marcia said, "Of course you should. I'm a doctor, after all."

"I forget that sometimes," Lucy said tactlessly. "Your job is so isolated from teething babies and over-protective mothers."

From reality, was what Lucy meant. Wincing inwardly, Marcia said, "Write down the phone number of the theater you're going to. If he's really upset I'll get in touch with you."

Lucy was chewing her lip; she looked tense and unsettled in a way Marcia was to remember. Troy said firmly, "Get your jacket, Lucy, or we'll be late." He then passed Chris to Marcia. "There's some stuff in the bathroom to rub on his gums. Thanks, sis."

Three minutes later the door closed behind them. Chris began to cry with a dedication that reminded Marcia of Tansy. She turned the radio to an easy listening station, then went to the bathroom, where she very gently rubbed his gums. He jammed his fist into his mouth. Crooning to him softly, she started making slow circles around the room in time with the music.

Half an hour later his forehead had drooped to her shoulder. He was heavy and her arms were aching. She was walking down the hall to put him in his crib when someone knocked sharply on the door. Marcia jumped. Chris's eyes jerked open and he let out a loud wail. Muttering a rude word under her breath, she went to see who it was.

Through the security peephole she saw Quentin standing on the other side of the door.

CHAPTER EIGHT

MARCIA'S heart gave a lunge in her chest. Clutching Chris to her breast like a shield, she unlocked the door and pulled it open. Quentin's face went blank with shock. Then joy blazed in his blue eyes and a grin split his face. "Marcia—so she invited you too! That's wonderful."

He was carrying a bottle of wine in the crook of his arm and he looked very handsome in a brown leather bomber jacket and faded jeans. Marcia stood back to let him in, watching as the joy in his face was replaced by puzzlement and then calculation. "You didn't know I was coming, did you? Where's Lucy?"

"Lucy and Troy have gone to a movie. I'm babysitting. I'll murder my darling sister when she gets home… Hush, sweetheart, it's all right."

Quentin closed the door behind him. "No dinner for three at seven-thirty?"

"No dinner at all. We ordered pizza and finished it off."

"Oh, well," he said cheerfully, "at least I've got a bottle of wine. Very good wine, if I do say so. I shall ply you with it."

"Babysitters aren't allowed to get sloshed, Quentin."

He quirked his brow. "You look utterly enchanting, dearest Marcia. I love the color of raspberries and your cheeks match your dress. What's wrong with Chris?"

"He's teething. He was nine-tenths asleep when you knocked on the door."

"He's not ten-tenths awake." Quentin shucked off his jacket; he was wearing a blue denim shirt under it, his body

hair a dark tangle in the V at his throat. "Here, give him
to me for a while—he's been slobbering all over your dress.
Is it a new dress?"

"I spent a whole lot of money between yesterday and
today," Marcia said with a touch of defiance.

He shot her a quick glance as he settled the little boy
into his shoulder. Then he said, "He's wet. Soaked. Come
on, Dr. Barnes, that's your department."

"I never noticed," she said, flustered. "We can change
him in the bedroom."

Chris's room was lit by a soft nightlight. As Marcia
washed and changed him his wails turned to a full-bellied
crying and his little face screwed up in misery. Quentin
watched as Marcia fumbled with the lid of the petroleum
jelly jar, dropped the baby powder and struggled with the
tabs on the diapers. "Bet you haven't done that since medical school," he said.

"Pour me a glass of wine, Quentin," she retorted. "I
can see it's going to be a long evening."

When she went back into the living room Quentin had
lowered the lights, and two glasses of wine along with a
hefty tuna sandwich were sitting on the coffee-table. A
tunafish sandwich didn't go with seduction any more than
a screaming baby did, thought Marcia. Not that Quentin
was making any attempt to seduce her. "I'll hold him while
you eat," she said.

Chris found his thumb and his screams subsided. She
waltzed him round the room until her arms got tired. Then
she sat down on the chesterfield a careful distance from
Quentin. When he'd finished the sandwich he took the baby
from her, easing him against his chest. "I won't bite, Marcia. Drink your wine and tell me about all this money you
spent."

The wine was a full-bodied burgundy. Marcia let it slide

down her throat and said, "I bought two outfits and a car, none of which is navy, brown or gray."

He gave a snort of laughter. "You don't do things by half measures, do you?"

Underneath her dress she was wearing raspberry-red lingerie. "No," she said demurely, "I don't."

"I find that encouraging… Hush, Chris, it's okay." Chris whimpered and attacked his thumb again; Quentin shifted himself more comfortably into the corner of the chesterfield and smiled at her. "You're sitting so far away I practically have to yell at you. Move over."

She gazed at him warily and took another gulp of wine, with scant respect for its quality. She looked very beautiful in her brave red dress, he thought; it made her skin creamy and darkened her eyes to purple. He said lightly, "I lust after you like a sailor who's been at sea for six months. Or an artist who hasn't been near a woman for a lot longer than that. But a ten-month-old baby who's teething is a most effective chaperon—I bet Lucy never thought of that when she set us up. So you're quite safe. I won't be seducing you on the chesterfield, the carpet or the coffee-table. More's the pity."

Marcia glowered at him. "I don't feel the slightest bit safe when you're anywhere in my vicinity."

"Tell me more. I like it."

She said in a rush, "I'm very glad you didn't go to Peru."

"So, right now, am I."

She was feeling rather peculiar; the spicy pizza was co-habiting with the red glow of the wine along with a strange ache somewhere deep inside her, which had nothing to do with food or drink and everything to do with the sight of Quentin holding her nephew. His big hand was curved protectively around Chris's body; Chris had butted his head under Quentin's chin, with his cheek lying on Quentin's chest. It was all too easy to imagine that she and Quentin were an ordinary married couple spending a quiet Saturday evening at home with their child; the ache increased in intensity.

"My mother's getting married again," she blurted. "To Henry."

"What brought that to mind?" he said softly.

"You have a positive genius for asking unanswerable questions! Did you like Henry?"

"I liked him very much. My left arm needs a counterbalance for my right. Come over here."

Marcia let another mouthful of wine course its way down her throat. Then she put her glass down and edged nearer, her back ramrod-straight. "It's not very romantic to entice a woman into your arms by calling her a counterbalance."

"Arm. Singular," Quentin said, and put it round her, his palm cupping her shoulder, his fingers beginning to caress it in a gentle, hypnotic rhythm. "Relax. I want to tell you a story."

Go for broke, thought Marcia, and drew her feet up on the chesterfield and let her head fall to his shoulder. His arm tightened instinctively. She closed her eyes, aware through every pore of the tautness of his muscles, the unyielding hardness of bone, the clean, masculine scent of his skin. "Not sure I'll be able to concentrate," she mumbled.

"Marcia…"

There was a quality in his voice that made her look up. His eyes were an unfathomable blue, and for a moment she felt a catch of fear. But when he found her mouth with his, fear dropped away as if it had never been. Wonderment and a bittersweet longing surged through her veins; she opened to the probing of his tongue and to a heat like that of a summer day.

He was drowning, Quentin thought, and wished Christopher Stephen Donovan a thousand miles away. Or at least asleep in his crib down the hall. She smelled so sweet, the silky brush of her hair against his cheek tantalizing all his senses. He felt her fingers creep up to stroke his nape, then bury themselves in his hair, and as his head began to reel he hoped fleetingly that Lucy was thoroughly enjoying the movie, because she'd sure done him a good turn.

Chris gave a little whimper, then sucked juicily on his thumb again. Nibbling at Quentin's lips in between her words, Marcia whispered, "I don't think babysitters are supposed to neck on the couch either... You were going to tell me a story."

"So I was."

As he lifted his hand to push her hair back from her face she saw that his fingers were unsteady. I do that to him, she thought humbly. I have that power. "Why me?" she burst out. "That's what I don't understand."

Was this really the right time to explain to her why he couldn't stay away from her? Or would it only frighten her away again? "That's what the story's about," he said. He leaned his head back on the chesterfield and closed his eyes, holding her close to his body. Where she belonged. He had to believe that.

"Once upon a time in the village of Holton there lived a boy called Quentin," he began. "He never had any brothers or sisters, but that didn't really bother him because he had the woods and the fields as his playground, and he'd spend hours watching deer and porcupines and birds— watching them and drawing them, because he always knew he was going to be an artist. And perhaps that was another reason he never missed having a sister or a brother. His other reason was because of his parents. They were as solid and dependable as granite, and as loving as the wild geese who mate for life and share the sky.''

She felt a sudden stabbing pain—for had she not lost her father when she was five? ''Yes?'' she prompted.

Without noticing, Quentin changed pronouns. ''I always knew there was something special about my parents—those two ordinary people who loved each other so passionately. The older I get, the rarer I think it is that a couple can sustain that kind of love through good times and bad... Lucy and Troy have managed to do it, although not without enormous difficulty. I expect that's partly why I'm friends with them.''

He looked down at the woman curled so intimately into his body. ''Ever since I was ten or eleven I've been sure I'd meet the right woman—the one who'd be my mate in the way my mother was my father's. My mistake was to ignore that certainty when I married Helen. But when you walked in the door of the gallery I knew you were the one. The woman I'd been waiting for most of my life.'' He cleared his throat. ''End of story. Or should I say beginning?''

Marcia sat up straight. ''You're in love with me? Is that what you're saying?''

''I suppose so. Although the words have become so damned trite I almost hate to say them. There's a connection between us, Marcia. Your blood calls to mine and mine to yours. Hell, I don't know how to say it—I deal in paint, not words.'' He thought for a moment. ''Your image is my heart's image...maybe that's what I'm getting at.''

Shaken, she said, ''You really mean it, don't you?''

''Oh, yes.'' He traced the elegant arch of bone in her cheek with one finger; her eyes were as wary as those of a deer that smells danger. ''I fought it for a while. Didn't think you were my type—control and detachment have never been high on my list, and Lucy had painted a picture of you back on the island that wasn't overly flattering." He paused. "It might have been an accurate picture then…but I don't think it is now."

Suddenly he'd had enough of words. Very deliberately his hand followed the slim line of her neck to her collarbone and the sweet rise of her breast, then fell to the flatness of her belly; when he reached the angle of her thigh he let it rest there, heavy and possessive on the soft raspberry-red fabric.

He heard her breath catch in her throat and watched her eyes dilate, and all the while she said not a word. "Red's the color of passion," he said softly. "Did you know that, Marcia?"

"We've neither of us made love with anyone for a long time, that's all this is!"

"You know better than that."

She did. "Are you saying I'm the woman you want to spend the rest of your life with?"

"Yeah," he said. "Yeah, that's what I'm saying."

"But we only met two weeks ago."

"Spend more time with me. That way we'll get to know each other."

She looked down at his hand where it rested on her leg; she already knew both its strength and its sensitivity. She reached over, picked up her glass of wine and drained it. "Why didn't you tell me this before?"

He felt his nerves tighten. "You weren't exactly receptive."

"You lied to me," she said sharply.

"I didn't! I just didn't tell you the whole truth."

"Now you're playing with words."

"Stop trying to pick a fight with me!" he roared. "You've got to be the most infuriating and obstinate woman that I know, and don't ask me why I'm in love with you because I don't have a clue—but just don't accuse me of lying to you because I won't stand for that.''

Chris reared his head up. His jaw was agape and his gray eyes full of astonishment. "Hi there, buddy," said Quentin in a more moderate voice. "You're cramping my style, you know that?"

Chris gave him a gleeful smile and blew a large, fat bubble. Marcia said helplessly, "I did it again. Lost my cool, I mean."

"Sexual deprivation—that's what it is."

She suddenly began to laugh, a delightful cascade of sound that made Quentin smile in spite of himself. "Take note," she chortled, "I'm actually agreeing with you, Quentin Ramsey. I'm announcing to the world that one of the effects you have on me—only one, mind you—is indeed that of sexual frustration."

With genuine interest Quentin asked, "What are the rest?"

She ticked off her fingers one by one. "Rage. Panic. Desire. Happiness. Misery. Jealousy. How am I doing?"

"You've left out detachment."

"Dear me, so I have."

Chris reached out for her, his smile revealing three pearl-like teeth and his red gums. Marcia took him in her arms, cuddling him and blowing down the neck of his pajamas. He gave his fat laugh and blew another bubble.

Quentin said in a peculiar voice, "When I see you like that it's all too easy to imagine Chris is ours. Can you picture yourself as the mother of my child, Marcia?"

With an honesty that entranced him, she announced, "Most of the time I'm with you I seem to be preoccupied to the exclusion of all else with the process that makes babies. But when I see you holding Chris I get this funny

ache inside.'' She grimaced. ''This has got to be the wack-
iest conversation I've ever had in my whole life. I've never
even lived with a man, Quentin. The day-to-day stuff. Who
does the dishes? Who cleans the bathroom sink? I bet we'd
drive each other crazy inside of a month.''

''One way to find out. Move out to the cottage,'' he said
promptly.

''You don't mean that!''

The mere thought of living with her made his throat tight
and his mouth dry. ''I sure do.''

She gaped at him much as Chris had. ''Do you know
what's really wacky here? That I'm actually considering
it.''

''All you've got to say is yes. Not a complicated word.''

His crooked smile did funny things to Marcia's heart-
rate, which was already erratic enough. As Chris seized a
handful of her hair she said unevenly, ''I think we should
give him a bottle and put him to bed. Lucy won't thank us
if we keep him up half the night.''

''Don't change the subject. Say yes.''

''Will you hold him while I warm his bottle?'' Staring
into Chris's slate-gray irises, so like his father's, she added
rapidly, ''I promise I'll give you an answer by the end of
next week. I promise. Don't rush me, Quentin...please.''

The soft lamplight feel on the swell of her breast and the
delicate hollow in her wrist; both filled Quentin with a
longing that made nonsense of patience and promises. A
longing he had to keep to himself so he wouldn't frighten
her away. He was rushing her. He knew he was. But how
could he help it? He got to his feet and tossed back the
better part of a glass of wine. Then he took the baby from
her, being careful not to touch her because she wasn't his—
not yet. And maybe never.

Her hand fell on his arm. ''When you look like that,

I…I'm sorry, Quentin, I know it doesn't make any sense to you to wait for a week, but I have to be sure I'm doing the right thing. This is serious, what we're talking about, and it scares me out of my wits. Please try and understand.''

He said roughly, "Do you know what I hate here? That I've got no choice. I'll wait because I have to wait. Because you're the woman I want and no other will do.'' He gave a harsh laugh. "When I was eleven it never occurred to me that love might feel like a trap. Closing in on me. Cutting off my options. How's that for male arrogance—not to realize that the woman I wanted might not want me?''

Frightened by the tone of their voices, Chris began to whimper again. Restlessly Quentin moved his shoulders, trying to work the tension out of them. "I think I'll go, Marcia. It's not fair to upset Chris, and we're getting nowhere fast.''

"I don't want you to go!''

"So we're both caught,'' he said heavily.

"Maybe love's only sweetness and light when you're not in it,'' Marcia said, not very sensibly.

"You don't get much of anything without a cost—I know that. I've always been a nomad, wandering wherever the spirit took me. Loving you means losing that freedom—although I'm not so sure that I wouldn't discover another kind of freedom.''

"I'd lose some of my independence,'' she said in a small voice. "Most of my life I've done what I want to do—no one else to consult, nobody else's schedule to consider. That would change, wouldn't it?'' She gave him a sly grin. "Knowing you.''

"We'd gain so much more than we'd lose,'' he said forcefully.

She began walking up and down, her skirt swirling round

her legs, her stockinged feet whispering on the carpet. "Do you know when my safe little world started to collapse? When Lucy and Troy's first baby died—Michael. I'd envied them their happiness—they were so in love with each other and then they had Michael, this perfect little baby. But Michael died and the marriage fell apart and they were both so unhappy—it was awful. Even though I was just an onlooker, I think that's when I finally started growing up."

Her hands were deep in the pockets of her skirt and her shoulders were hunched. Quentin stood still, each word she spoke making him more and more certain of the depths of passion buried in her heart. The red dress was no accident. He said quietly, "I love you, Marcia."

She stopped dead in her tracks. "It's too soon, Quentin," she said desperately. "I'm doing the best I can—but it's just too soon."

His impatience battled with his reason; the latter won by a narrow margin. "Let's put Chris to bed and then I'll get out of here. And maybe in the next couple of days we can have a date. An ordinary date." He smiled. "Pizza and a movie, for instance."

His reward was to see her smile back—a rather wan smile, but a smile nevertheless. "Sounds good," she said.

Half an hour later Chris was settled in his crib and Quentin had shrugged on his jacket. Marcia was standing in the hall, the overhead light shining on her face in which tension, uncertainty and a tremulous happiness all had their place. "I feel—" she began, then she suddenly flung herself at him, wrapping her arms tightly around his waist and hugging him as hard as if he were leaving for South America rather than the Gatineau Hills.

Quentin's heart was pounding in his chest like the thunk of an ax on wood. He strained her to him, lifting her off her feet and kissing her in fierce gratitude and even fiercer love, and evidently he felt her respond to him just as fiercely. He thrust with his tongue. As she dug her nails into his scalp and pressed her body into his he knew that he had already moved into that new freedom of which he had spoken.

Behind them a key turned in the lock. Quentin raised his head, watching the door open, and dropped Marcia unceremoniously to the floor. But when Lucy's head came round the door his arms were still linked around Marcia's waist, and her hands were clutching the front of his shirt as though that was all that was keeping her upright.

With rather overdone surprise Lucy said, ''Why, Quentin, how nice to see you.''

Marcia stepped back, her cheeks redder than any raspberry. ''He was just leaving,'' she said.

''The movie was awful,'' Lucy went on trenchantly. ''Neither of us could stand it, so we left.''

Troy looked from Marcia to Quentin in amusement. ''Take off your jacket and stay awhile, Quentin. How's Chris?''

''He settled down a few minutes ago,'' Marcia babbled. ''We gave him another bottle—I hope that was all right. He seemed to be hungry.''

''Whatever works,'' said Troy, the specialist in pediatrics.

Much as he liked Lucy and Troy, Quentin wasn't in the mood for small talk about movies and teething babies, nor for dealing with Lucy's curiosity about what had been going on between him and her sister. He said, ''I think I'll head back to the cottage. I'll give you a call tomorrow at Cat's, Marcia—take care.'' Without hurrying, he kissed her open mouth, smiled impartially at all three of them and let himself out.

He ran down the stairs, whistling loudly to himself. One

reason he didn't want to deal with Lucy was because he wasn't as sure as he'd like to be of what was going on between him and Marcia. He loved her. No question of that. If only he were as sure that she loved him back.

Still, he felt immeasurably more confident of the outcome than he had twenty-four hours ago.

And that, for now, was enough.

CHAPTER NINE

ON SUNDAY morning Marcia took the dogs for a walk. When she got back, the light on Cat's answering machine was blinking. She pressed the button and Quentin's voice surged into the kitchen.

"Marcia," he said abruptly. "I hate these bloody machines. I'm always afraid they're going to cut me off before I've finished. I'm going out in the canoe for a while—my dreams were such that I require large expanses of cold water. I'll call you later. Maybe we could have dinner together tonight? I never know whether to say goodbye—I mean, who the dickens am I saying goodbye to? You're not even there. I love you."

The machine beeped. Marcia picked Artie up, hugged him and put him down again. "Am I in love with that man?" she said. "This is nothing like the way I felt about Lester. Or Paul."

Artie woofed. Tansy whined. And Marcia put on a CD of operatic arias and warbled along with them as she cleaned up Cat's house and packed her own clothes. She showered and put on her new jeans and silk shirt, along with the Mexican belt and a big pair of silver and turquoise earrings. She then applied more make-up than usual and brushed her hair smooth. Not bad, she thought complacently, looking at herself in the bathroom mirror.

Would Quentin like her new shirt? Surely there'd be no harm in having a meal with him tonight. And Lucy had suggested that all four of them go out for dinner on Tuesday; Evelyn had offered to stay with her grandson so that

Henry could get to know him. Humming to herself, she made a salad and wished Quentin would phone. He'd been canoeing an awfully long time.

Was worrying about someone another side of love?

Was she in love with Quentin?

In love or not, one more thing the two of them had in common was impatience. She hated waiting, too.

Tansy was racing around Cat's small back garden, tearing up little chunks of sod with her claws, and Artie was sitting under the sundial, watching. She'd take them for one last walk to pass the time until Quentin phoned.

Not bothering to change, Marcia picked up the leashes and went outside. As usual, Tansy went nearly berserk at the prospect of an outing. After a brief tussle, which Marcia won, the three of them set off down the sidewalk.

The sun was shining and Marcia felt extraordinarily happy. She marched along, every now and then stopping to untangle Tansy's leash from whatever obstacle she'd wrapped herself around. Artie plodded phlegmatically at Marcia's side. She would miss Artie; she didn't think she'd miss Tansy.

Half an hour later Marcia turned around to go home. Thinking rather more about Quentin than about the dogs, she didn't see the lustrous-coated Great Dane standing on the opposite curb beside its elegant female owner, the pair of them waiting with equal poise for the light to change. But Tansy saw the Great Dane and her eyes lit up.

She made a sudden lunge for the street. Pulled off balance, Marcia was jerked out of her daydream. As she staggered sideways, grabbing for the lightpole, the leash was yanked from her hand. To her horror she saw Tansy leap into the road. "Tansy!" she yelled. "Tansy, come back!"

With a screech of brakes and a pungent smell of burnt rubber a black sedan came to a halt across the white line.

But not soon enough. As though it were happening in a dream, Marcia saw Tansy's hairy brown and white body make a lazy curve in the air and thud to the tarmac. For a split second she was frozen to the spot. Then she looked from side to side and raced out into the street, dragging Artie with her.

Tansy's eyes were closed. She was bleeding from a cut in her side. Marcia gathered the dog into her arms and heard a male voice say, "I'm most terribly sorry, but I really couldn't stop in time."

The driver of the black sedan was standing beside her. He looked rather as she had first pictured Quentin, she thought dazedly, right down to the tweed jacket, the pipe and the British accent. A younger man on a bicycle had begun competently directing traffic. The man in the tweed jacket said, "Please allow me to drive you to the veterinarian's—there's a clinic only two blocks from here."

The black sedan was a Jaguar. "Thank you." Marcia stumbled over the words. "I'll try not to make a mess in your car."

"This way, madam."

Within ten minutes the veterinarian on call was opening the door of the clinic and the man in the tweed jacket had driven away. Clutching Artie to her, Marcia sat trembling on the bench. Twenty minutes later the vet, a very pretty young woman, came back into the waiting area. "The dog will be fine," she said. "Concussion, so I'll keep her until tomorrow for observation, and ten stitches in her side. But no broken bones or internal damage. She was very lucky."

Holding tight to her self-control, Marcia paid the bill, left Cat's name and phone number, and took a cab back to her sister's house.

A yellow sportscar she would have recognized anywhere was parked at the curb and Quentin was sitting on the front steps of Cat's house. He stood up as she got out of the cab and started down the path toward her. Then he halted, and said in a strangled voice, ''Marcia, what's happened? There's blood all over your shirt.''

''It's Tansy's; she ran out into the road,'' Marcia said, and felt her body begin to tremble again.

''Sweetheart,'' he said, a note in his voice she hadn't heard before. ''Here, give me the key—and Artie.''

He put an arm around her waist, unlocked the door, let Artie in and stood aside so Marcia could enter. Cat had a large antique mirror in the hall. Marcia quavered, ''I bought this shirt the same day I bought the red dress. It's ruined.''

''For God's sake, it's only a shirt! For a minute I thought it was your blood.''

He did look pale, she noticed absently. Wringing her hands, she said, ''How will I ever tell Cat? It was all my fault. I wasn't thinking about what I was doing and Tansy ran out into the street and got hit by a car.''

''Was she badly hurt?''

''No—oh, no. She'll be fine. But I was responsible, don't you see?''

She looked utterly distraught. Quentin said carefully, ''Tansy is an unmitigated idiot and you'd have to be Superwoman to keep her under control.''

''I said I'd look after her. And I didn't.''

He wasn't at all sure what she was getting at. He rested a hand on her shoulder, but she pulled away from him. ''Marcia, what's going on here? Accidents happen and we all make mistakes—you're only human. How about putting some of the responsibility on Tansy's owner, who didn't train her, or on the kennels, who must have been inbreeding dogs for generations? Or even on Cat, who didn't really warn you what you were getting into.''

Marcia was backed against the wall, shrinking from him

as though he were an enemy. "I'm responsible," she repeated, and two tears dropped from her lashes to trickle down her cheeks.

Quentin couldn't stand to see her cry. He stepped closer, swung her into his arms and headed for the stairs. "What are you doing?" Marcia squeaked.

"I'm taking you upstairs. I'm going to start a bath for you, then I'll wash your shirt in the kitchen sink."

She was beating against his chest with her fists. "I don't want you taking over my life, do you hear me? Telling me what to do. Interfering all the time. Put me down this minute!"

"No," said Quentin. "Stop hitting me."

"Put me down and I will."

"For once you're going to do what I say and not what you want! A new experience, Marcia. It'll be good for you." Her fist hit his breastbone. "Ouch, that hurts."

"Good," she seethed as he pushed open the bathroom door with his foot and lowered her to the floor. "Go home, Quentin—I don't want you here."

He felt suddenly cold. "You don't mean that."

"I do! I've looked after myself for over thirty years—I don't need you doing it for me."

The muscles clenched in his jaw. "If you really mean that, I'll go," he said, each word like a shard of ice. "And I won't be back. Ever."

Blank shock replaced the fury in Marcia's face; her cheeks were as pale as the wall behind her. But Quentin had gone too far to back off. In a voice like a steel blade he said, "Love's not just good times, Marcia—babysitting and family dinners and movies. It's about crises and accidents and losses as well. It's about us sharing whatever happens, because that way each of us is stronger. You letting me see that you need me…me showing you how much

I need you. But if you won't let me near you there's no point.''

Although how he would live without her, he couldn't begin to contemplate.

She said incoherently, ''That's emotional blackmail, what you're doing to me.''

''If that's how you see it, then I'm out of here. For good.''

Her face crumpled. She sat down hard on the edge of the tub. ''You don't understand—I was responsible for Tansy and she could have been killed. I can't bear it, Quentin, I can't bear it!''

He knelt beside her. Tears were streaming down her face, and he was almost sure the pain in her drowned eyes had very little to do with Tansy. Or even with him. He said urgently, ''What can't you bear?''

She let her head fall to his shoulder, her back a long curve of surrender. ''My father died when I was only five,'' she whispered, so softly that he had to strain to hear her. ''There was a red-haired boy in my class—Kevin Meade. I hated him. He used to pull my hair, and on rainy days he'd throw my books in the puddles. He told me it was my fault my father died because I'd stolen some apples from Mr. Bates's trees on the way home from school. I knew stealing was wrong, so I believed him—I'd been a bad girl, and that was why my father had died and gone to heaven. It was all my fault.''

In his mind's eye he could picture a little dark-haired girl with pigtails, climbing over a fence and plucking a ripe red apple from the tree. ''Why didn't you tell your mother?''

''She went somewhere else when Daddy died. I don't mean physically…it was as though she was dead inside. Totally absent. I thought that was my fault too.'' She looked up, the tip of her nose pink. "I know it sounds silly. But I was only five years old."

"In effect you lost both parents."

Her eyes widened. "You're right—in a way, I did. I couldn't talk to Lucy, she was only three, and Cat was just a baby. So I tried very hard to be good so nothing else awful would happen. Good all the time. I was always top in my class, and I never broke any of the rules anywhere."

Quentin was beginning to think that he owed brainless Tansy a debt of gratitude, because Marcia had just given him the key to understanding her. "I think it's called control," he said.

She wiped her nose with the back of her hand. "I became a doctor, of course. Except for Lucy our whole family is nothing but doctors—and even she married one. I did everything right. Medals and scholarships all through university, research papers that attracted a lot of attention, guest speaker at important conferences. It wasn't until Michael died and I met you that I began to realize how unhappy I was. How empty. When I saw that painting of yours at the exhibition it was everything I've never allowed myself to be. I felt as though you knew me."

"No wonder you cried."

"Like a rainy day in April." She sagged against him, rubbing her cheek against his chest. "It's funny, I feel lighter, somehow, now that I've told you."

"Good," Quentin said prosaically, acutely aware of the softness of her breast against his arm.

"I do need you," she blurted. "But what happens if I need you and you're not there?"

"Marcia," he said, as strongly as if it were a vow, "to the best of my ability I'll always be there for you. I swear that."

"I'm going to cry again," she muttered. But as a fresh

crop of tears sprang to her lashes she also smiled at him so sweetly that his heart dissolved within him. "Cat's going to be back in an hour or so…and what are you doing here anyway? I thought you were off communing with the lake."

"When I came back and phoned you and got that damned machine again, I figured I'd come into town." He tweaked at her hair. "I much prefer the real person."

He got up, flipped the drain shut on the tub and turned on the taps. Then he surveyed the row of bottles on the shelf over the sink, opened one and poured a very generous dollop of pale blue liquid into the tub. Marcia gave a gasp of horror. "That's Cat's favorite bubble bath—it's horrendously expensive."

"She owes you," he said, and poured in some more.

Marcia giggled. "You won't be able to find me for bubbles."

"Try me," said Quentin, and reached for the buttons on her shirt.

For the first time since she'd trailed up the front path there was some color in Marcia's cheeks. She sat very still as, one by one, he undid the buttons. His fingers felt clumsy; his heart was pumping as if he'd taken his canoe down a whitewater river. He tugged the shirt free of her waistband, then eased it from her shoulders. Against the white bubbles of the bathtub her skin was palest ivory, as smooth as the silk shirt he had removed. Her bra cupped her breasts; through its white lace he could see the darker circle of her nipples, the tips as hard as the seeds of an apple. He said huskily, "I'd like to paint you like that— because I don't have words to tell you how beautiful you are."

Acting on instinct, Marcia lifted her face for his kiss, a long, deep kiss of mouth and tongue, of exploration and entry. His hands were roaming her shoulders, her arms, the hollow at the small of her back. Then his head dropped to her breast, and in a shaft of sweetness she felt the warmth of her face against her flesh. She pressed him to her, playing with his thick black hair, overwhelmed with emotions new to her. True emotions, she thought confusedly. Real ones.

Something cool and wet touched her spine. She glanced down and said, laughter warming her voice, "We're going to have a flood on our hands any minute."

The bubbles were rising over the sides of the tub. Quentin said a very rude word and turned off the taps. She stood up, the twist of her body in her jeans stabbing him with a complex mixture of lust and love. He said thickly, "I'd better get out of here or I'll be making love to you on the bath mat."

He was almost out of the door when she said clearly, "Quentin—thank you."

She was enveloped in a cloud of steam, a small, slim woman wearing jeans and a bra, who meant more to him than anyone he'd ever known. He nodded in acknowledgement, went out to the kitchen and doused her shirt in cold water. He should do the same to himself, he thought wryly, gazing out the window at Cat's tidy front garden.

He was glad Troy had bought Marcia the painting of the three carefree little girls running through the field. She'd lost that freedom much too young, and it had taken her all these years to admit it. Was he deluding himself to think that she would only truly rediscover herself in bed with him?

Half an hour later Cat arrived home. Artie woofed a welcome. Cat hugged her sister briefly and said, "Don't tell

me you've broken Tansy of her habit of devouring everyone who comes to the front door.''

Marcia said, ''Tansy's at the vet's,'' and described what
had happened. Quentin heard the quiver in her voice.

Cat said carelessly, ''I'm not surprised. I told you that
dog had a screw loose—I can't imagine why Lydia puts up
with her.''

''You didn't really warn me how badly behaved she is.''

''Don't make such a big deal of it, Marcie. I'm glad she's
all right—but you needn't blame yourself. Give me the vet
bill, though. You shouldn't have to pay that.''

Cat didn't have the slightest clue what the episode had
meant to her sister—and if she had, would she have cared?
Marcia said steadily, ''How was New York?''

Cat gave them an enthusiastic description of the plays
she had seen and of the exhibitions at the Met. Then Marcia
said, ''I've got to go, Cat, I'm tired. Glad you had a good
time.''

''Thanks for everything... I'll treat you to dinner soon
at that new place everyone's raving about. Bye, Quentin.''

Quentin followed Marcia down the path, carrying her
suitcase, angered by Cat's cavalier attitude and amazed that
three sisters could be so different.

After he had put the case on the back seat of Marcia's
new car he straightened, feeling the wind ruffle his hair,
watching it blow dark strands across Marcia's face. There
were faint mauve shadows under her eyes. His head was
telling him to leave her now, to go back to the cottage and
let her digest what had happened, but his gut was saying,
Stay—she's exhausted and vulnerable—now's the time to
make your move. He said flatly, ''You'll be all right, Marcia? I thought I'd head back to the lake.''

As her shoulders sagged infinitesimally with relief his
jaw clenched. Would the day ever come when she'd want

to be with him all the time? Was he a fool to hang around waiting for that day?

"Troy and Lucy want the four of us to go out for dinner on Tuesday," she said. "Would you like to do that?"

Two days before he saw her again. Forty-eight hours. "If that's your best offer."

With a touch of desperation she said, "I'll let you know on Friday whether I'll move in with you at the cottage—I promise I will." Impulsively she reached up and cupped his face, slowly tracing the jut of his cheekbones, the slight bump in his nose, the dark brows and the fan of lines at the corners of his eyes.

It was, he thought, almost as though she were seeing him for the first time. Memorizing him. Wondering if he'd ever be able to anticipate what she would do next, he rasped, "I'm not going to go away."

Her fingertips were clasping the angle of his jaw, her eyes as shy as a wild creature's; she kissed him softly on the lips. Then, bemused, she stepped back. "I'll see you Tuesday. We're meeting at Troy's at seven."

"I'll pick you up at ten to seven."

Her little car pulled away from the curb. Quentin stood there until it was out of sight, then drove back to the cottage, which seemed distressingly empty, and barbecued a steak that could have been made of plastic for all the taste it had.

He didn't want to go canoeing again, and he'd walked everywhere there was to walk. None of the books he picked up seemed to say anything that even remotely connected to the way he was feeling. He pulled a sketchpad towards him and began to draw.

The next morning he replaced the canvas on his easel with a freshly sketched one, smaller than usual, and began to work, cudgeling his brain to remember the photos in

Lucy's living room in Vancouver. On Tuesday afternoon, unshaven, his legs and back aching, he knew the painting was finished, and when he drove into the city he took it with him. Carrying it gingerly, because it was still wet, he tapped on Marcia's door.

She was wearing the red dress, gold earrings dangling from her lobes. He swallowed hard, because how could he detach the gift of a painting from the gift of himself? "I did this for you," he said.

Her face lit up like a child's. "A painting? For me?"

"It's wet. Is there somewhere I can prop it up?"

Marcia led him into the living room and moved some ornaments, watching him lean the oil painting against the wall and stand back. In silence she looked at it.

The focus of the work was the figure of a woman in a swirling red dress: herself. The woman was surrounded by a dark background from which emerged the faces of her mother and father, while almost hidden in the shadows was a red-haired boy; lastly, and here Marcia's eyes lingered, in one corner was a little girl who was also herself. Somehow the energy of the painting was such that all the faces were gathered into the lissome curves of the woman's body, inextricably part of her grace and beauty.

Almost inaudibly she said, "Will I ever be that woman, Quentin?"

"I think you already are."

Unconsciously she stood a little taller. "It's the most wonderful gift anyone has ever given me," she said gravely. "You've given me myself—and yourself too." Because—and she had seen this immediately—it was very obvious that the artist was in love with his subject.

She turned to face him, the radiance of her smile taking his breath away. "Your best suit," she remarked. "I'm flattered. And do you know what? Whenever I'm away from you, I can never believe that your eyes are that incredible blue. Gorgeous eyes.'' Her smile widened. ''Sexy eyes…bedroom eyes.''

''Dearest Marcia,'' Quentin said, ''you wouldn't be trying to seduce me, would you?''

Flustered, she replied, ''I'm out of practise. Heck, who am I kidding? I've never been *in* practise. But I suppose I am.''

''I love your technique, but your timing's atrocious— we're supposed to be at Lucy's in precisely five minutes.''

She glanced over her shoulder at the painting, in which her dress glowed like a ruby. She said slowly, ''You really do love me, don't you, Quentin?''

''I've been trying to convince you of that ever since I met you.''

In a low voice she said, ''I don't feel worthy of such a gift—and I'm not fishing for compliments and I'm not going to cry because I'll ruin my mascara.''

''Look how you've changed in the last three weeks,'' he said forcibly. ''Courage, passion, laughter—you've got them all. They just went underground a long time ago, that's all. Yes, I love you, and when my fingers are too arthritic to hold a paintbrush I'll still love you.''

''When you look at me like that,'' she sputtered, ''I want to strip off that very expensive suit you're wearing, not to mention your shirt and tie, and drag you off to the nearest bed.''

''Feel free,'' Quentin said, grasping her under the armpits and lifting her high over his head. He laughed exultantly. ''I'm going to enjoy being seduced by you, Dr. Marcia Barnes.''

''We'll be late,'' she said.

''Kiss me,'' he ordered, lowering her feet to the floor. As she did so, with unabashed delight, his body responded instantly and predictably. "Call Lucy and tell her that it's not food we're interested in eating."

She fluttered her lashes. "I hate to sound unromantic, but I didn't take time for lunch today. How about food first?"

"What's happened since Sunday?" he asked quizzically. "You're different."

She said with a violence that charmed him, "I'm sick to death of playing it safe. Winter's over and I'm tired of being underground… I want to be like those tulips all along the canal, with the sun on my face, and I suppose it's got something to do with telling you about my father. Quentin, we've really got to go. You know Lucy—she'll suspect the worst."

"If I have my way, her suspicions will be well founded as soon as possible," he said.

When they got to the apartment Evelyn was holding the baby, Henry was warming the baby's bottle, and Lucy and Troy were waiting for them—Lucy wearing her purple dress, Troy looking tall and distinguished in a charcoal-gray suit. "Shall we take one car?" Troy asked.

"Two," said Quentin, "so I can drive Marcia home."

Marcia blushed, Lucy looked at them speculatively, and Troy said affably, "Let's go."

The restaurant had a small dance floor and a menu that reduced Marcia to indecision. "I want one of everything," she said. "If I have the baked Brie I could have salmon steak, but if I have smoked salmon I'd go for the rack of lamb. What are you having, Quentin?"

"Fish chowder, if it hasn't got any shrimp in it—I'll check with the waiter. And the loin of pork with mangoes."

They ordered cocktails and Marcia finally settled on Brie and salmon, after which Quentin led her onto the dance floor.

Afterward she couldn't have said whether he was a good or an indifferent dancer, all she was aware of was the closeness of his body and the provocative shift of muscle under the fabric of his suit. As his arm curved possessively around her waist her imagination ran riot. She wanted the evening to end with him in her bed, this man whose blue eyes spoke to her so ardently of love and desire. Yet the wild excitement this prospect engendered was shot through with flashes of panic.

The music stopped. Quentin took her back to the table and a few minutes later Troy asked her to dance. As he waltzed her expertly round the floor he said, "Looks like Lucy's subjecting Quentin to the third degree."

"Troy," Marcia burst out, "did you know right from the start that Lucy was the woman you wanted?"

"Yep. Although I fought it pretty hard. Just about as hard as you're fighting Quentin."

"I'm thinking of giving up fighting."

"And that scares you, hmm?"

"You're a very nice man and I'm so glad you're my brother-in-law," Marcia said. "You bet it does."

"Quentin's straight, Marcia—he's been an honest and loyal friend to both me and Lucy, and you can't fake that. So if you're asking for advice, I'd say jump in with both feet." He twirled her in a complicated circle. "Love *is* what makes the world go round. Living with Lucy and Chris gives my life its meaning. Go for it, sis." He grinned at her. "By the way, I like you in red—it suits you."

But Marcia hadn't finished. "You and Lucy, you've known each other—what is it, more than six years?—and you both look more in love than you ever were. Will it last, Troy? Can you love one person your whole life through?"

"You sure ask difficult questions," Troy said in an

amused voice. "Quentin's got you all stirred up, hasn't he?"

She tripped over his toe. "Quentin and my hormones."

He thought for a moment, steering her between two other couples. Then he said, "If Lucy and I hadn't loved each other with the kind of love that's got a good dose of determination in it—the determination to last a lifetime, I mean—I think we'd have stayed apart after Michael died. We'd have divorced, I suppose." He grimaced. "We came perilously close as it was. But something held us together, which for want of a better word we called love...I'll love Lucy until the day I die—I know that in my gut. But I can't explain it in any way that makes sense."

"Maybe you don't need to." Marcia chewed on her lip. "It was when Michael died and you and Lucy separated that I started to realize how sterile my life was. How empty of love. I'd much rather he'd never died Troy—but in a way a little bit of good did come out of it."

Troy, who was an accomplished dancer, missed a step; for a moment Marcia saw agony lacerate his features. Distressed, she said, "I'm sorry! I should never have mentioned—"

He picked up the rhythm again and said evenly, "If good doesn't come out of bad there's not much point, is there? And I never want to act as if Michael didn't exist. I'm glad you told me—thanks."

She had her answer, Marcia thought. Troy believed in love that lasted forever and so did Lucy. She'd be willing to bet that Quentin did too. But what of herself? Was she capable of that kind of love?

The waltz ended and Troy accompanied her back to the table. But before they reached the others, he said, "Good luck, sis—give it the best you've got."

She braced herself to meet Quentin's inquiring look and

Lucy's smug one, and was relieved to see that the appetizers had arrived.

They ate and drank, they talked about everything under the sun and they laughed a lot. Marcia was having a wonderful time. Her earlier panic had vanished, sublimated in the sexual energy that crackled and danced between her and Quentin in every look they exchanged, in every small touch. When he bent to pick up the napkin she had dropped he said, for her ears alone, "You look like the woman in the painting, sweetheart." And that was indeed how she felt: graceful, sensual, fully alive.

The entrées were delicious, and while they were waiting for the dessert menu Marcia excused herself to go to the washroom and Lucy followed her. The bathroom was very elegant, with gold taps and a spray of orchids in a crystal vase on the marble counter. As Marcia gazed in the gilt-edged mirror at her sparkling eyes and flushed cheeks she scarcely recognized herself.

Lucy took out her lipstick and said, "You look fantastic, Marcie. You should wear bright colors all the time."

"I may do that," said Marcia, running a brush through her hair. She had already checked that they were alone in the bathroom. Gathering her courage, she said, "Lucy, can I ask you something really personal?"

Lucy was frowning at her lower lip, now neatly outlined in red. "Go ahead."

"I don't really… What I want to ask is… I mean, do you really like sex, Lucy? It's more than six years now…is it still okay?" Too embarrassed to meet her sister's eyes, Marcia fumbled in her evening bag for her own lipstick.

Lucy sat down on the marble counter, her lipstick brush in one hand, the tube of lipstick in the other, and gave her answer her full consideration. "It isn't always that dynamite stuff you read about in books," she said thoughtfully.

"But you wouldn't want a symphony to play loud all the time either, would you? It can be friendly and playful...or so full of tenderness you think you might die of happiness. And sometimes it's just plain old lust." She gave an unselfconscious giggle.

"Last week we made love up against the kitchen door while I was cooking supper...the carrots burned and the broccoli was soggy and we ended up ordering Chinese food." She was warming to her theme. "It's like anything else—you get what you give. Sometimes when Troy's schedule is exceptionally heavy we'll make a date, and all day we'll know that's what we're going to do when we're alone together...those times are wonderful. But, you see, we love and trust each other too, Marcia, and we're committed to each other—so there's always that running through it." She swirled the brush in the lipstick. "I'm talking too much. Is that any help?"

"I...guess so."

"Sometimes you just have to jump in at the deep end," Lucy announced.

"Take the plunge," Marcia riposted, smiling at her sister's reflection.

"Take the risk," Lucy said, sounding very fierce. "I learned that in the year Troy and I were apart. Don't push Quentin away because you're afraid, Marcie, that's the worst thing you could do—and now I really will shut up. Troy's always telling me I interfere too much." She filled in the rest of her lips and said casually, "My hair's a disaster—I must get it cut. Shall we go?"

But when they went back to their table Troy was sitting there alone. He pulled back Lucy's chair and said evenly, "They changed chefs this evening unexpectedly, so the waiter didn't know that the chowder had a shrimp broth in it—Quentin just left; he was feeling lousy. He knows the

symptoms by now and he said he'd be all right… He sent
his apologies and asked if I'd drive you home, Marcia.''

''Was he going back to the cottage?'' Marcia asked in
dismay.

''Yeah… I tried to persuade him to go to our apartment,
but no dice.''

''How long ago did he leave?'' she flashed.

''A couple of minutes before you came back. He said it
always hits him like a ton of bricks… Where are you off
to?''

Clutching her evening bag, Marcia was already halfway
round the table. ''I'll see if I can catch him in the car park.
He should go to my place, not all the way to the cottage.
If I'm too late, I'll be back in a minute.''

She dashed between the tables, grabbed her jacket from
the rack and ran outside into the warm spring evening.

CHAPTER TEN

QUENTIN had parked in an underground lot across the street. Marcia checked for traffic and sprinted across the road. There was a young man with a Vandyke beard in the booth. "Excuse me," she said breathlessly, "has a man in a yellow sportscar just left?"

"No, ma'am. No one's left in the last fifteen minutes."

"This is the only exit?"

"Yes, ma'am."

She'd wait here, then, she thought, ignoring his curious look, and heard the roar of an approaching motor. Blinded by the headlights, she stood to one side and saw that it was Quentin's car. As he drew up at the barrier and rolled down his window she took the ticket from him, thrust a five-dollar bill at the attendant and said, "Move over, Quentin—we're going to my place."

He looked ghastly—his features drained of color, his forehead beaded with sweat. "I'm not inflicting—"

"Or else I'll go to the cottage with you."

The attendant was trying to give her the change. She grabbed it and said impatiently, "Which is it to be?"

Quentin's fingers tightened on the wheel and his face contracted with pain. When he could speak, he said, "I'm better off alone. I don't want you—"

"This is about you needing me," she interrupted furiously.

"I never let anyone—"

"Our whole relationship has been about change," she cried, with no idea where the words were coming from.

134

"You've got to change too! Because need works both ways—it has to." She gave him a sudden rueful smile. "And I am a doctor, Quentin. In case you'd forgotten."

He swiped at his forehead and didn't smile back. "Why don't you get lost?"

Her lashes flickered. "No."

"Then get in, for God's sake," he snarled, clambering over the clutch and collapsing in the passenger seat.

Remembering to throw a smile of thanks at the attendant, Marcia opened the door, sat in the driver's seat and quickly checked the unfamiliar pedals. Quentin said nastily, "You win—how does it feel?"

His eyes were like chips of ice. She said, "If you hate me for winning, we both lose."

"Very clever," he sneered.

She eased out the clutch and managed to get up the incline without stalling. "You're just as bad as I am," she snapped. "About letting people close to you."

"I'm a man. It's different."

"Oh, sure. What are the skeletons in your closet, Quentin?"

Jerkily he wrapped his arms around his belly and hunched over in the seat. "Just get me to your place, will you?"

Quickly Marcia planned the shortest route to her condo; she drove as fast as was safe and whipped through two yellow lights. And all the while, despite the fact that she was almost certain Quentin would rather have been on his own, she knew that she was exactly where she wanted to be. So much for detachment, she thought, sneaking a sideways glance at her companion.

He was leaning back in the seat, his eyes closed; one hand was wrapped around the seat belt strap, the knuckles white with strain. "Two more blocks," she said in a neutral voice. "Tell me what to expect."

"I get these godawful cramps," he muttered. "Then I'll spend the better part of the night vomiting everything I've eaten for the last four days. No fun."

She parked on the street in front of her building and got out, locking the car. When she walked round to Quentin's side he was trying to stand upright. He staggered a little and she seized him by the arm, knowing that if he fell she'd never be able to get him to his feet. "Sorry, Doc," he said sarcastically, "I forgot to tell you about the dizziness."

"Let's go."

Fortunately there were only three steps to the lobby and they had the elevator to themselves. By the time they reached her door, Quentin was leaning most of his weight on her; she unlocked it and almost pushed him inside. He headed straight for the bathroom, closing the door behind him. She hung up her jacket and went into her bedroom, where she changed into leggings and a loose green sweatshirt and changed the sheets on the bed. Then she walked down the hall to the bathroom.

From inside she could hear Quentin retching; she clutched the doorframe, feeling utterly helpless and as miserable as though his suffering were her own. She paced up and down the hallway for fifteen minutes, then made herself a cup of coffee and poured it down the sink because she didn't feel like drinking it, and finally went back to the bathroom door. She heard only silence from within—a dead, waiting silence; in sudden terror she called Quentin's name.

As though he were in the next condo rather than on the other side of the door, he said, "Don't fuss—I'm fine."

He didn't sound fine. He sounded horribly weak. Marcia

tried the doorhandle and found it locked. In a surge of anger she said, "Quentin, let me in."

"I'll be in here for hours and there's nothing you can do... You might as well go back to the restaurant."

"And leave you alone?" she cried.

"I can look after myself."

It was an uncanny echo of her own words two days ago. I've looked after myself for over thirty years, she had told Quentin, and as a result he had threatened to leave her. Forever. That works two ways, she thought vengefully. "Cut out the macho stuff and unlock the door," she stormed, rattling the handle.

With a suddenness that took her by surprise the handle turned. As she stumbled inside Quentin was standing in the opening, leaning heavily on the door, his face with the hard pallor of marble. "Go away, Marcia. I haven't got the energy for arguing."

He looked terrible, and for a moment her anger faltered. But in some obscure way she knew that she was fighting for something vital to both of them. "I'm a doctor," she said shortly, "I'm not going to pass out if you look less than perfect. Plus I'm the woman you say you want to spend the rest of your life with. Is that just the good days, Quentin? Or is it your whole life, good and bad—the days when you're healthy and the days when you're sick as a dog?"

"I'm a doctor" seemed to be becoming a refrain in her life, she thought wildly, and waited for him to answer.

"There's not a goddamned thing you can do—will you get that through your thick head?"

Although she flinched from the anger in his voice, she stood her ground. "I can be with you," she said.

His throat felt like sandpaper and there was a vise squeezing his belly, making him dizzy and sick. But through the pain he could see a kind of stubborn courage superimposed on Marcia's delicate features. "You don't know when to give up, do you?"

She didn't think he meant that as a compliment. "Do you want me to?"

"That seems like one hell of a complicated question," he said muzzily. Then his face changed. "Vamoose."

She did as she was told. But when the horrible bout of sickness had ended she went back into the bathroom. He was sitting on the edge of the tub, his head in his hands. His hair, she saw with a pang of compassion, was wet with sweat and he was shivering. She went into her bedroom and came back with a multi-hued mohair sweater she had knitted a couple of years ago, draping it over his shoulder.

He turned his head into its soft folds. "It smells of your perfume... You made one like it for Lucy, didn't you? She had it with her on Shag Island."

She nodded, stroking his hair back from his forehead and trying to warm him with her body. He didn't push her away but he didn't hold her close either, and somehow she wasn't surprised when he muttered, "So much for our romantic evening."

"Quentin," Marcia said emphatically, "if you still want to, we'll make love. Not tonight, that's for sure. But soon. I'm just sorry you're feeling so awful, and that's got nothing to do with making love."

He looked up, his eyes sunk deep in their sockets. "If I still want to? I can't imagine that I'll ever stop wanting to. How could I, when I love you as much as I do?"

She was certain he was in no state to speak anything but the truth. So he was offering her the kind of love of which Troy had spoken, she thought in awe, and said shakily, "Why do some of our most intimate moments take place in the bathroom?"

"When I get my strength back, I'll remedy that."

"The bedroom would be a distinct improvement," she teased. "In the meantime I want you to drink something so you don't get dehydrated. I'll be right back."

The night wore on, the bouts of sickness gradually spacing themselves farther and farther apart, until finally she heard Quentin splashing water on his face and gargling with mouthwash. He walked out into the hall, leaning one hand on the wall. "At the risk of losing whatever remains of my macho image, I don't think I'm safe to drive home," he said. "Can I bunk down on your couch until tomorrow?"

"No," she said with a big smile, infinitely relieved to know that the ordeal was over, "you can bunk down in my bed. I'll take the couch."

"Marcia…" She looked pale and tired; it was three in the morning and he knew she hadn't slept at all. "Thanks," he said gruffly. "It was sweet of you to take such good care of me."

"Just obeying the Hippocratic oath," she said fliply.

Like a shadow, an indefinable emotion passed over his face, and she heard the words replay in her mind. She rested her palm on his chest and said, "Sorry, Quentin—that was the old Marcia speaking, wasn't it? The keep-you-at-arm's-length-at-any-cost Marcia. Hippocrates would have fired me tonight—I definitely did not maintain the proper attitude of medical detachment from my patient. Come and lie down before you fall down."

She had a three-quarter mahogany bed that had belonged to her great-grandfather, a thoracic surgeon. Her walls were painted ivory while the drapes and bedspread were softly patterned in spring flowers. It was a restful room, now lit only by a bedside lamp. For a moment Quentin looked around him; somehow he had expected something more stark, less welcoming. Then, to his enormous gratification, he saw that she had moved his painting of the woman in the red dress to her bureau, where she could see it from her bed.

Marcia said nervously, "You're the first man who's ever been in here."

Because his knees were giving out he sat down on the edge of the bed; his head was pounding and he felt very cold. "I trust I'll be the last," he said, watching her lashes lower to hide her eyes. Without finesse he added, "Sleep with me, Marcia."

Startled, she looked up. "I—I'd disturb you when I get up in the morning."

"After one of these sessions, it'd take a bulldozer to disturb me." His smile was twisted. "And sleep's all I'm capable of—this ain't no proposition, honey."

Blushing, she stammered, "Well, I—I guess so. If you— I mean, if you're sure that's what you want."

He loved it when she lost her cool. "What I want, I can't deliver. Not—" He broke off as he was seized by a violent fit of shivering; gritting his teeth, he fought to control it.

"Oh, Quentin, I'm a lousy doctor—just look at you," she cried, and started undoing the buttons on his shirt, her fingers awkward with emotion and haste.

He said thickly, "This isn't quite the way I pictured being in your bedroom."

Her hands stilled. With that rare, sweet smile that always smote him to the core, she said, "Nor I. But I wouldn't want you to be anywhere else."

His cufflinks were intricate and her fingers all thumbs, but finally she tugged his shirt from his body. After she'd undone his belt buckle and taken off his socks he managed to get to his feet again. Her tongue caught between her teeth, she fumbled with the zipper on his trousers. He said roughly, "You're the first woman I've ever allowed to look after me like this."

She gave him a faint ironical smile. "I have no difficulty believing that."

"A very different kind of intimacy than I'd planned."

"Is that why you were less than happy to see me when I turned up at the car park?"

"Yeah…sorry about that. I learned to be self-sufficient pretty young."

As his trousers slid to the carpet in a heap she said wryly, "So while you have grounds to fire me as a doctor, you won't fire me as a woman?"

"Full employment guaranteed." With a relief he couldn't hide, Quentin sank down on the mattress and hauled the covers up over his chest. "Which side do you sleep on?"

His lean hips and long, muscled legs had filled her with an agony of longing. "The middle, actually."

He rolled over until he was in the center of the bed. "Your sheets are like ice—hurry up and get in bed."

He sounded more like a husband of several years than an ardent lover, she thought. Whereas she felt like a timorous virgin. Grabbing her nightgown from under her pillow, she fled to the bathroom. But when she came back a few minutes later, Quentin was still awake.

She had bought her nightgown in the lingerie shop. It was made of thin flowered silk, with narrow straps and a loosely draped bodice that revealed the shadowed cleavage between her breasts; the fabric clung at waist and hip and thigh. For a moment Marcia hesitated in the doorway, for she'd been hoping he'd be asleep. But when she saw how his eyes flew to meet hers, as though she were his lodestar, she was suddenly glad that he had stayed awake.

With unselfconscious grace she hung up her red dress in

the closet, then sat down at her dressing table and removed her earrings and bracelet. She then smoothed off her make-up and brushed her hair, all her movements unhurried.

Quentin lay still. Because he had no physical reserves to draw on, all his emotions were so close to the surface that he felt naked and exposed. When Marcia walked over to the bed and reached for the switch on the lamp, the light shone through her nightgown, delineating the curves of her body; through the throbbing in his temples he knew he was bound to her for as long as he lived. Then darkness fell and he heard the small sounds as she slid into bed beside him.

He reached over and pulled her to him. She gasped, "You're freezing!"

"I love you," Quentin said jaggedly.

Marcia rested her head on his shoulder and wrapped one arm round his chest, her breasts soft against his ribcage. "I don't think I'm ready for that word yet," she whispered, "but I've never felt with anyone else the way I feel with you, Quentin. I want you to know that." As she eased one thigh over his, trying to warm him, she added with a throaty chuckle, "This is so weird—almost as though we've been married for years."

"It's bloody marvelous," said Quentin, and closed his eyes.

Within seconds his breathing had deepened and he was asleep. Intending to savor the intimate closeness of his body in her bed, the gradual warming of his flesh, Marcia closed her eyes...and when she opened them her bedside clock informed her that she was fifty minutes late for work.

Quentin was deeply asleep, curled into her back, his breath cool against her shoulderblade. She didn't want to get up. She wanted to stay here all day, in bed with Quentin, and see what happened when he woke up. Stealthily she edged away from him. He flopped over on his back, his hair black against her pillow, his big body taking up most of the mattress. We'll need a queen-sized bed, she thought, and with a small shock of surprise wondered if her decision wasn't already made.

Half an hour later, showered and dressed and chewing on a muffin, Marcia hurried out the door. She was reluctant to leave Quentin—although "reluctant" was scarcely an adequate word to describe the wrench of frustration as she locked the door behind her—but she was also reluctant to go to the lab in a way that was new to her. While she could usually immerse herself in her work to the exclusion of all else, the last two days had been nothing but rumors and counter-rumors about cutbacks and layoffs—the staff tense and edgy, the management staying well out of the way. Today she'd shut herself in her office and edit the paper she was to present at a conference in Brussels in September, she decided as she pulled out into the street.

Unfortunately she couldn't altogether shut out the world. Her secretary had heard that fifty percent of the junior research staff were to lose their jobs, the coauthor of one of Marcia's papers had it on good authority that there would be no layoffs at all and one of the janitors confided that his wife was sick and he couldn't afford to lose his job. It was no atmosphere in which to work, although Marcia did her best.

But at three in the afternoon she found herself gazing out the window of her office, her paper only half edited, her pencil idle. Fifty percent of the junior staff might include herself.

Her job was her life. She couldn't lose it.

Quentin, she thought. I'll go home to Quentin. I don't have to tell him what's going on. But if I'm with him, at least I won't be churning it over and over in my mind.

Her decision made, emotions washed over her as turbulent as the rapids on the Ottawa River. The rumors, upsetting though they were, really had very little to do with her inability to concentrate. All day, she thought, she had been worrying about Quentin, wanting to be home with him, wondering if he was feeling better.

Wondering if he still wanted to make love to her.

She pushed her papers in her drawer, shucked off her lab coat, threw her sweater over her shoulders and, with the air of a woman on very important business, ran out to her car. Fifteen minutes later she was unlocking the door of her condo.

Quentin was singing, loudly and unmelodiously, over the splash of water in the bathroom. Marcia closed the door behind her, a silly grin on her face, and called his name. He didn't hear her. She walked down the hall to the open bathroom door and stood there, her eyes meeting his in the mirror, her smile wider. He broke off his song in mid-bar. He had just finished shaving. He was wearing a pink towel swathed around his hips, and nothing else. Marcia said, strolling in the door, "You're a better artist than a singer."

"I'm dreaming," he said, his blue eyes blazing with such happiness at her appearance that her heart began to race. "Or else you're home early."

"You're wide awake, and here we are in the bathroom again."

"So we are." He dabbed at a cut on his chin. "Your razor is entirely inadequate for my beard, my love, and I haven't any clean clothes."

"Then maybe you should go back to bed."

"Only if you'll join me... After all, you were up half the night."

She pursed her lips. "Are you trying to tell me I don't look so hot?"

"You look extremely beautiful—although that skirt and top should be consigned to the back of your closet."

The skirt was brown, the top beige. "I spent enough money the other day without revamping my entire wardrobe, Quentin Ramsey. You must be feeling better—you're starting to complain again."

He rinsed off her pink plastic razor and turned to face her. "I slept the clock round—I feel wonderful. And I wasn't expecting you for another three hours."

"I couldn't concentrate."

"Because you were tired?"

"No, that wasn't the reason."

"Because it's really spring and the sun is shining?"

Take the risk...wasn't that what Lucy had said? "Because I wanted to be here with you," Marcia said.

He walked up to her, put his arms around her and kissed her. Her palms against his bare chest, aware of his nakedness with every nerve in her body, Marcia kissed him back, and with her mouth expressed the seesaw of emotions she had gone through in the last twenty-four hours—all the fear, compassion, tenderness and longing. As he covered her face with tiny kisses she tangled her fingers in his body hair. "You smell nice."

He laughed. "Your soap was a little too feminine for me—I don't think I'm the lily of the valley type. So I swiped your herbal shampoo and showered with that."

She nibbled gently at his shoulder. "The results are splendiferous."

"You have," he said huskily, "a wonderful way with words. You also have far too many clothes on."

He pushed her sweater from her shoulders, then pulled her short-sleeved knit top over her head. As he undid the zipper her brown skirt fell to her feet, and quickly she stepped out of her hose. Under her very ordinary work clothes she was wearing her raspberry-red lingerie. Quentin raised his brows. "You're full of surprises," he said, his eyes darkening as he took her breasts in his hands and teased their tips beneath the delicate lace.

She swayed toward him, parting her lips for his kiss, feeling their tongues entwined. As he clasped her by the hips, pulling her against a hardness that was both hunger and need, the towel slithered down to join the heap of clothes on the floor. Marcia ran her hand down his back, holding him by the jut of his pelvic bone, feeling the muscles tighten as he thrust himself between her legs. Heat enveloped her like fire. She threw back her head, frantic to join with him. He undid the clasp of her bra, the garment sliding down her body like flame; his tongue encircling her nipple made her shudder with desire.

For a moment Quentin raised his head, his gaze caressing her drowned features, her mouth so soft and seductive a curve from his kisses. Through the pounding of his heart and his own urgency, an urgency beyond anything he'd ever known, he said, "Don't you think it's time we moved our relationship from the bathroom to the bedroom?"

With overt sensuality Marcia drew her fingernails up his back, following the length of his spine, and spoke the literal truth. "I'm not sure I can walk that far."

"That's easily remedied," Quentin said, bending to pick her up.

She looped her arms around his neck, touching one fingertip to the cut on his chin. "We'll have to buy you a proper razor."

"We'll have to buy you one too—I ruined yours." His voice deepened as he walked into her bedroom. "But we can do that later. Right now I have more important things on my mind."

She traced his top lip, admiring its strongly carved line,

letting her finger come to rest in the little indentation below his nostrils. "Your nose has character," she said.

"It got broken in a fight when I was thirteen," he said, a fleeting shadow crossing his face. "It didn't set quite straight." Then he smiled down at her with such love in his face that Marcia forgot about his nose. "You wouldn't be attempting to distract me from the matter at hand, would you, my darling?"

"Oh, no," she answered fervently.

So he was laughing as he lowered her to the bed and covered her with the heat and weight of his body. With one hand he drew her last garment from her hips. She wriggled her legs free, feeling the rasp of hair on his thighs, watching his face convulse as she circled her hips slowly and suggestively beneath him. He muttered, "I'll look after contraception—you're driving me out of my mind doing that."

"Good," she said, and, raising herself on her elbows, brushed her breasts against the hard wall of his chest.

He dropped his head and licked the soft swell of her flesh, his tongue moving with such slow, deliberate sensuality that Marcia shuddered with pleasure, her throat stretched taut, her dark hair splayed on the pillow. As if time had stopped, she saw his curls black against the white of her skin, and felt the thrust of his erection against her inner thighs. How would she ever forget this moment? Or this man, who called her to a wildness that she had never suspected was hers?

When her breasts were aching and swollen Quentin moved down her body, parting her thighs and with his fingers gently playing with the petals of flesh between them. Sensation rippled through her, wave after wave, until she was almost sobbing his name. Then he stopped, so suddenly that she moaned in protest. He smothered her moan with another fierce kiss, rolling over and pulling her on top of him.

Marcia clung to him, panting for breath, her irises the dark purple of a sky at nightfall, her body throbbing with primitive, unfulfilled hunger. Slowly she raised her head. The blue depths of Quentin's eyes that she had so feared in her dreams were no longer frightening; the swirling currents of her sexuality had been liberated for her by this man lying beneath her, so loving, passionate and vulnerable.

She knelt over him, beginning her own slow exploration, laying her cheek to his chest, where his heartbeat vibrated like an ancient drum, letting her hands wander over the arch of his ribs and the concavity of his belly to his navel, where the dark hair funneled still lower.

Then, against her palm, she felt the silken smoothness of skin over a hardness like bone, and heard his harsh intake of breath. In a broken voice she would never have recognized as her own, she cried, "Quentin…I want you inside me."

He fumbled with the envelope on her bedside table; frantic with haste, she helped him as best she could. He kissed her again, a kiss as possessive as if he were setting his seal on her, the thrust of his tongue matched by the thrusting of his body. She opened to him, lifting her hips and feeling him slide within her as though they had been made for each other. I am both possessed and possessor, she thought distantly, and then abandoned thought for pure sensation, shaft after shaft of brilliant sensation, lancing through her whole frame until they joined into a dazzling brightness like that of sunlight dancing on water.

Deep inside her body she felt Quentin find his own throbbing release. He called her name hoarsely—once, twice. Then he collapsed on top of her, his chest heaving, his forehead falling to her shoulder. She held him close, kissing his hair, filled with a deep, all-encompassing happiness.

When he eventually looked up Quentin had no idea how much time had passed; it could have been seconds or minutes or even hours. He stroked Marcia's hair back from her face and said unsteadily, "From the very first time I saw you I suspected you were a passionate woman, and today you proved me right—you wanted me as much as I wanted you, didn't you, sweetheart? Do you have any idea how wonderful that makes me feel?"

"You can't possibly feel as wonderful as I do right now," Marcia murmured, stretching as luxuriantly as a cat.

"Watch it," he growled, "or you're going to get yourself in trouble."

"You mean I didn't satisfy you?" she asked, big-eyed.

"Witch—you know damn well you satisfied me. Which isn't to say I couldn't be tempted to do it all over again."

Her cheeks were flushed, her eyes very bright, and now that he had possessed her Quentin realized that somewhere deep down he had doubted that he ever would. Even now, he thought, and despite a lovemaking that had been as tempestuous as a spring storm, there was still something missing. In that same deep place he had hoped that in the heat of lovemaking Marcia would tell him that she loved him. She'd been generous and passionate beyond his imagining, but she hadn't spoken those three magical words—I love you.

So neither had he.

He lifted his weight from her, his gaze lingering on the pale slopes and valleys of her body that had been her gift to him. One woman's body; how could it hold so much of rapture and of promise? He said softly, "I'd like to paint you like that."

She blushed delightfully. "Not for that gallery owner to get her hands on."

"No. For us. We could hang it in our bedroom."

She could have said, What bedroom? She could have said, Don't make assumptions, Quentin. She could have said, I'm not sure I love you. Not like Lucy loves Troy. She said none of these. Instead she said, "Do you know what I'd like? An almond croissant from the little bakery down the road."

There was no need to feel frightened, Quentin told himself. Three weeks ago he hadn't even met Marcia, and not everyone fell in love at first sight, as he had. "Not sure a croissant will do it for me—I haven't had anything to eat yet today."

She sat up, her face full of concern. "Oh, Quentin, you must be starving... I wonder what I've got in the freezer."

"I'll take you out for dinner."

"Only if you promise to stick to steak," she said drily.

"And if you'll wear your red dress."

"I'll have to go shopping again; you'll be getting tired of it."

"That's not very likely," said Quentin, and kissed her.

They wandered hand in hand to the bakery and ate croissants with hot chocolate. Then they went to the drugstore to buy Quentin a razor and some soap, and to a men's store where he bought himself some casual clothes.

They then went back to the condo to change for dinner, in the midst of which they made love in an ardent and intent silence. Marcia fell asleep afterward. When she woke, she was alone in her bed; she could hear Quentin moving around in the kitchen, and a delicious smell of curry wafted down the hall.

She lay still, and could acknowledge to herself, now that she was alone, that underlying her happiness she was afraid.

Oddly, she felt as though she'd lost her virginity today. Nothing she had ever done had prepared her for an intimacy so total and so impassioned, so altogether undeniable, so much like a force of nature. I can't go back to the way I was, she thought. I'll never be the same again.

He's changed me. Whether I was ready to be changed or not.

CHAPTER ELEVEN

THE next day Marcia was only half an hour late for work. She sneaked into the building by the side door again, certain that one look at her face would tell all her coworkers exactly what she had been doing since they'd seen her last.

But the staff had other things to talk about; management had had a four-hour meeting the day before, and the rumors were as varied as they were unsettling. Marcia plugged away at her paper with her door closed; that way if she found herself gazing at the wall with a silly smile on her face, or blushing at images that had a tendency to pop out of nowhere and that bordered on obscenity, no one could see her.

At four o'clock she entered the last change on her computer, and by four-thirty she was climbing the stairs to her condo. She had left Quentin with a key so he could come and go as he pleased through the day. Hoping he was home, she opened the door, stepped inside and gave an audible gasp of surprise.

The hallway was festooned with wide strips of paper that had been taped to the walls. The paper was covered with charcoal sketches, drawn with an irresistible energy and vitality, of a man and a woman making love. Herself and Quentin.

Marcia walked slowly toward the kitchen, looking from left to right, her cheeks scarlet because Quentin had not censored any of their activities and there was a great deal of bare flesh. Her mouth curved in a smile that, as he came out of the living room, turned into helpless laughter.

SANDRA FIELD   153

"What if I'd brought the chief of police home with me?" she gurgled. "We'd be spending the night in the clink."

Quentin grinned. "I was arrogant enough to think you'd want me to yourself."

"Oh, I do, I do. But Lucy could have dropped in...or my mother and Henry."

"I wouldn't have let them past the door."

Marcia's eyes had been busy. In the sketch next to the living room door she was stretched out on the bed in languorous abandon, her body a series of graceful curves from shoulder to ankle: a portrait of a woman well loved. "I'm not that pretty."

"You haven't looked in the mirror lately."

Her gaze flicked to the opposite wall where, between the doors to the kitchen and the bathroom, she was depicted in a particularly compromising position. "Oh, my goodness, did I really do that?" she said, pressing her hands to her red cheeks and then answering her own question. "Yes, I did, and I loved every minute of it. If you ever decide you're tired of being an artist, you could go into the wall-papering business—you'd revolutionize it. Oh, Quentin, what am I going to *do* with you?"

"Marry me," he said.

"What?"

"You heard. Marry me."

She said spiritedly, "The last I heard, you wanted me to move in with you. At the cottage."

"If that's all I wanted, I was fooling myself as well as you. Yes, I want to live with you. Here, or at the cottage, or in Vancouver—the location doesn't matter. But as my wife, Marcia."

The laughter had faded from her face. "I told you I'd give you my answer on Friday."

Quentin tried to tamp down his anger. "Today's Thursday. What's going to change by tomorrow?"

"How do I know? Change seems to follow in your wake. Anything could have happened by then."

"You love me. I know you do."

His certainty for some reason infuriated her. "Then you know more than I do," she said coldly.

As though they had been recorded on tape, she heard her words play back to her—words spoken in anger. Suddenly she stamped her foot. "I hate this! I don't want us to argue." Her voice shook. "I just want to be in bed with you, that's all."

He hardened his heart against the stubborn curve of her jaw and the appeal in her eyes. "I love you," he said. "I'm not going to pretend that I don't."

Unexpectedly her lips quirked. She looked up and down the length of the hall and said with a tiny chuckle, "I'm glad you told me—because I never would have guessed."

Her anger had ignited his own; her laughter defeated him. He gathered her into his arms, kissed her thoroughly to their mutual satisfaction, and steered her into the bathroom. "I bought you a bottle of the same kind of bubble bath that Cat had—want to try it out?"

With the sense that something momentous had been averted, Marcia said, "That was sweet of you, Quentin."

He had put a big spray of larkspur and delphiniums in the corner of the bathroom, and a pile of fluffy purple towels by the tub. As it was filling with hot water he started undressing her. "How did work go today?" he asked, undoing the buttons of her new silk shirt. "You're home early again—you're ruining your reputation as a workaholic."

Knowing she was going to keep the rumors and tensions at the institute to herself, Marcia said, "I finished editing the Brussels paper. I've got another one to do, but I decided

I'd start it tomorrow rather than today." As his hands brushed her bare breasts she added impetuously, "All day I've wanted to be home with you, and I'm not sure my bathtub's big enough for two."

"We'll manage," Quentin said, with a note in his voice that she already recognized and that set her heart racing as if she'd run all the way home.

When they were both naked, Quentin sank down into the froth of bubbles and pulled her down on top of him. As she lay back, her head tucked under his chin, the water rose alarmingly high. "There's an overflow valve—I checked," Quentin said, and began stroking the wet peaks of her breasts.

Content to surrender to his touch, Marcia closed her eyes, feeling desire uncurl within her and spread through her whole body until she was nothing but desire, her low moans of pleasure interspersed with the water's soft lapping against her skin. When his hand slid between her thighs, the bittersweet ache of desire became naked hunger, strong and hot and imperative; whimpering, she moved her hips to his skillful, tormenting fingers, until with a cry torn from her throat she was seized by the compelling rhythms of release.

Quentin could feel the frantic racing of her heart against his arm; her breasts rose and fell with her agitated breathing. He kissed her ear, murmuring little love words to her as gradually she quietened. Then she whispered, "Each time I'm with you I feel as though it's the first time I've ever made love."

Touched, he wrapped his arms around her. "You're getting cold; we'd better get out."

She scrambled out of the tub, then gave him her hand to help him out. When they'd dried each other Marcia led the way to her bedroom, his hand still clasped in hers. In the

doorway she stopped dead. The room was a bower of flowers—chrysanthemums, snapdragons, roses, cosmos and
daisies. At some point Quentin had run out of vases, so
some of the flowers were in plastic ice cream containers;
the overall effect was of an exuberant and colorful muddle.

She turned to face him, her eyes dancing. "You're a
crazy, wonderful man, you know that?"

"I'm the kid who grew up in rural New Brunswick,
where we had frosts in June and September. So every time
I go near the market and see all those flowers, I want to
buy the lot."

She looked around the bedroom again; her bed seemed
to have shrunk, surrounded as it was by blossoms. "I think
you're close to achieving your aim," she said solemnly.
"You could add interior decorating as a sideline to the
wallpapering business." Then she looped her arms around
his waist, her voice suddenly trembling with intensity.
"You make me feel so cherished. And you're so beautiful
to me, Quentin—the feel of your muscles, the warmth of
your skin, the smell of you... Make love to me. Now."

Her body was trembling too, in a way that inflamed him.
He said unsteadily, "Nakedness, so I'm discovering, has
almost nothing to do with clothes... Tell me how I can
please you, dearest Marcia."

She drew his head to her breast. "This...and this, Anything and everything... Oh, God, Quentin, can one faint
from pleasure? Die from it?"

"Let's find out," he said, and lifted her to the bed.

Whether it was the profusion of flowers in all their vivid
hues, or her growing trust and familiarity with this man
who was her lover, Marcia felt freer than she had ever felt
in her life: free to experiment, free to ask Quentin what he
wanted and then to do it for him, free to cry out with wanton pleasure and laugh with sheer, voluptuous delight. Their

climax had all the tumult of ocean waves on a deserted shore—a deep drowning and a slow, eventual surfacing to the separation that was reality.

Clutching Quentin by the shoulder, because she didn't want to be separate from him, Marcia said faintly, "How can an act of the body ravish the soul?"

He had both ravished her and been ravished by her. He said, speaking the simple truth, "Because we're soul-mates."

"My life will never be the same."

"You think mine will?"

Her eyes were downcast, as if she was afraid of where her words had taken her. She licked the saltiness of sweat from his shoulder, tugging gently at his chest hair with her fingers; her lips were swollen from his kisses. "I love your body," she said.

I love you, Quentin wanted to say, but said evenly, "Body and soul—they come together. Package deal."

Her nostrils flared. "You don't let up, do you?"

"I can as easily stop loving you as stop breathing." He cupped the rise of her hip in one palm and said more temperately, "Marcia, we're not going to fight. Not now. For one thing, I don't have the energy." He glanced down at his arm, where he could see the faint parallel marks her fingernails had left, and recalled in graphic detail the precise moment she had done it. "I feel as if I've been in bed with a tiger."

She blushed. "I didn't mean to hurt you."

"I wasn't complaining."

"I should hope not," Marcia responded with a demureness that ill-matched her pink cheeks and her nudity.

Amused, Quentin said, "You're a very vocal lover."

"I never used to be." She gaped at him. "There was nothing much to say."

"I can't imagine you and I suffering from that particular deficit."

Neither could Marcia. So what was stopping her from telling Quentin that she loved him? And how was one more day going to change that?

An hour or so later, Marcia and Quentin went out for dinner. Marcia wore her red dress and Quentin his very expensive suit, and they went to a chic French restaurant whose chef personally assured them that nothing Quentin chose from the menu had come within ten feet of a shrimp. Afterward they walked home, went straight to sleep and made love at dawn. Marcia was late for work again.

Her secretary, a rather flighty young woman called Rosemary, said, "The director wants to see you at two, in his office."

Her curiosity was ill-concealed. Marcia swallowed a flutter of fear and said easily, "Thanks, Rosemary. Any mail?" She then went into her office and turned on her computer. Why would the director want to see her on a Friday afternoon?

By lunchtime she'd found out that three others of the junior staff also had appointments, after hers; this didn't make her feel any better. She could have phoned Quentin. She didn't.

She slogged through her paper, checking her data and redesigning a couple of the tables, and promptly at two presented herself at the door of the director's office.

Dr. Wayne Martell was overweight and ruthlessly efficient; Marcia respected him without liking him very much. "Marcia," he said, closing the door behind her. "Sit down, please."

Outwardly composed, she did as he asked, folding her hands in her lap. He sat down heavily in his swivel chair.

"You will, I'm sure, have heard the rumors of financial cutbacks," he said. "Unfortunately they're true. Our budget has been drastically reduced, and myself and the board have come to the conclusion that we have to lay off a number of staff members. We do this, as I hope you will understand, with deep regret and only out of the direst necessity." He paused, fiddling with his gold cufflinks; she had never realized before what a plummy voice he had.

"As you are aware," he went on, "you joined us seven years ago, which places you in the junior category—and it is that category which must be reduced. The institute will suffer from the loss of your extremely valuable contributions to our research program. We only trust that you yourself will not suffer."

He paused, looking at her expectantly. He wants applause, she thought wildly. Admirable job, Dr. Martell. You should fire people more often. She said, without visible emotion, "Are you telling me I no longer have a job here?"

"As of the middle of the month. You will, of course, receive full benefits up until that time."

Thanks a lot, she thought, and struggled to find some dignified way to get out of his office. He added, his voice deepening, "I can't tell you how sorry I am to be doing this, Marcia."

"Yes," she said. "Is that all?"

He stood up, extending his hand across the desk. Reluctantly she took it; after Quentin's lean fingers, his hand felt pudgy and damp. She could think of absolutely nothing to say. Nodding at him, she turned on her heel and marched down the corridor, her face expressionless. Rosemary, thank goodness, was on her coffee-break. Not bothering to leave her a note, Marcia picked up her purse and left the building.

She got in her car and discovered that her knees were

shaking. It took two tries to get the key in the ignition. She then headed for the Queensway, all her movements automatic, her brain as blank as her face. From the Queensway she took Route 17 east. The sun was shining and it was warm; she opened her window and let the wind blow through her hair. The traffic was fairly heavy. She wasn't the only person going east this sunny Friday afternoon. Probably many of the drivers were heading for their cottages along the river.

Cottage… *Quentin.*

She closed her mind against those two words, just as she had closed it against Dr. Martell's words, and drove steadily for two hours, leaving Ontario and entering Quebec, following the wide, lazy curve of the St. Lawrence River. Her gas gauge was getting dangerously low. She pulled in to a gas station, asked for a refill and went to the washroom. As she paid for the gas she picked up a bottle of ginger ale and a bag of chips, then took to the road again.

Behind her the sun sank lower in the sky. She'd had only a bowl of soup for lunch, and the chips and pop were pretty thin fare. At a quarter past six she stopped at a roadside restaurant that had several eighteen-wheelers parked outside; truckers always knew where the good meals were to be had.

The restaurant boasted vinyl-covered booths, rock music and a haze of blue smoke. Very different from where she'd eaten last night, thought Marcia, and as though someone had physically punched her she felt the words penetrate her consciousness. She looked at her watch. Six-eighteen. Quentin would have expected her home by now.

I can't phone him, she thought. I can't.

I've been fired. I've lost my job. I'm unemployed.

Acting on instinct alone, she went back to the phone booth by the entrance, using her calling card and dialed

Lucy's number. Troy answered. She said rapidly, "Troy, it's Marcia. Something's—something's happened and I need a little time to myself. Will you phone Quentin and tell him not to worry. I'll—"

"What's the matter?" he asked sharply.

"Tell him I'm all right. I'm just not sure when I'll be back, so—"

"Marcia, you sound terrible. What's happened?"

"Please, Troy, will you do that for me? I just need to be alone for a while, that's all… I've got to go, bye." She crashed the receiver back on the hook and went back into the restaurant. The volume of the music appeared to have gone up by several notches. She ordered the roast turkey dinner, choked it down, and followed it with two cups of excellent coffee. She then went back to her car and turned onto the highway, driving away from the sunset.

Losing all track of time, Quentin had spent the day sketching: strange, surreal sketches that were both an abstraction and a mythicizing of what Marcia had called his wallpapering efforts. At some deep level that pleased him immensely. When the grandfather clock in the hall chimed five, he dropped the stub of charcoal with an exclamation of dismay and shoved back his chair. Marcia would be home any minute.

He went into the kitchen and within fifteen minutes had reduced it to the kind of tidiness he knew she preferred. He then made the bed and gathered up the petals that had dropped from the flowers. He'd leave the papers on the wall for one more day.

He showered, cleaned up the bathroom and went back in the kitchen, opening a bottle of red wine and putting out some pâté and crackers. The better part of an hour had passed. She was late.

Although he picked up his sketchpad again, he couldn't concentrate, because subconsciously he was listening for the sound of her key turning in the lock and waiting to hear her voice. It was Friday, he thought. Today she'd promised to give him her answer. Whether she'd live with him. Or marry him.

Absently he poured himself a glass of wine and ate some pâté, going through the sketches one by one. With an inner certainty that had never yet failed him, he knew that they were good. What would Marcia think of them?

He wished she'd get home.

At six twenty-five the telephone rang in the kitchen. He ran for it and, not waiting for her to speak, said, "The wine's poured, the bed's made and all I need is you."

There was a small silence. Then a man's voice said non-committally, "It's Troy speaking, Quentin. I just had a phone call from Marcia, and she asked me to get in touch with you."

Quentin's breath seemed to have lodged somewhere in the vicinity of his larynx. "Yes?" he croaked.

"She said something had happened and she needed some time alone. She's all right and you're not to worry."

"What the hell do you mean? *What's* happened? Where is she?"

"She wouldn't say."

His imagination running riot, Quentin rapped, "Maybe some guy had her at gunpoint."

"You're way off base, Quentin—Marcia would have found some way to let me know if that had been the case. This was something personal, I'd say."

"Where was she?"

"She didn't say and she rang off before I could ask. A public place of some kind—rock music, voices in the background—could have been a restaurant. A car pulled up while she was talking to me.''

Quentin's frustration exploded in his voice. ''That could be any bloody restaurant the width of the country.''

Troy said carefully, ''She did say you weren't to worry.''

''Sorry,'' Quentin said. ''Don't shoot the messenger, huh? But goddamn it, Troy, what's going on?''

''You've had a whirlwind romance—what's it been, three weeks? Maybe she just needs time to catch her breath.''

''Then why call you and not me?''

''I don't know... She'll probably get in touch with you later,'' Troy said.

Her answer, Quentin thought. She didn't want to give him her answer because she knew he wouldn't like it. So she'd run away.

Her answer must be no.

Troy was saying something. Quentin fought to concentrate. ''...in all evening if she calls again.''

''You'll let me know if she does? I'm going to ring off, Troy, in case she's trying to reach me. Thanks.''

He put down the phone and went back into the dining room. The sketches he'd been so proud of looked like messages from another country, meaningless scrawls not worth the paper they were drawn on. He drained his glass of wine and for the better part of an hour stayed where he was, willing the telephone to ring. Then he stood up, walking over to the window and staring out at the tidily arranged houses and the dull green waters of the canal.

He couldn't leave the condo in case Marcia phoned. Or came home. He was trapped in a square brick building in the middle of a city because he wanted a woman with hair like burnished wood and eyes the color of pansies. Wanted her more than he'd ever wanted anything in his life.

He'd lost his freedom.

What if he'd lost Marcia as well?

CHAPTER TWELVE

AT EIGHT-THIRTY that evening Marcia stopped at a small mall by the roadside and bought some toiletries, a night-gown and a change of clothes. At nine-thirty, exhausted, she booked a room in a motel, where she flicked on the television and sat mesmerized in front of the news channel for nearly an hour. One of the major oil companies was making layoffs. She buried her head in her hands and finally let the feelings that she'd been working so hard to repress wash over her.

She'd been fired. Her job was gone—the job that had been her life for seven years and the goal of her life all through university. Her job was her identity, she thought in terror. What would she be without it?

No one in her family had ever been fired. What would her great-grandfather, a thoracic surgeon, or her grandfather, a neurosurgeon, have thought of a member of the family who'd been ignominiously laid off?

Not much. And what of her clever, successful mother and her equally clever sister?

I'm ashamed of myself…I feel like a failure. The first tears slid down Marcia's cheeks. She cried for a long time, tears of anger and frustration and pain. Then she curled up in a ball on the bed and fell into a stunned sleep.

When she woke in the morning, she was reaching for Quentin. She had shared her bed with him for only two nights, and already she was used to him being there. Quentin wanted to marry her. But how could she marry him when she didn't have a job? Would she sponge off him?

Put her hand out for money every time she needed anything? She couldn't do that. She wasn't cut out to be a kept woman. She was too independent.

Yesterday, she realized with an ugly lurch of her stomach, was the day she was to have given him her answer. On Thursday, in bed with him, she had wondered what might change between Thursday and Friday. She now knew. She couldn't possibly marry him. It wouldn't be fair to either one of them.

The pain she had felt last night was nothing to the pain she felt now, a pain that was beyond tears. With grim efficiency Marcia showered, breakfasted in the motel restaurant, and got back in her car. One thing had become clear to her in the night. She now knew where she was going. She was going to Holton, the little village in the Kennebecasis Valley in New Brunswick where Quentin had grown up.

She didn't know why yet, and rationally it made no sense at all. But it was her destination.

The miles rolled by, her little red car purring along smoothly. She reached the New Brunswick border, ate a late lunch at another truck stop, and by early evening had turned off the main highway into the valley. The river wound through open fields that merged into gentle wooded hills; red-winged blackbirds were singing in the reeds and bobolinks burbled above the tall grass of the meadows. There was an old-fashioned covered bridge over the river; she felt almost as though she were entering another century.

Holton consisted of a cluster of houses and a few farms, a post office, a gas station and a general store. Now that she was here, Marcia wasn't quite sure what she was going to do. She went into the general store and bought a chocolate bar, and said to the teenaged girl behind the counter, who was busily picking flakes of red polish from her fingernails, "Can you tell me where Quentin Ramsey used to live?"

"Never heard of him."

"I've come a long way," Marcia said. "Is there anyone else who could tell me?"

"I'll give Margie a call." She rolled her eyes. "Margie knows everyone in these parts."

After a lengthy conversation she put down the phone and said to Marcia, "Go right and follow the dirt road until you come to a yellow house. Ed and Kaye Miller. They'll tell you."

"Thanks," Marcia said, and hurried outside. Now that she was here, she was filled with a strange impatience. She soon found the yellow house. It was rundown, but there were big clumps of daffodils along the driveway and red-feathered hens pecking in the dirt by the porch. She took a deep breath and knocked on the front door.

It was flung open by a gangly old man with the most rambunctious eyebrows she'd ever seen. She said weakly, "I'm trying to find out where Quentin Ramsey used to live, Mr. Miller, and someone called Margie sent me here."

"You don't want to believe one word that comes out of that woman's mouth," he barked. "Worst gossip in fifty miles."

She took a step backward. "You can't help me, then?"

"Now, did I say that? Come along in—hurry up, else the house'll be singin' with mosquitoes. And call me Ed. Kaye!" he bellowed. "We got company... She's not feelin' that good—got a sore finger. I bin hollerin' at her all week to hike herself in to see the doctor, and does she listen? No, sirree."

He was tramping through a parlor complete with an upright organ and a horsehair sofa. Marcia followed him into the kitchen, which was clearly the hub of the house, with

windows full of tall scarlet geraniums. Then footsteps shuffled into the room. Kaye Miller was wearing a print dress
with a handknit cardigan; her hair was pure white, her eyes
a gentle blue and her smile warm.

Marcia said quickly, "My name's Marcia Barnes. I'm
from Ottawa, Mrs. Miller. I'm sorry to bother you, especially if you're not feeling well, but I was hoping to find
out where Quentin Ramsey grew up, and I was directed
here."

Kaye sat down in the rocking chair by the oil stove,
nursing her right hand. Her face lit up with pleasure. "Well,
now, how would you know Quentin?"

"We're—er—we're friends."

"Such a dear little boy, he was."

"Full of the old Nick," Ed growled.

"All boys are mischievous. And he's done so well for
himself, painting those pictures."

"Them colors he uses—I wouldn't put 'em on a barn."

"Now, Edward," soothed Kaye. "What did you want to
know, dear? Edward, why don't you put the teapot on?"

Amused to notice that Ed instantly headed for the stove,
Marcia said, "I wondered if his parents were still alive, and
where his house was."

"Ah, well…no, dear. His parents died when he was
twelve. It was very sad, they drove off the road in a snow-
storm. It changed him overnight; I do have to say that. Got
real quiet, he did. The nearest relatives were in St. John,
so he had to go and live in the city. Worst place in the
world for a boy like him, who loved the outdoors so
much."

"Ran wild from the time he was old enough to run,"
said Ed, getting three mugs from the cupboard and a can
of milk from the refrigerator.

"The house had to be sold, of course—they left no

money, not even for the funeral." Kaye sighed. "So the furniture went to auction and the Martins bought the house."

"Riffraff," Ed snorted.

"They weren't very nice people, certainly. The house burned to the ground a year later, so there was nowhere for Quentin to come back to—even if he'd been able to. We wanted to take him, but the uncle wouldn't hear of it."

Ed's opinion of the uncle was unrepeatable. "Now, Edward," said Kaye, and sighed again. "Not a good man, dear. We heard Quentin got in a lot of fights in the city. The townies always give the country boys a hard time. Broke his nose, and his wrist too, so we were told." She cheered up as Ed poured tea the color of coffee from the pot. "He always comes to visit us once a year, though. Such a lovely-looking man, isn't he?"

"Yes, he is," Marcia gulped, and blushed rosily.

The shame she'd felt over the loss of her job was nothing to the shame she felt now. She'd never even asked Quentin if his parents were alive; she hadn't asked about his broken nose or his childhood, or the village where he'd grown up. She'd been too absorbed in all the changes in her own life.

Selfish bitch, she thought venomously. How could she have been so mean-spirited, so self-centered?

So unloving.

Ed said testily, "You drove a long way to find this out. You plannin' on marryin' him?"

His question tapped into all her shame and confusion. But how could she evade those fiery old eyes. "He—he's asked me to."

"You could do a lot worse," said Ed.

"Now, Edward, you mustn't interfere. But why don't you get out some of the old albums? Perhaps Miss Barnes would like to see some photos of him when he was a boy."

"Please call me Marcia...and I'd love to."

But as Ed passed Kaye an old leather-bound album it slipped from his fingers and banged against her right hand; she gave a tiny shriek of pain. "What's the trouble?" Marcia asked in quick concern. "I'm a doctor—why don't you show me?"

The finger that Kaye showed her was puffy and inflamed. "That should be drained," Marcia said. "As soon as possible. I can't do it—I'm not a practising physician. Where's the nearest doctor?"

"Other side of the valley," Ed said promptly. "Ole Doc Meade—he'd take a look at it."

There had been no sign of a car outside the yellow house. "Why don't you check with him and I'll drive you there?" Marcia offered.

"Oh, we couldn't do that, dear."

"Friends of Quentin's are friends of mine," said Marcia, and knew that the simple words held a deeper meaning, one that was all-important to her.

One that she'd had to drive all this way to discover.

Since Troy's phone call on Friday evening, Quentin had passed the longest twenty-four hours of his life. The grandfather clock had ticked away the minutes and chimed the hours. His guts churning with an uncomfortable mixture of fury, desperation and anxiety, he had paced up and down, trying to eat a tuna sandwich that had tasted like sawdust and endeavoring not to drive himself crazy with worry.

His brain was a quagmire of questions, none of which he could answer. What in God's name had possessed Marcia to run away? How could she have shared her bed and her body and then simply disappeared without even speaking to him? Was she afraid of him? Was that it?

These were not comforting thoughts. And as the time

passed with agonizing slowness the telephone had remained deafeningly silent.

At two in the morning he had fallen asleep on the chesterfield because he couldn't bear to use the bed. His sleep had been riddled with nightmares that woke him again and again to the harsh sounds of his own breathing and to a loneliness blacker than any he had ever known. Today had crept by at a snail's pace, until suddenly, at four in the afternoon, he couldn't stand the silence and solitude of his vigil any longer.

He'd gambled all his happiness on a woman he'd been convinced was his soulmate, and he'd lost. He loved Marcia with every fiber of his being. But she didn't love him, and had lacked the courage to tell him so. The sooner he faced up to that, the better.

Moving very slowly, Quentin began to gather his belongings. Picking up his clothes in the bedroom, he flinched from the sight of the bed in which he had both found and given—or so he'd thought—such felicity. He'd been wrong there too, he thought dully. So much for intuition. So much for his certainty that he'd found the one woman who was his completion.

Although every movement felt as though he was pushing his way through mud as thick as that on the banks of the Kennebecasis, he persisted until there was not a single mark left of his brief occupancy. Somehow, during this activity, the patterns of years reasserted themselves; he now knew exactly what he was going to do.

He walked into the kitchen, looked up a number in the phone book, picked up the telephone and began to dial.

Marcia, Kaye and Ed left together for the doctor's. Ed was in the back seat, which in no way impeded his tongue.

"Marcia, how come you ain't a proper doctor?" he demanded.

"I've been doing research ever since I graduated."

"Humph," said Ed. "Real people not good enough for you?"

Marcia remembered Jason falling from the step, and Quentin being so sick, and now Kaye's sore finger. On each occasion she'd said, I'm a doctor, and each time she'd been of use. I'm changing again, she thought in mingled excitement and panic. What's going on now?

"I got fired from my research job yesterday," she said, and somehow the words weren't difficult to say at all.

"Places in the backwoods, like Holton, they need a good doctor nearby. When ole Doc Meade passes on, Kaye an' me'll have to go into the city."

Quentin wanted to live in the country, so he could build her a house there. West coast or east, the country would have people like Ed and Kaye. "I haven't told Quentin I got fired."

Ed roared with uncouth laughter. "He got fired from every job he ever had. First sunny day, he'd take off to the woods. Bosses don't take kindly to that sort of thing."

"So you don't think it would matter to him?" she said blankly.

"Not likely!"

"I was ashamed to tell him. So I left town." Feeling as though a black pit had just opened in front of her, she gasped, "I ran away for nothing."

"You got that right," Ed remarked.

"Do you think he'll ever forgive me?"

"Of course he will, dear," Kaye said comfortingly.

"Tell you somethin' else," Ed put in. "I bet Quentin'd be a whole lot happier if you were a proper doctor—he was always lookin' after some scruffy ole raccoon, or an owl that one of the Martin kids had shot at. That research stuff—that's for people who ain't got the guts for real life.''

Dr. Martell would not agree. But Marcia didn't work for Dr. Martell anymore. For the first time since she had gone into his office yesterday afternoon, she gained an inkling that it might be possible for her to view being fired as an opportunity for change rather than solely an occasion for shame.

''That's Doc Meade's place,'' Ed announced. ''The next driveway.''

Dr. Meade had his office in the basement of his house. Once Kaye and Ed were ushered in, Marcia sat quietly in a rickety wooden chair, going over all the events of the past two days in her mind. She now knew why she'd run away. The old Marcia had taken over—the woman who never shared her feelings with anyone. Especially the bad ones.

Quentin had threatened to leave her the last time she did that.

She looked around the room but there was no sign of a phone. I've got to talk to him, she thought frantically. I've got to tell him I made a terrible mistake and that I'm sorry.

Because I love him. I love him the way Lucy loves Troy. Good times and bad, for the rest of my life.

A beatific smile on her face, she sat very still. How could she have been so blind? So ignorant of her own feelings? Of course she loved Quentin. It had been staring her in the face for days.

As for Quentin, he wasn't in love with her salary or her position. He wasn't that kind of man. He was in love with her, the woman. A woman who might well become a country doctor. And if her change of career were to cause her great-grandfather and her grandfather to turn over in their respective graves, too bad. Lucy would approve. So would Troy. And so, she was certain, would Quentin.

She wanted to laugh and sing. She wanted to dance around the shabby little office between the worn wooden chairs. But most of all she wanted to tell Quentin she loved him. She wanted to hear his voice. To feel his arms around her.

It was a twelve-hour drive back to Ottawa.

In an agony of impatience she waited for Ed and Kaye. But when they came out they had Dr. Meade with them, a delightful old gentleman who didn't share Ed's low opinion of immunologists and wanted to hear all about her latest research. As briefly as good manners would allow, Marcia told him, then said craftily, "I should get Kaye home—it's been a long day for her. Nice to have met you, Dr. Meade. Goodbye."

As soon as they got home, Kaye sat down in the rocking chair and Ed put the kettle on again. Not sure if her digestive tract would survive more of his tea, Marcia said, "Do you mind if I use your phone? I have to talk to Quentin."

"Maybe we could have a word with him too, dear," Kaye said placidly. "We can tell him how kind you've been to us."

The telephone was attached to the kitchen wall. Marcia dialed her own number. It rang five times, then her answering machine clicked on. He's not home, she thought in despair, and said into the silence after the beep, "Quentin, I'm at Ed and Kaye's. I'll be back on Sunday. I love you. I'm *sorry* I ran away." She then replaced the receiver and tried the cottage. The phone rang and rang and no one picked it up.

Biting her lip, aware of Ed ostentatiously washing the mugs in the sink with a great clattering and splashing, she dialed Lucy and Troy's number. Troy answered. Marcia said in a rush, "Is Quentin there, Troy? It's Marcia."

"No, he's not," he said in a peculiar voice. "Where are you?"

"I'm in New Brunswick. In the village where Quentin grew up. Where is he, do you know? I've got to talk to him."

"You're too late," Troy said.

Her body went cold. *"Too late*?" she whispered.

"Sorry, sis, I didn't mean to scare you," Troy said hastily. "But he left two or three hours ago. He was going back to the cottage to get his gear, then he was catching a flight to Baffin Island."

"Baffin Island?" she repeated blankly.

"Yeah…he has friends in Clyde River he thought he might visit."

"He didn't wait for me," Marcia said in a hollow voice.

"He wasn't in the mood to listen to reason. He'd figured out that you didn't want to marry him and that he'd pressured you too much, and he said he had to get the hell out of the city; it was driving him nuts sitting around waiting for you to come home when you obviously weren't going to. He was a tad angry that you'd run away too."

"I bet that's an understatement," said Marcia.

"We tried to talk to him… Well, you know Lucy, she didn't just talk, she lost her temper and yelled at him, but it didn't do any good. He left anyway."

"Oh, God," said Marcia. "I love him, you see. But I didn't know I did until tonight. And don't ask me to explain that because I can't. Do you know the names of his friends?"

"No. You could try paging him at the airport—I'll give you the number. It's the flight to Iqaluit…it might not have left."

''Thanks, Troy.''

She dialed yet another set of digits, and when an official-sounding male voice answered she asked him to page Quentin Ramsey. ''It's very important,'' she implored. ''Please hurry.''

But the slow minutes ticked by and Quentin didn't answer the call. When the official came back on she said numbly, ''Thank you for trying. Goodbye,'' and leaned her forehead on the wall.

He'd gone. He'd left her because she hadn't had the guts to tell him she'd been fired.

He thought she didn't love him.

He thought her answer was no.

CHAPTER THIRTEEN

KAYE said tentatively, "Are you all right, Marcia?"

Remembering where she was, Marcia turned around. Kaye was watching her with concern and for once Ed was speechless. "Quentin's left," Marcia said. "He thinks I don't love him. So he's gone to Baffin Island. Baffin *Island...*" she finished in despair.

Ed snorted. "Kind of looks to me like he's got it all wrong. Or else you're a real good actress. You'd better hike yourself right after him."

Her jaw dropped. "Baffin Island's a big place."

"You'll find him," Ed said. "You don't even have to take vacation, 'cause you got fired."

Incredibly Marcia felt her mouth curve into the beginnings of a smile. "He has friends in Clyde River."

"Then you kin go there for starters. And you make sure when you find him you tell him right out that you love him—don't you go beatin' round the bush."

"You're right," said Marcia. "Am I a woman or a mouse? I really want that man, so I'd better make darn sure I do find him. There's not that many places in the Arctic, and he does tend to stand out in a crowd."

"You must stay the night," Kaye said pragmatically. "It wouldn't be safe for you to start out now. Ed's up before the rooster crows, so you can get away in good time in the morning."

So Marcia spent the evening looking through photo albums and listening to the two old people reminisce. Her heart ached at some of the shots of Quentin, a lanky boy

176

with wiry black hair and laughing eyes, who'd lost parents and home and been consigned against his will to a city school with bullies who didn't like country boys. His intensity was the more easily understandable, as well as the darkness in so many of his paintings. No wonder he'd always been a nomad. No wonder he'd left Ottawa today to seek out the space and silence of the north.

Considering the amount of caffeine she'd drunk, she slept well, and by six-thirty the next morning she was ready to leave. "You make sure we get an invitation to the weddin'," Ed said.

"If there is one."

His brows positively bristled. "You cut out that 'if' stuff. I'll tell you, if I was younger I'd pound some sense into that fella myself—takin' off on a fine young woman like you. Kaye took a real shine to you—and she knows people, my Kaye does. And you make sure you stick to proper doctorin'."

"Yes, Ed," Marcia said meekly. Laughing up at him, she started her car. "I'll be in touch," she promised. As the hens scattered and the rooster charged down the slope in pursuit she drove onto the road and waved goodbye.

She didn't spend the whole day being as optimistic as Ed would have liked. The nearer she got to home the more she was convinced that Quentin wouldn't take her back, that she'd learned her lessons too late. She didn't cry, because she was possessed by a desperate urgency to get home, and she couldn't cry and drive at the same time. But her stomach was like a chunk of ice and her eyes burned and her hands were cold on the wheel. By the time she reached the outskirts of Ottawa, she felt sick with fear.

At the cloverleaf there was a sign for the airport. Without even thinking she followed it, turning off Route 17. She'd go there now and book a ticket on the first flight to Baffin

Island. She didn't have the courage to go back to her empty condo without the ticket in her hand. Not when every room would be haunted with memories.

But what if she went all the way to Clyde River and Quentin didn't want her any more? What then?

At the airport Marcia parked her car and ran a comb through her hair. She looked awful, she thought dispassionately. She was wearing the blouse she'd worn to work on Friday along with the jeans and sweatshirt she'd bought at the little mall; the sweatshirt was purple with neon-tinted lupins drooping across her chest. The shadows under her eyes were also purple.

The lupins reminded her of the flowers Quentin had put in her bedroom. I won't cry, she told herself fiercely. I will not.

She locked her car and walked to the terminal, her legs protesting at the exercise. Her back ached. Her brain was in overdrive. As for her emotions, in the last forty-eight hours she'd surely made up for a lifetime of suppression.

On her way to the ticket counter she passed the television screens that listed arrivals and departures. Her eyes flicked over them. A flight had arrived from Iqaluit twenty minutes ago. Like a woman in a dream she sought out the signs for the baggage carousels and hurried toward them, her face set. When she got to the baggage area the crowd was thinning under the carousel labeled with the Iqaluit flight number, and not one of the passengers was Quentin.

Through a crushing disappointment she scolded herself for being such a fool. Quentin had only just gone there. Why would he turn around and come straight back?

Especially if he didn't love her any more.

It was a good thing Ed wasn't here, Marcia thought, holding tight to the remnants of her composure; Ed would have given her merry old hell for thinking so negatively.

She turned on her heel to go back to the ticket area, and as though her need had conjured him up she saw the man standing in front of one of the telephones on the far wall. Although his back was to her, she would have known him anywhere. He had just dialed a number and was waiting for the connection, the cold fluorescent lighting falling on his untidy black curls. He was wearing a dark blue sweater and jeans, hiking boots on his feet. Her heart crowding its way into her throat, she stood frozen to the floor.

He slammed the receiver down and ran his fingers through his hair. Then he slung the duffel bag that had been at his feet over one shoulder and headed for the exit. He looked in worse shape than she was.

He hadn't seen her. "Quentin!" Marcia shouted in a cracked voice. "Quentin!" And as if it were happening in slow motion she saw his head turn. Paralyzed by a storm of emotions, the uppermost of which was terror, she found herself quite unable to move, her feet like lumps of lead. Their eyes met, and for a moment that seemed to last forever he stood as still as she. Then he started toward her, his face unreadable.

He loves me, he loves me not, she thought idiotically, and watched him come to a halt two feet away from her. Letting his bag slide to the floor, he said in a level voice, "I just tried to phone you."

"I'm not home."

The ghost of a smile crossed his face; his eyes were deepset, bruised with fatigue, and his jaw stubbled with a dark beard. "I see that, Marcia. What are you doing here?"

"I came to the airport to buy a ticket for Clyde River. I don't even know where Clyde River is."

"East coast of Baffin Island," he said, his features carefully blank. "Why were you going there?"

"You're not making this any easier," she complained. "And you look even worse than I do."

"I've just been through the worst two days of my entire life, and I've had a few bad ones to compare it with. You don't look so hot yourself. You should give that sweatshirt away—not that anyone would take it."

"I'd better hold onto it," she said, "considering I lost my job on Friday."

Something flared in his eyes and was gone. "Did you, now? For being late three days in a row?"

"No, Quentin. Government cutbacks."

"So did you hide at the institute for the weekend? Where, of course, all the telephones were out of order?"

She had known he was angry, but not quite this angry. "I spent last night with Ed and Kaye," she said roundly.

Surprise, fury and relief followed each other across his face. "Now what did you do that for?" he asked with spurious calm.

She blurted, "Quentin, do you still love me?"

"Do you think I flew to Iqaluit and back in the space of twenty-four hours for fun?" he exploded. "Of course I still love you. I'm stuck with loving you for the rest of my goddamned life."

He did not look happy at this prospect. "Oh," Marcia said in a small voice, her heart beginning to sing in her breast, "that's good. Because I love you too."

"Listen to me, Marcia Barnes—I'm dirty, unshaven, hungry, thirsty and exhausted. Don't play games with me— I'm not in the mood!"

"I'm not playing games," she retorted, and repeated in less than lover-like tones, "I love you—I finally figured it out." In an effort to get rid of the crippling tension in her chest, she raised her voice over the whining of the carousels and the clatter of baggage carts. "I love you, Quentin Ramsey! I love you right now, I'll love you tomorrow and all next week, and I suspect that I, too, am stuck with loving you for the rest of my life. Goddamned or otherwise."

There was a smattering of laughter from some passersby. Quentin looked around, baring his teeth in a raffish grin. "Let's see if you'll put your money where your mouth is. Will you marry me?"

She said pertly, "Would you marry me in this sweat-shirt?"

"God help me, I would."

"Okay," she said.

The line of his jaw relaxed a little. But he had yet to touch her. He said abruptly, "This is all very amusing, but I hate airports. Let's go home."

"Where is home? I don't even know that any more."

"I don't think either one of us is capable of driving to the cottage right now. Your place?"

She nodded. "My car's outside."

"So's mine. Let's go."

Marcia stood her ground, her heart thumping underneath the lupins. "Quentin, kiss me."

He took her by the shoulders, planted a passionate and passionately angry kiss on her lips and stood back, his chest heaving. Then he hoisted his bag over his shoulder and started for the door.

Marcia followed, trotting along behind like an obedient wife. His beard had scraped her chin, and unless she was mistaken they were headed for the biggest fight of their not particularly placid courtship. All right, she thought, if that's the way you want to play it, I'll be glad to oblige, and said coldly, after they had crossed to the car park, "My car's over there. I'll see you in a few minutes."

He gave her a curt nod and strode off between the closely packed rows of cars. Twenty minutes later, when Marcia took the elevator to her floor, Quentin was already unlocking her door. His gaze far from friendly, he said, "Who's first for the shower?"

"You shave and I'll shower, then I'll dry my hair while you shower," she said, and walked inside. "You took the drawings down!"

"I burned them. At the cottage."

She stalked down the hall to her bedroom, not surprised to find it bare of floral offerings. The whole place looked bare; he'd removed every trace of his stay. She grabbed a very unsexy cotton nightgown from her drawer along with an old terry robe she'd had for at least six years and headed for the bathroom. Stripping off her clothes, not caring if he was watching her or not, she stepped into the shower.

The stingingly hot water diluted her temper and relaxed her muscles. She wrapped her body in one towel and her hair in another, and stepped out onto the mat. Quentin was bent over the sink, rinsing his chin; he was naked, his back curved like a bow, his long legs arrow-straight. She fled to her bedroom and dried her hair in front of the mirror. Belting her robe tightly round her waist, she then went into the kitchen.

She hadn't eaten for what felt like a very long time. And Quentin had mentioned hunger among his list of woes. She banged a saucepan on the stove with unnecessary force and heard him say, "What are you making?"

"Oatmeal with raisins, brown sugar and cream," she announced. He was wearing his jeans slung low on his hips and nothing else; her eyes skidded away. "Comfort food. What did you do with all my flowers?"

"I trashed them," he said. "I'll make myself a tuna sandwich. My aunt made oatmeal three hundred and sixty-five days a year and I haven't touched it since."

Her fingernails were digging into the rim of the saucepan. "How old were you when you left them, Quentin—your aunt and uncle, I mean?"

"Sixteen. Minimum legal age."

She had known the answer before she asked the question. "I love you," she said helplessly. "I love you, and we're behaving like a couple of stray cats."

He walked up to her, detached her fingers from the saucepan and held them captive in his own, his blue eyes piercing through all her defenses, his voice harsh. "Why didn't you tell me you lost your job? Why did you run away?"

At some level Marcia had known this was the question he would ask, to which he deserved the most honest answer she could give. She rested her free hand on top of his and let him see all her bewilderment and pain. "There'd been rumors flying all week, but I never really believed they'd affect me. Then on Friday at two o'clock I was told I was out of a job. Just like that.

"I come from a family of achievers, Quentin—physicians back four generations—and I'm the first one ever to be fired. I felt humiliated and ashamed, as though I wasn't worth anything. It was also quite clear to me that I'm not cut out to go asking you for money—I'm too used to being independent. So—"

"I don't give a damn if you've got a fortune stashed under the mattress or if you're penniless! That's never been an issue. It's *you* I love. Not your money or your career."

"I was too upset on Friday to realize that."

"You could have asked," he said with dangerous softness. "You could have told me what was going on."

"I'm *sorry*. I didn't even think—I just ran."

"And phoned Troy instead of me. How do you think that made me feel?"

"I was too humiliated to talk to you!"

"Do you know what I thought had happened?" he said, his voice rising. "I thought your answer was no—you didn't want to live with me or marry me. And you'd lacked the courage—or the common courtesy—to tell me face to face, so you'd run away. That's why I stripped this place bare of every mark I'd made on it, and that's why I headed north. I'd misjudged you ever since I'd met you. That's what I thought."

Briefly she closed her eyes. "I'm more sorry than I can say. But for the space of twenty-four hours I felt as though I'd lost my identity, as though I didn't know who I was any more... It took Ed Miller to knock some sense into me. I don't know why I headed east on Friday afternoon; it wasn't a conscious decision. But don't you see, Quentin? Even while I was running away from you I was running toward you too."

He let out his breath in a long sigh, the muscles rippling across his bare chest. "Yeah..." he said. "I only wish I'd known what was going on."

"I wish I'd had the courage—or the smarts—to tell you," she said stonily.

He brought her hand to his mouth, pressing his lips into the hollow at her wrist where the veins showed blue and her pulse bumped against her skin. "So you went straight to Holton?"

She nodded. "I've never asked you about your childhood, have I? Or what happened to your parents. I felt ashamed of myself for that too. But from Ed and Kaye I found out why you've always been a nomad and how much you must love me to have stuck it out with me in a condo in the city." With passionate intensity she added, "I'll do my best never to take away your freedom, Quentin."

His heart was thudding in his chest. "You traveled a long way," he said obliquely. "If I was less than friendly at the airport it was because I discovered when I got to Iqaluit that freedom for me now means being with you. I couldn't stay there. I had to come back. But all along I'd given you the very best gifts of my body and my talent and my heart, and they hadn't been enough—you'd run away. When I saw you at the airport, I was so strung out I figured I was hallucinating."

"Oh, no," said Marcia. "I'm real." Raising his hand to her cheek, she added, "Ed suggested—and I think he's right—that I should become a real doctor. A proper doctor. Like ole Doc Meade."

"Is he still around?" Quentin threw back his head and laughed. "The day I had the brush with the porcupine, he picked quills out of my knee for a solid hour. You'd make a great Doc Meade, Marcia."

"I might have to go back to university for a year."

"That'll give me time to build our house."

"You really do want to marry me?"

His arms found their way around her waist. "Yes," he said.

A sheen of tears in her eyes, she confessed, "By the time I'd reached the Quebec border, I'd convinced myself you didn't love me any more. Quentin, I won't ever run away again—I swear." Her brow furrowed in thought. "I don't know why I had to go to Holton to find out that I love you. But now that I know I do—why, that makes you my safe haven, doesn't it? The one person I can tell anything to… Am I making any sense?"

He said succinctly, "You learned a lot at Kaye and Ed's."

"Ed wants an invitation to the wedding."

"I wouldn't think of getting married without him." Quentin pulled her closer and kissed her with lingering sensuality. "Dearest and most adorable Marcia, I love you. I suspect our marriage will never be dull and tomorrow morning I'm going to buy you a housecoat that's just the tiniest bit sexier than the one you're wearing. And some more flowers.'' He moved his hips against hers. ''But right now you have a choice to make. Oatmeal or me.''

Fluttering her lashes and linking her hands behind his neck, she said, ''Are you saying you prefer me to a tunafish sandwich?''

''I think that's what I'm trying to get across.''

Desire flooded her, hot and compelling. ''You're succeeding,'' she said. ''You're very definitely succeeding. I can always have oatmeal for breakfast.''

Unbelting her robe, he caressed the soft swell of her breasts. ''Someday soon I'll ravish you against the stove,'' he said. ''But not tonight. Tonight I think we both need to be in bed.''

So they went to bed and made love. They then got up and made tunafish sandwiches and oatmeal. They phoned Lucy and Evelyn and Cat and Ed and announced their engagement. They went back to bed and made love again.

And two months later, when they'd come back from their honeymoon in New Brunswick and were packing all their belongings in a moving van to go out west—where Marcia was to do a residency in family medicine and Quentin was to build a house—there were three paintings in crates in the van: the woman in the red dress, the three little girls running through a field and a big canvas covered with spirals of vibrant color—the canvas that had been Marcia's first introduction to the man she loved.

Kim Lawrence lives on a farm in rural Anglesey. She runs two miles daily and finds this an excellent opportunity to unwind and seek inspiration for her writing! It also helps her keep up with her husband, two active sons, and the various stray animals which have adopted them. Always a fanatical consumer of fiction, she is now equally enthusiastic about writing. She loves a happy ending!

Kim Lawrence has some fantastic books coming out this year in Modern Romance™. Look out for:

AT THE PLAYBOY'S PLEASURE
– May

THE ITALIAN PLAYBOY'S PROPOSITION
– September

THE SEDUCTION SCHEME

by

Kim Lawrence

CHAPTER ONE

THE waiter lifted the lid of the silver tureen with a flourish. A closet romantic at heart, he gave a smile of satisfaction when the attractive young woman gasped in surprise.

Rachel was surprised. She'd known Nigel was going to propose tonight—he'd dropped enough hints—but she hadn't expected a gesture as theatrical and grand as this. Mouth slightly open, she stared at the diamond nestling on the velvet cushion as if it might leap out and bite her any minute.

Nigel Latimer leant forward eagerly in his seat; well satisfied with his companion's reaction, he nodded the waiter away with a conspiratorial grin.

'It doesn't bite,' he said, reaching over and taking hold of her hand. 'Try it on,' he urged. 'My God, Rachel, you're trembling.' Rachel, who was always so composed and in control. He was delighted and faintly surprised that his efforts had made such an impact.

Rachel tore her eyes from the sparkling ring to the spot where her hand was covered by a larger one. 'This is such a shock,' she lied shakily. It would offend him if she snatched her hand away, so being a considerate young woman she didn't.

Actually it had been obvious for weeks that this moment would arise; she'd thought about it a lot and now the moment was here she still didn't have the faintest idea what she was going to say! What a time to become indecisive.

She looked into Nigel's handsome, confident face, at his nice clean-cut features, the silvered hair that gave him the distinguished air that went down so well with his patients—

he looked every inch the successful, competent surgeon. Shouldn't it be excitement, not consternation that made her stomach muscles spasm? Some people didn't know when they had it good—and she, apparently, was one of them!

He expected her to say yes—and why shouldn't he? He was the answer to most women's prayers: good-looking, kind, wealthy. She sometimes wondered how a man like him had stayed single into his forties. Rachel found it unsettling when he called her the perfect woman he'd been waiting for all his life. His expectations of her were very high, so that she always felt almost as if she was playing a part for him. Perfect women always said the right thing at the right moment. How would he react if he discovered the less than perfect side to her nature?

He must love her to distraction to pursue her in the face of extreme provocation from Charlotte, her daughter. Did she love him? Did it matter? Weren't other things like companionship and compatibility more important? She was thirty now, past the age of expecting the fulfilment of adolescent fantasies.

The thoughts flickered through her mind in the blink of an eye. She felt a trickle of sweat slide down between her shoulder blades as she tried to respond the way she ought to. What's wrong with me? she asked herself. The first signs of concern were beginning to appear on Nigel's face when the waiter reappeared and apologetically announced that there was an urgent phone call for Miss French.

It wasn't just a desperate desire for a breathing space that made Rachel leap to her feet; the only person who knew she was here was the baby-sitter. What was Charlie up to now? she wondered in alarm.

She returned a few moments later and it was immediately obvious to her escort that all was not well.

'What's wrong, darling?' Nigel was at her side in a second. Rachel bit back a terrified sob. 'Charlie's disappeared!'

'There you are!' Benedict Arden flinched as a pair of small arms suddenly snaked around his leather-clad middle. 'See, I *told you* I wasn't alone.'

This last comment wasn't addressed to him but was thrown defiantly in the direction of a prosperous-looking middle-aged couple who were regarding him with dubious disapproval.

Having presented the sort of appearance for almost all the thirty-four years of his life that would dispose people like this couple to regard him in a benevolent light, Benedict permitted himself a small ironic smile at this fresh reminder of how important first impressions were before his thoughts returned to the more pressing issue: who the hell was this kid?

'This is your father?' Pity was mixed with scepticism in the woman's voice.

'Good God, no!' Revulsion flared in Benedict's voice as he took a step backwards.

He was relieved to find his wallet was where it ought to be, in the breast pocket of his leather jacket. The jacket was air force issue; he'd inherited it from his grandfather and it proved that he hadn't just inherited the face of a man he'd never known, but his build too.

The jacket combined with hair that had become long enough to be troublesome, plus a liberal sprinkling of dark stubble over his angular jawline, gave him an almost sinister aspect. At first glance, Benedict would be the first to admit, not the sort of character anyone would expect to find hugging a child, but then he wasn't doing the hugging.

The thin arms unwound and a pair of reproachful blue eyes looked up at him. Looking down into a delicate face, Benedict realised for the first time that the child was not, after all, a boy, but a girl—a girl dressed in androgynous jeans and tee shirt. The realisation didn't soften his expression; the menace that would have made sensible souls cross the road didn't appear to make any impact on the child.

'He's my brother,' she continued, not taking her remarkable china-blue eyes from his face. 'My stepbrother, actually; my father married his mother,' she elaborated, warming to the theme. A furrow developed between her brows as she mentally composed a full family history. 'His father's dead now.'

Benedict blinked as his parent was heartlessly disposed of. This kid was unbelievable. You had to admire her sheer cheek, even if she was mad or dangerous, or possibly a combination of both! His lips quivered.

'It was probably the drink.' This, if recent comments had been true, was the direction his son was driving him in—so long as the vintage was good, of course. Nothing but the best for Sir Stuart Arden.

He felt the swift exhalation of relief that made the child's slight frame shudder and immediately regretted this frivolous response as the blue eyes smiled approvingly up at him. He wanted to groan; the last thing he wanted to do was encourage this lunatic child. As far as she was concerned he'd become some sort of co-conspirator. Like an idiot he'd let the obvious opportunity to deny absolutely all knowledge of her to pass him by. Well, he'd soon rectify that! He had plans. He thought it unlikely that Sabrina had been pining away for him, despite her assurances, and there had been a dearth of single female company on the property his grandmother had left him in the Australian outback.

'Do you think it's responsible to allow a child like this to wander around the city at this time of night?' The woman's lips pursed in distaste as she looked him up and down. The man's expression showed no less disgust, but more caution.

He was also keeping a safe distance from the dangerous-looking character.

'No, I don't,' Benedict replied honestly. He could readily share this woman's sense of outrage. His eyes narrowed in anger as he thought of the irresponsible parents who robbed children like this one of their innocence by letting them roam the streets alone.

'Y-yes, well…' she stammered, thrown off her stride as much by the glint of anger in his dark eyes as his unexpected agreement.

'They tried to make me go with them, Steven.' The child had a very clear and penetrating voice. The male half of the couple looked embarrassed and alarmed as several people on the pavement, which seethed with a cross-section of humanity, glanced in their direction. 'Mum says I shouldn't talk to strangers!'

'We only wanted to take her to the police station.'

'Be my guest.' He felt dawning sympathy for this pair of Samaritans. He wanted nothing more than to hand the responsibility for this disreputable child back to someone who was obviously more qualified, not to mention more eager than himself. The joke had gone on long enough. As he took a step towards them the man backed hastily away.

'Well, all's well that ends well,' he said, taking his more reluctant wife's arm firmly. 'Goodnight.' The woman continued to cast suspicious glances over her shoulder as she was led away. Benedict watched their departure with dawning dismay.

'I thought they'd *never* go.' The skinny child abruptly released the hand she'd been holding. 'You were very useful.' She nodded towards him.

Benedict sighed; a conscience was a very uncomfortable thing to have sometimes. 'They were only trying to help. That's pretty commendable.'

'I don't need help.'

'The police station seems a good idea to me.' No matter how streetwise this kid seemed, he couldn't leave her to her own devices in an area that was crawling with undesirable persons. The child's next words made it obvious she considered him one of those undesirables.

'The police would have believed *them*.' She nodded in the direction where the couple had been swallowed up by the assorted bodies that thronged the pavement. '*You* don't look like the sort of person the police would believe at all. I picked you because you look scruffy and mean,' she told him frankly. 'I'd say you were trying to kidnap me and I'd scream very loudly. They'd believe me; that man thought you were going to hit him,' she ended triumphantly.

The kid's logic was flawless and her self-possession was staggering. A glance at his reflection in the plate-glass window told him she was right.

Recoil in horror had about summed up his mother's reaction to her younger son's appearance. His father had been less restrained. 'My God, he's gone native' and 'Get that bloody hair cut!' had been a selection of the more moderate pieces of advice he had offered. His teenage sister's response had been less predictable.

'You'll be mobbed by women who want to see if you're sensitive and misunderstood under the dark, dangerous exterior. Sexily sinister,' she'd said, quite pleased with her alliteration.

He'd found such perception in one of such tender years worrying; accustomed to female attention, he had already been aware of a subtle difference in that attention since he'd got back home—women were strange creatures. And talking about precocious—he had a more immediate problem than his hairstyle to worry about.

'If you don't want to go to the police station…' Maybe

this kid was already well known there, he surmised. He felt a stab of fury at the sheer injustice that any child's future could be so depressingly predictable. 'How about home?' He doubted home meant the same thing to this child as it did to him.

She still kept her distance, but his comment seemed to make her pause. 'The taxi driver said I didn't have enough money to go all the way home. I'll walk the rest of the way. I wanted to be back before…' The shrug was pure bravado. 'I'll be all right.' She bit her lip.

Despite the stoical exterior she couldn't keep the small tremor from her voice. It occurred to him that maybe she wasn't half as blasé as she pretended to be. The poor kid was probably scared stiff.

'I'll pay for your taxi.'

'You?' The young lips curled with scorn.

'You don't think I'm good for it?'

'I'm not about to get into a car with a stranger.'

'I'm pleased to hear it. I'm not going in your direction.' Walking through a minefield had to be easier than this!

'Why do you want to help me?'

Good question, Ben. This child certainly had an unnerving ability to cut to the heart of the matter. 'Such cynicism in one so young.' He suddenly remembered he was talking to a child. 'Cynicism is…' he began kindly.

'I know what cynicism is; I'm a kid, not an idiot.'

And that puts me in my place nicely, he thought, stifling an urge to smile in response to the youngster's scornful interruption. 'And I'm your guardian angel, so take my offer or leave it.' He made it sound as though he didn't give a damn.

'I think you're mad, but I do have a blister.' She looked down at her feet. 'New trainers,' she added, scuffing her toe on the ground.

*   *   *

'Follow that cab!'

The driver was quite happy to oblige once Benedict had paid up front. He'd be prepared to pay a lot more just to have the opportunity of telling that scrap's parents what he thought of them! Something about those eyes had made his protective instincts kick in with a vengeance.

The building the black cab drew up in front of was not in the sort of neighbourhood he'd expected. Rows of Edwardian villas lined the roads, and there was an air of quiet affluence. He watched as the kid walked up the driveway of a house as he got out of the cab.

She didn't see him until she had the key in the lock of the ground-floor flat. 'What are you doing here?'

'I'd like a word with your father.' Actually he'd quite like to throttle the irresponsible idiot.

'I don't have a father.' Her whole stance said, Want to make something of it?

'Well, your mother, then.'

'She's out. She won't be back until very late.' The door opened a crack and, slippery as an eel, she disappeared inside, closing the door behind her. 'Her boyfriend's going to propose to her tonight!' The last words were muffled as the door swung closed.

Images of a heartless, selfish woman so involved in her own pleasure that she neglected her child made his chest swell with righteous indignation. He'd heard definite tears in that tough little voice as the door had closed. Without actually thinking past his need to tell this woman exactly what he thought of her, he leant hard against the doorbell.

The baby-sitter had begun to scream again at the mention of the police.

'Police? Is that really necessary, Rachel?'

Rachel French rounded on her escort, her grey eyes smouldering with anger. 'Necessary! It's eleven-thirty at night, Nigel, and my ten-year-old daughter is not only not in bed, she is not in the flat, or the building. She could be anywhere!'

Actually, considering the discussion they'd had earlier in the day, Rachel had a pretty shrewd suspicion where her errant child was heading. This knowledge only increased the wholesale panic that threatened to reduce her to a gibbering wreck. Fear lodged like a physical presence in her chest; she could smell it and taste it. She glanced at the baby-sitter who had collapsed onto the sofa. She couldn't lose it now; one incoherent wreck was enough! Her fingernails gouged small half moons in the soft skin of her palms, but her expression stayed composed.

'It w-wasn't my fault!'

'I didn't say it was. Charlie is very…resourceful. Did you say something, Nigel?' she enquired icily as a disparaging sound emerged from his throat.

'Resourceful is one word for her; I could think of others…' He'd been goaded by the frustrating events of an evening which he had planned so meticulously into forgetting his usual tactful reticence.

'At another time I'd be only too delighted to hear your opinion…'

'Rachel, darling, I'm—'

'In the way,' she supplied, her urgency making her brutal as she shrugged off the unwanted protection of the arm he had draped across her shoulders. 'Susan, what time was it when you last actually saw Charlie? Not just heard the music in her bedroom, actually *saw* her. I know you're upset, but it's very important.' She stifled her natural impulse to wring the information out of the girl and forced herself to sound calm and reasonable. It took every ounce of her will-power. 'We need to know how long ago she left.'

'I...I'm not sure,' the girl sniffed. 'I was revising...the finals are next week.'

Rachel bit back the scathing retort that hovered on the tip of her tongue. To say her interest in this young woman's academic future was tepid would have been an exaggeration.

'You were being paid to look after the child, not study.' Nigel's accurate but ill-timed observation reduced the young woman to incoherent sobs once more.

'Nigel,' Rachel snapped, 'will you be quiet?' The loud and continuous sound of the doorbell interrupted her. 'Charlie!' she breathed, hope surging through her body.

'Will you stop that and go away?' The door opened a crack. 'I didn't want Susan to know I've been—'

'Charlie!'

'Mum!' The child released her hold on the door and Benedict took the opportunity to push it open. The source of the first cry stood at the other end of the hallway. A slim-fitting lavender-coloured floor-length gown was gathered in one hand, a mobile phone in the other. She let go of both; one slithered around her shapely calves and the other hit the big, distinguished-looking man with the silver-grey hair directly on the nose.

'I'll kill you, you little wretch,' the low, intriguingly husky voice that evoked a response like fingers gently moving up his spine announced lovingly.

Benedict didn't think this was likely, unless you could hug a person to death. The woman had dropped onto her knees and the child had walked straight into her arms.

'Are you all right? How *could* you?' Rachel was torn by equally strong desires to berate and kiss her daughter. 'Hush, it's all right now,' she murmured as the slender frame was shaken by silent sobs.

Rachel noticed the man standing behind her daughter for

the first time. How sad—the lights were on but there was
definitely nobody home! It instantly struck her as tragic that
someone so sinfully beautiful was lacking the intelligence to
lighten those heavy-lidded, almost black eyes. She pressed
her daughter's damp face into her bosom and looked briefly
into the blank face. Jaw slack, eyes glazed and vacant, he
stared back dully. Latin extract, she decided; there was nothing Anglo Saxon about his olive-toned skin and glossy black
hair.

'Who's this, Charlie?'

'That's…Steven. He fetched me home. I thought I'd get
back before you were home, Mum. How did you know…?'

'Susan rang us, of course.'

'Susan doesn't usually look in after John arrives. Just my
luck!'

'*John?*' Rachel turned her attention to the baby-sitter who
hovered nervously in the background.

'My boyfriend. He sometimes comes to keep me company.
He had to go home early tonight.' Her tear-stained young
face turned an unattractive shade of red as she studiously
avoided Rachel's eyes.

'How fortunate for us he had a prior engagement.' Rachel
pushed the wing of soft brown hair that had escaped her
smooth chignon from her face and the sparkle of anger faded
from her eyes. She could afford to be magnanimous now she
had her daughter back. Her fingers slid down Charlie's silky,
jaw-length blonde hair and she felt weak with relief. Things
could have been so different.

Her eyes returned to the magnificent hunk in the doorway.
A very unlikely Samaritan, she thought, gratitude misting her
eyes.

Benedict hoped the groan was only inside the confines of
his skull—*incredible* eyes! Pale skin that had an almost trans-
lucent quality and slightly slanted almond-shaped eyes that

made the onlooker overlook the fact that her features weren't strictly symmetrical.

'I'm sorry, Miss French; it's just John and I don't get to see one another much. We've both got part-time jobs to supplement our grants and—'

Rachel's weary voice cut through the young woman's babble. 'I've no objections to you having your boyfriend's company, Susan. I just don't like you neglecting Charlie. It's been a long night. Perhaps you should be going home.'

'Right…sure, I'll get my things.'

She turned her attention back to her daughter, noting the sure signs of exhaustion in the delicate young face. 'Well, young lady, was it worth it?' The post-mortem and the chastisement would come later.

'You know where I went?'

'It didn't take a genius, love.' The argument they'd had over her standing with hordes of equally youthful, adoring fans in front of a theatre in the hope of catching a glimpse of her favourite boy band as they arrived at an awards ceremony had dragged on for two days. Charlie had capitulated rather too easily, which ought to have set the alarm bells ringing.

'Actually there was such a crowd, I couldn't see a thing,' Charlotte confessed. 'The taxi driver overcharged me and there were these nosy people…'

'Quite a little adventure,' Rachel murmured with great restraint. She knew it didn't do any good to dwell on what might have happened, but it was hard to control her wayward imagination.

'Is that all you're going to say?' Nigel asked incredulously.

Mother and daughter turned with identical frowns to look up at him. Although there was little physical similarity, at moments like this their relationship was very apparent. Rachel straightened up gracefully, her arms around her daughter's shoulders, the two of them unconsciously presenting a united front.

'At this precise moment, yes,' she said quietly.

'The child needs punishing; she needs to know what she did was wrong.'

'It's none of your business!' Charlie flared, pulling out of her mother's arms.

Rachel sighed. 'That's no way to speak to Nigel. He was very worried about you.'

'No, he wasn't! He doesn't even like me.'

Rachel winced as her daughter slammed the sitting-room door behind her. 'Sorry about that, Nigel.' She noted with dismay the pinched look around his nostrils.

Even though she knew Nigel's ill-judged comments stemmed from the best possible intentions, Rachel couldn't help but sympathise with her daughter's viewpoint. It had been just the two of them for so long, she couldn't help but resent his well-meaning efforts to share the burden of responsibility herself at times. Do I want to share the responsibility? a tiresome voice in her head piped up.

'Are you?' He ran a hand through his well-ordered hair and sighed. 'I'm sorry, Rachel,' he said stiffly. 'It's just tonight was meant to be special...'

'Well, we're not likely to forget it.' Her impish grin faded as there was no glimmer of answering humour in his handsome face. 'Perhaps we should just forget tonight ever happened.'

'Are you trying to tell me you *don't* want to marry me?' Incredulity filled his voice.

'Of course I'm not.' *Am I?* The thought filled her with guilt as she looked at the hurt expression on Nigel's face.

Her intention to kiss him, Rachel moved forward. She'd kicked off her high-heeled shoes earlier and the silky fabric of her long gown caught a loose nail in the skirting-board.

'Damn,' she muttered as the fabric snagged. 'Oh, thank you.' A large, capable-looking hand had freed the hem with surprising delicacy. Irrelevantly she noticed that despite his dishevelled appearance the shapely hands seemed very well cared for. As the young man straightened up his dark eyes looked directly into her face; the smile on her lips frayed ever so slightly around the edges.

She mentally binned her earlier label of simple but kind. There had been nothing simple or even particularly kind in the dark glance. Her stomach muscles quivered and she waited a little breathlessly for the sensation to stop. She'd never been this close to so much sheer *maleness* in her life. The distant noise in her ears sounded very similar to warning bells.

She was still grateful but her gratitude was now tempered with a degree of caution. There had been intelligence in those midnight-dark eyes and a confidence bordering on arrogance, a complacency common to all attractive male animals who knew they were the cream of the crop. It wasn't a confidence she associated with someone who worried about where his next meal was coming from.

Come to think of it, he didn't look undernourished—far from it. She felt an unexpected wave of heat under her skin as she assimilated his lean, muscular build and broad, powerful shoulders. It didn't matter what clothes he was wearing—he'd stand out in a crowd. Stand out in crowd nothing—the crowd would part to let him pass! He had an indefinable aura of someone who'd never been jostled in his life.

'I don't know how to thank you.' Angry that she could be distracted by anything as inconsequential as a well-developed thigh, she thought her voice came out crisply prim. *For heaven's sake, Rachel, this man has saved Charlie from God knows what and you're sounding snooty because he stands out in a crowd? You can't hold the fact that he oozes sexual magnetism against the man.*

What could she do to thank him? It was beneath him to even think it, but Benedict couldn't stop mentally forming the obvious trite response. At least he could think again, even if the thoughts were too crass to share! He'd experienced lust at first sight before, but never anything quite so mind-numbing as those first few moments when he'd set eyes on this woman—Rachel. He liked the name, he liked—

'For your trouble…'

Benedict stared at the notes in the boyfriend's outstretched hand and his narrowed eyes moved slowly to the older man's face. Forty if he was a day, he thought in surprise. What did she see in him? Apart from the air of affluence, he thought cynically.

'I don't want your money.' He didn't bother to disguise his contempt.

Rachel elbowed Nigel in the ribs and glared at him as she brushed past. 'Please don't be offended,' she said urgently. 'Nigel only meant—'

'Pay off the loser—he lowers the tone of the neighbour-hood?'

'Now look here…' She wasn't surprised Nigel didn't sound his usual confident self. That thin-lipped smile and dark stare would dent anyone's assurance. Rachel doubted he was accustomed to being regarded with such dismissive contempt.

'Nigel!' she remonstrated in a tone betraying more exasperation than sympathy. He was acting as if this were his house, his daughter, his debt to repay. Couldn't he see he'd trampled on the man's pride? Her tender heart was wrung with empathy. 'Perhaps it would be better if we said good-night now. Charlie—'

'Are you asking me to go? Fine…'

'Don't be silly, Nigel.' It was unfortunate he sounded like a sulky schoolboy.

'You're very considerate of *his* feelings.' This accusation took her breath away. 'What about me?' The childish whine was back. 'One of the things I like about you is your unemotional, level-headed attitude, Rachel, but just occasionally it would be nice to get a response that's not… Forget it!' he said, compressing his lips and throwing one last glance in the stranger's direction.

'I'll ring in the morning, Rachel, and don't forget we're dining with the Wilsons on Tuesday. Wear something a little less…' his eyes dwelt critically on the loose, soft, low cowl neckline of her dress '…revealing. You know how conservative Margaret is.'

The apology died dramatically on her lips as Nigel left. Usually she could ignore his comments about her clothes. They were normally couched in such subtle jocular terms that it wasn't possible to take offence, but this time it wasn't possible to disregard the criticism.

With a frown she peered downwards. The shoestring straps had made it impossible to wear a bra beneath the dress, but it wasn't as if she was displaying a vast expanse of cleavage—she didn't *have* a vast expanse of cleavage to display! Not that she was exactly flat-chested. She plucked at the folds of fabric and squinted down at the shadowy outline of her firm breasts.

'Oh, damn and blast it to hell!' she said defiantly, letting the fabric fall back into place. Trying to please Charlie, trying to please Nigel, she was tired of walking a damned tightrope. She was also pretty tired of feeling constantly guilty.

The faint indentation between her arched eyebrows deepened and her head fell back, revealing the graceful curve of her lovely throat. For a split second Benedict wondered what she'd do if he kissed her on that fascinating spot where the

pulse visibly beat against her collarbone. Scream bloody murder, you fool, he told himself sternly, putting a lid quick
smart on this foolish fantasy.

'Was that my fault?'

Her eyes flickered upwards and he could see she'd forgotten he was there. A flood of self-conscious colour washed
over her pale skin. She glanced nervously down to check that
the gown was covering what it ought and Benedict's lips
twitched.

'No, of course not. I really am very grateful, you know,
and I'd like to say thank you, without...'

'Bruising my feelings?' he suggested. His words brought
a rueful smile to her lips and a twinkle to her eyes.

'How can...?'

'I missed my dinner bringing...Charlie home. A sandwich...?' He accompanied his words with a smile that had
been melting female hearts since he was five years old.

Invite a man that looked like this into her home? Cautious
instincts instilled from an early age fought a brief battle
against her deep sense of maternal gratitude.

She gave an almost imperceptible nod. 'Follow me.'

He'd already proved himself trustworthy when he'd
brought Charlie home. So he looked dangerous with his long
hair and unshaven face, not to mention those sexy dark eyes,
but all that was just superficial and she'd told Charlie often
enough not to judge by appearances... All the same she
couldn't dismiss the flutter of uncertainty in the pit of her
belly. It did seem a lot like inviting the wolf into your house
when you ought to be boarding up the door.

Charlie appeared as they entered the sitting room and
Rachel's heart twisted as she saw how tired her daughter
looked.

'Has he gone—?' She broke off when she saw the tall
figure behind her mother. 'What are you doing here?' She
sounded more curious than critical.

'Mr.… Steve is hungry.'

'So am I.'

'Bath and bed in that order.' To Ben's surprise, Charlie shrugged, grinned and obeyed the instruction. 'Have a seat,' Rachel then invited.

He did, and looked around with undisguised curiosity. 'Nice place.' If it was true that a room reflected the personality of the owner, Miss Rachel French's lovely exterior hid an uncluttered, unpretentious but warm interior. It was a lot easier to live with than the seventies retro look the designer he'd let loose on his own place had left him. He spread his long legs in front of him and gave a satisfied sigh. It was too late to go to Sabrina's now anyhow.

'Do you…do you have a place?' She removed her eyes self-consciously from the tears in his worn jeans. Her vivid imagination had conjured up some sordid squat.

He looked into her concerned grey eyes; she looked almost embarrassed. Obviously she thought he was comparing her good fortune to his lack of it.

'I have a place.' She looked relieved and he felt a bit of a rat, but not enough of a rat to come clean. 'Not as nice as this,' he said sincerely. If she knew his address she wouldn't believe his sincerity.

'I didn't meant to pry; it's just there's a lot of homelessness…'

'Are you a do-gooder, Rachel?'

She was instantly conscious of the casual way he used her name. He had a nice voice—deep and easy on the ears. Well, a bit more than easy on the ears, really, she admitted ruefully. It probably came in very useful in the seduction stakes.

'You make it sound like an insult. Some people do genuinely care, you know,' she said earnestly. 'I'm know I've been fortunate and I also know that pity isn't a very constructive emotion.'

'But it's a very natural one,' he said. Somewhere along the line the roles had got reversed. Wasn't she supposed to be putting him at ease?

'It's a bit late to be talking about social inequalities,' she said lightly. 'I'll make you that sandwich.' Suddenly she felt the need to escape those velvety brown eyes.

'Can I help?'

Rachel was alarmed that he'd followed her into the small galley kitchen. His presence made the small space seem even more confining. Whatever his domestic circumstances, there was nothing wrong with his personal hygiene; if there had been she'd have known it in the confines of the tiny room. He didn't ladle on the masculine fragrance with a heavy hand like Nigel, thank goodness! He smelt so male, she thought, breathing in appreciatively. Abruptly her spine stiffened. What am I doing? she thought in confusion.

'No, it's fine. Will cheese do? I don't have much; tomorrow's shopping day.' As if he was interested! She knew she was babbling and couldn't stop.

The chances were he was well accustomed to the effect he had on women—he probably traded on it. He knew his way around the female psyche all right, and probably the female anatomy too! She suddenly imagined the long, sensitive fingers that lay lightly on her work surface touching pale skin, and she shivered.

'Cheese will be fine. Charlie tells me you're getting married.' Elbows bent behind him, he leant back on the countertop.

Rachel bent down to retrieve the knife she'd dropped, the action hiding her flushed cheeks. Just how much had her daughter confided to this stranger? she wondered in alarm. Her alarm was given an extra edge because she realised that the skin she'd been visualising his hands touching was her own! Lack of food was obviously affecting her brain! She pushed a slice of cheese into her mouth and hoped this would give her flagging blood sugar a boost.

'Children don't miss much,' he said with the comforting certainty of someone who knew about these things. Actually he didn't know much about children; his sister would be insulted to be included in that category and his niece was a baby of seventeen months whom he'd not seen above twice in her young lifetime. 'And I couldn't help but overhear...'

'Charlie doesn't miss much.' Rachel dropped the knife in the sink and pulled a clean one from the drawer. 'She's very bright—with an IQ that makes me feel inadequate sometimes. It's easy to forget how young she is on occasion.' She had begun to wonder whether it had been a good move coming to the city to be close to the school that specialised in 'gifted children'; Charlie didn't seem to be settling in at all.

'And are you?' Getting married, that is?' he added.

'I don't know.' Now why the hell did I tell him that? she wondered. Perhaps it was just a relief to speak to someone who didn't have a vested interest.

'It must be hard bringing up a child alone,' he mused casually. 'I suppose it would be a relief to find someone to share the responsibility with, especially if he's loaded...'

'I'm not looking for a father for Charlie. Or a meal ticket.' She felt her defensive hackles rising. Was he trying to get a rise, she wondered suspiciously, or was he just plain rude?

'Just as well—the father bit, I mean.' She gasped audibly and he smiled apologetically into her face over which a definite chill was settling. 'The cosy rapport was noticeable by its absence. She seems to hate his guts.'

Rachel found herself responding with a rueful smile even though she felt vaguely uneasy at the intimacy developing in this conversation with a total stranger.

'Charlie has very definite views,' she admitted. 'But, as much as I love my daughter, I don't let her vet the men I see.' *'Men'* made her social life sound a lot more interesting than it was. Over the past ten years how many had there been? No calculator required, she thought wryly. 'Mayonnaise?'

'Yes, please.'

'Help yourself,' she said, sliding the plate in his direction.

'Thanks.' Benedict pulled out one of the two high stools that were pushed underneath the counter. 'Aren't you eating?' Two stools, he noticed, not three; boyfriend didn't stay over too often, then. He felt a surge of satisfaction.

Rachel thought of the meal she'd never got to eat. 'I lost my appetite somewhere between losing my child and fighting with my fiancée.'

She glanced down at her finger and realised she'd never actually picked up the ring. She'd never actually said yes. She didn't believe in fate, but it did seem as if someone was trying to tell her something. Perhaps there was enough of the romantic left in her to wish she could marry someone she genuinely didn't want to live without. Someone whose touch she craved. A man with whom she could share her deepest dreams and fears—who would make her feel complete.

'Do you do that much?'

For a horrified split second she thought she'd spoken out loud. It took her another couple of confusion-filled seconds to realise he wasn't referring to her fantasising and then make the connection with her earlier comment.

'I don't make a habit of losing Charlie.' What a night; it's no wonder my concentration is shot to hell, she thought.

'I meant fighting with your boyfriend—though he's hardly a boy, is he?' He took another healthy bite of the sandwich and watched the angry colour mount her smooth cheeks. He'd touched a nerve.

'Nigel is forty-two,' she snapped back, her fingers drum-

ming against the work surface. 'I've not the faintest idea why
I'm justifying myself to you!' she muttered half to herself.

'Don't worry…'

'I wasn't!'

'You probably feel uncomfortable about the age gap.'

'Age gap!' she yelped. This man was stretching her maternal gratitude to its limit. 'I'm thirty.'

'Really? You don't look it.' Time might blur the edges of
her beauty in the distant future, but with a bone structure like
that the ageing process would be graceful.

The dark, direct stare was deeply disturbing. 'Am I supposed to be flattered?' she asked sharply to hide the fact that
this unkempt man was making her feel flustered and more
self-conscious than she could recall feeling in years!

'I can do better than that…'

'I'm sure you can.'

'But I wouldn't presume.'

Her brows drew together in a straight line as she looked
at him. 'I find that difficult to believe.' He had the look of a
man who'd do a lot of presuming.

'Has he ever been married?'

'As a matter of fact, no. And he's *not* gay!'

'I'm sure you did the right thing asking.'

'I didn't ask! Nigel is a cautious man, and he's seen lots
of his friends' marriages break up.' She didn't add that Nigel
had always seemed more appalled by the financial havoc this
wrought when he'd mentioned the marital failures of his
peers. 'There's nothing wrong with caution.' She winced at
the defensive note in her voice. There wasn't a single reason
why she needed to justify herself to this man.

'Not a thing. Not unless it makes you deaf to gut instinct.'

'Nigel isn't too big on gut instinct,' she said drily. She bit
her lip, immediately feeling disloyal for voicing this opinion.

'And you?'

'Pardon?' The icy note in her voice didn't alert him to the fact that he was being unacceptably personal. Wasn't that just typical? Just when you needed them, the tried and tested remedies let you down…

'I suppose there are times when a lady like you just can't afford to listen to her gut instincts,' he reflected slowly. She searched his face suspiciously; she was certain, despite the gravity of his expression, she was being mocked. 'I mean, you couldn't just date any guy who wandered in off the street.' This time there was no mistaking his reference. 'Do you have a list? Suitable professions, salary, that sort of thing?'

'If you want to say I'm a snob…'

'I'm not really sure what you are,' he confessed. 'I'm feeling my way.'

'I don't want to be *felt*!'

'That explains Nigel's frustrated expression.'

'If you've finished eating…?' she said pointedly. She could see from his expression she was wasting her breath. Her haughtiness was passing right over his dark head.

'Has it always been just the two of you?'

'Are you always this curious about strangers?'

'Charlie made me feel like one of the family.' The flash of laughter in his eyes was reflected by the lopsided smile that tugged at one corner of his mouth. He didn't let her into the private joke.

'Really?' Her arched eyebrows shot up. 'That's not something she makes a habit of.'

'It's like that sometimes, don't you find? You meet someone and it feels as if you've known them for ever. You just click.'

His voice had a tactile quality when he lowered it to that soft, intimate level; it was almost as if he'd touched her—stroked her. She pushed aside this disturbing notion briskly, because the idea of being touched by this man was *extremely* disturbing!

'I try not to make snap decisions.' Panic was developing into an uncomfortable constriction in her throat. 'I'm sure you do a lot more…clicking than me,' she said tartly.

It occurred to her belatedly that it might be a mistake to swap sexual innuendo with someone she wanted to keep at a safe distance. She didn't want to give the wrong impression.

A laugh was wrenched from his throat. 'That sounded a lot like a snap judgement to me.'

'I didn't mean…' she began, horrified. She stopped; that was *exactly* what she'd meant. He had the look of a man who put his charismatic personality to good use with the opposite sex. A sensible woman naturally distrusted a man with such raw, in-your-face sexuality.

'Many a sexual athlete lurks behind horn-rimmed specs and a geeky exterior,' he warned, amusement in his face. 'So is it my social standing or physical appearance which places me in the no-go zone?'

He'd dropped the veiled pretence that this conversation was impersonal. Usually someone who welcomed straight speaking, she felt light-headed with an adrenalin rush that made her want to lock herself safely behind a closed door.

'I don't enjoy this sort of conversation.'

'No, I don't recall having a conversation precisely like this one before.'

'Mum, I'm ready.'

Rachel turned, an expression of false vivacity on her face. For once Charlie's timing was immaculate.

'Right,' she said briskly. Love swelled in her chest as she looked at the small figure. How could you feel cross with a child who looked at you with eyes like Charlie's? she wondered. Especially when those eyes were underlined by dark rings of exhaustion. 'You'd better say thank you to Mr…'

'Steve will do just fine.' A man called Steve wasn't born with a silver spoon firmly pushed down his throat…a man named Steve didn't choke on family obligations. He held out his hand and the sleeve of his jacket fell back to reveal the face of his Rolex. Casually he shook his cuff down. A pair of bright blue eyes followed his action.

'Thank you…Steve?' Small, delicate fingers were laid in his own; the guileless glance was knowing and slightly smug.

'I'll just see Charlie to bed for the *second* time tonight.'

Benedict watched them go, his expression thoughtful. Charlie didn't miss much at all, he mused.

Rachel had half expected her guest would be difficult to get rid of. She'd been rehearsing tactful ways to make him leave in her head. She felt vaguely deflated, and relieved of course—yes, she *was* relieved—to find him standing in the sitting room obviously waiting to go when she re-emerged from Charlie's bedroom.

'Thanks for the sandwich.'

'You didn't tell me where you found Charlie or how…' He hadn't actually told her much at all. She'd done all the revealing.

'You could say she found me,' he said. The statement made him grin for some reason.

'I'll never forget what you did.'

'But you'll forget me?'

She decided to ignore this challenge. Kissing him would be open to misinterpretation so she clasped one of his hands firmly between both of hers.

'I can't tell you how relieved I was to hear that doorbell. I've no doubt you think I'm the world's worst mother.' He was looking at her hands with a peculiar expression so self-consciously she let his hand go.

'For about two seconds, but first impressions can be misleading.'

She misunderstood the significance of his words. 'I expect you get a lot of that. I mean looking the way you do…' She closed her eyes and drew a deep breath. When you've dug a hole, Rachel, stop before it's too deep to climb out of, she told herself. 'There's nothing wrong with the way you look.' She couldn't resist trying to repair the damage.

'And there's nothing wrong with the way you look, no matter what the boyfriend says.' There was amusement rather than offence in his deep warm voice. 'A man who tells you what to wear will likely tell you what to think if you give him the chance. Goodnight, Rachel.'

'I won't let anyone do that.'

'Good girl.' He took her chin in his hand and placed his warm lips over hers. If this chaste salute was meant to keep her wanting more, it worked! The sensual impact left her body so taut and strung out, she might well have responded like some sex-starved idiot if he'd touched her again. He didn't.

'I won't say goodbye. I think we'll meet again very soon.'

Rachel watched him go with a dazed expression. She knew they were just words, but it didn't stop her wondering just what she'd do if he turned up on her doorstep one day.

CHAPTER TWO

'OH, WELL, if she's on loan from Albert at least she'll be easy on the eye.' Benedict's mouth twisted into a dissatisfied grimace. He wasn't happy at the idea of working with a stranger; Maggie's anticipation of his needs bordered on the psychic. 'All the same, Mags, I think it's pretty mean of you to desert me on my first day back.'

'I could stay to hold your hand if your sojourn down under has turned you soft. I don't understand a word of German, but I could look intelligent.' His secretary cast him an unsympathetic glance as she continued to flick through a file. 'Here it is! I don't know how it got there!' she exclaimed, retrieving a sheaf of papers. 'I want to leave everything as it should be for Rachel.'

The reminder of a familiar name brought a reminiscent smile to his lips. 'Would you really do that for me—cancel your holiday?'

'No, I can't wait to kick off the dust of this place,' came the frank rejoinder.

'So nice to see someone who enjoys her work.'

'Huh! Listen to who's talking. I didn't see you hurrying back. Besides—' the fashionable specs were pushed firmly up her retroussé nose '—I'm a legal secretary, not a slave— subtle difference, I know, but…'

Benedict sat down on the edge of his desk. 'PA sounds much more dynamic.'

'I'm not feeling too dynamic right now.'

'You'd *really* prefer to lie on a tropical beach with your husband than stay here?' he said incredulously.

31

'Call me peculiar… Ah, is that you, Rachel? Come along in!' she yelled as she heard a sound in the adjoining room. 'Rachel French, this is Benedict Arden. You probably haven't met; I think he was on walkabout when you started.'

Disbelief froze the polite smile on Rachel's lips. The possibility that she'd met a *doppelgänger* or long-lost identical twin was speedily dismissed—*it was him.*

Rachel wasn't sure how long the shock lasted or when it became full-blown fury. A wave of humiliation fanned the flames of her anger. Her thoughts all ended in a big question mark. Sick joke…? Well, whatever it had been she'd certainly been sucked in.

'Well, I'll leave you two to it. I've already shown Rachel the layout and I've warned her you'll work her to a shadow of her former self, and unlike me Rachel needs all the pounds she's got! So be nice to her.' She glared at her employer, affection thinly concealed beneath the spiky exterior.

'I will, Mags.' This could work out quite beautifully—then again maybe not, he thought, meeting the frozen hostility of his new assistant's eyes.

'He works so hard himself he doesn't realise the rest of us have a social life.'

Maggie hadn't noticed anything, Rachel realised incredulously. She maintained her tight-lipped silence; if she said what she wanted to she just might lose her job! Screaming abuse at the big boss's son had a habit of doing that. *Social life?* The way she'd heard it Benedict Arden, son of Sir Stuart Arden, the head of Chambers, managed a very creditable social life. The sort of social life beloved of society pages. What the grapevine hadn't told her was that he got his kicks from humiliating those on a less elevated social plane.

Whilst her features remained immobile her scorn spilled out into the grey of her clear eyes as they flickered briefly in his direction. That suit probably cost more than two months of her salary. In her head she'd furnished his home with rising damp and peeling paintwork—when she thought of the anxiety and guilt she'd felt when she'd pictured him in those surroundings! Her hands unconsciously balled into two fists. She was only vaguely conscious above the buzzing in her ears of Maggie's departure.

'So you work for Albert.'

'I do.'

'His secretaries always do have excellent…office skills.'

He wasn't looking at her office skills. 'Are you implying I got my job on the merits of my legs?' It was pretty hard to miss the fact that his eyes were on her legs, their slender length disguised by tailored fine black wool trousers.

'Don't get defensive. I don't think you're sleeping with the boss. Everyone knows Albert only ever looks; he's a happily married man.'

'That's a weight off my mind; I wouldn't want you to get the wrong end of the stick.' That was it, after this dignified silence, she promised herself.

'I expect you're wondering…'

'Not at all. Maggie has brought me up to speed. I've already provided translations of all the relevant documents. I don't know if you've had an opportunity to read them yet…?' she said briskly.

The heavy lids had drooped slightly over the alert dark eyes and he levered his long frame from the edge of the desk, straightening his spine. He was one of the few men she'd ever seen who could get away with long hair past their teens and he was further past his teens than she'd imagined. But why should this surprise her when nothing else she'd imagined about him had been accurate?

The newly shorn hair combined with the clean-shaven look revealed a deeply tanned, blemishless skin stretched tightly over a stunning bone structure. Fate and generous genes had arranged all those strong planes and hollows in exactly the right places, giving him a masculine beauty that was in no way soft or pretty.

'We've got to work together…'

'Maybe.' She made it sound as though she had some choice in the matter, which they both knew wasn't the case. 'I'll reserve my judgement on that. You do *look* the part.' The way he looked was the way hungry young executives all over the city dreamed about looking—from his highly polished handmade shoes to his tasteful silk tie. 'But then you're good at that…'

Why did I say that? she groaned inwardly. Anyone would think I want to get the sack! A mental picture of all the bills she needed to pay before the end of the month flashed before her eyes. Be cool, professional, she told herself; he's not worth the energy of losing your temper.

'So possibly we should clear the air?' he continued, as if her acid observation had remained where it ought to—in the privacy of her mind.

Rachel discovered resentfully that an eloquent quirk of one dark brow could make her feel childish and petulant. 'I'm a secretary; I don't require explanations, just instructions.' Pragmatism lost out to the sort of antipathy that made her skin sprout invisible thorns.

'Fine,' he said, some of the lazy tolerance evaporating from his deep voice. 'Instruction one, sit down!' He grasped the back of one pale wooden Italian-designed chair and dragged it across the carpet.

'How dare you speak to me like that?' she gasped.

'*Please,*' he said, with a smile that made her realise the guise she'd last seen him in had only revealed a danger that was already in the man—disguised now by perfect tailoring and a cultured air, but it was there all the same…bone-deep.

'That's better,' he approved as she reluctantly sat down in the chair he'd indicated.

His fingers brushed against the back of her neck as he released his grip on the chair and she tried not to react. She prayed the sensation that crawled over her skin was revulsion—anything else she couldn't cope with!

'Why are you angry?'

She automatically twisted her head to look at him—was he being serious? 'I'm not.'

'Surprise,' he continued as though she hadn't spoken, 'amazement, curiosity... I experienced those when you walked through the door. I can identify with the gobsmacked state—'

'You didn't look very gobsmacked to me.'

'I hide my emotions behind a suave exterior,' he said blandly.

'Are you laughing at me?' This very definite suspicion only increased her deep sense of misuse.

'Why the anger, Miss Rachel French? And don't bother denying it; your eyes have been flashing fire since you first saw me.'

To hell with office politics—she was going to tell him what she thought of him: walking into her life and disappearing just as abruptly, leaving a vague sense of dissatisfaction and restlessness in his wake...

'I *hate* frauds.' To think he'd infiltrated her thoughts enough to make her wonder, at the most unexpected moments, what he was doing. Now it turned out his lifestyle was indeed far removed from her own, but not in the direction she'd imagined! She doubted he wanted rescuing from his pampered, privileged existence.

'I didn't lie precisely.' A quick mental review confirmed this was correct. His ethics weren't so irreproachable that he wouldn't have bent the truth a little if required.

'Steven…?'

'That was Charlie's idea.'

'Why would my daughter make up your name?' she said scornfully.

'It had something to do with claiming me as her long-lost brother. I took to it right off; there's something solid and dependable about a Steven. Admittedly I'm not Steven, but I'm still the man who rescued your daughter—despite her opposition, I might add.'

He had to remind her, didn't he? Rachel chewed her full lower lip distractedly; she couldn't deny the truth of his observation—at least the bit she could follow. The part about brothers made no sense at all.

'You were laughing at me—us. I'm sure you'll dine out for the next month on the story: "what happened when I went slumming". I felt *sorry* for you!' She couldn't have sounded shrill if she'd tried but indignation did make her rather deep, husky voice rise an octave.

'Pity is a very negative emotion,' he reminded her. 'Sorry, photographic memory. Only pity's not all you felt.' The way his dark eyes moved over her face alarmed her almost as much as the soft accusation. To her relief he didn't pursue it. 'I find it curious that you approved of me more when you thought I was one of the great unwashed. An unforgivable sin, I know, to turn out to be neither a paid-up member of the underworld nor a thug with a heart of gold. Has it occurred to you that your craving for a bit of…how can I put this delicately?…rough—' an inarticulate squeak of outrage escaped Rachel's pale lips and he reacted as if she'd uttered soothing words of encouragement '—could be a reaction against the sort of man you date? You're looking for someone outrageous and slightly dangerous.'

'I'm not looking full stop!'

'When I meet a woman she generally knows what I do,

who my family is and can usually hazard a fairly accurate guess at my bank balance...'

Rachel watched as he straddled a chair that was twin to the one she was sat upon. 'My heart bleeds...and you just desperately want someone to love you for the *real* you.' Her voice fairly dripped with sarcasm. 'Which is no doubt why you roam the streets looking like a drug dealer!'

'Do you make a habit of inviting drug dealers into your home?' he enquired with interest.

The fingers that were laid lightly along the back of the chair were very long and elegant, she noticed irrelevantly, and his hands were shapely and strong. His words made her hospitality suddenly seem worryingly reckless.

'I was grateful—' she began defensively, before his urbane, polished tones interrupted her.

'Was?'

'Am—I *am* grateful,' she said from between clenched teeth, sounding anything but. 'I was sorry for you if you must know.' That will teach me to get all sloppy and sentimental, she thought.

'You shouldn't blame yourself, you know. Your body is chemically programmed to find a mate. Hormones aren't too concerned with financial prospects or social standing.'

'Leave my hormones out of this!' she yelled.

'Fine,' he said, with a languid smile that made her want to scream. 'I can work with pity. As ulterior motives go, I think I prefer pity to avarice.'

'Only someone from an obscenely privileged background could say anything so stupid.'

'You have strong opinions about wealth, Rachel?'

'No, just you. I think you're a spoilt...irresponsible—' She broke off, biting down hard on her lower lip to stop further imprudent remarks escaping.

'I sense you were just warming to your theme,' he said,

with a provoking smile. 'Don't let the fact I'm your boss cramp your style.'

'Temporary boss.'

'Thank God, she breathed fervently?' he surmised.

'You're very intuitive.'

'And you're very suspicious, Miss French. Let's get a few things straight. When I met your daughter she was about to be carted off to the police station by a concerned couple. Being a child with limitless resources and a cool head, she decided to claim me as her brother. Apparently I looked mean enough to lack credibility in the eyes of the law *and* to get rid of the nice people—'

Rachel's angry glare turned slowly thoughtful. That *did* sound awfully like something Charlie would do. 'That doesn't explain the way you looked or the fact you made me think…' She shook her head doubtfully. 'Why didn't you just tell me?'

'If you work here you'll know I've just come back from a six-month stint on a cattle ranch in Queensland, and that's the only reason I lacked a certain sartorial elegance. The conclusions about my background were all yours and your charming companion's. How was dinner at the Wilsons'? Did you wear something suitable?'

Rachel stiffened, warm colour seeping under her skin. 'Nigel has a cold; we didn't go,' she ground out.

'I put Charlie in a taxi and followed her with the express intention of giving her delinquent parents a piece of my mind. It took me about ten seconds to realise I'd misread the situation, and less than that to be rendered speechless by your beauty…'

Rachel gritted her teeth and opened her mouth to tell him in no uncertain terms that the only desire such ridiculous statements evoked in her was one to throw up! Suddenly she recalled that vacant expression that had first made her think he was a bit challenged in the intellectual department. He couldn't actually be telling the truth—*could he*? For some reason this absurd notion impaired her ability to think straight.

'Don't say things like that!'

'This is the new me, open and transparent.'

'I'm not beautiful, I'm passably attractive.' Letting him see she was rattled seemed a bad idea. It wasn't too difficult to see how he'd achieved his reputation as a womaniser.

'As they say,' he remarked with an almost offhand shrug, 'it's all in the eye of the beholder, and this beholder,' he said, touching his chest with an open hand, 'sees beauty. I also see a kind heart.'

'A fact you ruthlessly exploited,' she reminded him, trying hard to cling to her sense of outrage.

'I was tempted,' he admitted, 'but I didn't think your charity would extend as far as a bed for the night.'

She gave a gasp of outrage. 'You were right!' Had he *no* shame?

'I feel much better now we've sorted that out,' he confessed with a sigh. 'I was wondering how I was going to bite the bullet and tell you I'm actually quite respectable. I was hoping my disreputable appearance didn't account for all of the attraction, and if you have a thing about leather...'

'*Respectable!*' she choked incredulously. 'Am I supposed to believe you'd ever have remembered me except as an amusing story to relate over dinner?'

'Oh, believe it,' he said, placing his chin in one cupped hand that rested on the chair-back. Suddenly he wasn't laughing at all. Rachel thought the expression in his eyes should have carried a government health warning; happily she was immune to shallow flattery. She could be objective about the ripple of movement in her belly and the rash of gooseflesh that erupted over her hot skin.

'It also makes it all much simpler to ask you out to dinner,' he added cheerfully.

'I'll speak slowly and clearly because I can now see my first impression of you was correct…'

'What was your first impression?'

'Muscularly overdeveloped and intellectually undeveloped—a beautiful imbecile!' she flared in a goaded voice. She realised too late the revealing nature of this confession. 'I have a fiancé,' she hurried on swiftly. 'I don't date other men.'

'I don't see a ring,' he remarked sceptically.

'We have an understanding.'

'He didn't seem to understand you too well the other night. Nice bloke, no doubt, but a bit lacking in the imagination department.'

Of all the arrogant, *impossible*… 'For your information Nigel is *very* imaginative,' she spat back.

'I'm happy for you,' he said solemnly. Confused, Rachel stared back. 'A good sex life *is* important.'

'I didn't mean Nigel is imaginative in bed!' She hated knowing he'd made her flush to the roots of her hair.

'I didn't really think he was,' Benedict responded, nodding sympathetically.

The blood was pounding in her ears. 'Nigel is worth ten of you!'

'That's being a bit severe,' he remonstrated. 'I did detect the very early stages of a paunch, but that's to be expected in men of a certain age. He seemed very well preserved to me. Tell me, are your parents still alive?'

This apparently inexplicable change of subject tipped the balance away from inarticulate fury and towards confusion. 'No, they're not; my aunt Janet brought me up.' Janet French had been there all her life and the recent loss of the lady with the indomitable spirit still hurt badly.

'An all-female household,' he said triumphantly. 'I thought so, and now there's just you and Charlie. You're looking for a father substitute, not a lover, Rachel.'

'Lame-brained psycho-babble.' Her lip curled with genuine scorn. 'This is sexual harassment.'

'This is mutual attraction; we both knew that from the moment we set eyes on each other. If I wasn't a gentleman I'd have done more than kiss you goodnight. Only I wanted to know if the attraction wasn't totally the forbidden fruit thing. I see now it isn't.'

'Your ego is unbelievable!' she gasped. 'I wouldn't have you if you came gift-wrapped.'

'Is that a fetishist thing? he enquired. 'Because I have to tell you I'm not really into that sort of thing.'

'And I'm not into smutty innuendo!'

'If you prefer, we'll keep our personal and professional relationship strictly separate. That's fine by me. A freak set of coincidences is the only reason this conversation is taking place in the work environment. We needed to clear the air.'

And he thought the atmosphere was clear! The only thing that was clear to her was that she ought to keep her dealings with Benedict Arden to a minimum.

'We don't *have* a personal relationship,' she felt impelled to point out.

He was persistent; you had to give him that. If her circumstances had been different she might even have been flattered. Be honest, Rachel, he *is* extraordinarily attractive, she told herself.

If she'd been a carefree, single thirty-year-old, who knew? Temptation might have overcome good sense. But she wasn't. She had a child, responsibilities. She didn't act on impulse—she *couldn't* act on impulse. She'd done that once when she was a naive nineteen-year-old and she knew all about consequences—not that she'd ever regretted the decision to keep her child.

'We will, Rachel,' he said with an unshakeable confidence she found disturbing.

'I'm a single mother.'

'So? I'm not applying for the post of father. Do you only date potential daddy figures, Rachel? Had you decided what you were going to do when Steve knocked on your door?'

The sly question slid neatly under her guard. 'You! Given a choice, I wouldn't have you within a fifty-mile radius of my daughter!' His words had held an edge of mockery that made her long to hit him. What did Benedict Arden, the self-confessed hedonist, know about bringing up a child alone?

'You know something? You're even more shallow and two-dimensional than office gossip has led me to believe. It may shock you but it's not all that unusual for people to consider someone else's feelings other than their own.'

'You want to know what I think?' He remained palpably unmoved by her passionate annihilation of his character.

'Would it make any difference if I said no?'

'I think you'd decided to open the door to Steve, and not just to prove you're not a snob.'

Rachel fixed a scornful expression on her face, though she knew his words would return to haunt her when she was alone later. Steve hadn't existed but this man did and he had all the same bold sexuality. She instinctively knew that Benedict Arden was the more dangerous of the two.

'You're flesh and blood, not a machine; you can't control your feelings. You're a single woman who happens to have a child. You're never going to marry good old Nigel, because when it comes right down to it, despite all his admirable qualities, he bores you rigid.' He nodded with satisfaction as a revealingly guilty expression crept across her features. 'I'm not asking you to do anything that will emotionally scar your daughter, I'm asking you to break bread with me and possibly open a bottle of wine—even two if you're feeling reckless.'

'Do you always do *exactly* what you want?' she asked resentfully.

An odd expression flickered across his face, deepening the lines around his mouth and bringing an inexplicable bleakness to his eyes. 'I'm here, aren't I?' he said cryptically. He pulled at the silk tie neatly knotted around his neck as if the constriction suddenly bothered him. 'Are you free tonight?'

'I don't even like you.' His mercurial temperament made it hard to keep up with his chain of thought.

'Liking will come—I'm a very likeable guy; ask anyone.' His smile held an attractive degree of self-mockery. 'We could settle for mutual attraction for starters. Think about it,' he advised. He glanced at the Rolex on his wrist. 'The meeting with Kurt is in twenty minutes—right?'

Rachel glanced at her own watch and realised with a sense of shock that she'd forgotten completely about the morning's tight schedule.

'Yes,' she said uncertainly.

'When I had dealings with him last year he brought his own translator; you must have made an impression. You're fluent in German?' He stood up and Rachel followed suit. The switch into impersonal mode had been subtle but distinct.

'German, Italian and French,' she confirmed. When the translator hadn't turned up she'd enjoyed the opportunity to utilise her skills.

She ought to have felt happy now they were on ground she felt confident about; she knew she was good at her job. Albert had taken over a portion of Benedict's work, which was mainly corporate law, whilst he'd been out of the country, but this particular client had worked with Benedict before and wanted him to take charge now he was back in harness. She'd had the impression that Albert had been more than happy to relinquish the complicated case.

The client also wanted her, so she'd been transferred too to stand in for Benedict Arden's PA who was taking annual leave. At the time she'd been quite happy to agree. At the time she hadn't known who Benedict Arden was.

'Why aren't you working as a translator?'

'I did when Charlie was a baby—manuscripts mostly.'

'From home?' She nodded. 'That must have been quite an isolating experience.'

His perception startled her. 'When childcare became easier I worked for a law firm near home.'

'Where's home?'

'Shropshire.'

She paused, realising with a sense of shock how adept he was at drawing out information without revealing anything himself. Or maybe not—the memory of that bitter expression in his eyes when he'd implied he would have preferred not to be here flickered into her mind. She wondered whether she'd interpreted his economic words correctly. Was he already disillusioned with his career or did it simply interfere with his taste for the high life?

'That's where the aunt brought you up. And would I be way off the mark if I suggested this aunt wasn't too keen on men?'

'Experience taught me to be cautious, not indoctrination.'

'Charlie's father?'

'My daughter is not a subject I discuss with strangers.'

'You're the subject I'm interested in, but if it makes you feel happier I'll put that on hold.'

It didn't make her feel happier but she welcomed the breathing space. She soon learnt, as she worked in close contact with him throughout the day, that, though she might doubt his dedication, his competence was undeniable. He caught on fast and had a knack of homing in on small but significant details that would take most people hours of arduous toil to discover. There had been none of the languid playboy about the man she'd worked with today, and despite herself she found the seeds of admiration germinating.

'We work well together, don't you think?' She slid the last file into its place and didn't respond even though she was overwhelmingly conscious of his presence. 'Don't tell Mags I said that; she'll think I'm being disloyal. What time shall I pick you up?'

'Pick me up?' She couldn't delay looking up; there was nothing left to fuss about with on her neat desk—where was an errant paper clip when she needed it?

'For dinner.'

'It's a girls' night in with a pizza take-away, and even if it wasn't I don't want to go out with you.'

'Staying in would suit me.'

'I'm trying to be polite.'

'Don't worry about manners; you should have left half an hour ago. This is your own time—be as rude as you like,' he said generously.

'Why are you doing this?'

He seemed to consider the question seriously and she had the fleeting impression that he was almost as puzzled as she was. 'Hormones?'

It wasn't the reply she'd expected and she almost laughed out loud. That might be construed as encouragement, however, so she carefully wiped all trace of amusement from her face.

'Are you just not used to being knocked back? Is that what this is about? Are you one of those men who's more interested in a difficult chase? You lose interest once you've caught your prey?'

'In answer to your first question I've had my fair share of rejection…'

'Sure…' she drawled.

'Your disbelief is very flattering.'

'It wasn't meant to be.' Her aching jaw told her she was grating her teeth again.

'I'd enjoy accepting your surrender as much as you'd enjoy offering it.' The heat coursed through her body so unexpectedly, the breath was trapped in her suddenly tight chest. She was angry with herself for allowing the sudden mental image of 'surrender' to throw her into such total confusion.

'But all that stuff about the chase being more fun is pure junk. As to the endurance of these feelings, who can ever tell how long that will last?'

Surrender! Was she really some sort of pathetic creature who fantasised about surrendering to male dominance?

'Give me strength.' The ring of defiance she heard in her own voice was deeply disturbing. 'Are we talking hours or days here?' she hurried on, wanting to erase the sound of her own lack of conviction.

'Does durability lend respectability to sex? I can guarantee quality, not—'

'Staying power?' she suggested, sliding her arm into the tailored jacket that matched her trousers.

'Here, let me.' She either had to comply or indulge in an undignified scuffle so she willed herself to accept his help passively.

'Can't I tempt you?'

There was the faintest tremor in her fingers as she fumbled over the buttons of her jacket. Benedict remained standing behind her, his hands still at either side of her shoulders. Despite the gap of air that separated them she could almost feel the imprint of his fingers; it was quite a bizarre sensation.

Was this the same sort of phantom pain amputees suffered? What a ridiculous analogy, she told herself, irritated by the whimsical idea; he's not part of my body. *He could be.* Shock at the mental picture that accompanied this maverick thought made her suck in air through her flared nostrils and extinguished the dreamy, unfocused expression in her eyes.

Even as she turned to look at him and firmly shake her head in refusal, the honest answer to his question was ringing in her mind. Not only could he tempt her, *he did.* Even though she knew he was shallow, deceitful, self-indulgent and definitely not for the likes of her, she actually wanted— no, *wanted* didn't begin to cover the craving that had taken over her body. Her treacherous hormones had conspired against her.

As devastating as this sudden self-awareness was, she was determined to keep it in proportion and not be over-whelmed—she *could* cope. Her intellect and emotions weren't involved; she could rise above what amounted to basic lust.

'Tell Charlie that Steve sends his love,' Benedict called after his secretary.

It looked to him as though she was about to break all records for escaping from the building. Or was it just him she was trying to escape? Whistling softly to himself as he pondered this question, he walked back into the inner office.

CHAPTER THREE

'WHERE are you off to?'

Rachel registered that the solid object she had walked into was the chest of her temporary boss. 'S-sorry,' she gasped. So much for the cool, professional distance she'd vowed to keep. After a single morning of detachment she was flinging herself into his arms.

She was seized by a sudden strong and bizarre urge to blurt out her troubles. This is the wrong person and wrong place to indulge in an orgy of shared burdens, Rachel, she told herself firmly as she attempted unsuccessfully to pull clear of the protective circle of his arms. She'd learnt to handle life's crises alone some time ago.

'Is it the appeal of sandwiches in the park? I'd join you myself if I hadn't already promised to lunch with the revered parent.' The quizzical, teasing expression left his face as he took in her pale features. 'What's wrong, what's happened?' he demanded, taking her by the shoulders. The smell of the soft, lightly floral perfume she used tantalised his nostrils. That haunted expression in her wide eyes was doing the strangest things to him.

'I'm sorry but I have to go… Charlie…it's an emergency. I left you a note… I have to go.'

Hands flat against his chest, she tried to push past. God, what must he think of her? Only their second day working together and she was running off. She didn't care what he thought of her; there was such a thing as priorities. He'd have to wait for explanations.

'Hold on, what's wrong?'

'I know it's not convenient, but I—'

'Forget about what's convenient and tell me what's wrong.'

'The headmistress rang; Charlie's at the casualty department…'

She didn't get any further. 'Which hospital?' He nodded when she told him. 'Come on, I'll take you.'

'What…?' On the very few occasions when her meticulous childcare arrangements had not stretched to cover a domestic disaster that required her presence, at best her previous bosses had displayed impatience; at worst they'd been openly critical of her lack of professionalism.

'I thought you were in a hurry.'

'I am.' A sudden smile of pure relief spread across her face. The journey by underground and taxi would have taken her over an hour, with every second an agony of anticipation. 'I can't impose,' she began doubtfully.

'Shut up, Rachel; I'm trying to show you what a nice guy I am. Don't spoil it. A lift should be good for at least a dinner date.' His mouth curved in a lopsided smile and when she looked half suspiciously into them his eyes were kind and concerned, not predatory.

'On me,' she promised fervently.

Seeing the glow of gratitude in her marvellous eyes, Benedict decided he might just have undervalued his services. She didn't object to the light touch of his guiding hand on her shoulder as they left the building.

He racked his brains to recall one instance when he'd actually put himself out to please one of his lady friends and failed, but then the disasters in his previous lady friends' lives had tended to lean in the direction of broken nails or an inability to get a hair appointment, not hospitalised children!

Rachel pulled aside the cubicle curtain to reveal a pathetic sight.

'Oh, *Charlie*!'

'I know I look terrible, but the hair will grow back; they had to shave off the little bits to stitch up the cuts. The blood's from my nose.' She touched the gory front of her once pristine school shirt. 'I'm not cut anywhere and I didn't break anything.'

'Congratulations,' Rachel said drily as she sat down on the edge of the trolley.

'They want to throw me out so I must be fit.'

'And does Mrs Faulkner want to throw you out too?' When Rachel had left the headmistress in the reception area with Benedict the lady had looked almost as stressed as she felt.

'I hope so. It's a crummy school. They all think they're so smart.'

'And you don't?' Charlie's new punk-spiky hair made her look incredibly young.

'That's different,' she said impatiently.

'But *fighting*, Charlie?'

The thin shoulders hunched defensively. 'He was much bigger than me; I wouldn't hit a little kid. And I didn't hurt him; I fell down the steps before I had the chance to,' she admitted honestly.

'Mrs French?' The nurse stepped into the room. 'If she gets any of the symptoms on this card—' Rachel skimmed anxiously over the card which was pushed into her hand '—bring her back. Ten days for the sutures. Your GP will remove them; here's a letter for him. Sorry to rush you but we're busy this afternoon.'

She'd whipped the paper sheet off the trolley which Charlie had just vacated and disappeared before Rachel could mumble her thanks.

The headmistress was deep in conversation with Benedict when they returned to the reception area; she looked almost animated as she listened to what he was saying and a lot more relaxed. For once Rachel had reason to be grateful for his effortless charm; she needed the head mistress as softened up as possible. This was one tête-à-tête she wasn't looking forward to.

'Miss French, perhaps we could have a word?' Her eyes slid to Charlie. *'Alone?'*

'I know you don't get into cars with strangers, Charlie, but with your mother's permission perhaps you'd like to look over mine,' Benedict said.

'What do you drive?'

'A Mercedes.'

'What sort?'

He told her, and her eyes widened in admiration.

'Wow!' She looked hopefully in her mother's direction.

When Rachel returned to Benedict's car a few minutes later her daughter was deep in what appeared to be a technical discussion with Benedict.

'Sorry to keep you waiting,' she said, looking through the open window of the passenger seat.

'I wasn't bored,' Charlie said happily. 'He doesn't know *anything* about this car,' she informed her embarrassed mother.

'I do now,' Benedict said drily.

'I was apologising to Mr Arden, not you, Charlie. We'll get a taxi home of course.'

'Don't be stupid, Rachel.' Before Rachel had an opportunity to complain at this form of address she was distracted.

'Rachel!'

She spun around, startled at the sound of a familiar voice. 'Nigel!' she said, staring at him in blank amazement. 'What are you doing here?'

'I work here, remember? More to the point, what are *you* doing here?' His expression changed as he recognised the small, spiky-headed figure in the front seat of the car. 'Charlie's been in the wars, I see. Why didn't you ring me, darling?'

So that was why the name of the hospital had sounded so familiar. The sound of the endearment made her feel oddly embarrassed.

'It was all such a rush. I got a phone call at work and Mr Arden kindly offered me a lift. How are you feeling? Is the cold better?' How could she admit she hadn't even thought about Nigel? She'd forgotten he even worked in the hospital!

'I'm fine…fine,' he said hurriedly. 'That was kind of Mr Arden. Have me met?' he asked, looking directly at Benedict, a puzzled frown pleating his brow.

Rachel held her breath.

'It's possible,' Benedict admitted calmly. 'Ben Arden's the name.'

'Any relation to Sir Stuart Arden?'

'My father.'

'I can see the resemblance.' Benedict nodded neutrally; he knew he was a genetic throwback to his Italian maternal grandfather and bore no resemblance to his very Anglo-Saxon-looking parent. 'We're in the same golf club,' Nigel explained affably.

Rachel could see the umbrella of social acceptability obviously extended to Sir Stuart's offspring.

'Give me a minute, Rachel, and I'll take you home.' He reached in the breast pocket of his white coat to retrieve his urgently buzzing pager.

'Don't worry yourself; it's on my way,' Benedict assured him.

Rachel met Benedict's benign smile with a look of seething frustration. Now that the immediate panic was over the last thing in the world she wanted was to get in that car with him.

'That's very good of you,' Nigel responded, with a grateful smile. 'I'll ring you tonight, Rachel.'

Whilst she was receiving a peck on the cheek—Nigel wasn't the most tactile person in the world—she was overwhelmingly aware of the brown eyes watching her every move. This awareness probably had something to do with the fact that she turned her head and kissed a somewhat surprised Nigel full on the lips.

He looked bemused but pleased, and Rachel immediately felt guilty for using him. She was going to have to put a stop to this—she should have already. The knowledge weighed on her conscience like a stone.

'Slide into the back, Charlie, and let your mum sit up front.'

Rachel saw that Nigel looked a bit startled when the child immediately did as she was bid. 'Maybe a knock on the head wasn't such a bad thing,' he joked softly to Rachel as she slipped reluctantly into the soft cream leather upholstery beside Benedict. Nigel waved them off cheerfully.

'What did he say to make you look so murderous?' Benedict asked curiously as they pulled away.

'It was nothing,' she said shortly, avoiding his probing eyes. She told herself she was being over-sensitive—Nigel had only been joking. She knew she shouldn't compare Benedict's light touch with her daughter to Nigel's heavy-handed approach, but it was hard not to contrast their very different styles.

'I prefer Steve. *Benedict*.' Charlie screwed up her small nose, her expression speaking volumes.

'My friends call me Ben if that's any help.'

'Ben.' She tried it out experimentally. 'Not bad,' she conceded. 'I thought it was cool when Mum said she was working for you.'

'Mr Arden to you,' Rachel put in sharply. Trust Charlie to

take a shine to him; that was *all* she needed. Where was that well-known disagreeable personality when she needed it?

'Mum was really mad when she found out you'd fooled us,' Charlie piped up from the back. 'I don't think she's forgiven you yet.'

'Is that so?'

'Take a nap, Charlie; you look tired,' Rachel observed hopefully. She knew from experience that short of gagging her child there wasn't much chance of stemming the flow of indiscreet comments.

'I wasn't worried about you, like Mum.'

'You weren't?'

'No. I saw the real expensive watch you were wearing so I knew either you were a good thief or an eccentric rich guy.' With a satisfied smile she settled into her seat.

'You worried about me?' Rachel could hear the slightly smug smile in his deep, expressive voice. Why did this man's voice have the same effect on her as half a bottle of red wine? she wondered resentfully. It did have a marvellous texture; she found herself whimsically likening his warm, rich tones to being wrapped up in a rich, luxurious velvet sheet and pulled herself up short. The less she thought about sheets and Benedict Arden in the same context the better!

'No more than I do any other destitute social outcast,' she observed with a dispassion she was far from feeling.

She'd never admit it was the man more than his condition that had got under her skin, but fantasising about someone she'd never meet again had seemed a fairly harmless thing to do. There was safety in distance and she found herself wishing she had more than a couple of feet to protect her right now.

They continued to travel in silence for several minutes. In the back Charlie fell asleep. When she noticed this Rachel worriedly fished the card the hospital had given her out of her bag and scanned it.

'''Sleepy or difficult to rouse''.' She read the words out loud and glanced anxiously at her sleeping daughter. 'Do you think…?'

'She's just asleep, that's all, Rachel. She's had quite a day.'

Strange how a second opinion made things slip back into perspective. Rachel's smile was strained; she took a deep breath and tried to calm down. She tried really hard not to be a fussy, over-protective mother, but sometimes…

'I expect you think I'm just a neurotic mum.'

'I think you've perfected the mum part, Rachel, but I think you've neglected the woman part.'

His words startled her and made her feel uneasy. 'You're saying I'm not feminine.'

'You're about the most feminine female I've ever met.'

Her stomach went into its now familiar acrobatic contortions as his dark eyes moved warmly over her face and lower… Give me strength—*please*, she prayed without much confidence that anyone was listening. In the wider view her libido probably came pretty low down priority-wise.

'You're just overcompensating for being a single parent. When did you last do something for yourself?'

'What do you mean?'

'I mean something spontaneous, selfish…'

'I'm not a spontaneous sort of person.'

'You must have been once.' She saw his eyes touch the image of her sleeping daughter in his rear-view mirror and her expression grew chilly.

'I don't think that's any of your business.'

'Granted,' he acknowledged easily. He changed tack. 'How do you think Charlie will feel if in eight years' time she realises that you've built your whole life around her needs?'

'I haven't, I don't!' she protested angrily. He knew nothing about her—nothing! She recalled uneasily that Aunt Janet—more tactfully, of course—had insinuated something similar last year.

'It's highly likely she'll feel guilty when she wants to be independent and go her own way. You're not doing her any favours by living your life vicariously through her.'

'I don't!'

'Not yet, but you have definite leanings in that direction.'

'You know nothing about being a parent.'

'Perhaps an impartial critic is what you need.' It occurred to him that the impartial bit was getting less accurate by the minute.

'Charlie will *always* be the most important person in my life,' she breathed passionately.

He nodded slowly as if he understood her passion. His next words took her totally by surprise.

'Have you *got* a life, Rachel?'

'I used to think so until you turned up and with a few words of worldly wisdom showed me the error of my ways.' She shot an acid look at his perfect profile. '*You* telling me *how* to live! If it wasn't so ridiculous it would be laughable. You don't live on the same planet as the rest of us; you're just a pampered—'

'I realise a few distinguished grey hairs and a nice line in pomposity would lend me more credibility on the advice front…'

The dig made her jaw tighten. 'Am I supposed to believe all this interest and concern is totally altruistic?'

He flicked an almost amused look at her heated face as he pulled up in front of her flat. 'I never imagined you were naive enough to think that,' he observed with provocative gravity. 'Why do you get so aggravated when I'm nice to you, Rachel? Are you by any chance afraid of liking me?'

It was so obvious she couldn't understand why she hadn't figured it out for herself. Afraid? She was petrified! He wouldn't intend to destroy her life but then she didn't imagine tornadoes had inherently evil intentions either.

Benedict was the sort of man people loved—she mentally sidestepped the chasm that opened up at her feet. The sort of man who would leave a great gaping hole when he moved on. Already Charlie liked him, and she was an intense little creature who didn't let people close often—but when she did... No, it was totally irresponsible to let a man without staying power into her life. He hadn't even attempted to disguise the fact that his intentions were of the dishonourable kind.

She laughed, achieving a brittle sort of condescension that she was proud of. 'You're so charming...' Hand on the door, she swivelled slightly in her seat to look at him.

There was a movement behind the liquid darkness of his eyes that said even more clearly than the febrile contortions of the erratic muscle beside his mouth that she'd succeeded in aggravating him. She hadn't wanted him to like it, had she? So what was the problem?

'Perhaps you could let me practise it on you.'

Oh, help! What sort of can of worms had she opened now? That would teach her to be smart. Getting out of the car was definitely the right thing to do. If only her legs had been in full working order. If only he weren't looking at her in that wolfish way.

'You could give me a few tips on how to bring my performance up to scratch. It would be a generous gesture.'

'Ben...'

'Progress! She's said my name.' His gesture was too expansive for the confines of the car and his fingertips collided with the luxuriously upholstered roof. 'It wasn't so difficult, was it? Now, about my lessons…'

'You're b-being foolish,' she stammered, unable to tear her hypnotised eyes from his face. 'Charlie…' She wielded her daughter's presence as a last line of defence.

'Is sleeping like a baby.' His right hand was on the angle of her jaw; his thumb moved over her cheek, tracing the sweeping curve of one high cheekbone. Abruptly his expression intensified and grew into something breathlessly intimate—she was certainly pretty breathless, anyhow, and his breathing had noticeably picked up tempo!

'I really want to kiss you, Rachel French. Tell me you've thought about it too.' The muscles in the strong column of his neck worked hard as he swallowed.

Her own throat ached with emotion. 'It's safer to leave it there—in your mind,' she said huskily. A small corner of her brain informed her disapprovingly that she'd just made a confession.

The lethargy that had invaded her body screamed a different message entirely from the one she spoke. He had altogether the most fascinating mouth she'd ever seen. What would it feel like? Her mouth grew dry as she waited in breathless anticipation to have her question answered.

'Safer but frustrating.'

The sexy rasp of his voice made her tremble harder. This had to stop. 'Oh, for heaven's sake!' she snapped as the sexual tension reached breaking point. 'Get it over with.' She closed her eyes and leant forward.

There was a second's startled silence and then, to her amazement and chagrin, she heard the sound of his laughter; it began somewhere in the depths of his chest and emerged deep and uninhibited.

'My God,' he gasped, leaning back in his seat and wiping his eyes. 'You really know how to break a mood, Rachel.

You looked like a sacrificial virgin in one of those cheap B horror movies.' He started to laugh again.

Eyes fully open, she glared at him. 'I'm not a virgin.'

'I'd guessed that,' he confirmed gravely, the laughter now confined to his dark eyes. Eyes that had been smouldering seconds earlier.

To say she felt piqued was an understatement. Ridicule, rejection... He was heartless and insensitive to boot! So her technique had been lacking in a certain amount of finesse. She'd wanted him to...she still did, she acknowledged angrily. Well, if he wouldn't kiss her she'd just have to...

Half kneeling as she leaned towards him, she took his face between her two hands. Breath coming fast and hard, she deliberately covered his mouth with her own. Benedict froze, and as his lips remained passive and unresponsive under her own Rachel realised the enormity of the mistake she'd just made. Lips still pressed to his, her eyes opened.

She met his startled gaze and wanted to die of sheer humiliation. Even as she began to pull back the expression in the dark, hooded eyes changed. Seeing the change was like watching spontaneous combustion.

'Don't!' She felt the harsh command against her lips. Even had she felt the inclination, the strong arms that had moved across her back prevented her from withdrawing.

Eyes still holding hers, the pressure of his lips slowly parted hers. Suddenly a whole mindless, exciting world was within her grasp. Very slowly his tongue traced the silky outline of her lips. When her tongue darted out to meet his tentatively she could see the flash of sultry approval in his eyes. She was close enough to see the gold tips of his extravagantly long lashes and the fine lines around his eyes which would one day become permanent. Permanent and Ben weren't compatible terms.

The silky thrust of his tongue wrenched a deep groan from

her as it penetrated deep within her mouth. His dark features swam out of focus and her eyes closed.

Her arms wrapped themselves around his neck as if it was the most natural thing in the world. For several mindless, frantic moments they explored hungrily with lips, tongues and hands. She could hear the gasps and weak, bleating moans but didn't actually associate them with herself.

Though she'd managed to plaster herself very firmly against his impressive upper torso, it didn't feel nearly close enough to satisfy the fire in her blood. Her fingers pressed deeply into the sculpted outline of his broad back as she squirmed sinuously in his arms.

'Rachel...?'

She lifted her lips from the side of his neck and looked in a dazed fashion into his face.

'I think Charlie's waking up,' he said thickly.

Remembering who she was and where she was was a painful business. Horrified, she looked into the back seat where her daughter was stretching sleepily.

'Are we home?'

'Yes. How are you feeling?' Well, I've really done well on the keep-my-distance campaign, haven't I? she mocked herself inwardly. She couldn't even claim the excuse of moonlight and a romantic location. It was broad daylight and she'd been behaving like... She felt the skin of her neck burn as she remembered exactly how she'd been behaving. And *she'd* started it!

'I feel sore.'

'Where?' Benedict asked.

Charlie stretched and considered the question. 'Everywhere.'

Apprehensively Rachel stole a furtive glance in Benedict's direction. The smug satisfaction she'd half expected was absent; he looked... Distracted was as good a word as any to describe his expression. As she watched he inhaled deeply and ran a hand roughly through his hair. Recalling that she was responsible for the ruffled condition of the short, sleek style brought a fresh wave of mortification.

'Are you all right?'

'I'm falling apart at the seams' probably wasn't the response he was expecting so she smiled politely if distantly. *Now* I'm distant, she thought wryly.

'You must be in a hurry to get back to the office.'

'Anxious to get rid of me, are you?'

'I wouldn't be so rude.'

'The impeccably mannered Miss French,' he drawled slowly. 'I think you'd be quite a lot of things that would surprise both of us—given favourable conditions.'

This thinly veiled reference to her recent wanton behaviour was enough to send her almost tumbling from the car in her anxiety to escape. He was almost as fast as her and much better co-ordinated; by the time she'd opened the rear door to help Charlie out, he had already scooped the uncharacteristically passive child into his arms.

'Lead the way,' he said cheerfully. Charlie giggled as he swung her around.

'You'll make her throw up.' Rachel pursed her lips and refused to enter into the spirit of things.

She didn't like being manipulated and she fumed quietly whilst she did as he requested—at least it had sounded like a request, but she knew an order when she heard one, no matter how sneakily it was dressed up.

She was doing it again—letting him into her home—and this time she knew exactly how dangerous he was! If she'd been the sort of young woman to indulge in misty optimism Rachel might have told herself that nothing had changed, but she had a much more realistic approach to life. She knew that walking away from that short burst of beautiful hormonal insanity back there would require good judgement and careful handling. She was pretty sure she wasn't capable of either just now.

'Make yourself at home, won't you?' she said sweetly as, much to her annoyance, he placed Charlie at one end of the sofa and claimed the other end for himself. For once Charlie seemed prepared to tolerate adult foolishness as he tickled her feet which lay in his lap.

'Sure I'm not intruding?'

'Would it make much difference if I said yes?' What did a few kisses mean to him? A great big nothing—the answer was depressingly obvious.

He strolled into the kitchen a few seconds later and spoilt her efforts to regain her serenity. 'Charlie sent me to say she would like a milkshake, preferably chocolate.'

'I'm not at all sure I should reward her after what she's done.' She continued to clatter around.

'What are you doing?'

'Making a cup of tea.'

'Looks to me like you're just rearranging the cups.'

'I don't recall inviting you into my kitchen. It's too small and you're…you're too…too big,' she ended feebly.

What was she supposed to say? Having you this close is driving me to distraction? All I can think about is the way you tasted, the way you felt…?

'I'm a genetic throwback to my grandfather,' he explained apologetically. 'He was Australian, of Italian extraction—a big man by all accounts. My sister's the same, but Tom, my big brother, never made it past five ten. I think it's the scent that's heightened in an enclosed space.' The words emerged suddenly and his eyes widened with shock as though he was as surprised as she was to hear them.

'What?'

He wasn't looking at her; his eyes were fixed grimly on

his own hands, and that muscle beside his mouth had begun
to throb again. 'Even after you've left a room it lingers, but
in an enclosed space like this—or the car—it drives me crazy.
It's so distinctive—not the pretty flowery stuff but that warm
female smell that comes off your body.' His words emerged
in uneven staccato bursts and his fingers, as they gripped the
stem of a glass he'd idly picked off the draining-board, were
white. Suddenly the stem cracked with a noise like a pistol
shot.

'Sorry.'

'You're bleeding,' she said hoarsely as she watched the
scarlet drops land on the white counter. He was watching the
flow of blood with a peculiar lack of interest. 'Here, put it
under the cold water.' She grabbed his wrist and thrust his
hand under the tap.

'Florence Nightingale.'

'I could hardly watch you bleed to death in my kitchen,'
she said gruffly. His forearm was covered in fine dark hairs;
they felt surprisingly soft under her fingers. Stroking couldn't
be designated as first aid, she told herself firmly, stifling some
very strong urges in that direction.

'It's only a scratch.'

'That's very brave and macho of you, but it looks pretty
deep to me,' she said worriedly. 'I've got a first-aid kit in
the bathroom; don't go away.'

'It's good to be wanted.'

Wanted? If he knew the half of it…! Then again she'd not
been exactly subtle so he probably did. As she rushed
through the living room Charlie was engrossed in her favourite video. She ought to be concentrating on sorting out
the latest disaster in her child's life—*fighting*, for heaven's
sake! Instead what was she doing? Mooning over some beautiful body dangerously attached to a cunning mind.

She'd never be able to pick up her perfume without being

reminded of his words—words that had filled her with a savage exhilaration: he was hurting as much as she was. There was another, less palatable and unflattering explanation—he might just be recycling old and well-tried lines. He'd had so many women it wasn't reasonable to expect originality.

All the same he'd have to be a *very* good actor to fake that raw need in his voice. The downy hair over her body stood on end as she relived those breathless few seconds.

'Sorry if that hurts,' she said a few moments later as she applied pressure to the dressing to stem the flow of blood.

'It takes my mind off the other pain.'

'Which…?' She raised her eyes to his face and immediately wished she hadn't.

'I think you know what pain I'm talking about.'

She did now: his eyes were very eloquent. 'I won't offer you the use of my cold shower; I'm sure you've got a perfectly good one at home.'

'You'd consign me to seventies retro? Black tiles and mirrors on the ceiling? Cruel, cruel woman.'

'If you don't like it…' she began curiously.

'When asked my opinion I made the major error of admitting I didn't give a damn.'

'Why would you do anything so stupid?' She finished securing the light dressing with tape and stood back to observe her handiwork.

'Because I didn't care.'

'What a peculiar attitude.'

'You've done this before,' he said, turning over his bandaged hand.

'You've met Charlie—are you surprised? Though she's never gone in for fighting before.' A worried frown creased her wide, smooth brow.

'I'd listen to her story before you tell her off,' he observed casually.

The unspoken overtones almost jumped out and bit her on the nose. 'Why do you say that?' she asked suspiciously. 'Has she said something to you?' The idea of Charlie confiding in someone who was almost a total stranger— Heavens, I'm jealous! she realised. When did I get so sour and disgustingly twisted?

'Sometimes it's easier to talk to someone who's not part of the...'

She could almost see him mentally back-pedalling.

'Part of the problem?' she finished grimly.

'She's very protective of you.'

'You've got to tell me now, Ben.'

Benedict sighed, looked into her lovely face. which was flushed with emotion and tight with tension, and nodded. 'Granted. It seems they had this lesson at school where everyone gave a potted biography of their father. When it was Charlie's turn, she told everyone her father came from a sperm bank.'

'She *what*?'

'I take it this information didn't come from the horse's mouth?'

'What do you think I am?' she gasped.

'It's what Charlie thinks that's the problem.'

'And *you* know what she thinks?' She didn't even bother to hide her antagonism to the idea.

'Don't kill the messenger, Rachel. Shall I make the tea?' he offered, after looking at her pale, drawn features.

'Why not?' She was redundant in every other way—why shouldn't he take over the domestic tasks too? She knew she was being ungrateful and petulant but for the life of her she couldn't stop it.

'This particular boy started making some nasty insinuations about your...er...sexual preferences and, as I said, Charlie's very protective.'

Rachel closed her eyes and groaned; it got worse. 'She's never asked about her father.' If she had what would I have told her? she thought. How would I have explained about Raoul?

'Didn't he want to be involved…?'

'He's dead,' she said in a flat, emotionless tone.

'I see.'

Rachel lifted her elbows from the counter and straightened up, glancing at Benedict as she did so. What did he see? A tragedy that had separated young lovers? Whatever he thought it couldn't come close to the truth.

Had she let that youthful disillusionment sour her attitude to men? Where she'd imagined she was cautious had she actually been distrustful? Had she encumbered her daughter with her own prejudices and insecurities? Had she taken self-reliance too far? The disquieting questions refused to stop.

'My confidence in my parenting skills has just taken a nosedive.'

'Don't knock what you've done, Rachel. Charlie's an exceptional kid. It must have been hard alone…'

'I wasn't alone,' she put in impatiently. 'The money I inherited from my aunt Janet meant I can live here in relative luxury—not up to your standards possibly, but most people wouldn't complain. When Charlie was small Aunt Janet was always there for us. It was she who made me continue with my education; I had it easy compared to a lot of single mums. I had a safety net…'

'And a sense of proportion?'

'What?' She faltered; he looked disconcertingly bored.

'Don't you think you're going a bit overboard with the unfit parent stuff?' he drawled.

'That's rich coming from you,' she gasped incredulously. 'You've only just finished telling me all the things I'm doing wrong!'

'Rachel, what I know about childcare could be fitted on the back of a postage stamp. Of course I'm going to tell you you should be expanding your social horizons; it's in my best interests. We both know I've got an ulterior motive.'

'You have?' Responding at this point might be construed as encouragement but the words that trembled on the tip of her tongue wouldn't be censored.

'I want to be your lover, Rachel.'

'Just like that?' she choked. She'd steeled herself for something much cleverer and more subtle. The simple brutality of the truth was totally devastating. She knew her colour was fluctuating in tune with the violent changes in body temperature she could feel taking place. 'You're very sure of yourself.' It was more a croak than an indignant sneer, but it was the best she could do.

'The only thing I'm sure of, Rachel, is that we'd be good together—*very* good.' Her seared nervous system reacted as violently to his husky tone as if it had been a caress.

'Nigel…'

'Oh, yes, Nigel,' he mused. 'I think you should tell Nigel it's over, don't you?'

Her mouth opened but no sound emerged. His arrogance was literally breathtaking. 'Why should I do that?' It didn't matter a jot that she'd known since the night he proposed that the days of her comfortable relationship with Nigel were numbered. What right did Benedict have to instruct her?

'I'd prefer exclusive rights…'

'To what—my body?' She sucked in air wrathfully. 'I'm no radical feminist but that's the most outrageous thing anyone has *ever*…'

'You might not be political, but you *are* the most stubbornly independent female I've ever met.'

'You mean I don't hang on your every word.'

'Don't get me wrong; I like independent. I'm all for a girl taking the initiative,' he purred suggestively.

This unsubtle reminder of her earlier lapse made her set her chin stubbornly despite her flaming cheeks. 'One kiss and you take a lot for granted. You get exclusive rights to my body and I get what…? Nigel wants to marry me…' She let her words trail off provocatively. That ought to send him running; the prospect didn't make her feel as happy as it should have.

'I'm not proposing.' He didn't appear as intimidated by the suggestion as she'd expected—he didn't seem fazed at all.

'You *do* surprise me,' she snapped sarcastically. 'Tell me, do women usually do exactly what you tell them? They must do; nothing else could account for your incredible arrogance.'

'I gave up comparing you to the other females of my acquaintance within the first thirty seconds of meeting you. Fortunately I like a challenge. I like you.'

'You do?'

'Don't sound so surprised, Rachel. Of course I like you. If you give it half a chance you might find I'm not totally without redeeming features.'

'I don't have time in my life for—complications.' Or heartbreak, she thought, firming her weakening resolve.

'So you admit I'm a complication.'

'We don't want the same things out of life, Ben.'

His mouth thinned and an unexpected spark of anger smouldered to life in his eyes. 'And when did you become such an expert on what I want out of life?'

She stared at him, perplexed by his obvious annoyance. 'I'm not. I couldn't be, could I? You never tell me anything.' As she warmed to her theme his anger seemed all the more perverse. 'You're very clever at worming personal information out of me, but what do I know about you?' Her expansive gesture sent a copper pan suspended decoratively on the wall clattering noisily to the floor. 'A big fat zero. But if office gossip is anything to go by your life follows a fairly predictable pattern.'

'All you had to do was ask. For you I'm an open book. What *do* they say about me on the office grapevine?'

'Depends on who you're talking to—male or female,' she responded sweetly. She wasn't about to bolster his already inflated ego.

'Ouch!' He winced, with a grin.

'I'm taking Charlie her drink,' she announced, turning her back firmly on him and this disturbingly intimate conversation.

CHAPTER FOUR

'AND then Mum kissed him. They thought I was asleep…'

'Charlie!'

'Oh, hiya, Mum. I let Nigel in. You didn't hear the door-bell. I expect you and Ben were—'

'That's enough, Charlie; go to your room!' Rachel said quietly. The tone in her mother's voice made the animated expression fade from her daughter's face.

'But…'

'*Now!*'

The expression of hurt incomprehension on Nigel's face was making her feel like a bitch—which, looked at from his perspective, she was! He looked like a man whose belief in Santa Claus had been dashed.

She couldn't really lay the blame at Charlie's door, even though she was under no illusions that there had been any-thing artless about those confidences. She ought to have con-fessed her true feelings or lack of them sooner. With the ruthlessness of the very young Charlie had seized on the op-portunity to get rid of someone she disliked irrespective of the hurt she might be inflicting.

'Do you want me to stay?'

Rachel raised her eyes to Benedict who had entered the room in her wake. 'I don't think so,' she said quietly. That would be rubbing salt in the wound.

'My God!' Nigel got to his feet, an expression of incre-dulity contorting his regular features. 'He's the thug with the attitude…the barrister you're working for.' His gaze slid from Benedict's impassive features to Rachel's face, which was coloured by a guilty flush. 'Black leather and role-playing…I didn't know sick games like that turned you on, Rachel.'

The contempt in his voice made her feel grubby and if possible even guiltier. 'It was just a coincidence, Nigel.'

His scornful laugh rang out. 'Please; I may not be one of life's intellectual giants, but give me some credit. I don't believe in coincidences.'

What could she say? Neither had she a few days before. Rachel clasped her hands in distress. She hadn't wanted it to end like this. Why, oh, why had she let things drag on? Why, oh, why had she kissed Ben? A thousand 'whys' rushed through her mind.

'I don't suppose you *didn't want to rush things* with him.' He looked at her with fastidious distaste as he caricatured her tone.

'Ben and I—we're not… I mean, we haven't…' She looked to the tall, silent figure at her side for inspiration.

'Yet. We haven't *yet*, sweetheart,' Benedict said, clarifying the point helpfully.

'Thank you!' she snapped from between clenched teeth. He was probably enjoying this.

'I'm just glad I found out now, before it was too late, what sort of woman you actually are. I was prepared to make allowances for youthful indiscretion.'

Rachel stiffened at this patronising allusion to her daughter. Benedict's arm moved lightly around her waist and she was grateful for the contact. His splayed fingertips moved over the bony prominence of her hip. The slow, sensuous, soothing movement took the edge off her anxiety. It did a lot of other things too, which, given the circumstances, said a lot about her susceptibility to this man.

'If I'd known your tastes ran to perversions…'

Nigel's thin lips curled as he openly sneered at her and

Rachel's temper flared. Guilt would only compel her to accept so much. Perversions indeed!

'I'm sorry if I've hurt you, Nigel, but that's just plain ridiculous and you know it! I can't marry you, Nigel. I should have told you.'

'Do you think I'd want *you*?' He gaped at her as if she were mad. 'I'm just glad now that we've never slept together…'

That was just in case Ben had missed the previous hints, she decided, repressing a groan.

'You and me both,' Benedict murmured softly in her ear. He tucked a strand of soft brown hair behind her ear and sent a jolt of neat, toe-curling electricity all the way to her feet.

Nigel's eyes were riveted jealously on the apparently intimate gesture. 'I thought you were something special,' he spat. 'I put you on a pedestal. I can see now that Jenny was right about you.'

'Jenny?'

'She's Ted Wilson's cousin. She was very sympathetic on Tuesday.'

'The Tuesday you had a cold.'

'If you must know I felt we needed some time apart for…'

'You to sulk?' she suggested. 'And regale the dinner party with my shortcomings?'

'I didn't know the half of it then.'

It was something about the defensive note in his voice that made her gasp suddenly. 'Is it possible that you've been seeing this sympathetic person? What was her name?'

She'd always accepted work commitments as the reason for him pulling out of a number of arrangements at the last minute. Now it looked suspiciously as if he had been keeping his options open all along!

'Jenny,' he responded, tight-lipped, looking annoyed that she'd introduced the subject. 'It's all perfectly innocent.'

'Is that what you told her about us?' The unattractive shade of crimson that washed over his fair complexion was more revealing than any words.

'I asked you to marry me,' he responded in a disgruntled tone.

'Flip the coin again.' She felt a whole lot less wretched knowing that Nigel wasn't the saint she'd thought him.

'Promiscuous women like you are ten-a-penny, and then these days there's the question of contamination simply on medical grounds.'

'That's it.' Benedict's voice was suddenly decisive. 'A bit of bile is acceptable when you've just been kicked where it hurts, but I think Rachel has grovelled guiltily for long enough. Cut your losses, mate, and clear out.' His tone was unfailingly polite but the hard light of warning in his dark eyes told another story. 'Don't be tempted to indulge in any more colourful insults or I might just be tempted to—'

This intervention was too much! Rachel pulled clear of his arms. 'I'm quite capable of sorting out my own problems.'

He shrugged and held up his hands in mock submission. 'I never thought otherwise.' His smile held a caressing warmth that robbed her anger of its impetus.

She cleared her throat. 'Good.' She grabbed her scattered wits by the scruff of the neck. 'Nigel…'

'Don't worry, I'm going. I can see how things are.' He looked from Rachel to the tall man at her side. 'I'm not blind. Don't bother—I know my way out,' he said bitterly. The slamming of the front door reverberated through the flat.

'Poor Nigel.'

'Don't become too attached to that hair shirt, Rachel; it doesn't suit you. *Poor* Nigel has a filthy mind and a substitute in the wings—crafty old Nigel..'

'He's not like that, really; he was hurt and humiliated.'

Benedict found her defence of her former lover irritating,

though it seemed the 'lover' part hadn't been strictly accurate.

'Why didn't you sleep with him?'

'Is it obligatory?' She could hardly tell him she was a cautious individual with a low sex drive after the way she'd behaved with him!

'When you're going to marry someone it usually is,' he confirmed drily.

'I didn't say yes.'

'He mentioned that.'

'I mean I didn't say I'd marry him.'

'Didn't he think it was a bit odd?' Benedict continued with what she considered insensitive persistence.

'He was sensitive and understanding.'

'Dead from the neck down, more like!'

'You can be very coarse and vulgar,' she observed frigidly.

'I can,' he promised warmly.

The warmth as much as the promise made her step backwards. The impetuous movement brought her into direct collision with a coffee table over which she fell in a tangle of arms and legs.

'Don't touch me!' she commanded urgently as he bent forward. 'I can't think when you touch me.'

'That's the nicest thing you've ever said to me,' he told her as she got to her feet, straightened the coffee table and wished she'd been wearing trousers. She smoothed her skirt with slightly unsteady fingers.

'Well, cherish it because that's as good as it's going to get,' she said nastily.

'I cherish every kind word you say to me, Rachel, and a few of the insulting ones too.'

An unwilling laugh was torn from her throat; he was impossible! Shaking her head slowly from side to side as she looked reprovingly at him dislodged the last remaining hairpin and her gently waving, glossy hair cascaded slowly around her face.

'Blast!' she cried impatiently as the heavy weight came to rest at shoulder-blade level.

'Is it as soft as it looks?'

The tone of his voice as much as the taut, hungry expression on his face warned her of the imminent danger of this situation. She turned a deaf ear to the reckless voice that told her to walk straight into the path of that danger. Nothing in her life had prepared her for the physical pain of denial.

'I think you should go too, Ben. I'm very grateful for your help today.' Both the wanted and the unwanted, she thought, but now wasn't the time to quibble. 'I'm tired; I want to go to bed.' The sudden wicked gleam in his eyes made her rush on swiftly. 'And I need to talk to Charlie,' she said with as much dignity as she could muster.

Dignity wasn't usually something she had to work at—she had buckets full of the stuff. Calm, unruffled composure was her trademark; she knew it, and liked it. It kept unwanted attention at bay. What had happened to her? She wasn't the sort of girl who needed a shoulder, strong or otherwise, to lean on. She wasn't the sort of girl who kissed unsuitable men who looked on women as a way to pass a few hours pleasurably.

'About her father?'

'I don't know,' she said honestly. 'I imagine we'll touch on artificial insemination,' she said drily. It was time for the 'warm loving relationship' speech and she wasn't looking forward to it. It that area she hadn't been the best role model in the world.

'And us?'

'I'll see you in the office tomorrow,' she replied, deliberately misunderstanding him.

'With your hair neatly secured…I know,' he said, his tone

laden with an irony that brought a self-conscious flush to her cheeks. At the door he turned abruptly. 'Wear your hair loose for me tomorrow, Rachel,' he said impetuously.

She was still digesting this ludicrous request when he left, his departure a good deal quieter than Nigel's. Wear my hair loose indeed, she snorted. What exactly would he make of it if she did? He'd see it as some sort of silent admission—a surrender.

Surrender… A sudden shudder racked her slim body and she was conscious of her aching breasts and the way they chafed against the white shirt she wore. She'd be mad to pander to his private fantasies; it was all about control and domination and she wasn't about to buy into that sort of thing—not for a minute!

Her confrontation with Charlie was delayed until the morning. When she entered her daughter's room she was sprawled face down across the bed. Rachel removed her shoes and pulled the quilt over her before telephoning the neighbour who looked after Charlie for the couple of hours after school before she finished work. Fortunately she was happy to have her the next day. She'd have loved to stay at home the next day, but being a working mother, she'd already discovered, required a lot of compromise.

Benedict's eyes went immediately to his secretary's desk as he walked into the outer office. The morning sun fell directly onto the corner from where the efficient hum of the word processor issued.

'Good morning.' Rachel cradled a phone against her cheek. 'Your father rang; he's on his way down.'

Not even the royal visitation could cloud this morning. Benedict nodded. 'Thank you, Rachel.'

Rachel would have known his appreciation wasn't directed at her ability to convey a message even if his eyes hadn't been fixed on the cloud of hair which rippled over her shoulders.

She'd almost been late this morning. First she'd gone all the way back to the flat to pin up her hair, then there had been the last-minute visit to the ladies' room to demolish her previous efforts.

Why shouldn't a girl change her hairstyle if she wanted? If Benedict wanted to read anything into it that was his problem. She could rationalise as much as she liked, but she'd still been waiting with baited breath for his arrival. He'd been pleased, if the savage satisfaction that had flared in his dark eyes could be interpreted as pleasure.

'How's Charlie this morning?'

'She sends her love.' This was the literal and worrying truth.

'Is anything the matter?'

His perception was as acute as ever. I don't want my daughter to get too fond of you, would have sounded churlish, but it was true. From their conversation earlier this morning she'd noticed that Charlie was exhibiting a dangerous tendency to attach the label 'father figure' around Benedict's neck.

She'd tried tactfully to discourage this development, but she was gloomily aware that her words hadn't fallen on fertile ground. Her own heart would have to take care of itself but she didn't want to take similar risks with her daughter's. She had no right to throw caution to the winds.

Her fingers suddenly itched to twist her hair into a neat knot. What am I doing? she thought angrily. I might as well pin a sign around my neck saying 'Just whistle'! Talk about a pushover!

Stuart Arden didn't make a habit of knocking and Rachel was taken completely unawares, and, if the expression on his face was anything to go by, so was Benedict.

The sudden sight of the very slim, very tall, very *young* blonde throwing her arms around Benedict's neck was a traumatic shock to her system. If she'd had a pair of scissors handy she might just have hacked off her hair at that moment and left him to make what he would of that symbolism.

Sir Stuart Arden, looking every inch the powerful pillar of the community, stood back with an expression of approval on his face.

'I thought I'd surprise you with Sabrina,' he said as his son emerged from the thorough embrace.

'Gift-wrapped, I see.' Benedict's expression didn't give away anything, but Rachel was pretty sure he didn't object to this form of greeting—what man would?

'Do you like it, darling?'

Rachel observed the crimson fingertips and the lime-green and lilac striped sheath dress with distaste. She was the sort of girl who called everyone 'darling' indiscriminately. Only in Benedict's case she probably meant it. Her proprietorial air with him spoke of a close relationship. The thought of how close made Rachel feel nauseous.

'I hope they charged you by the yard,' he observed, eyeing the length of leg revealed.

'Try and think metric, darling. I was telling your father, I've hardly seen you since you got back from that horrid farm.' She pouted attractively up at him.

Rachel, who had seen exactly where his masculine gaze was resting, would have bet money that that hateful laugh had been practised for hours to get that perfect sexy intonation.

'Considering the amount of time you've spent behind a desk, Benedict, I was quite surprised.'

Rachel was immediately conscious, despite the casual tone, of the tension in the air between father and son. Aware that his absence yesterday had been on her account, she hoped this wasn't responsible for the friction.

'Have you, or any clients, got any complaints about my work?' Benedict already knew the answer. His father was no sentimentalist.

He had never made any secret of the fact that he wanted one of his sons to carry on the family tradition of heading the prestigious law firm which had been founded by their great-grandfather, but it had been shrewd judgement rather than nepotism that explained Benedict's presence.

He was here because he was the best of his year's crop of law graduates and this firm always wanted the best. He'd refused offers from rival law chambers and his father knew it, although he never referred to the fact.

'You'd know if I had,' Stuart Arden confirmed. 'I was talking to your father last night, Sabrina; he was telling me you've graduated with flying colours from your cordon bleu course.'

'I was going to practise my skills on Benedict.' She glanced upwards through her heavily mascaraed lashes at him.

I just bet you were, Rachel thought with a fresh spurt of self-disgust. What am I doing? I don't want any part in this tacky scenario. I'm not going to compete for a man's attentions like this; it's so demeaning.

'Only he stood me up,' Sabrina continued with a sigh. She tapped his hand playfully. 'I was devastated. Did Daddy tell you he's going to set me up in my own little catering firm?'

'Well, if we can put any work your way…'

That was how it worked, Rachel thought, when you knew the right people—so simple. This was Benedict's world, not hers; the gap between them had never been more apparent. Her hands were clammy as she struck the keyboard and tried to pretend she wasn't listening to every word. To the Sir

Stuarts and Sabrinas of this world secretaries were just part of the furniture. They probably hadn't even noticed she was there. However, the next words blew a big hole in this theory.

'You're not Maggie.'

'Pardon?' She didn't immediately realise that this remark was addressed to her. 'No, I'm not.' The great man stood waiting expectantly and she knew she was looking more and more foolish with each passing second, but her vocal cords had seized up.

'I thought you arranged the temporary transfer, Father.' Benedict came unexpectedly to her rescue.

'Did I? I do a lot of things around this place.'

'And with your failing faculties you can't be expected to recall them all,' Benedict observed in an understanding manner.

'You're such a tease,' Sabrina remonstrated. 'I wish half the so-called *young* men I know had half Sir Stuart's energy and dynamism.'

Rachel had never understood why intelligent men who had given up reading fairy tales years ago fell for such blatant flattery. It works every time, she thought, watching the distinguished-looking peer try to hide his pleasure. He puffed out his not insubstantial chest.

'I only popped in to invite you out to lunch. You will come, won't you, darling Ben?'

That endearment had the same effect on Rachel's nerve-endings as a dentist's drill. She clenched her teeth and bent blindly over her desk, giving a passable imitation of intense concentration.

'Sorry, but I'll have to take a rain-check, Sabrina. I've got something else on.'

'Anyone I know?' she enquired archly, and the Cupid's-bow mouth tightened noticeably.

'Let me walk you out.'

'I'll wait for you in the office, Benedict. Perhaps Mrs French could get me some coffee?'

'Miss French.' She wondered with a spurt of militancy what he'd say if she pointed out that coffee-making wasn't included in her job description.

'*Miss* French.' He inclined his leonine head slightly as he moved past her. 'I stand corrected.' And that didn't happen too often, she surmised, repressing an inappropriate urge to laugh—obviously nerves. 'Are you enjoying working for my son? Is he a considerate boss?' he enquired casually.

'It's nice to have an opportunity to use my linguistic skills.' Rachel had the distinct impression that nothing this man said was unplanned.

'Very diplomatic. I've heard you're a *clever* young woman.' Rachel frowned. The way he'd said 'clever' sounded almost like an insult. 'I have a friend who works in Brussels who's always on the look-out for people with your sort of expertise in languages. You'd be in great demand over there.'

Suddenly he knew a lot about her, she thought as she smiled noncommittally back.

'Have you ever thought about moving?'

'I have a child, Sir Stuart.'

'Boarding-school's the answer; it makes them independent. Our lot thrived on it. I take my coffee black,' he added abruptly as he stalked into Benedict's office.

This sudden concern for her future rang alarms bells in Rachel's head. What was behind this interest? She suddenly didn't feel at all comfortable.

'This is for my father, I take it?'

Rachel wondered whether he ever dropped the formal 'father'. She nodded.

'I'll take it in.' Benedict took the cup from her hand. 'An urgent call in…' he glanced at his watch '…shall we say

seven minutes? Don't look so shocked, Rachel; where do you
think I learnt my tactics?'

Rachel stared as he closed the interconnecting door. Being
orphaned too early to recall her parents hadn't made her the
world's leading expert on family dynamics, but what
Benedict had with his father didn't seem like your typical
father-son relationship.

Stuart Arden had seated himself behind his son's desk. The
gesture was inspired more by habit than a belief that it would
help him intimidate his son; he knew his offspring too well
for that. Benedict's independence had been an infuriating
characteristic even when he was a baby. He often thought
he'd got all his elder brother's share. The only time Tom had
ever shown any backbone was when he'd refused to take his
bar exams and follow in his father's footsteps.

'What can I do for you, Father?' Benedict placed the cup
down on the desk and strolled towards the window. He didn't
notice the small red light that indicated his father had
switched on the intercom.

'There's been talk. Talk about you and that French
woman.'

'You must have been listening hard to hear any *talk*,'
Benedict observed sceptically.

'Something's been wrong with you since you got back and
you left the office with her yesterday and cancelled all your
afternoon appointments. It doesn't take much imagination...'

'Not much, just a particular type.' Benedict spoke without
any discernible inflection. Head slightly inclined to one side,
eyes narrowed, he moved across the room and looked at his
father thoughtfully. 'So you pulled her file and scurried down
here to check her out. Her name is Rachel.' Benedict was
too familiar with his parent's *modus operandi* to sound surprised by this discovery.

'There's a company policy about that sort of thing.'

'That's a new one on me,' Benedict observed with interest.

'Are you sleeping with her?'

'Is this exchange of intimacies meant to bring us closer? I hate to disappoint you but I've already got a best friend to share my secrets with.'

'Huh! Share, *you*? That I don't believe; you've never voluntarily given away any information in your life. You always were the most evasive child…'

'I was only being polite,' Benedict admitted. 'You know me so well. "Mind your own business" sounded so…bald and lacking in respect.'

Stuart Arden gritted his teeth. Benedict was the one who was meant to be on the defensive. He tapped his fingers impatiently on the desk. That infuriatingly languid tone of Benedict's always irritated him—he did it deliberately, of course…

'She works for you, she has a child… You're going to raise…false expectations; of course she's eager. I'm not saying she's set out deliberately to snare you.'

'That's very generous of you.'

'You can sneer, Benedict, but you have to look at the facts. In her position who could blame her for…? You're a *catch*, so they tell me. You'll make her a figure of fun when you've finished with her.'

'What an exemplary employer you are,' Benedict breathed admiringly. 'So considerate towards your employees. I'm curious about your sources. Is this fatherly instinct or surveillance talking now?' The resigned humour had been replaced by a definite thread of hard anger, but his father continued, oblivious to the change.

'Why go looking for trouble when there are any number of suitable young things like Serena…?'

'Sabrina,' Benedict corrected him drily.

'Whatever.' His father brushed aside the interruption im-

patiently. 'The right sort of wife is very important for someone in our position. If you'd been married you wouldn't have
been so eager to spend six months sorting out a manager for
that damned property. I'm sure she only left you the place
to spite me!' he added in a disgruntled tone.

'Knowing Gran, you're probably right,' Benedict conceded
with a sudden grin. 'I'm surprised you married Mum, considering her shaky pedigree. The word hypocrite springs to
mind for some reason.'

'That's entirely different.'

'It would be, of course. But have I got this right? The
consensus is I should marry…sooner rather than later. How
do you know I'm not considering it…?' Even though his
only intention when he'd opened his mouth had been to taunt
his father, by the time he closed it a number of things had
fallen into place in his mind.

'*You*, lumbered with another man's cast-off?'

'Are we talking child or mother here?' Benedict let this
slur pass unpunished. His heart wasn't wholly committed to
the verbal combat any longer; he was still reeling from an
unexpected discovery.

'Both! It would be social suicide. Have you any idea how
many skeletons a woman like her is bound to have? A High
Court judge needs to have a blemishless background…'

An unwilling laugh was torn from Benedict's throat. 'High
Court judge! So that's what I want to be when I grow up, is
it, *Daddy*?'

'You've got a brilliant future ahead of you; everyone says
so,' his father said defensively, aware that he'd gone further
than he intended in the heat of the moment.

'Thank you, Father.' A smile that worried his parent no
end curved the stern outline of Benedict's lips.

Feeling old, the elder man levered himself slowly from the
leather swivel chair. 'Thank me for what?' he said suspi-

ciously. Emily had warned him to leave well alone. You'd think he'd have learnt by now—his wife usually knew what she was talking about, he reflected grimly.

'For reminding me it's *my* life.'

'My life? What sort of talk is that? You're an Arden, boy; you're my heir.'

'So long as I toe the line?' Benedict suggested lightly. 'You've got other children.'

'Your brother is happy being a country solicitor.' He shook his head, unable to comprehend how his first-born was happy with such an existence.

'Nat...'

'Natalie is a girl.'

'Open your eyes. Nat is a girl with enough drive and ambition to light up the national grid; is a girl who is as well endowed in the brains department as me.'

'Did she gain entrance to Oxford when she was—?'

'Oh, I know she hasn't gone through school three years ahead of her peers, but that's only because you didn't think it worthwhile to constantly urge her onwards and upwards— she being a mere girl.'

'You didn't complain!'

'Maybe you don't know what things are really important until it's too late,' Benedict observed thoughtfully. He wasn't assigning blame. So certain aspects of his childhood might have been better—the same could be said for a large proportion of the population. He was much more interested in the present.

'I tell you something, Father, you really should take a good look at Nat one of these days—you might be pleasantly surprised. She's certainly hungry to prove herself to you.'

'Unlike you.' He sounded disgruntled but Benedict could see his father was looking thoughtful. 'About that woman...'

'Rachel,' Benedict said firmly.

'I'm only thinking of your best interests.'

'A twelve-bore might be less destructive than your concern,' Benedict told him frankly but without heat. 'If it makes you feel any better she isn't interested in me…'

His father laughed ruefully. 'Perhaps she's got something about her after all.'

'Parental approval—I feel *so* much better.'

'I'll thank you to keep a civil tongue in your head, young man, and I'm not approving of anything.'

'Were you rude to her?'

'As a matter of fact I was extremely civil.'

'Oh?'

The narrow-eyed suspicion from his offspring provoked an exasperated sigh. 'It's possible I might have accidentally flicked on the intercom whilst we were…'

'Whilst *you* were calling her a gold-digging opportunist. I suppose you made sure she received a strictly expurgated version.'

'Naturally when I happened to see the red light I switched it off.'

Giving his father a hawkish look that shook the older man deeply, Benedict turned his back and strode purposefully out of the room.

Surprise, surprise, the outer office was empty. He couldn't go back into his office; he didn't trust himself to look at his father, let alone speak to him. He'd been entirely too tolerant of the manipulative old man over the years.

Where would she go? he wondered. Her half-opened bag lay beside the desk. Of course—the answer was obvious. Where did women always go when they wanted to shed a tear in private?

'Good morning, Ben.' The latest female pupil to be recruited to the chambers stared at him, startled, as he walked confidently past her into the ladies' room.

'Morning, Sarah.'

A quick survey revealed there was nobody standing beside the mirrors that ran the length of the plushly carpeted room. One cubicle door was closed.

'I know you're in there, Rachel, so you might as well come out. You only heard what my father wanted you to.' His voice echoed in the high-ceilinged room. 'I know you can hear me, Rachel. I need to talk to you. Come on out. Damn it, woman, if you don't come out I'll knock the door down!' he warned.

His head fell back as relief flooded through his body at the sound of the bolt sliding back. 'Rach—' The eager smile faded dramatically from his face as the occupant fully emerged.

'Sorry to disappoint you, Ben, but it's only me.' A solicitor with whom he'd worked on several occasions stepped forward, trying without much success to hide her broad grin.

'Carol. Hello. I thought you were someone else.'

'So I gathered,' she observed, with a limpid look. 'I had no idea you were so romantic…or forceful…' A twinge of envy mingled with her amusement as she finally succumbed to mirth, but she was talking to empty space.

CHAPTER FIVE

'SORRY I'm late.'

Kurt Hassler got to his feet, his hand extended. 'Don't worry, Ben; Rachel explained about your emergency. We've been well looked after.'

'I'm sure you have.'

Rachel's eyes slid self-consciously away from the dark, ironic gaze. 'I'll see you all after lunch, gentlemen,' she said with a smile as she got to her feet.

'It's a working lunch; I think it would be beneficial to have you with us, Rachel. Besides, it's going to be a long session this afternoon; we don't want you fading on us before we're through.' He turned to the other men. 'These young women and their apples and yogurt. Always dieting.' There was a general male wave of agreement and a flurry of compliments on the perfection of her figure.

Rachel's smile became strained as she thought vicious thoughts about where she'd put her apple had she had one to hand. She was sure that Ben knew exactly how much she hated this patronising, pat-her-on-the-head sort of situation.

'I don't diet and I've never had any complaints about my staying power.' She positioned herself between the solid bulk of Kurt Hassler and Benedict. 'However, there's no way I'm going to turn down a free lunch.'

There was also no way she was going to let Benedict know she'd heard the start of the humiliating conversation with his father. At least she could stop worrying about the possibility that she was going to cave in to temptation. After the things Sir Stuart had said she had no doubt Ben would steer clear of her. A dalliance with a mere secretary—especially one, horror of horrors, with a child!—wasn't worth risking his brilliant prospects for.

And after that afternoon she had no doubt he had a brilliant future. He had cut a path through the legal maze which had made Albert despair. The clients went away happy, knowing they'd been saved a very costly court battle, and she could go home knowing her stint as Benedict Arden's PA was going to be much shorter than she'd anticipated.

'So you're still here?'

'Ask the same question in ten seconds and you'll be talking to fresh air,' she promised, heaving her bag onto her shoulder. 'You must be pleased with how things went today.'

'What happened to my seven-minute phone call?' Benedict growled unexpectedly. He sat down on the deep window seat and she thought he looked to be in a foul humour for someone who'd just achieved miracles.

Calmly she buttoned her dark tailored jacket to the neck. The very precise way she did so seemed to irritate him—his irritation was hard to miss. Some perverse imp made her go back and flick off an invisible speck then smooth a sleeve once more.

'Albert's temp was having a problem this morning locating a brief,' she explained, with a final glance around her clean desk. 'You don't mind that I slipped down to help, do you?'

'Why should I mind?'

'You look a bit…on edge,' she observed innocently. She met his hard scrutiny with a bland indifference that gave no hint of the churning misery in her stomach. Was he seeing the same scheming bitch his father evidently did when he looked at her now? Was he wishing he'd never shown any interest?

'On edge,' he mused. 'That's as good a description as

any.' For some reason the thought seemed to amuse him. 'Are you surprised? You've met my father...'

'On several occasions,' she admitted, compressing her lips. 'I didn't know I'd made a deep impression, but today he seemed to know an awful lot about me.'

'You did hear, didn't you? Look at me, Rachel,' Benedict said, and she could hear the urgency in his voice.

'Hear what?' she said in a bewildered tone.

'You heard what my father said—heard what he *intended* you to hear. Didn't you?'

'It's no big deal,' she said, making a big show of looking at her watch. 'What I did hear made very good sense.'

What a fool she'd been to imagine she'd ever been anything but a passing fancy. Men like Ben Arden didn't take women like her seriously—she was a novelty to a jaded palate, that was all. She ought to be thanking Stuart Arden for making her wake up.

Walking through the corridors of the old, luxuriously furnished building today, she'd been hard-pressed not to assume that every quiet conversation she came upon was about her. Rationality didn't come into it; the seeds of doubt had been planted and she felt conspicuous, as though everyone knew about her lustful fantasies. Fantasies that had almost become reality.

When he spoke Benedict's deep voice vibrated with anger and frustration. 'You and my father are on the same wavelength, it would seem.' His nostrils flared and the sensual curve of his lips was outlined by a thin white rim of anger. He came around and placed his hands palm down on her desk. The sturdy oak trembled slightly under the pressure, but not nearly as much as her knees trembled.

'Do you mind?' she asked coldly, catching hold of the creased corner of a document under his hand.

As he leaned forward the warm male smell of his body

assaulted her nostrils. She could see the faint dark blur of body hair through the fine white cotton of his shirt. Despite the air-conditioned coolness of the room sweat trickled down the valley between her breasts. Her hostility was almost submerged by the scorching thrill of arousal that swept through her.

With a sweeping movement he knocked the whole pile she was attempting to straighten onto the floor. 'Will you stop that?'

For a moment she'd thought he had been privy to her prohibited thoughts. The flush of mortification faded when she recognised his meaning.

'It's what I'm paid to do!' She hadn't even realised she'd been sharpening a pile of pencils that lay neatly on her desk. 'You won't get anywhere with me by acting like a thwarted child!'

The veneer of indifference was abruptly torn away and suddenly she was trembling with suppressed emotion—with humiliation. What did he think it felt like to hear herself discussed like a...an object? He might not like being reminded that at the end of the day it was daddy who called the shots, but at least he hadn't heard himself spoken of like some sort of grasping tart!

'How will I get somewhere with you?' The husky query made her quiver.

This was a question she decided it was politic to avoid. 'Why didn't he just sack me?' she wondered out loud. She bit down firmly on her trembling lower lip.

'Because that would leave him open to an accusation of unfair dismissal,' Benedict said gently. He didn't doubt his father would have used this method had it been an option.

'I hope you told him he had nothing to worry about. A kiss, a bit of mild flirtation...I'm sure you're much more pragmatic than he thinks. It would certainly take more than me to distract you from your great future.'

'I'm much more selfish than either of you think.'

She didn't quite know what to make of this cryptic utterance, and mysteriously Benedict's expression wasn't showing much of the relief she'd expected after she'd so generously let him off the hook. She didn't think for a minute he'd consider the effort of continuing to pursue her would be worth the aggravation.

Her slender shoulders lifted fractionally and she gave a brittle laugh. 'I'd hate to be the cause of dissent.'

'Dissent is the natural state between my father and me.'

'Fine, if that suits you, but I don't feel happy being in the middle of your private battleground.' Her eyes filled slowly with tears and angrily she blinked back the stinging heat. 'Hearing you discuss me…it made me feel soiled and…' She shook her head as she swallowed the constriction in her throat.

'Hurt,' Benedict supplied gently.

'No matter,' she said with a sniff. Hurt implied she cared to begin with. 'I know some people think just being a single parent automatically means that you're on the look-out to rectify the situation.' She swallowed and cleared her throat. Losing her cool now wasn't going to help. 'About lunch; shall I book you a table for two for tomorrow?' She could be the perfect secretary for a few more days, maybe less—how hard could it be?

'What makes you think I'll need a table for two?'

'I thought you might want to lunch with Sabrina; she did leave a message to that effect. Didn't you get it?'

'I did.'

'She looks a very persuasive sort of girl.' Perhaps I can take night classes in eyelash-fluttering, she thought viciously as she smiled generously.

'She's also a great cook,' he agreed readily. 'It makes you wonder why I settled for an indifferent cheese sandwich instead of the full works, doesn't it? Yes,' he agreed, folding his arms across his chest as she looked up with a startled expression. 'I was on my way there when Charlie kidnapped me. Can you take a letter?'

'Of course,' she replied, her professional dignity stung as she knocked all the neatly sharpened pencils onto the floor.

'It's a letter of resignation,' he continued calmly as she scrabbled about on her knees, retrieving the scattered pencils.

'A what?' she yelped, straightening up and hitting her head on the desk. 'Ouch! You want me to resign?'

'*My* letter of resignation.'

'You can't resign because of me!' she said in a horror-struck tone. She sat back on her heels, wondering how she'd managed to get caught up in the middle of this chaos.

'I'm not resigning because of you.'

'Oh! Of course not.' That's what happens when you get ideas above your station, my girl, she told herself. If the father could humiliate her, why not the son?

'Although I can see that would be quite a gesture.' His frivolous tone made her frown.

'I think you should think very seriously about this, Ben.'

'I know you believe I'm a capricious party animal, incapable of sober reflection.' The ironic flick of his eyes made her flush guiltily. 'But I have actually thought this out. It's something I've been thinking about ever since I came back from Australia. I'm going back…'

And there was me thinking I had something to do with his decision. The dark irony was like a dagger-thrust.

'I see.' It's about time you opened your eyes and did just that, girl, she told herself sternly. 'And how you spend your leisure time is nothing to do with me. You're single, eligible, and it's very natural that you like to let your hair down.'

These pragmatic words succeeded in focusing his eyes on her own hair, which fell softly around her shoulders. 'The London social scene will probably grind to a halt without you,' she added quickly.

'That sounds a bit impersonal; I'd prefer to picture pillows wet with tears.'

I just bet you would, she thought, inhaling deeply to steady herself. 'The world is full of impressionable females.' Her tone made it quite clear she didn't categorise herself as one of these.

She was getting her message across loud and clear. 'Your world might be full of them, but I meet precious few,' Benedict responded drily.

'Perhaps you'll have more luck in the outback?' He was actually serious; it finally filtered into her consciousness. He was going. Would he *really* give up a lifestyle most people would envy?

'Australian women are certainly refreshingly open.'

'Are they the main reason you're going there?'

'Careful, Rachel, you're sounding jealous,' he pointed out smoothly. He ignored her strangled squeak of denial and continued smoothly. 'My grandmother left me a cattle station in Queensland when she died four years ago. I put in a manager and left it to take care of itself until last year when he walked out and it became painfully clear he'd been siphoning off profits.'

'Oh!'

'Oh, indeed, especially as Nina left me land but very little capital. Remember we're talking a different scale; put the station in Britain and think a small village. A lot of people's livelihood depends on its continued prosperity. Overstocking plus drought had left the place in a pretty bad way. I went out to sort out the legal wrangles and put another manager— one I could trust—in his place. If it wasn't for my mother's sentimental attachment to the place—she was brought up on the Creek—I might well have put it on the market. It was just one big hassle.'

'Was?'

Benedict grinned and she realised she'd never seen his eyes burn with quite that sort of enthusiasm before.

'It still is, but the place has a way of getting under your skin. My life has always been so predictable: pass exams before and with higher marks than the next guy; be the first, the best... It stopped being a challenge years ago. Connor's Creek is different; the land is...' He gave an almost self-conscious shrug. 'To cut a long story short I kept putting off finding a manager and in the end I didn't bother.'

'You never intended staying here?' Did I come under the heading of time-filler—a handy stopgap? she wondered bitterly.

'I left my options open.' Deep down he knew that wasn't really true; he'd always known he was going back.

'I can't see you...'

'The suit does come off...remember? I had a hard time convincing the people there I was serious too. Some people go too much on appearances.'

She *did* remember what he looked like without the suit and suddenly it wasn't so hard to think of him getting his hands dirty working under some vast, alien blue sky. She could imagine him relishing shrugging off the constraints of civilisation and undertaking a task that required not just his mental tenacity but also his physical endurance.

'Your family won't be happy.' Why did she feel like this—so *empty*? She was physically attracted to him, nothing else. His leaving was a perfect solution in many ways to her own problem. No Benedict—no problem.

'Dad's got an heir apparent; he just doesn't realise it yet.'

'What about law—your career?'

'It'll survive without me. To be honest this has always bored me.' His shrug took in their surroundings.

'Perhaps that's why you throw yourself so wholeheartedly into the social whirl—you're compensating for your stifling professional life? Pardon me for saying so, but that all sounds a bit glib. Who's to say you won't get bored with playing cowboy in few years' time?'

'Leave the bitter irony to me, Rachel; it doesn't suit you.' His quiet tone made her feel uncharitable and plain mean. 'Not many people find a place they know they're truly meant to be. When I make up my mind what I want I'm not easily deflected.'

The warning in his words made her shiver. If she didn't tear her eyes away from his, critical meltdown was imminent!

If anyone had told him a year ago that a man could become emotionally attached to a place, a piece of land, he'd have laughed. Now he knew differently. As he'd explored the vast expanse of land they called the Creek he'd found himself envying the men who had settled this area, who'd been the first. This rapport with the land wasn't something he could put into words—wasn't something he could explain to anyone.

'It's a big step to take,' she said huskily.

'They're the only ones worth taking, Rachel.' He extended his hand and she realised she was still sitting on the floor, her fingers clutching a pile of papers. Her hand slid inside his and he pulled her to her feet. With a tiny jerk of his arm he drew her closer and she automatically raised her eyes to his.

It was a mistake. He was going to the other side of the world; it wasn't something she was likely to forget but she thought this was an opportune moment to remind herself of the fact while her nervous system was plugged into its own personal high-voltage system.

He knew how he made her feel—he knew *exactly* how he made her feel; he was too experienced to miss the obvious signs she was transmitting. Walking away from Benedict Arden with her pride intact might be a small step when compared to what he was doing, but it was going to be one of the hardest things she'd ever done.

'Is what you've told me public knowledge, or do you want me to be discreet?'

When she'd tried to step back he'd slid his fingers down to the curve of her elbow. It was stand still and take the agony that being this close to him was giving her or dislocate her shoulder. On reflection maybe dislocations weren't that bad!

'You're the only person I've told.' She could feel the web of intimacy his soft words were weaving around her. Illusion, she told herself—wishful thinking. 'Will you be sorry to see me go, Rachel?'

'I'm only your temporary secretary,' she reminded him lightly. 'It doesn't really affect me.' I'm a temporary everything, she thought with a surge of self-pity.

'I was forgetting,' he said smoothly. His eyes were on the small creamy V of skin where her shirt was modestly unbuttoned at the neck. She half expected the delicate gold chain she wore to melt under the hot, smoky scrutiny. 'And I suppose on a more personal note it might even help my cause.'

'How exactly?' she asked uncertainly. It occurred to her that if anyone walked in right now the gossips would have something more substantial than hearsay to sink their fangs into.

'You don't like the fact that Charlie likes me. You're afraid of her getting attached to me. This way there's no chance of that happening now, is there? I'm just passing through.'

'You always were,' she snapped bitterly. 'And anyway it's not true!' The quirk of one eloquent dark brow made her subside into slightly resentful silence. A mother's job was to protect her child; she refused to feel apologetic.

'It's a natural enough response. You like to keep men on the outside—strictly no admittance to the enchanted circle. That's probably why you took such a shine to good old Nigel—you knew there was no possibility of him cracking the code. I don't think your home has stayed a male-free zone by accident.'

'What a load of rubbish!' she shouted. What was wrong with being emotionally independent? He made it sound like a disease. 'I'm old enough to realise that some relationships are transitory—shallow; Charlie isn't. I don't want her to be hurt. You're nice to her and she's reading all sorts of things into it. She's used to men who run a mile when they know you have a child; she can cope with them.'

'Be serious, Rachel. Look in the mirror.' He took her chin in his hand and examined her profile greedily. 'Most men would put up with a tribe of juvenile delinquents if you were part of the bargain.'

'Most men want a shallow, superficial relationship.' Her defiance was weakening. If he'd chosen that moment to kiss away her objections she'd have been a goner.

'And isn't that exactly what you wanted with *Steve*...me? Didn't you fantasise just a little bit about making love to a total stranger—no questions, no complications? You were attracted to him—me. I've never seen a more obvious case of lust at first sight. Anonymous sex—didn't you think about it? You could safely surrender to male dominance; I'm sure that was tempting. You'd be completely free with a stranger to express your needs in any way you chose.'

The emotions his throaty, insidious words stirred up made

her head spin—with anger, she told herself. 'Sex with a
stranger is not my idea of safety,' she said unsteadily.

'Perhaps a safety valve would be a more appropriate description,' he conceded calmly. 'A release for all your repressed sexual feelings. It wouldn't surprise me if the last
person you slept with was Charlie's father,' he jeered provocatively.

Seeing the expression on her face, he froze. 'Good God!'
he breathed hoarsely. 'It's true, isn't it?' Under the healthy
glow of his olive-toned skin he'd gone white with shock. 'A
hard act to follow, is that it?' Learning his competition was
six feet under was not one of the greater moments in his life!
Ghosts could do no wrong.

She was so amazed at his interpretation, she didn't reply
at all. At nineteen, and working as an au pair with a delightful
couple in the South of France, she'd reacted the way most
teenage girls would have on meeting the famous brother of
her host. Raoul Fauré had been a Formula One driver as
renowned for trophy girlfriends as he was for his racing tro-
phies. His reckless skill on the circuit had brought him ad-
ulation from the public and envy from his peers.

She'd have been happy to worship from afar, but he hadn't
kept his distance; he'd told her she was the most beautiful
girl in the world and she'd believed him. His declaration of
love had been the fulfilment of all her adolescent fantasies—
what followed had been inevitable.

The next week he'd come back to the villa, only this time
he'd had a lovely young actress on his arm and in his bed.
He'd treated her with the same avuncular affection as his
brother; it was as if he genuinely didn't remember. It was
only later that she understood. At the time she'd been bewildered and miserable; her youthful idealism had suffered a
death-blow. She'd developed a convenient dose of terminal
homesickness about then and the Faurés had been sorry to

see her go, but understanding. Happily for them, they were nice people; they hadn't suspected anything.

'Chastity has a lot going for it. Sex just isn't important to me.'

'Is that a fact?' he said, not bothering to hide his scepticism.

'I just said so, didn't I?'

She realised about two seconds too late how easily her vaguely belligerent stance could have been interpreted as a challenge. It was one Benedict seemed very ready to accept. His mouth was hot and urgent—almost angry as it covered her own. The taste of him detonated an equally violent response within her; it ripped away all the elaborate barriers she'd constructed.

Her body arched as his strong arms lifted her upwards until her toes were the only things still in contact with the ground. His hard thighs ground rhythmically against her softer, more fragile frame. There was salty moisture on her skin as his dark head moved to touch, taste and torment her. Her fingers clenched tight in the dense thickness of his hair and a startled cry escaped the confines of her tight throat as her back suddenly collided with the wall.

He lifted his head at the sound. For a moment they were eye to eye and she saw the blaze of savage triumph in his dark, passion-glazed eyes. He nipped slowly at her trembling lip, letting his tongue slide into the sweet moistness within.

'You're…' she whispered hoarsely. She could hardly breathe; this sweet ache was smothering her. Hunger, viscous and warm, nibbled away at her restraints.

'I'm what? What am I, Rachel?' he persisted. As she turned her face into his shoulder he drew back fractionally; with a finger under her chin he forced her to face him. 'Tell me.' His free hand slid up her thigh, pausing momentarily only when his questing fingertips made contact with the edge of her hold-up stockings. She felt the tension that coiled in his muscles hike up a notch and heard his razor-sharp gasp.

His hand settled around the curve of her taut buttock. 'You're cruel and very…very beautiful, Ben.' He was cruel to make her want him like this…make her love… She gasped and suddenly went limp in his arms.

'This wasn't meant to happen here,' he said thickly as he stared down into her face. Her eyelashes flickered against her cheek; she looked barely conscious. But she was alive; the vigorous rise and fall of her breasts were evidence of that.

It wasn't the only thing that wasn't meant to happen, she thought in dazed disbelief as his thumb and forefinger moved up her neck before coming to rest on the pointed angle of her firm chin. His right arm was taking almost all her weight.

'Nothing's going to happen,' she said dazedly as she looked up at him. His taut features made it quite clear he was firmly in the grip of rampant desire. The evidence of this was pressed against the cradle of her hips. Trying to twist free only increased the intimate pressure. The heavy, dragging sensation had pooled low and deep in her abdomen; it was treacherously sweet.

'I've heard of denial but this is ridiculous.'

She felt the deep shudder through his body and the shivery, hot sensations in the pit of her belly responded with mindless pleasure to this evidence of his own lack of control. The dark excitement didn't respond to her wishes—at least not the wishes she consciously acknowledged.

She could see the dark pupil had swallowed up the colour of his iris completely. There was a faint sheen over his finely textured olive skin. Without thinking she reached out and ran a finger down his lean cheek. The light shadow on his skin had a fascinatingly abrasive quality. She pressed her damp finger to her lips and shivered as she tasted the faintly salty moisture.

The only flicker of movement in his entire body was the faintest stirring of his eyelashes. He didn't even appear to be breathing—this fact was confirmed when he did eventually take a deep, shuddering breath.

'Ben…'

'Hush,' he ordered huskily. His finger traced the outline of her quivering mouth before sliding inside her parted lips. The intimacy was totally devastating. 'I love your mouth. You try and make it all prim and proper and all the time it's just saying, Taste me, kiss me.'

She moaned out loud and pressed the back of her hand to her lips as he ran his tongue over the finger he'd just used to explore her mouth.

'You taste so sweet. I really like the idea of you tasting me. Would you like that?' he persisted throatily.

The erotic picture his sinful words were building made her dizzy. Her fingers tightened convulsively on the fabric of his shirt and several buttons came adrift. She felt the fabric part and even though she tried desperately not to she found herself looking downwards.

The skin over his washboard-flat belly was smooth and the tan was too dark to be attributed solely to his olive complexion. She wanted to touch him so badly, tears stung the back of her eyelids. Her body was convulsed by a feverish shudder.

'Perhaps you're right. I should just have sex with you!' The words emerged suddenly, loud and harsh. She didn't have many defences left. 'Get it all over and done with and things can go back to normal with your giant-sized ego intact—after all, no woman can refuse Ben Arden, superstud!'

Benedict lifted his head. Melting capitulation would have been nice, but Benedict wasn't a man easily discouraged. He knew a last-ditch effort when he saw one.

'There's no *perhaps* about it,' he replied huskily.

The sexy rasp combined with the suggestive heat in his eyes made her want to endorse his view. Hold on, Rachel, she told herself, harnessing her runaway tongue firmly; you're trying to defuse this situation, not ignite it!

'It's probably the simplest way to get this out of your system.' She tried to imply she was nothing but a disinterested observer—it wasn't easy.

'Is this the point where I'm supposed to be so offended by your icy detachment that I retire, my ego irretrievably bruised?' To her horror he looked amused.

'I'm just being realistic. Would you prefer I got all emotional?' Perhaps she should just confess she'd fallen in love with him—that should be more than enough to make him back off, she thought bitterly.

'Of course this strategy of yours only works if you endow me with finer feelings. If I don't recoil in disgust and say "Yes, please", you've just shot yourself in the foot,' he pointed out helpfully. 'As for a *superstud*?' He shook his head from side to side reprovingly and grimaced. 'I might just have such a high opinion of my sexual prowess that I'm confident you'll come running back for more. Or I might be callous and selfish enough to turn a blind eye to your obvious lack of interest in the whole sordid business if it means slaking my terrible lust. I really don't think you've thought this one through properly, Rachel.'

'I wouldn't actually go to bed with you!' she protested weakly.

'On the other hand,' he mused, 'if your surrender is couched in those terms you can rationalise it as being the only logical solution to a trying problem—a sacrifice for the greater good. Can it be I was doing you an injustice?' he wondered out loud. 'This removes any nasty nagging problems about how you're going to explain to yourself that you *want* me in your bed. And you just can't do that, can you, my love?'

'I'm not your love,' she choked, using up her last reserves of defiance.

'And you'll probably hate me tomorrow,' he agreed with a placidity that was contradicted by the fierce predatory glitter in his eyes.

'I hate you now.'

'That's a start.'

'Are you mad?'

'The jury's still out.'

'What are you doing?' she yelped as he swept her up into his arms. God help me, I'm enjoying playing the weak, defenceless female! she thought.

'My office has a lock and a sofa.'

The idea of a locked door gave her a completely false sense of security. 'And you have the key?' she asked, breathing hard; she'd abandoned all pretence of rejection.

'No,' he said, pressing something cold into her hand. 'You have.'

Rachel discovered the sofa was softly upholstered and the material was smooth against her naked back. The lacy bra she wore was almost but not quite transparent, and Benedict found the *almost* part incredibly arousing—at least that was what he said and his actions thereafter tended to confirm this statement.

He was kneeling beside the sofa and seeing his dark head against her as his mouth closed around the outline of her nipple where it showed dark through the flimsy fabric was incredibly erotic. She wore only the lacy pair of pants that matched the bra but he was still fully clothed, although his jacket did lie somewhere at the side of the room where he had impatiently thrown it.

Without warning he suddenly touched the skimpy triangle

of lace that barely concealed the soft, protective thatch between her legs. She jerked with shock at the intimate touch and wound one pale thigh protectively over the other.

'Don't you like that?'

She did; she liked it very much. Eyes on his, hardly able to credit her own daring, she straightened her legs.

'Yes,' she said throatily as she parted her thighs for his touch. The act of symbolic submission felt thrillingly erotic.

'It gets better,' he promised huskily. It did; the sight of his dark head bent over her, the feel of his mouth moving against the thin fabric was almost unbearably exciting. His fingers quested sensitively towards the hot core of her desire.

'Stop,' she pleaded. 'I can't bear...'

'So long as you remind me where I was...later,' he conceded. 'I think you could do with room for expansion up here,' he mused as he lifted his head. His thumb moved rhythmically against her flattened nipple; the burning sensation made her stomach muscles contract violently.

Holding his eyes, she leant slightly forward and unhooked the bra fastening. 'Is this better?'

His nostrils flared and the muscles of his throat worked as he stared at the gentle sway of her pale-pink-tipped breasts.

'It's perfect; you're perfect,' he groaned thickly. 'The first time I saw you you weren't wearing a bra under that blue dress...'

'Lilac.'

'And I could see how lovely and full and firm you were then. When you bent forward I could see just enough to...' He cleared his throat noisily. Benedict Arden blushing? That couldn't be right. 'Let's just say enough to drive me crazy. Take them off.' He hooked a thumb in the elasticated waist of her lacy pants.

'Do it for me?' she pleaded huskily.

The agonisingly slow progress of his fingers down her

thighs was almost unbearable. Free of the confinement, her hips stirred and rotated as, eyes tightly shut, she imagined him moving inside her…filling her… The choking sound he made forced her to open her eyes. The molten ferocity of his tense features convinced her he was sharing her fantasy. He looked as if he was on the brink of losing control. The idea was both exciting and appalling.

'Now come here and let me finish what I started,' she purred huskily.

He looked on with half-closed eyes as her trembling fingers slid free the remaining buttons on his shirt. The glitter she could see within the slits of his eyes made her even more clumsy. She dragged the fabric back to reveal the broad expanse of his bronzed torso; the faint sheen of moisture made his satiny skin glow. His body was built on truly magnificent lines, though his impressive musculature was not unduly bulky; he was built for flexibility, speed and grace, not just strength.

Fingers splayed, she laid her hands on him and sighed deeply. Mesmerised by the texture of his warm skin, she let her fingers move sensuously, delighting in the sharp contractions of his muscles. Her fingers slid under the waistband of his trousers and she felt a tiny quiver of uncertainty. She looked up and the expression in his eyes sent her confidence soaring.

His trousers had slipped down to his lean hips and she could see the line of hair that narrowed to a dark line that disappeared beneath the white cotton he wore underneath.

'Are you all right?'

Suddenly he sounded concerned and she lifted her head sharply, sending her thick hair fanning cloud-like about her flushed face. She tried to speak and realised that her breathing had become a series of staccato, uneven gasps. She pressed

her hands to his shoulders to steady herself and tried to draw
adequate breath into her lungs.

'I'm fine.' Then, in a rush of honesty, she admitted, 'I
don't know my own body, not when you touch me, or I touch
you. I don't recognise any of the things I'm feeling, Ben.'

She'd not acted on impulse since she was a green teenager
but something compelled her to do so now. This was something she just had to share with him.

'It feels as if this is happening to someone else.'

The feverish, reckless glow in his eyes deepened. 'Perhaps
I should make this more personal—more *real*.'

'There's plenty of room here.'

'Slow might not be an option once I join you there,' he
confessed, looking at the narrow space she patted with sultry
invitation.

'It's a risk I'm willing to take.'

'Comfortable?' he asked as he cleverly insinuated his body
under hers.

'Not really the word I'd use,' she gasped, finding herself
sitting astride him. His back was against the arm of the sofa
and they were eye to eye.

Then she wasn't using any words at all because he was
guiding her nipple into his mouth. The slow, sumptuous friction of his tongue and lips was agonisingly arousing.

Rachel gave a deep moan and her body jerked violently
before sagging against him. One of his hands rested in the
small of her back and the other sank into her hair. The sweeping motion as his fingers sank into the luxuriant growth
pulled her head backwards, leaving her neck sinews taut. His
mouth moved upwards to the irresistible temptation of the
graceful curve, leaving a trail of burning kisses. The warm
scent rising from his skin made her body ache almost as
much as his expert touch. *Expert*.

'What's wrong?' he asked, picking up on her sudden mental withdrawal almost instantaneously. His breath was hot against her cheek as his tongue moved in lazy, teasing circles over the ultra-sensitive skin beside her ear.

Chin resting against his shoulder, her body leaning bonelessly against him, she slid her arms tightly around his middle, pulling tightly as if the contact would ease the sudden flurry of insecurities.

'I'm not exactly experienced…I haven't done this for…' Before she hadn't really been a participant at all. Her contribution had been compliance. Ben wanted more than that. What if she disappointed him? 'My body isn't perfect…I've had a child.'

'Do you think I'm asking for perfection?' He sounded angry and when he forced her chin up he looked it, too. His dark eyes were filled with a resentment she didn't quite understand. 'Do you think making love can be rated on a scale of one to ten? There hasn't been a measurement invented that can accurately describe the way it feels to touch your skin.'

'Try,' she said, intoxicated and immensely relieved by the sincerity of his words. 'Try and tell me?'

'It's easier if I show you.' He firmly guided her hand downwards to the painfully congested area between his thighs. His response to her light touch made her gasp and smile with greedy, erotic satisfaction. Lips parted slightly, she lifted her passion-glazed gaze to his face.

'This thing limits our options.' He banged his head against the upholstered arm before sliding dramatically downwards and pulling her with him. 'It's either you up there and me down here, or me up here—' her soft shriek was smothered by the erotic imprint of his marauding mouth '—and you down there. The choice is yours.'

'I'm easy.'

Deep laughter vibrated in his chest. 'Would that were true. What are you…?' He inclined his head to see her drag his already loosened trousers and his shorts over his hips. She felt the hot, hard tip of his arousal nudge against her belly and fought hard to retain control. The gap between consciousness and dark oblivion was dangerously close.

'I'm showing initiative,' she said, lifting her head just close enough for the tip of her tongue to lap back and forward over the dark stud of one male nipple. She reached up and pulled his shirt, which flapped around them, a couple of inches down over the flexed muscles of his shoulders. The fabric didn't give and the constriction caused him to collapse down on his elbows.

'I'll squash you,' he warned hoarsely.

'I like being squashed by you,' she reassured him. She hooked her legs up and around his waist, locking her ankles firmly over his back.

'Rachel!' he rumbled in warning, the contorted expression on his face reflecting the strain he was under. He slid between her thighs because there was nowhere else for him to go. 'I can't move.'

'You can. You can move exactly where I want you to go.'

'I've never made love with my shoes on. My clothes.'

'Don't worry, we can work around them.' Only one thing could satisfy her now.

'Work around!' A hoarse laugh emerged from his dry throat. 'You're a very bad girl, Rachel,' he said thickly. 'You mean I'm on top, but you're in charge?'

'Now you come to mention it...' The air was expelled from her lungs in one long sigh as he slid firmly into her body. All thoughts of domination and control vanished at the precise moment her body expanded to accommodate his pulsing masculinity.

'You're—' She gasped, sliding her arms beneath his shirt to grip the slick, warm flesh of his back.

'I'm what?' he asked thickly, his voice almost unrecognisable. Rachel was beyond words; she only wanted to absorb him, feel him move within her.

He couldn't resist her pleas and any restraint he had vanished under the onslaught of her inarticulate entreaties and encouragements. He could no longer control the aggression of his thrusts as he gave her what she asked for—all of him.

'Oh, God, I didn't use a condom!'

As post-coital sweet nothings went this really ruined the mood.

'Don't worry, it's not a fertile time of my cycle.' If the sofa had come supplied with sheets she'd have used them to cover her vulnerability. And a whole lot more than her vulnerability was showing just now! She edged as far away from his sweat-covered body as possible.

'That's not the point.'

'It isn't?' She wanted so badly to touch him. Would it be so bad? she wondered wistfully.

'I wouldn't want you to think I'm normally reckless.'

'Relax, I don't.'

'Next time—'

'There won't be a next time.'

She felt the sofa groan as he raised himself on one elbow. Under the circumstances it was impossible to avoid his eyes. 'Oh?'

His eyes ran slowly over her slim body, still flushed from their strenuous lovemaking.

'I'm not blaming you.'

'That's good of you.' The droll smile that lifted one corner of his mouth wasn't reflected in his eyes.

'But it can't happen again.'

'If you're willing to give me ten minutes and some encouragement I think you'll find it can.'

The heat tore through her body as her imagination responded to the vivid images conjured up by his words. 'I need to go home.'

'Let me guess, I'm not the sort of man you want to take home to Charlie.' He didn't look or sound amused.

'I don't want to raise her expectations, Ben. She's fond of you...'

'And her mother?'

'You're a very attractive man.'

'I can hear a "but" in your voice.'

'Don't be like this,' she begged unevenly. 'It's not as if you're planning to share your life with me, is it? We've nothing whatever in common and I've not the mental attitude that makes a happy harem member.' She dredged the light laughter up from somewhere when he didn't respond with a firm proclamation that she was the one and only girl for him— she hadn't really expected him to.

'It's better for everyone concerned if we return things to a professional basis. I'd like to get dressed now.' It was probably too late even now to save herself from all the classic symptoms of addiction, but she had to make a token effort to escape.

'At this point am I supposed to avert my eyes while you make yourself decent? Sorry, Rachel, I like looking at you nude. Surely you don't begrudge a man something to remember when we're back to a professional basis?'

'Do you always make situations like this so awkward?'

'It may surprise you, Rachel, but even with my varied, much documented love life I've never found myself in this situation before. I wasn't expecting slavish adoration...'

'No?' The sooner that little time bomb was skirted the better! 'Just applause possibly? I think you're just peeved because the women you date wait for *you* to call it a day.' Anticipating the fact that he was about to get a lot more physical, she slid sinuously off the sofa and landed on her bottom.

He leaned over the edge and she reached for her discarded shirt, pulling it protectively over her breasts.

'Date! What date? You did promise me dinner when I took you to the hospital… I think you'd like me better if your first impressions had been right and I was some penniless bum on the prowl. You were falling over yourself to dole out the tea and sympathy then. The fact I've got anything to offer you is obviously a big turn-off! Does a relationship on equal terms scare you that much?'

Equal? Was he serious? She dreamt about equal. She sat on her heels and jerkily shoved her arms into the shirt. 'Offer me! When did you ever offer me anything?'

'There doesn't seem much point when you throw every gesture back in my face.'

'Fine! If you want dinner, I'll buy you dinner, and you can bring me flowers to say thank you. I promise I won't throw them back in your face. It's not that I didn't enjoy…' she began awkwardly.

'I know that.' He watched as she unsuccessfully tried to tug the shirt over her hips and his anger seemed to subside. He tugged up his trousers but didn't bother fastening the belt. 'When?' She looked at him blankly, worried by the rather calculating expression on his face. 'Dinner,' he reminded her.

'What? Oh, tomorrow if you like.'

'Good girl; get it over with as soon as possible. I bet you always ate your greens before the good bits. Good strategy. Are you looking for these?' Swinging his legs to the floor, he held out a pair of lacy pants at arm's length.

She lunged automatically and he withdrew his hand. 'That was tomorrow, was it? Eight o'clock?'

'Yes, yes!' she replied as he dangled the scrap of material

just out of her reach. She gave a sigh of relief as he released his grip.

'Our first date,' he said, raising an invisible glass to his lips. 'I'll return this at a later date,' he added, audaciously tucking her bra into his pocket. 'You look much better without it. I'll let you put it on so that I can have the pleasure of taking it off.'

'Our only date,' she choked defiantly.

CHAPTER SIX

'I NEED to go to the ladies' room.' Charlie laid her napkin to one side. 'Don't let them take that away,' she added, frowning suspiciously at one of the zealous waiters. 'I haven't finished yet.'

'It continually amazes me how much you can pack away,' Rachel said, getting to her feet.

'I'm not a *baby*. I'm quite capable of going on my own.'

'Pardon me…' Rachel kept her expression grave, to avoid giving any impression that she was laughing. A ten-year-old's pride was a delicate thing.

'Besides, you'll *have* to talk to Ben if I'm not here.'

And look who's laughing now, Rachel thought, staring after her daughter's retreating back.

'Out of the mouths of babes…' Benedict drawled, leaning back in his seat and enjoying the expression of discomfiture that spread across Rachel's face.

'Are you suggesting I brought Charlie along as a…a…?'

'Shield? Perish the thought.' His dark brows lifted in sardonic assurance. 'I'm sure it just slipped your mind when you issued the invitation to mention that we weren't going to be alone.'

'I owed you dinner…this is dinner.' Even if he'd seen through her somewhat transparent ruse he might have tactfully not said so.

'Was I complaining?' He grinned and reached across the table and took hold of her hand. 'Relax,' he advised as she stiffened. 'I'm having a great time. Charlie's great.' He shrugged and his ironic smile deepened. 'She hogs the conversation, but the same has been said of me. We have a surprising amount in common, you know; I was a so-called "gifted" child too. I've been through the whole hothouse thing.'

That explained the rapport. 'What hothouse thing?' she asked, ultra-sensitive to implied criticism.

'You know, skipping the bud stage and going straight into full bloom. That's the system these schools who cater for the *crème de la crème* specialise in.' He cast a knowledgeable glance at the militant light that had entered her eyes. 'And lower those prickles, darling; I don't want to fight.'

'You've got a funny way of showing it.' She had enough insecurities about her decision over Charlie's education without him making her feel even less sure about her move to the city.

'I know how it must be; on one hand you don't want to be a pushy mother, on the other you don't want to stifle her potential. It's a classic no-win situation so relax and play it by ear. Right now,' he confided, 'there's only one thing I want to ask you about Charlie. What time will she be safely in bed?'

Rachel recognised a leading question when she heard one. 'On weekends her bedtime's flexible.'

'You could always prop her up in the corner if she dozes off.' His sarcasm stung.

She snatched her hand away. His thumb had been inscribing slow, sensuous circles over the palm of her hand; her nerve-endings were jangling and she found it impossible to concentrate on anything above the clamour.

How, she pondered bleakly, was it possible for this man to do more damage to her nervous system with such an innocuous caress than anyone else could manage with a full-scale seduction?

'You'll be gone long before then,' she said pointedly.

'Are you trying to tell me something, Rachel? It couldn't be you're scared of being alone with me, could it?'

Rachel gritted her teeth and displayed them in a brilliant smile. His smug confidence really got under her skin—especially as she had a sinking feeling it could well be justified.

'I am alone with you and see—' she held out her hand for his inspection '—not even a tremor.'

'Steady as a rock,' he agreed admiringly, 'but very much prettier.' He bent forward and touched his lips to the back of her extended hand.

She gasped; she couldn't help it; the neat electricity made her toes curl tightly in her elegant high heels. Benedict raised his dark head slowly and she pulled her hand back, nursing it protectively in her lap—not even the best will in the world could have kept the tremors at bay now.

'There are things I need to say to you that are better said in private, Rachel.'

'I don't think I want to hear them,' she confessed, too flustered to compose a less truthful reply.

'Why?'

Through the protective shield of her lashes she watched him fill up her glass with wine which she had no intention of consuming—she needed all her wits about her tonight.

'You're going away.'

Too late for me, she thought grimly as she hung grittily onto what composure she had left. She could see it might be nice for him to have some blatantly besotted idiot to while away the time with before he packed his bags and moved to the other side of the world, but she wasn't going to be that idiot.

'And does that bother you?' The dark eyes were fixed with unnerving intensity on her face.

'If you're waiting for me to say I'll be devastated, don't hold your breath,' she returned calmly.

'I really like that in you.'

'Like what?'

'You're a fighter, a real scrapper.' Elbows on the table, he rested his chin in his hands and allowed his eyes to wander admiringly over her flushed face. 'Only you ought to accept there are some things you just can't fight.'

'Really?' she said, compressing her lips and suppressing the urge to run—well, she was still sitting anyhow.

'You were about to say, Such as? Only you thought better of it.'

'Now you're a mind-reader too.'

'Last night we both seemed to be doing a lot of that.' The slow, husky drawl, only a notch above a whisper, had a resonance that vibrated through her tense body. She couldn't tear her eyes from the lips that had formed the words and once she started looking the remembering was inevitable. She remembered how those lips, applied in various imaginative ways, had reduced her to a… She shook her head to clear the images that flooded through her disorientated mind.

'I thought we'd agreed that that was a one-off thing,' she said harshly.

'I didn't agree to anything; you agreed for us both,' he reminded her. 'I didn't think you were the sort of girl who went in for one-night stands, Rachel?'

'Neither did I,' she admitted with a flash of honesty. She suspected he knew as well as she did that that put her in a situation where she had to say no; one night would no longer be an appropriate description.

'Would it make a difference if I wasn't going away?'

The sly question threw her shaky balance completely for six. 'Naturally I'm flattered you haven't got bored with me just yet. But…don't you think you should get a bit of practice with normal relationships before you contemplate the long-distance variety?' She and Benedict didn't want the same things from relationships. She knew what she wanted, but it wasn't on offer.

'And if I wasn't leaving would you offer to repair that gap in my education?'

'My spare time's pretty full at present.' The linen napkin was crushed beyond salvation in her fingers. 'I don't think you're ready for the sort of…'

'Commitment.' He pounced almost eagerly on the opening in her faltering explanation.

Rachel had already heard his opinion on longevity and permanence; she didn't want to offer him the opportunity to rub salt in the wound. She didn't want to join the legion of women who pursued him.

'Here's Charlie…'

The fleeting expression of seething frustration that flickered through Benedict's eyes made it quite clear that the levity in his manner had been masking deeper, more urgent emotions. Only Rachel didn't see it because her attention was riveted on the man beside her daughter. Good God, he was talking to her.

'Rachel?'

Concern replaced frustration as she continued to stare beyond him. She looked, he thought, as though she'd seen a ghost. He automatically turned to see what was causing her such alarm.

It looked innocuous enough; Charlie was handing an empty glass to a tall guy who was patting his damp shirt-front. He looked to be taking the incident in his stride. The Italian proprietor's laid-back attitude to children had obviously rubbed off on some of the patrons too.

Rachel saw his body freeze as Charlie straightened up. He said something quickly and she saw Charlie nod towards their table. Her heart thudded as they moved closer. It was a long time since she'd wondered if this situation would ever arise. The chances of her meeting one of the Faurés were remote, but remote had happened.

'Hello, Rachel.'

'Christophe, this is a surprise,' she said huskily.

'For me too,' he said heavily.

The guy had one of those French accents females found attractive. Benedict tried not to hold the accent against him; after all, he was an open-minded sort of guy. However, despite his open-minded attitude he found he couldn't stretch to a smile when the older man glanced in his direction.

'You are married, Rachel?'

'No, no…this is Benedict Arden. Ben, this is Christophe Fauré.'

'And I have met Charlie.'

It was then, as he smiled down at the child, that it finally clicked: the eyes. Charlie had his eyes! That was why he'd looked familiar. No wonder Rachel had looked as if she was seeing a ghost; she *was* seeing a ghost. Benedict had felt a similar sensation when a cricket ball had hit his unprotected adolescent manhood when he was thirteen.

'Are you in London alone?' This was a nightmare, Rachel decided; a waking nightmare. Christophe knew; of course he knew. He was seeing his brother as he looked at Charlie. She didn't have the faintest idea what his reaction would be.

'Annabel stayed at home. She has an exhibition next month. My wife,' he said, glancing politely at Benedict. 'She is an artist.'

'So you're married.' The hostility would have been hard to miss.

'Yes.'

'A question occurs to me.' This was Benedict at his most bland and Rachel, who hadn't thought things could get much worse, thought she might be sick. 'Were you married when you and Rachel last…met?'

'I was.'

'And when might that have been?'

'*Ben!*' She frowned reprovingly at him. He was behaving like a heavy parent, for heaven's sake! Or a jealous lover… She pushed this notion and the accompanying spurt of dangerous gratification firmly away.

'Eleven years ago.' Christophe's eyes repeatedly strayed to Charlie as he went on, 'Your mother was our au pair, Charlie. She kept house for us for a while. She was not very much older than you really.'

God, what was he going to say next? she wondered with alarm. She could almost hear the questions forming in Charlie's mind. If Charlie was going to hear the story she was going to hear it from her mother's lips.

'Dance with me,' she said, urgency lending her inspiration. Christophe looked startled. '*Please*, Christophe?' Her smile was all teeth and terror. She had to get him away from Charlie.

'I'd be delighted.'

'Sorry,' she said a few minutes later as she trod on his toes for the second time.

'She is Raoul's of course,' he said, breaking the silence.

Silently Rachel nodded.

'He was my brother and I loved him but he was a selfish.…'

Rachel's French was good enough to translate the unflattering epithet accurately.

'And I was a silly girl,' she added, not disagreeing with his harsh assessment of his dead brother's character.

'Did he know?'

'No.'

'That's something, I suppose. I'd like to think it would have made a difference if he had…' He left his doubts unspoken. 'You were living under our roof,' he continued in a severe voice. 'Our responsibility. I should have guessed and been more vigilant; I knew how Raoul was—without honour.' His lips twisted in disgust. 'Charlie is my niece—my blood; I could have helped. I hope you didn't tar us with the same brush as Raoul. I would understand if you did.'

'No, of course not; you and Annabel were very kind to me. I was ashamed, frightened. I didn't want anyone to know I'd been so stupid. Later, when I heard about the crash, I thought about letting you know, but I thought you might think I was after... Well, it would have looked pretty suspicious: I pop up complete with child when Raoul is no longer there to deny or confirm my story.'

'Charlie's eyes are all the proof you needed,' he said, his frown deepening. 'My family have done you harm, Rachel. Helping you would have been a privilege, not just a duty.'

Rachel's throat was suddenly choked with emotion at the sincerity in this man's voice. It was amazing that two brothers could be so dissimilar, she reflected sadly.

'And this man who looks at me with murder in his eyes— what is he to you?'

'Benedict! He wouldn't...' There was only one other couple on the dance floor and she had an unobstructed view of their table. She saw Benedict's face and changed her mind— it looked distinctly possible that he would! There was nothing sophisticated about his expression—it was one of crude, violent disapproval.

'Perhaps he doesn't like you dancing with other men.'

'It's none of his business who I dance with,' she responded, her mouth settling into a combative line. He expected her to get her mind around his colourful past; how perverse could you get? Even if he had assumed that Christophe was her former lover—and from his confrontational attitude that seemed very likely—he had no right to come over all possessive.

A sceptical expression stirred in Christophe's eyes, but he maintained a diplomatic silence. 'I would like to make amends—too late, I know. Don't!' he said, pressing a finger to her lips, which were parted to refuse. 'The request is selfish also. Annabel and I couldn't have children.' Behind the stoical acceptance Rachel had a glimpse of pain and her tender heart ached.

'There is no young blood in our family and the sound of a child's voice would bring us all delight. Don't deny my mother her only grandchild, Rachel. You and Charlie could visit us in France; we could all get to know one another.'

'Charlie and I don't have any family either.' She couldn't believe it was this simple! Suddenly there was a grandmother, a whole family Charlie had never met. Not in her wildest dreams had she pictured such ready acceptance.

Christophe sighed. 'Thank you, Rachel,' he said simply. 'Now you'd better tell me your address before I return you to your young man.'

'He's not mine '

'I think he might dispute that,' came the dry reply.

'I want *Ben* to say goodnight.' Charlie wielded her dripping toothbrush like a conductor's baton and her attitude was just as imperious.

It's nice to be wanted, Rachel thought as she watched Ben sketch a courtly bow. 'Your wish, my lady, is my command,' he said solemnly.

She bent to receive her daughter's kiss, worry behind her strained smile. It would be kinder to Charlie if she severed her connections with Benedict Arden cleanly. She'd never seen Charlie take such a shine to anyone before. It would be selfish and weak to listen to the insidious voice in her head that told her to forget her pride and enjoy what little time they had together. Deep down she had no doubt that had she been single that would have been exactly what she would be doing now—and to hell with the consequences!

When Benedict reappeared a few moments later the careful words of her 'it was nice while it lasted' speech fragmented. Looking at him made her feel weak and irresolute.

'Ben, I…er…that is…' She bit her lip and tried to reassemble her thoughts. The emptiness inside hurt now. It had always been there, but it was only since Benedict had got a handhold in her life that she'd recognised it for what it was— loneliness. He was going to go away anyway; she might as well feel the pain now as later.

'He didn't know about Charlie, did he?'

There was no question in her mind concerning the identity of the 'he' he referred to. The abrupt, expressionless accusation had robbed her of what little brain function she had left. He knew…how?

'No,' she heard herself confess. 'I never expected to see him again. He and his wife…'

'Oh, yes, the wife.'

She hardly noticed the sneer in his voice. Perhaps, she reflected, it would help sort things out in her own mind if she discussed the situation with someone. And Ben seemed to know so…

'They can't have any children so Christophe—'

'*I don't believe this!*'

She watched in confusion as Benedict ground his balled fist into the palm of his other hand. 'Why would he lie? He's no reason—'

'No reason!' he yelled. 'That's the truth, isn't it? You're obviously prepared to take everything he says at face value. One word from *him* and you're prepared to forgive and forget. Haven't you learnt anything from the past?' he asked incredulously. His dark eyes moved angrily over her face.

'It wasn't Christophe's fault,' she protested. She couldn't blame the man for his brother's misdeeds.

Benedict sucked in his breath and his slanted cheekbones jutted even harder against the taut flesh of his face. Everything about him seemed tight; the explosive quality in him was tangible.

'In my book,' he ground out, 'a man—an *older, married* man—who seduces a young girl—scarcely more than a schoolgirl—who is living under his own roof is…' He tilted his chin to one side as if considering the problem. *'Responsible,'* he drawled, his eyes shooting smoky fire. 'I'd say that about covers it. He's a lot of other things too,' he lashed from between clenched teeth. 'But I won't offend your delicate sensibilities by listing them. Only your feelings aren't too delicate where he is concerned, are they? The bastard was all over you.

'How are you going to explain her father's miraculous resurrection to Charlie? He gets a ready-made family—convenient, to comfort him in his declining years. And they're not too far away,' he added viciously. 'You really do have a thing about older men, don't you? You've got to admire the man,' he drawled, betraying no sign of that particular emotion. 'He really does seize the opportunity.'

Too late she realised that Christophe hadn't been the only one to notice the family resemblance. Whilst Christophe didn't resemble Raoul in any other way they did share the same distinctive blue eyes—Charlie's eyes. She'd been so distracted by his unexpected appearance, she hadn't realised that Ben had seemed unusually withdrawn and quiet on the way home. All the signs had been there—how could she have been so blind?

'Ben,' she said urgently.

'I never had you pegged as gullible, Rachel.' Obviously listening wasn't high on his list of priorities. He had a lot to say, though, and the delay in getting it out of his system hadn't helped any. 'God, woman, you're not a green nine-teen-year-old now. What is it about this guy that sends your judgement haywire? You've been suspicious enough of *me*. You continually endow my most innocent action with sinister motives.' Jaw taut, he shook his head disbelievingly. 'I suppose if he asks you to go to France with him…'

'He already has.' She knew now what she had to do.

It might break her heart, but using his misinterpretation of the situation might be the simplest—no, *only* way she was going to get Benedict Arden out of her life, and get him out for Charlie's sake she must. Her admission had stopped him dead; it had hurt too, she could see that. Even if his pain could be attributed solely to hurt pride it still made her want to explain.

'He doesn't waste much time,' he said slowly, breaking the stunned silence that had followed her words. 'And you said— No, don't bother telling me; it's obvious what you said.' He picked his jacket up from the back of the sofa and flung it over his shoulder. 'You may think you're mistress material, Rachel, but you're not.'

Suddenly she couldn't bear to let him go away thinking… 'Ben,' she said urgently, 'it's not the way it seems.'

'Men like that don't change, Rachel. Women just like to think they're the one who will break the pattern.'

His words stopped her in her tracks. 'You should know,' she agreed. Could he really not see the irony of his warning?

'Sure, I've seduced women and been seduced in my turn, but I've *never* destroyed anyone—I'm not a user. He'll break your heart, Rachel—he's done it before—and who's going to pick up the pieces?'

'Not you; you won't be here.' You're the one breaking my heart, you stupid, *stupid* man, she wanted to scream.

'But I'm here now.' A thoughtful expression she didn't

trust entered his eyes. The way his glance moved suggestively over her body was an insult. Insults didn't usually have this effect on her body, though. His smile was hatefully *knowing* as she raised her crossed arms to cover her tingling breasts which were only covered by a thin layer of silk. 'He's not.'

'I wish you weren't,' she responded with feeling.

'You weren't so anxious to get rid of me before the blast from the past reappeared.'

'You make it sound as though I laid down the red carpet. The way I recall it you've conned your way in here each and every time. Never use the truth when a lie will get you where you want to be,' she sneered.

It hit her forcibly that she'd just given a fairly accurate description of her own behaviour in enforcing Ben's belief that Christophe was Charlie's father. If he wondered why she suddenly subsided, blushing guiltily, he didn't ask.

'Where I want to be,' he mused slowly.

Oh, help! Her ribs didn't feel substantial enough to cage the wild tattoo of her heart. His eyes had turned her resistance to molten desire.

'I want…' he said, catching his breath sharply as she nervously touched the tip of her tongue to her dry lips. 'I want to be feeling your bare breasts against my chest and I want to be hearing your voice begging…pleading. I want to be inside you, Rachel. Will the truth get me where I want to be this time?'

'You can't talk to me like that,' she gasped. 'It's…it's offensive.'

'It's the truth, and you're not offended, Rachel. You're aroused.'

The achingly erotic words were swirling around in her head, gathering impetus rather than losing impact as, eyes wide and fearful, pink lips slightly parted, she stared help-lessly back at him.

'So am I.'

Rachel willed her eyes not to drop from his face. She could fell the faint beading of perspiration break out over her upper lip. The conflicting emotions were tearing her to pieces.

'I'll take your word for it,' she managed hoarsely. I'll show him I can cope with sexual innuendo—not that there had been much innuendo about his comments, she thought ruefully. Advances didn't get much more direct!

'Not just when I'm with you—when I see you. Just think-ing about you is enough.' He gave a sudden hard laugh. 'And I think about you a lot, Rachel. It conjures up a picture of adolescent excess to bring a smile of superiority to your lovely lips. You're not smiling. Doesn't it make you feel powerful?'

Powerful! That was the last thing she felt. She'd never felt so helpless in her life. She felt weak, needy, out of control and likely to fall victim to spontaneous combustion any sec-ond. Tiny black specks began to dance before her glazed eyes. It took an immense effort to make the buzzing in her ears diminish to a dull roar.

'Perhaps, Rachel…' His tone had dropped to a husky, in-timate drawl. The jacket he'd unceremoniously dropped was trampled underfoot as he covered the space between them. She had a whimsical image of him trampling all over her will-power with his handmade size elevens. Rejection wasn't what he read in her face or body and it showed in his self-assurance.

'Perhaps my gross, offensive words make you feel hot and…' He drew a sharp, shuddering breath that involved all the muscles of his impressive chest. 'I like to think of your body warm and moist…ready for me.' Hands resting on her shoulders, his fingers stroked her neck.

'It is.' Whatever residual defences she'd had had crumbled at the first rasp of his erotic confessions.

He reached for her then, pulling her against him with a hungry desperation. His mouth was greedy and hot as his tongue made a slow, lascivious meal of the inner recesses of her parted lips.

'Rachel…Rachel.' He was mumbling her name in between open-mouthed kisses and tantalising soft bites. His hands moved jerkily over her body. One arm swept her closer as it tightened around her slender waist until her weight was almost wholly supported by the strength of his braced legs.

She clung, she whimpered as their embrace grew more frenzied and urgent. The sensual maelstrom carried her along until she had no thought in her head that didn't involve the taste and texture of the man who held her.

'Where?' he said, one arm half out of the shirt she had unbuttoned. 'Where is your room?' he panted.

'Over there.' She gestured vaguely behind her and her arm was still elegantly curved in a graceful arc over her head as he picked her up. Head back, her body curved with sinuous grace, she felt the dragging weight of her hair as it obeyed gravity.

'I don't have a double bed,' she commented, looking up at him with sultry speculation from her narrow single bed. What would he do next…? Each individual nerve fibre in her body was tensed in pleasurable anticipation.

'We'll cope,' he said confidently, straddling her over his knee. 'This is pretty; I like this.' His fingers worked at slipping the rouleau loops that held her pale blue camisole together. He didn't remove it; he just pushed aside the fabric to reveal the peaks of her engorged breasts. 'But not as pretty as these.' He laid his hands at either side of her breasts and examined his prize with enraptured eyes.

Rachel groaned in languid ecstasy as his clever tongue set

about paying homage to these twin symbols of her femininity. Her head fell forward, her chin angled against the top of
his bent head. She let her hands slide, palms flat, from his
shoulders down the marvellous sculpted perfection of his
back. The action brought her up on her knees. Face still buried between her breasts, Benedict growled and slid his hands
under her raised buttocks and a sharp jerk brought her hard
against the pulsing evidence of his arousal.

His hands still cradled her hips as he fell backwards on
the narrow mattress. Rachel found herself astride his half-
naked body. 'Take my clothes off, Rachel; undress me,' he
commanded throatily. He reached up and took the weight of
her breasts in the palms of his hands. He gave a deep grunt
of male satisfaction.

His dark hands against her pale skin—skin that had ac-
quired an opalescent sheen in the semi-darkness—was incredibly arousing. The way his thumbs moved softly over the
hard peaks made her breath escape from her lungs in one
silent whoosh. He caught her hands in his.

'Let me show you how. Shall I show you how, Rachel?'

Her fingers turned within his light grasp and she raised
one hand to her lips. His fingers flexed until the bones
cracked as, open-mouthed, she kissed the slightly calloused
palm of his hand. Her tongue traced a delicate damp pattern
against his flesh.

'I'd like that. Teach me, Ben.'

'You've worked out a nice line in torture all by yourself,
lover,' he groaned.

'Don't you like it?' *Lover*—it sounded good, she decided
dreamily. Why shouldn't she be his lover? Was it asking too
much to have this time with him—the man she loved?

A laugh rumbled in his chest at the husky note of sulky
pique but his eyes were fierce. 'You seem to know what I
like, Rachel.'

'It's easier if you tell me.' She hooked one finger into the curling hair that was sprinkled over his chest and belly and bent closer to lap tentatively at his flat masculine nipple. He gasped hard and sucked in his belly, emphasising the solid slabs of muscle.

'That's good,' he breathed thickly, catching hold of the back of her head and urging her back down. 'We could start there.' He closed his eyes as the lash of her delicate tongue began once more. Periodically she raised her head to peep with sultry satisfaction at the tense, almost pained expression that contorted his features.

'I like this,' she sighed, tucking her damp hair behind her ears and throwing him another hot, hungry look.

'Let's find out what else you like.' Abruptly he tipped her pliant body backwards and Rachel found herself flat on her back with him kneeling over her.

'I didn't finish,' she said, tugging at the buckle of his leather belt.

'Two sets of hands make light work,' he said. He yanked his trousers down his legs and kicked them clear.

The excitement moved low in her belly at the sight of his arousal. The pain was sharp, the emotions deep and suffocating. The weight of hot, unshed tears stung her eyes. Nobody but Ben could ever make her feel like this—it wasn't possible.

'I'm glad.'

His words startled her; she hadn't been conscious of speaking. 'Shall I touch…?' She reached out and paused, suddenly not quite the sultry temptress she'd been playing.

'Yes—oh, yes!'

The red sparks that danced before her eyes seemed visible evidence of the sexual energy that crackled around them. The husky encouragement was all she needed to soothe the flurry

of uncertainty. She was now sure that what she wanted to do
was what he wanted too.

The room was filled with sharp gasps and hoarse groans
as he moved against her hand until the moment came when
his hand covered her own. She made a sound of protest.

'I'm a marathon man myself; I like to appreciate the journey. But if you keep that up…'

'You're saving yourself for a sprint finish?' she suggested
with an impish grin.

'Only if you behave, you little witch,' he said, responding
to her teasing with a mock growl. He pinned her arms to her
sides. She squirmed, not from any desire to escape but because it felt good to have his heavy body pressing against
her.

'Do you really want me to behave?' she asked, panting
from the exertions of their mock combat. His breath stirred
the downy hair on her cheek; he smelt distinctively of Ben.

'Naturally—I want you to behave naturally, Rachel.'

She could do that, she thought happily; at least, she could
with Ben. He obeyed the implicit plea in her passion-
saturated eyes and kissed her.

Rachel wasn't conscious of shedding her remaining clothes
but it wasn't very long before his elegant, sensitive fingers
were moving unimpeded over her smooth flesh. His clever
fingers roused her past and beyond thought; she was all feeling and sensation. The primitive regression was complete and
now she needed him—needed him badly to finish what he'd
started.

'Yes…yes…yes!' she cried as he slid into her. Feeling her
body adapt and stretch to accept him was a breathless, marvellous sensation, and when he began to move she wrapped
her legs around him and let everything happen. It did happen
perfectly.

Sleepy and languid in the aftermath, she couldn't feel regret. She burrowed like a kitten against him. Tiny aftershocks still tightened the muscles in her pelvis but she hadn't forgotten the moment of release; she never would.

'I wasn't going to do this again,' she murmured sleepily.

'Is that what you thought?' he replied indulgently.

'I don't say goodbye to everyone like this, you know.' A faint whimsical smile curved her lips. Her languid state of mind didn't register the sudden tension in the arms of the man who held her.

'Goodbye?' Rachel didn't hear his harsh question; she'd finally released her tenacious grip on consciousness.

'I think it's best if you leave now.'

The sleepy look on Ben's face made him look younger than his thirty-four years. The impulse to wrap her arms around him was strong. It would have felt good to have him wake up next to her. His dark head had been comfortably settled against the slope of her breasts before she had stealthily slipped from the warm bed.

Benedict dragged his fingers through his tousled dark hair and the sheet slid down to reveal his hair-roughened chest and flat belly.

'You're saying basically "Here's your pants; get lost"?' He jackknifed into a sitting position and from his alert expression his brain was no longer burdened by fatigue—it was firing on all cylinders.

'I'm saying it would be better if you left before Charlie wakes up. She'll be confused...'

'That'll make two of us.'

He didn't look confused; he looked angry. She'd hoped he wouldn't react like this.

'Be reasonable. I'm the one who'll have to field awkward questions,' she reminded him tensely.

'Are you sure it's the thought of Charlie's questions that's got you running scared, Rachel? Wouldn't it be more honest to say it's your own questions you're prepared to go to any lengths to avoid?' He flung back the quilt and swung his long legs over the side of the bed. The sight made her sensitive stomach muscles go into spasm.

Why don't you go ahead and drool? she asked herself angrily as she tore her glance from the sight of his athletically sculpted thighs.

'It's a perfectly legitimate request,' she said, tightening the sash on her smoky blue floor-length gown. He got up and walked across the room. There was no hint of self-consciousness in his graceful stride. He was as close to perfection as it came, she thought, watching him with covetous eyes.

'It makes it pretty clear that you're ashamed of last night.'

'Last night was just a…a…'

'The definitive term escapes you, does it?'

She glared resentfully at him. He appeared to get some savage satisfaction from seeing her floundering helplessly. 'I'm just being practical,' she insisted.

'Does the idea of sex full stop bother you, or is it just sex with me that becomes sordid and tacky in the cold light of day?'

There was a depth of anger and disillusionment she hadn't expected in his expression. She stifled the flicker of uncertainty before gritting her teeth and continuing in a patronising, amused tone, 'Don't worry, this is no reflection on your masculinity. I'll go on record as saying you're a fantastic lover.' She smiled and lifted her shoulders in a tiny gesture intended to reflect on the fragile ego of the male.

He stepped into his white cotton boxers and his brows drew together in a hard line of displeasure. 'Did I measure up to your idealised memories of your first love? Fantasies are so much neater, don't you find? There's no body to get rid of in the morning.' He smiled unpleasantly at her. 'Thank you,' he added as she passed him the errant sock which had been eluding him.

He only raised a brow when she jerked her hand away before their fingers touched, but it was enough to make her flush self-consciously. If he had any idea of how much she feared a simple contact like that and why, she'd die of sheer humiliation.

'Unlike you I don't consider sex a leisure sport. I'm sure some people can be satisfied...'

'I thought you were. You screamed something to that effect, as I recall.'

'Must you be crude and vulgar?' she asked, her cheeks ablaze. 'I'm trying to say I can't justify sex without love.'

'Well, you're not doing a very good job of it. Practical's a good line,' he mused. 'You stick to that, darling,' he advised. 'Anyone can say "I love you".'

'I don't.'

'I'd noticed,' he said with a savage inflection. 'I'm sure your Gallic charmer did—bilingually, probably—and look where that got you. At the end of the day actions speak louder than words; words are ten-a-penny.'

'When you say them I'm sure that's true.'

'You mean I wouldn't have been welcomed back to bed if I'd sworn undying love?' he asked incredulously. He gave a strange twisted smile as though the black humour in his eyes was aimed at himself.

'I'm not *that* gullible.' To hear him joking about something about which she'd nursed improbable fantasies cut deep.

'Just as well I didn't waste my breath, then, isn't it? It obviously hasn't occurred to you, but if you were a man kicking his partner out with indecent haste at five a.m. it would be a different story.'

'I don't believe this! Are you implying *I'm* using *you*?' She gasped incredulously at this novel interpretation of the situation.

'Weren't you?'

'My motivation didn't seem to bother you much last night.'

'I wanted you.' The raw confession made her body sway like a sapling struck by an unexpected gust of wind. Her nerves were vibrating like over-stretched violin strings. 'I wasn't in a position to make conditions last night.'

'And you think you are now? This is my home, Ben, and I decide who stays and who leaves. I'm not trying to pretend last night didn't happen...' She wished he'd fasten his shirt; it was making a difficult situation even more trying to be faced with the expanse of golden-tanned skin.

'*Really?*'

'We should learn from our mistakes.'

'What a healthy, well-balanced attitude.'

'And I can do without your snide remarks,' she hissed, hot-faced.

'Sorry,' he said unconvincingly. 'Tell me, what have you learnt from our...*mistake*? Or are you just clearing the decks for lover boy—off with the new, on with the old? Are you really so sure he's still the right fit for you, Rachel? You might discover you've done some growing.'

'I'm not trying to deny I find you physically attractive.'

'Pity; I could do with a good laugh.'

She refused to be sidetracked by his biting sarcasm. 'There's never been any question of anything more.' He'd said as much by omission himself. 'The future doesn't really come into the equation when we both know you're only here for a matter of weeks. You were right...'

'There's a first time for everything.'

She gave a dignified sniff. 'When you said I'm not mistress material.'

'You think he'll leave his wife for you, because of Charlie? Grow up, Rachel; if having children meant more to him than her he'd have deserted her years ago. His sort always go back to the wife.'

'For God's sake,' she snapped, 'I'm not talking about being Christophe's mistress, I'm talking about being yours!'

He froze, and she had the fleeting impression he was biting back his instinctive response. When he spoke it was very slowly and precisely.

'I don't recall asking you.' Eyes narrowed, he rocked on the balls of his feet and stood waiting for the inevitable explosion.

She gave a gasp of anger. Of all the smug, arrogant, self-satisfied rats! 'There's no point in trying to be civilised with you, is there? Get out!' she yelled. 'Now! *Mistress* was too formal a commitment for him! He thinks he can have me whenever he wants, and I haven't done much to discourage his theory so far, she thought bitterly.

Her anger seemed to have lifted his spirits; he grinned at her with every sign of pleasure. 'Are you going to throw that?' he enquired with interest, nodding at the hairbrush she was waving to emphasise her point.

'If I'm going to throw anything it will have a sharper edge than this.'

Still grinning, he shrugged on his jacket without bothering to fasten his shirt. The picture it presented was somehow decadent and erotic. Let's face it, girl, you'd find Ben Arden in a bin sack a turn-on; it's pathetic, simply pathetic, she told herself.

'For a woman who doesn't want to disturb the child you've turned the tiniest bit shrill.'

'You've not heard anything yet,' she promised grimly.

'Relax; I wouldn't dream of staying where I'm not welcome.'

'You finally got the message.'

'Put it down to the conflicting signals,' he said drily. Hand on the door handle, he turned back. 'Believe me, darling, it's your loss—I'm a morning man.'

The hairbrush hit the closed door.

CHAPTER SEVEN

'STOP there.' She must have this wrong. Fortunately he'd offered her a seat before he'd enlightened her as to the reason for this meeting or she might just have been stretched out on the ankle-deep Aubusson carpet by now.

There was no way Sir Stuart Arden could be saying what she thought he was. She'd probably feel extremely silly later for saying this.

'You want me to sleep with your son?'

She tried to make a joke of it but failed miserably; the persistent tremor reflected her bewilderment. He wasn't laughing and he wasn't looking furious at her presumption either.

'I didn't say that.'

'You implied it!' She was apparently to offer her body as inducement to Ben. Outrageousness seemed to be a congenital condition in the Arden family.

'You're a very blunt young woman, Miss French. I like that.' He beamed with generous approval at her.

'I thought I was unsuitable material for...' she began drily.

'I admit I might have been a bit hasty. I didn't like the idea of my son being saddled with a ready-made family.'

'I assure you that I'm not on the look-out for a rich husband—rich, or any other sort!'

'Since then I've been watching you.' Now there was a very unsettling thought, she reflected wryly. 'And I'm impressed by what I've seen.'

She judged it was time to put an end to this farcical situation. 'You've got this all wrong, you know. Ben isn't leav-

138

ng because of me,' she said earnestly. As mistakes went this
one was up there with the big boys. The ever-present bleakness settled around her heart like a steel band.

She could see she hadn't convinced him. It was made more
difficult when he was pretty well sold on the popular theory
of his own infallibility. When she'd been instructed to go to
the big man's office several scenarios had crossed her mind—
instant dismissal was one, a leave-my-son-alone lecture was
another. Use your feminine wiles to make my son stay home
hadn't been in the running!

'You're not the usual type he goes for at all.' Benedict's
father obviously considered this a clinching argument but the
significance remained unclear to Rachel. 'It's obvious he
thinks he's in love.'

'Your son isn't in love with me.' She was able to say this
without a blush; unfortunately she didn't have the same control over her heart as she did her complexion, and it hurt—
it hurt a lot to actually acknowledge this.

With a slow nod of his head he conceded she might be
right. It obviously didn't occur to him that it was tactless to
concur. Rachel's exasperation was increasing by the second.

'He might *think* he is, though. He's not used to rejection.'

His surveillance network wasn't infallible, then. *Rejection!*
Hysteria wouldn't be far away if she dwelt on that one too
long!

'Benedict made this decision before he even came back to
England.'

'Hah!' he said triumphantly. 'He's confided in you; I
thought as much. Benedict doesn't do that—it just goes to
prove it.'

'Prove what?'

'He's serious about you.'

'I really don't have any influence with your son.'

'You've got more than me.' For the first time she glimpsed

the depth of his frustration and anxiety. 'I'm asking you to use it to stop him making a terrible mistake. He'll thank us for it eventually.'

'I don't think Ben would thank anyone for conspiring behind his back.' If he ever found out about this little tête-à-tête she didn't want to be around.

'Conspiracy is a harsh word.'

'But accurate,' she insisted firmly.

Stuart Arden wasn't used to asking anyone for anything and it showed. She felt something she'd never imagined she'd feel for this man—she felt sympathy. It must have cost him a lot in pride to come to her and ask for her help. He must really be desperate to keep Ben in the country. However, she kept a tight hold on the sympathy; it wouldn't do to forget that behind the concerned father was a ruthless man who would do anything and use anyone to get his own way.

'I don't think Ben has taken this decision lightly.'

'Have you got any idea how gifted he is?' he asked, banging his fist down on the desk. 'He has a brilliant future to look forward to. He's throwing it all away! And for what? Some dry dustbowl!' he said scornfully. 'You must be able to see how ludicrous the idea is. This is a whim, nothing more. Do *you* want him to go?' She averted her face too slowly. 'I thought not.' He gave a triumphant grunt of satisfaction.

'What I want doesn't enter into it.'

'Are you lovers?'

Rachel got to her feet with as much dignity as she could muster. 'As my employer you have a number of rights, but asking that isn't one of them.'

'Don't be offended, my dear.' The transition from interrogator to kindly uncle was made with bewildering speed. 'If you want the man why don't you fight for him? You have weapons in your arsenal that I lack.'

Rachel's nostrils flared in annoyance. She didn't trust the crocodile smile one little bit. 'I think I should go,' she said firmly.

'A child—a baby—would make Benedict see where his responsibilities lie.'

Halfway to the door Rachel froze. She looked at the man behind the big desk with white-faced astonishment. 'Are you actually suggesting I get *pregnant* in order to keep Ben in the country?'

'It must have occurred to you.'

'You think so?' He *was* serious.

'There are in-built disadvantages to being a woman—no old-boy network, prejudices in the workplace—but there are also advantages, and I've always admired women who use their femininity to get what they want. A hint of cleavage can be just as affective as an old school tie.'

'Even if I did agree with you—which I don't—I hardly think what you're suggesting is comparable,' she croaked hoarsely.

'I'm only suggesting you utilise all the weapons at your disposal. If you don't like the idea of actually getting pregnant I understand. The mere possibility would be enough to bring him to his senses and lots of women lose babies…' His voice trailed off suggestively.

'You want me to pretend I'm pregnant?'

'Naturally I'd leave the details up to you.'

Her mouth worked and no sound came out. 'You expected me to go along with this idea?' All emotion was leached from her voice.

'Well, we both have something to gain.'

She took a deep, wrathful breath, her bosom swelling impressively as she did so. 'I'll *encourage* Ben to leave the country if it means he'll be clear of your devious machinations!' she announced, chin up, eyes blazing. 'What you've suggested is monstrous and immoral. I would never, *ever* use a child, or even,' she drawled sarcastically, 'the idea of a child, to trap a man. I think you've got a very warped idea of what love is, Sir Stuart. The sort of love I believe in doesn't manipulate and control a person.'

'Then you do love my son.' Sir Stuart looked thoughtful.

'I doubt very much if you know the meaning of the word.'

He laughed suddenly. 'You know, my wife said that to me the first time I proposed. She had that same look of disdain on her face when she said it, too,' he recalled with a nostalgic sigh.

'How did you get her to say yes? Threaten to bankrupt her father, or did you just kidnap her sick granny?'

To her amazement he appeared to find her sarcasm amusing. 'Perhaps she'll tell you one of these days, my dear. I hope there are no hard feelings; it was worth a shot. I'd do anything to keep Benedict from ruining his career,' he said simply.

'Maybe you justify your actions under the mantle of parental concern, but I don't swallow it. I think you're more concerned with how *you* feel, Sir Stuart.' She turned on her heel and left a very startled peer of the realm staring after her.

'Did Charlie really take the news well?'

'Better than I expected,' Rachel assured him. This evening was going better than she'd expected too. Christophe really was a pleasant companion. The natural awkwardness had faded quickly. He was an amusing, interesting companion, and a naturally kind man. 'She's fascinated by the idea of relations she's never met. I left her curled up with a book of French grammar—light reading, you know?' She laughed.

'A mixed blessing being so bright?'

She nodded at his perception. 'Sometimes,' she confessed.

'She milked me dry for details about your family. I hadn't realised until recently how much she wanted to know about her father. If I had…who knows?' She gave herself a sharp mental shake; it was never useful to reflect on paths you hadn't taken. 'I think she wants to interrogate you now.'

'You scare me.'

'I said she could stay up late to see you again—if you'd like.'

His smile deepened. 'I'd like. Annabel wanted to fly over, but I said it was probably better to play things slowly. I don't want to overwhelm her.'

'Charlie isn't easily overwhelmed,' Rachel said drily. 'But I think slowly is the best way to play this.'

'That looks marvellous.' Christophe breathed in the aroma appreciatively as the waiter placed his steaming dessert before him. 'Are you sure you're not tempted?' He rubbed his hands together in gleeful anticipation of the calorific delight.

Rachel grinned as he attacked the mammoth-sized portion with the enthusiasm of a schoolboy. 'I imagined we'd be dining somewhere very French,' she teased. The restaurant he'd brought her to specialised in traditional, unglamorous English cuisine.

'What could be more glamorous than a steamed suet pudding?' he asked indignantly, spoon poised halfway to his mouth. 'I have a weakness for English nursery food; do I have the expression right?'

She nodded. 'You have, only I imagine a cardiologist might have another name for it.'

'A little of what is bad for you occasionally can do no harm, Rachel.'

She was in a position to dispute that. A little of Ben had been *very* bad for her. Her concentration was shot to hell. It was getting hard to disguise the fact that she had no appetite. She had decided, rather harshly, that her face was looking quite gaunt tonight. As for sleep, she'd forgotten what it was to do anything other than toss and turn. It wasn't going to last, of course, she knew—she reminded herself of this fact a hundred times a day—only it didn't help.

She was just grateful for her premature return to Albert's office. Mr Arden apparently no longer had need of her services—or so the curt office memo had informed her. Pity he hadn't explained this to his father before she'd been subjected to that horrific interview, which got more bizarre and surreal every time she reconstructed it in her mind. She'd seen Ben just once in the distance; there had been no mistaking his broad back or the sound of Sabrina's high-pitched giggle.

'Will you have coffee?' Christophe asked for the third time.

'Sorry, I was miles away.' She unfolded her white knuckles from the wine glass and forced herself to smile. She wasn't about to tell him where she'd been or with whom. She listened as he patiently repeated himself.

'I do a passable coffee. Would you prefer to go back to my place? It will give you more time with Charlie.'

It was after midnight before she said goodnight to Christophe. She was only halfway up the stairs when the doorbell rang once more. He must have forgotten something, she decided, skipping back down the stairs two at a time.

'What's…?' The smile died dramatically as she recognised the tall figure who loomed out of the darkness. 'Go away!' Despite her determined attempts to close the door in Benedict's face the large size eleven got in the way. A well-muscled thigh followed the foot and she found herself thrust back against an unattractive umbrella stand which stood in the hallway.

'Don't bother closing that door—you're leaving,' she said grimly.

'Not until you've done a bit of explaining.'

'You're the one who should be explaining. What do you think you're doing barging in here?'

'I waited until Fauré had left. I thought that was very considerate of me.' Benedict's affable expression was somewhat spoilt by the waves of anger emanating from his lean body.

'You've been skulking out there waiting!' she accused, going cold all over at the thought. 'Spying on me!' she squeaked in outrage.

'*I know.*'

Whatever he knew it didn't seem to be affording him much pleasure. In fact the pulse that visibly throbbed in his forehead looked about ready to pop. Explosive described fairly accurately his state of mind at the moment.

'I'm happy for you. At least I would be if I had the faintest idea what you were talking about.' She picked up the assorted umbrellas and placed them back in the Victorian stand.

Hands thrust deep in his jeans pockets, he looked down at her with open contempt. 'And I don't suppose you went to see my father either?' he said in a voice calculated to wither hardier blooms than Rachel.

She turned to face him, a red brolly still clutched in her bloodless grip.

'Did you think he wouldn't tell me?' Benedict noticed she'd gone bluish around the lips. The floor was hard, unyielding mosaic tile; he'd have to move fast if she fainted.

'Actually I didn't think he would,' she confessed eventually. Her head was spinning. Stuart Arden wasn't the sort of man who did anything unless he thought he could get something out of it. For the life of her she couldn't imagine what advantage he imagined this confession would give him.

'Why the hell did you go to him, not me?' he demanded in an anguished voice. He swept an impatient hand through his hair—hair that had been soaked by the light summer shower. Dampness made his shirt cling to the contours of his upper body, emphasising his powerful physique.

Rachel's confusion deepened. For some reason he seemed to think she'd instigated the interview. Was it possible that Sir Stuart had, for his own reasons, made her the instigator?

'I know you're angry, and I don't blame you, but you can't blame me.'

'Blame you?' he echoed blankly. The deep red coloration seeped slowly until it covered every scrap of his skin she could see. 'Is that what you think of me?' he asked hoarsely. 'You thought I'd be angry?'

'Well, you are angry, aren't you?' she pointed out, somewhat mystified by his reaction.

'Because you didn't tell me, not because you're—'

'But couldn't this have waited until morning, or better still Monday? I really do think you're overreacting, Ben.' Her thoughts raced as she tried to quell the rising sense of panic. If he came in, if he touched her... She had no will-power where he was concerned. One thing she knew she *couldn't* do was say goodbye again.

'You think I'm...' Words appeared to fail him at this point. 'I'm sorry if my emotional outburst offends you but it's not every day I learn I'm about to be a father. Perhaps you can be blasé about it, having been there once, but this is the first time for me.'

It was Rachel's turn to be rendered speechless. She tried to interpret his words first one way then another way, but the meaning kept coming out the same.

'You think I'm...? Your father told you I'm...?'

'For once in his life my father did the decent thing. Something you obviously don't think I'm capable of.'

The irony struck her as being hilariously funny. She laughed, a wobbly giggle that swiftly crossed the border into hysteria. In her youth she'd had to overcome this embarrass-

ng response to moments of high emotional drama. Laughter
had frequently caused offence at numerous delicate moments
and she could see she hadn't lost her knack—he looked ready
to throttle her!

'You find this situation funny?' he enquired coldly.

She gasped for breath. 'I'm hysterical, you idiot!' she
gasped. She clutched her aching stomach muscles as tears
began to run down her cheeks.

'Do you prefer right cheek or left?' he asked, touching her
chin and examining each profile in turn. 'Isn't that the traditional remedy?'

'You w-wouldn't dare!' She hiccuped as she gradually re-
gained control. He didn't deny or confirm this accusation,
just smiled in what she considered to be a sinister manner.

'Didn't you think I had a right to know? Didn't you think
I was sufficiently involved to be informed?' he grated sarcastically. 'You've already deprived one child of her father.
I can't believe you were going to do it again. Well, whatever
plans you had, Rachel, you'd better include me.'

'This is ridiculous, Ben. Will you listen to me?'

'I've accepted you think I'm some lightweight party animal with no depth, but did you *really* imagine that I wouldn't
care if a woman was carrying my child?'

The way his eyes ran over her body and came to rest on
her flat belly with a fierce, possessive expression made her
feel…*excited*? That's sick, Rachel—stop it! she told herself
firmly. This wasn't the time to forget this pregnancy was a
fantasy spun by a devious, warped mind.

'Or did you just not take my feelings into consideration?'

'Oh, so this is all about *you*, is it?' Hands on her hips, she
let her scornful glance travel to the top of his dark head.
'Your fragile male pride.'

'Miss French, are you all right?' Clad in pyjamas, the occupant of the ground-floor flat opened his door. 'It's just I

heard some noise…' The retired accountant had to take a step back to see Benedict's face. He pushed his wire-framed spectacles up his thin nose and devoutly hoped Miss French wouldn't want any help.

'I'm really sorry we disturbed you and Mrs Rose,' Rachel began, wiping away the last remnants of moisture from her face. That might be the last time she laughed in a long time, she thought bleakly.

'I told her not to have the second bottle of wine. She gets a little…shrill when she's over-indulged,' Benedict said in conspiratorial undertones. 'We'll take ourselves upstairs. Do you need a hand, my love?' he enquired solicitously.

Rachel gritted her teeth and looked from the confused face of her neighbour to Benedict. If she didn't want to include half the neighbourhood in her troubles she didn't have much choice.

'I can manage, thank you,' she said from between clenched teeth as she shrugged off the hand on her elbow which was much more to do with restraint than solicitude.

The door upstairs was still ajar and she ducked under Benedict's arm as he held it open. *'Thank you,'* she grated sarcastically. 'God knows what he thinks now. He saw me go out with one man and come back with another!' she fumed.

'Worried about your reputation, Rachel? It's a bit late for that, isn't it?'

'I've done nothing to be ashamed of.'

'I'm pleased to hear it, because if you had…' He gave a thin-lipped smile and his eyes glittered as he let his glance dwell on her face. 'Shall we just say it saves me the bother of ruining his expensive dental work?'

'If I decide to sleep with the entire English soccer team it's nothing to do with you! Clean up your own act before you start interfering in mine.'

'Are you trying to tell me it's my debauched reputation

hat's behind your decision to keep me in the dark?' he enquired cynically.

'What gives you the idea I'm even *slightly* interested in
your reputation?' she enquired scornfully.

'I'm crushed,' he remarked, looking anything but. 'I've
spent all my adult life polishing my depraved image. Is
Charlie asleep?' he asked, looking around the room.

Rachel nodded reluctantly; after her late night Charlie had
gone out like a light.

'She met Fauré?' His eyes touched the large elaborate bouquet on the dining table and his lip curled contemptuously.
'A little ostentatious,' he commented, with a quirk of one
dark brow.

'They got on very well.' She wasn't about to tell him that
Charlie's approval of Christophe had contained a significant
rider: 'I don't like him as much as Ben.'

'You decided it was too complicated to cope with two
fathers at the same time?'

'You're not my child's father, Ben.'

'Prospective father, if you're going to be pedantic.'

'I'm not pregnant, Ben.'

'Can't you do any better than that?' His scorn was cor-
rosive enough to strip metal. 'Don't treat me like a fool,
Rachel.'

'It's the truth.' What else could she say to convince him?

'Did you enjoy single parenthood so much you want to go
through it again? Or are you hoping Fauré will accept this
child as his too? If you have any ideas along those lines,
Rachel, drop them now.'

She embraced the anger; it was easier to cope with than
impotence. 'I shouldn't really blame you for sounding like a
tinpot dictator. I suppose your father has always spoken to
your mother like that. But if you use that tone with me once
more, so help me…'

For the first time she saw a flicker of amusement. Momentarily it lifted the sombre expression on his strikingly handsome face.

'What's the joke?'

'After you've met my mother you'll understand.'

'I'm not going to meet your mother.'

His expression was the visual equivalent of a patronising pat on the head and she wanted to scream very badly. The only thing stopping her was the child sleeping in the next room.

'I suppose you were relying on the fact that I'll be leaving the country. You mistakenly thought that Dad would be on your side as he was so anxious to warn me off you. You miscalculated; one thing he feels passionate about is family!'

'Oh, I know all about your father's concern for his family. I'd say he'd go to any lengths to preserve it. Can you imagine your father as a cosy grandfather, Ben?' Anyone would think he *wanted* to believe his father's story.

'This is about us, not my father.' He pushed aside her dry observation impatiently.

'Would that were true.'

'He said you didn't intend telling him. He said you were very depressed and you just blurted it out.'

'"He said! He said!"' she mimicked, wishing the unscrupulous old man were here so she could tell him exactly what she thought of him. 'You're not listening to *me*, are you? How could I be pregnant?'

If he paused long enough to think he'd see that it wasn't possible. 'I told you the first time it was safe and then we took precautions.' She was annoyed that the reference made her flush like a schoolgirl, not a thirty-year-old mother. 'Besides, it was only three weeks ago.' The argument was pretty watertight, she thought, giving a relieved sigh. The relief proved premature, however, as she listened to Benedict proceeding to punch holes in her neat logic.

'The only fail-safe form of contraception is abstinence—we've not been very abstemious.'

Greedy, she decided, was a more accurate description; the thought brought an unwelcome reminder of the fact that some things hadn't changed. She still felt *greedy*. She lowered her eyes self-consciously before the scorching recognition surfaced in her eyes.

'And these days a testing kit can tell you if you're pregnant when you're hours late.'

'I wouldn't know.'

'I have friends who were desperate to get pregnant. Tom could have written a consumer column on kits that tell you when you should or shouldn't and others that tell you when you are or aren't. Or did you just know? Some women do.'

'Stop it!' she yelled, placing her hands firmly over her ears. 'I'm not pregnant! Your father was lying.'

'He can, and does, but why would he lie now? And why *this* lie? What would he have to gain?'

At last! Here was her opportunity to explain. 'He thinks if I get pregnant you won't leave the firm and you won't leave the country.' Even to her own ears the idea sounded preposterous.

'Is that the best you can do, Rachel? Why would he think that? I can't think of a better place in the world than the Creek to bring up a child.'

She would like to be watching when Benedict revealed this to his father. It wouldn't make up for what he'd done, but it would certainly help! Despite all his father's underhand tactics Benedict still had no intention of continuing with his legal career! At any other time the irony might have made her smile.

'Charlie will love it too,' Benedict continued persuasively. 'After we're married…'

'Married?' she echoed hollowly.

'I've no desire to be a part-time father, Rachel.' He looked at her as if he were stating the obvious and sank his fingers into the dark hair above a forehead pleated in a deep frown.

The gesture was implicitly weary; she could almost see him physically push aside the fatigue as his hand fell away. She had to do the same with the warm, mushy feelings that made her a push-over where he was concerned. He's tough, girl; he doesn't need you to mop his tired brow! she told herself.

'What happened to the "include me in your plans, Rachel"?' she enquired pointedly. 'Suddenly it seems as if *I* don't have any say in the matter.'

'Not a pleasant feeling, is it?' His resentment seemed momentarily overridden by concern as he examined her pale face. 'For God's sake, woman, sit down before you fall down.'

'Will you stop that? I don't want to sit down!' she snapped as he all but manhandled her into an oak carver chair she'd inherited from her aunt. Her hands curved around the smooth, worn wood of the arms; the solid familiarity was strangely comforting.

'You have to look after yourself,' he said gruffly, backing off.

This, she realised, was Benedict's version of the kid-glove treatment. She ignored the wistful sigh somewhere in the back of her mind. If this were for real it might be *quite* nice to be cherished by Ben Arden. The idea of carrying his child for real was dangerously seductive. Ever since his father had planted the germ of the idea she hadn't been able to stop imagining.

'I'm not ill!'

'Pregnancy isn't an illness,' he agreed gravely. 'Did you have an easy time with Charlie—any problems? I saw the scar.'

She started. Recalling the circumstances in which he'd noticed the almost invisible scar made her stomach muscles clench. Trying to cover her tingling breasts would only draw attention to the effect his casual words had had.

Though she didn't know why she was bothering; Ben had obviously already lost interest in her in *that* way. Naturally she'd been relieved when he hadn't continued to pursue her and Sabrina, by all accounts, was helping him fill his social calendar. Now she was nothing more than an incubator!

'I had a Caesarean.' Serve him right if she did treat him to the nitty-gritty.

'Does that mean that—?' he began uncooperatively, displaying much less embarrassment than she was feeling with the topic.

'I'm not pregnant, Ben,' she breathed, with an exasperated sigh. Much more of this and she was going to start believing it too!

'If you had a tough time I can understand why you want to deny it, but this is happening, Rachel.'

'I don't want your understanding! You're going to feel really stupid when you realise I'm telling the truth,' she said, not without relish.

'My God!' he said suddenly, his eyes narrowing in suspicion. 'You're not thinking of abortion, are you? Because I have to tell you… No, you couldn't do that.' Just as she was getting ready to throw something large and painful at him his expression cleared. 'You wouldn't.' His sudden supreme confidence brought a lump of emotion to her throat.

'I don't know what to say,' she sniffed, and found a man-sized handkerchief pushed into her hand. Nothing short of divine intervention, it seemed, would convince him she wasn't pregnant.

'I know.'

'You don't, Ben.'

'I do. I was shocked, especially when I heard it from the source I did. It's not something I'd planned to happen right now.'

Or ever, she thought, quite touched by this display of consideration for her feelings.

'But the idea of the life I planted growing in you…it's… The whole idea is *incredible*,' he grated thickly.

Something moved deep inside her as she listened to the depth of emotion throbbing in his voice. He dropped to his knees and gripped her thighs. It was impossible to look away from his searching eyes.

'If by incredible you mean implausible I couldn't agree more,' she croaked.

'By incredible I mean astounding, miraculous, wonderful, extraordinary—' His big hands tightened around her slim thighs.

'There's nothing extraordinary about pregnancy; it's commonplace.'

'Not for me, Rachel. I want to share this. Don't try and push me away.'

The stumbling analysis of her feelings revealed a shocking truth—she wanted it to be true. Part of her wished that his child were growing in her belly. Part of her wanted to have a legitimate reason to follow him to Australia, start a new life together. Was this what his father had reckoned on—her weakness?

Right now he didn't love her, but he didn't hate her either, and he would if she was crazy enough to follow her baser instincts.

'Leaving aside the fact I'm not pregnant for the moment,

what makes you think that I'd want to follow you to the other side of the world? I know there's a body of opinion that still thinks, even in this enlightened age, that a woman should follow her man...' She filled the pause with light laughter and saw the muscles around his sensual mouth tighten. 'But even they would agree that these extravagant acts of sacrifice have to be inspired by love. We've shared a lot of unbridled lust,' she said candidly, 'but *love*? I think I'd have remembered if you'd dropped that into the conversation.'

'And if I had?' It was hard to tell from his expression if he'd found her frankness insulting.

In my dreams you did... 'You didn't, I didn't and I'm not marrying anyone I don't love.'

'Then perhaps I'll just have to make you love me.' She had the impression she'd succeeded in getting under his guard this time. Seeing the implacable light in his eyes, she wasn't so sure this had been an altogether sensible thing to do.

'Don't be stupid.'

'You sound nervous, Rachel.'

'I'm not nervous, I'm tired. You can't *make* someone fall in love. They either do or they don't.' *I should know.*

'Then you've nothing to worry about, have you?'

'I'm not worried. As for this talk of marriage, you'll realise shortly that it was just a knee-jerk reaction.'

'Would it surprise you to learn I've been thinking of getting married quite a lot recently?'

'Yes,' she said flatly, 'it would. If you're going to wheel out some pathetic story that you're really desperately in love with me—don't!'

An expression she didn't understand flickered across his face. 'Did I say it was you I was considering marrying?' Head tilted slightly back, eyes half closed, there was nothing lazy about the way he watched her.

She stuck out her chin and determined to tough out the wave of hot mortification. 'You have a novel way of making a girl fall in love with you.'

'I'm trying to lull you into a false sense of security.'

'It's a mistake to reveal your tactics. As for security, just think how secure I'll feel when you start taking other women out.'

His lips twitched as he acknowledged her saccharine-sweet words. 'Sabrina is a lovely girl, but can you see her on an isolated property in the outback? You've no need to feel jealous of Sabrina.'

'You're on the look-out for a female with a strong back and good child-bearing hips? I'm flattered.'

'That's an interesting suggestion. Especially the bit about the hips.' His hands slid upwards until his thumbs came into contact with the sharp, jutting crests that delineated her slim pelvis. Through the contact he felt the shiver that affected her entire body. He smiled. 'And you've already got a proven track record in the fertility stakes.' He shook his head slowly and grinned at her outraged little gasp.

'I think I might have given you a false impression of the Creek, Rachel. The conditions are not exactly primitive, you know. And whilst we are isolated a plane really does cut down the distances. Despite what my father likes to imply, it's not exactly a tin shack and life is a long way from being a cultural desert.'

'You can fly?' She was fascinated despite herself. It was something she'd always wanted to learn.

'Nina, my grandmother, gave me flying lessons for my eighteenth birthday. I got the bug, which was no doubt what she intended. In her own way Nina was as crafty as my father; she made no secret of the fact that she wanted me to take over from her.'

'And now you are.'

'She's probably up there somewhere laughing.'

'Pardon me for not joining in with the merriment but being treated like a pregnant piece of livestock has had a detrimental effect on my sense of humour.'

'You didn't think I was serious for one minute,' he chided. 'At least you're not denying it now—the fact that you're pregnant. That's something.'

'I am not!'

'I'd say, Are too, but I'm trying to create a mature and responsible impression.'

'Are you implying I'm being immature?'

He anchored her flailing arms securely in his hands before replying. 'I'm saying that you being pregnant changes things whether you like it or not,' he said soberly.

And, despite his assurances to the contrary, he *didn't* like. Nothing he'd said or done had convinced her otherwise.

'You've done a good—no, a *great* job of bringing up Charlie, but you know better than most that a child needs two parents.'

'Two *loving* parents.'

'We can love pretty sensationally.'

'I'm not talking about *sex*,' she said witheringly. 'Even *sensational* sex isn't a basis for marriage!' She examined the foot she'd just unintentionally directed a bullet at and winced.

'Thank you, Rachel; I thought it was too.' He looked as smug as your average sleek predator when it sank its claws into dinner. 'Charlie likes me too.'

'That's really low—using a child's feelings.'

'I'm telling it the way it is, Rachel,' he said with no trace of remorse. 'Charlie would be better off with me providing the male influence in her life. You've got to admit Fauré isn't much of an improvement on a test-tube!'

'Isn't that the tiniest bit inconsistent? You're the one getting all defensive about a biological father's rights.'

'He's married. He forfeited any rights he might have hàd,' he said, nostrils flared in distaste. 'That's a fact I intend to convey to your friend very soon.'

'No! You can't do that!' she gasped. She could imagine poor Christophe's reaction if he thought she was spreading the story that he was Charlie's father. What if the story got back to Annabel?

'I'll make a deal. I'll keep away from Fauré for now if you agree to stop pretending. I can't talk to you about practical arrangements if you keep denying you're pregnant.'

She bit back the denial. Perhaps it would be sensible to go along with him, just for tonight, if it meant keeping him from confronting Christophe! Tomorrow she was going to confront Stuart Arden and make him confess that he'd been lying through his teeth.

'Practical arrangements?'

'Obstetrician's appointments; I'd like to come with you.'

'I haven't got an obstetrician.'

'Have you been to see a doctor at all?' He frowned in disapproval when she shook her head. 'Well, firstly I think we should—'

'I'm sure you're right, Ben, but I'm really very tired right now.' It wasn't hard to convey lassitude when mentally she was close to complete exhaustion. She saw the concern on his face and felt a spasm of guilt when he touched a solicitous hand to the side of her face.

'Tomorrow, then?'

She nodded mutely; the impulse to turn her cheek lovingly into his open palm was overwhelmingly strong. Her feelings were ambiguous when he did remove his hand.

After he'd let himself out of the flat she could feel the impression where his fingers had touched her face. Even the dampness from the tears didn't diminish the sensation.

CHAPTER EIGHT

'SIR STUART isn't at home.'

'I'll wait.' Boldly Rachel stepped into the vast hallway. Her heels echoed on the marble floor. She glanced casually around; this wasn't the moment to be intimidated by insignificant things like chandeliers the size of her living room and several paintings by an artist she'd never seen outside a museum.

'I'm afraid, madam, that won't be possible.'

Rachel squared her chin; it was going to take more than a sneer from a professional flunky to put her off. 'If you tell him I'm here he'll see me.'

'Is there a problem, David?'

Rachel automatically looked in the direction of the light musical voice. Tall and slim with dark red hair tied back in a ponytail at the nape of her neck, the figure on the curved staircase ran gracefully down the remaining steps. She was dressed for riding and the scarf at her neck was the same vivid green as her eyes.

'This person wishes to see Sir Stuart.'

'This person', Rachel thought, her lip curling. How delightfully 'Jeeves'.

'I have told her he isn't at home. I don't know how she got past Security.'

Rachel held up the official-looking papers in her hand bearing the authentic letterhead of the chambers. 'I said I was a messenger from the office.' She didn't want anyone to get into trouble on her account.

'And aren't you?' the redhead asked with interest.

'I work there.'

'For my husband?'

Husband! Rachel blinked. 'You can't be!' she repudiated hotly, feeling as if a fist had been jabbed into her solar plexus.

Aware that the lady of the house was regarding her with concern tinged by alarm—and who could blame her?—she tried to re-establish herself as a reasonably safe person to open the door to. When she paused to think, not react, her mistake was obvious. No, if Ben had had a wife, especially one as photogenic as this, it would hardly have escaped public notice.

'You look too young to be Ben's mother,' she added impetuously when she had established the woman's identity by means of elimination. 'That is, I thought you'd be—' Stop while you've only one foot in your mouth, Rachel, she told herself. Nothing so far was going according to her mental plan. She just hoped her words hadn't been interpreted as an attempt to ingratiate herself. The thought made her cringe.

It was unsettling to have her mental image of a well-bred doormat replaced by the vibrant, confident woman before her.

'I am Emily Arden. You work for Ben, do you? Is it him you're looking for?'

'No! I don't want to see him!' Horror-struck at the possibility that he might appear, she couldn't prevent herself from glancing nervously over her shoulder.

'Then you'll be pleased to hear he's not at home.' If she felt surprise at her visitor's obvious aversion to the notion of seeing her son her polite expression didn't reveal it.

Rachel's tension eased down a notch. 'I really do need to see Sir Stuart. It's personal.'

'About a personal matter? Should I be worried?'

Rachel looked at her blankly for a moment before blushing vividly. 'Not that sort of personal.'

'I'm only teasing, my dear. My husband has many faults, but chasing young women is not one of them. One of them, however, is a habit of becoming invisible when it suits him,' she added drily.

'Are you saying he's not at home?' Rachel tried to keep her voice steady and failed. He *had* to be here. He had to explain to Benedict. She'd worked herself up to this confrontation and now the anticlimax was tremendous. She suddenly felt a feeble shadow of the strong positive, young woman who'd sailed in here on a cloud of determination.

'Why don't you come through and have a drink, my dear? You look as though you need it. Look after these, David.' She took the file of papers from Rachel's limp grasp and handed them to the butler. 'Could you organise some coffee in the drawing room? Come along.' Rachel found herself meekly falling in step with the lady of the house.

'It's a lovely room,' Rachel said miserably on entering the drawing room.

'Yes, isn't it?' She noticed Rachel's eyes were fixed on an aerial photograph set in an elaborate frame. 'I was born there,' she said with an affectionate smile.

'Connor's Creek?' When Benedict had said it wasn't a tin shack he hadn't been joking. She could have lived there, she thought, gazing at the well laid out paddocks around the sprawling house. If she'd been willing to lie and cheat, that was.

'That's right. I'm afraid it isn't so green just now.' Emily Arden recovered her composure smoothly. The unhappy young woman's instant recognition had surprised her. 'Sit there; that's right. Now, tell me why you need to see my husband.'

'I need him to tell Ben the truth; he won't believe me.' If she'd been truly prepared she'd have had a cover story ready; as it was, the truth would have to do.

'What won't he believe?'

'That I'm not pregnant.'

The green eyes blinked twice and the slim, beautifully manicured hand gripped the chintz-covered chair-arm a little more firmly, but that was the only visible response to this statement.

'Perhaps I'm a little slow, but why does he think you are?'

'Because his father told him I am,' she choked.

'Isn't that just typical of Stuart? He creates chaos and leaves me to sort it out!' Emily Arden folded her arms across her bosom and pursed her lips. 'He does insist on meddling.'

Rachel stared; she couldn't quite believe the older woman's ready acceptance of her story. She hadn't even asked why her husband would do such a bizarre thing.

'You believe me?' she said incredulously. 'I could be anyone. I walk in here saying I'm—'

'I know; it's a shock. As a mother of two sons I was always prepared for a girl to walk in and announce she was pregnant, but to say she's not! I didn't have the speech prepared for this eventuality.'

'It's not a joke.'

The attractive face melted into a smile that was so kind, Rachel had to bite her lip to hold back the tears. 'I can see that, my dear; forgive me.'

'It's awful,' Rachel sniffed. 'He wants to marry me,' she explained in an outraged tone.

The dark eyebrows lifted towards the smooth hairline, but her serene expression stayed intact. *'Really?'*

'Only because of the baby.'

'But there is no baby.'

'Try telling him that. He won't take no for an answer.'

An expression of irritation flashed across Emily Arden's face as the sound of voices through the open French doors grew louder. 'Dry your eyes, my dear,' she advised softly. 'I think we're about to be invaded. I think you'd better tell me your name before I introduce you to the rest of the family.'

'Rachel—Rachel French.'

'Nat, darling, don't bring those animals in here; they smell disgusting.'

'I like wet-dog smell.' The tall, dark-haired teenager looked curiously at Rachel. 'Hi!'

'This is Rachel French; she works with your brother. Rachel, this is Natalie, and this is Tom, my eldest.' The slim, auburn-haired man carrying a sleeping toddler smiled warmly at her. 'And his wife, Ruth.' Ruth had hair the same pale colour as the sleeping child; she also had a lovely smile. 'Oh, and this is Sabrina—a friend of the family.'

Rachel wasn't sure whether wishful thinking supplied the certain reserve in the older woman's voice when she made her final introduction.

'I've seen you somewhere. I know, you're the secretary person.' This discovery was expressed in a bored, well-bred drawl. 'Is Ben here too?' Sabrina asked, her voice suddenly much more animated than it had been.

'I'm afraid not,' their hostess said smoothly. 'A family get-together without two male members of the family and with the addition of two unexpected guests. Par for the course,' she observed philosophically.

'I'm not staying,' Rachel said, getting to her feet. Her skin wasn't really thick enough for this intrusion stuff. If Sir Stuart wasn't here there wasn't much point in her staying, and there was always the worrying possibility that Ben would appear. 'In fact I think I should go now. I'm very sorry to intrude.'

'Here's coffee now. You must join us. I insist.' Beneath the smile Rachel could see the definite glint of steely determination. At least Sir Stuart didn't get entirely his own way at home. This thought offered her small comfort as she desperately tried to think of a reason for her immediate departure.

'But my friend is picking me up.' She glanced down at her wristwatch to illustrate the imminence of this event.

'Well, we'll get them to send him up to the house when he arrives. It is a he?'

'Yes. His name's Fauré.' She decided to be gracious in defeat.

'French!' The dark-haired daughter of the house pushed a dog off the sofa and installed herself cross-legged in its place. 'I think continental men are simply delicious. So much more sexy than boring Brits.' She flashed her brother a meaningful glance. 'Especially Frenchmen. All my lovers shall be French or maybe Italian.'

'Thanks a lot,' her brother said drily. 'I'll just take Libby up to bed; she's due her nap.' He patted the sleeping child on his shoulder gently on the back. He murmured a soft aside to his wife and she nodded.

'Get them to ring down to the gate about Rachel's friend, Tom.'

'Will do.' He nodded, before turning his attention briefly back to his sister. 'If I can't excel as a Latin lover—' he struck a mock-heroic pose and then slumped his shoulders pathetically '—I'll just have to earn my keep being useful round the house. Incidentally, Nat, maybe you should wait until you've got the ironwear off the teeth before you start working your way through the continental studs. A moment of passion and their crowns could be dust.'

'Shut up, you; I don't know how Ruth puts up with you!' his sister yelled after him. 'I shall have beautiful teeth,' she observed, tapping the metal framework around her front teeth.

'You will, my dear,' her mother confirmed. 'Ah,' she said,

inclining her head to one side in an attentive attitude. 'I recognise that slam. I do believe Benedict is back.'

'Oh, excellent.' Sabrina got to her feet slowly and regarded her reflection in an ornate mirror on the wall opposite with a smug smile.

Rachel got to her feet, too, like a puppet whose strings had just been jerked particularly viciously, but she wasn't smiling. She was still wondering if she could make it safely through the French windows before he entered the room when the door was pushed open.

'Darling.'

'Sabrina, what are you doing here?' Benedict's response would have dampened more sensitive spirits than Sabrina, who smiled seductively and glided across the room. 'Good God, *Rachel*!' He literally froze.

Someone released the tension on those invisible strings and her knees started to quiver. 'I'm just going, Mr Arden.' Her voice showed a tendency to quiver too. She heard it and Benedict did too; she watched his lips curve into a cruel smile. He looked to be in one hell of a temper.

'*Mr Arden?*' he echoed mockingly. '*Miss French*, no, you're not leaving!'

'Really, Ben, darling, it is the weekend; I'm sure the girl has better things to do than—do whatever secretaries do.'

Sabrina, Rachel thought despairingly, was probably the only person in the room that hadn't read, and personally translated, the undercurrents. Lurid reading those versions probably made, too.

'I'm not his secretary!'

'She's not my secretary!'

The two hot denials emerged simultaneously and seething grey eyes clashed with smouldering brown ones.

'What is she, then? And why is she here?' asked the

blonde, with a disgruntled expression. She didn't like conversations that didn't include herself.

The crinkly lines Rachel loved around Benedict's eyes deepened as he regarded her with narrow-eyed interest. 'Good question. What are you, and why are you here, Rachel?'

He was gloating, enjoying her discomfiture. Later, when she was rehashing the day's events, she might be able to come up with the perfect cutting rejoinder that would wipe that smug grin off his face, but right now she had to rely on the transparent subterfuge which had got her in here.

'I brought some papers for your father to sign.'

'What papers? Where are they?' He looked around the room, apparently confident he wouldn't discover any.

'I expect they're on your father's desk, Benedict. You look terrible.' Rachel thought he looked sinfully gorgeous but she could see what his mother meant. His eyes were definitely bloodshot and he hadn't shaved; in fact he looked more like Charlie's guardian angel than the sleek legal eagle. 'What have you been doing with yourself?'

Rachel shot a grateful glance in Emily Arden's direction. She needed all the support she could get.

'I've spent the best part of two hours camped out on Rachel's doorstep.'

'You can hardly hold me responsible,' Rachel said indignantly in response to his smouldering glare. 'If you choose to waste your time that's your affair.'

'Talking of affairs…' he drawled.

He wouldn't! The dark eyes shone mockingly back at her. *He would!* Her stomach churned in misery and embarrassment. 'What am I supposed to do—wait in on the off chance you might want me?'

'I don't think there's any *might* about it.' His wry tone left no room for misinterpretation. She knew what he was think-ng as his eyes made the journey from her toes to the top of her head with dramatic pauses to enjoy certain aspects of her figure, and so did everyone else in the room! She'd never felt so humiliated in her life—or as angry!

The slow, contemplative smile on his face broadened as the hot colour flared in two angry bands of red across her cheekbones.

'If you don't care about my feelings you might at least have the common courtesy not to embarrass your family,' she choked furiously. The bland look she received in return didn't display any signs of remorse.

'I'm not embarrassed,' Natalie observed chirpily.

An expression of shocked comprehension crossed Sabrina's face. 'But she's...' Her perfect nose wrinkled in confusion as she compared her own willowy reflection in the mirror with Rachel's slightly shorter, more curvy figure.

'*She's* going,' Rachel snapped. She didn't need the blonde to remind her of the disparity in their claims to beauty. And unlike Sabrina there was no way she could ever hope to match Benedict's sophistication. How he must be cursing the moment of madness that had tied him to her. She could imagine how relieved he'd be when he knew that there was no need to do the 'right thing'. His father certainly knew which buttons to press, she thought bitterly; Benedict wasn't the most obvious candidate for old-fashioned values.

'Not till I say so, you're not,' he replied in a cold, clear voice from which old-fashioned chivalry was noticeably absent.

Rachel heard a collective startled gasp and a nervous giggle, but she didn't notice from where it had originated. Her head was filled with the dull roar of the blood pounding in her ears.

'I'll go when and where I like, and if you try to stop me you can...'

'I can what?' he goaded.

She looked around and saw that all the audience was waiting for her answer with bated breath. Well, he might not mind providing a floor show for his nearest and dearest but she did!

'You know something, Ben? Meeting you is right up there with mumps and acne. You're the most insensitive, self-centred, manipulative...' She made a sound of disgust low in her throat. 'I wouldn't marry you if my life depended on it.'

'What makes you think it doesn't?' If anything the aggressive tilt of his square jaw had grown even more pronounced.

'You were right, Ruth. I owe you a tenner. He proposed! Well, I'll be—'

'Tom!' Benedict snarled, evincing no sign of brotherly love as he swung around to face the man who'd entered the room behind him. 'As a matter of fact I have. I've proposed and been refused. Thinking of offering me advice, are you?'

The eldest of the Arden brood bit back a grin and arranged his mobile features into a suitably sombre mask. 'Actually I just came to tell Miss French—Rachel—that her lift is here.' His green eyes sparkled with lively interest.

'Show him in, Tom,' Emily Arden instructed. 'Them in,' she corrected herself drily as the door swung open and Charlie walked in, followed at a more sedate pace by her uncle.

Charlie looked calmly around the room, completely unfazed by the unknown faces. 'This place looks like something off a magazine cover,' she remarked admiringly. She grinned at her mother. 'Hi, Mum!'

'She must be *old*.' Sabrina's chagrin was almost comical. She looked indignantly from Rachel to Charlie and back to Rachel again as if she expected to see her age before her eyes.

It was then that Charlie saw Benedict.

'Ben!' Her small face lit up and she ran like a heat-seeking missile straight at him.

That's what I want to do. Rachel felt the dull pain of ac-knowledgement. For a split second all she felt was deep envy for the ability to display such spontaneous pleasure.

Hiding her feelings meant she had to consider every word, every gesture. The expression on Benedict's face as he bent forward and lifted her high brought a heavy, emotional con-striction to her aching throat. There could be no doubting the genuine nature of his feelings where Charlie was concerned.

His family watched with varying degrees of shock as Benedict swung the youngster up into the air before placing her back down on her feet and ruffling her halo of damp golden-blonde hair.

'I was wondering where you were.' He saw for the first time who had followed Charlie into the room. It was as if someone had flicked a switch. He was projecting such intense hostility, you could almost see the waves of loathing ema-nating from his eyes.

'I was with Uncle Christophe.' Charlie's vivid blue eyes turned happily to the figure who had so far been silent. 'We went swimming.'

'Ah, yes, *Uncle* Christophe.' His dark eyes met Rachel's. The contempt she read there made her jaw tighten and her chin go up in automatic defiance.

He obviously thought she'd created another story to spare herself Charlie's awkward questions, but she couldn't squash his nasty theory without revealing the fact that she'd let him believe a lie. Her glance moved worriedly to Christophe and she wondered how the older man would respond to Ben's hostility. She knew she only had Charlie's presence to thank for Benedict's restraint so far.

'Charlie is an excellent swimmer.' Christophe smiled warmly at his niece.

'When I go to France I shall swim in the sea—it's warm there—won't I, Mum?' Not daring to look in Benedict's direction, Rachel nodded weakly.

'And when is this trip arranged, Charlie?' Benedict asked, no discernible expression on his face.

There was no question of drawing blood from a stone; Charlie was only too happy to reveal her plans to Ben. Rachel listened with deepening resignation as her daughter told him their plans in tiresomely meticulous detail.

'Wouldn't it be great if Ben could come too, Mum?'

That really did focus her attention!

'Great!' she echoed hollowly. 'But he's a very busy man and he'll probably be in Australia by then.' She met the glittering mockery in Benedict's eyes with as much dignity as she could muster.

'My schedule is flexible.'

'My plans aren't.'

'We have an open house; any friend of yours is welcome, Rachel.'

She silently mouthed 'no' to Christophe and grimaced to indicate this wasn't a good idea. All her furtive pantomime achieved was to make Christophe look even more confused. She wished now that she'd given him an explanation for her trip here this morning.

With her luck the way Benedict's mind was working he'd probably think poor Christophe was inviting him to form part of some sort of *ménage à trois*! Before Rachel could divert Christophe's native hospitality Benedict spoke up.

'Open…?' he mused slowly. The derision seeped around the edges of his languid drawl and Rachel instinctively moved to stand protectively in front of Christophe. 'Myself,

I like boundaries. In homes, in jobs, most importantly in marriages. It cuts down on confusion.'

Christophe Fauré looked bemused and Rachel could understand why. She just hoped he'd stay that way. As he was completely innocent of marital infidelity, Benedict's heavy-handed irony wasn't likely to prick his conscience.

'Why doesn't Ben like Uncle Christophe?' There was an embarrassed silence as Charlie glanced enquiringly at her mother. She tugged imperatively at the loose white shirt Benedict wore tucked into his blue denims. 'He's nice, Ben.'

'I'm sure he is, Charlie.' He visibly reined in his aggression. He flexed his fingers as they unfurled from the balled fists which had rested suggestively at his sides. His breathing was almost normal as he smiled reassuringly down at the child.

'Well, I think Frenchmen are very nice.' Natalie got to her feet and crossed the room towards her brother. Her mother smiled on proudly as, displaying maturity beyond her years, her daughter successfully took the spotlight off her sibling.

'Thank you, *mademoiselle*.'

'I'm Natalie.' With a self-confident smile she extended her hand and eyed this mature example of the breed with open approval. She gave a laugh of delight as it was raised to his lips. 'Watch and learn, boys,' she advised her brothers.

'Are you Ben's sister?' Charlie asked curiously.

'For my sins.'

'You look alike.'

'So I've been told,' she replied, with a grimace. 'But, unfortunately, he's much prettier than me.'

'You're too kind,' her brother responded drily.

'Do you like horses, Charlie?' Natalie continued in her friendly manner. She squatted down until she was at eye level with the little girl. 'I was just on my way out to the stables…'

'I used to ride,' Charlie explained, her eyes sparkling in response. 'But we live in the town now.'

'Would you like to come and see them?'

'I'm afraid we've intruded long enough.' Rachel ignored the reproachful spaniel look her daughter threw in her direction. 'Christophe has an appointment in town this afternoon.' If he didn't pick up her desperate signals this time she'd just die.

'Yes, unfortunately I do need to leave.'

Rachel sighed with relief and sent him a grateful smile.

'That's no problem; I can give you and Charlie a lift back later, Rachel. I was going that way anyway.'

Fear was supposed to sharpen your wits, lend an extra edge to your mental faculties. I must be the exception to the rule, she thought, unable to tear her eyes away from Benedict's gaze. The insolence in those dark eyes was deliberate; he was daring her to get out of that one. She'd have loved to rise to the occasion but her brain was the consistency of mush.

'I…that is.…'

'That's settled, then. Shall I show Mr Fauré to the door?'

'It's a bit late to play the perfect host, Benedict,' his mother said lightly. 'Mr Fauré, let me do the honours and possibly persuade you to come and visit again when things are less…' she eyed her son thoughtfully '…volatile?'

'Come on, Charlie,' Natalie said, chivvying the dogs with a piercing whistle. 'We'll go and see the horses.' She leant close to her brother. 'This will cost you big,' she said softly.

'I know.' Benedict's eyes didn't leave Rachel's face for an instant.

'And I expect a blow-by-blow—'

Benedict did look at her then with indulgent tolerance. 'Get a life, Nat,' he advised, not unkindly.

'Some chance of that; you want to try being sixteen,' she

ossed back, taking Charlie by the hand and leading her out
nto the garden.

'Weren't you going to show us those photos of the big
ɔash for your brother's engagement, Sabrina?' Tom shot a
slightly apologetic look towards his wife as he pulled her to
ıer feet. 'Ruth was amazed when I told her who was there.'

This was enough to draw Sabrina's resentful eyes from the
silent tableau of the two remaining figures in the room. 'Did
I tell you that…?' She began ticking off all the minor members of royalty and media personalities who had been there
on her carmine-tipped fingers. 'And she's much fatter than
she looks on TV.' Rachel never did discover who this was:
the doors in the Arden mansion were very solid.

'Alone at last.'

'I didn't say goodbye to Christophe. He'll think…'

Benedict's expression grew harsh, his jaw clenched in anger and his eyes were obsidian-hard. 'He's history,' he said
with a dismissive shrug. 'And if he's got an ounce of intuition he knows it, and if he hasn't…' His sensual lips thinned
to an unpleasant line.

She could hardly believe this was the same man with a
solution to the most complex of legal problems who was
displaying an amazing willingness to solve this problem with
his fists. Violence was implicit in every line of his athletic,
power-packed body.

'How dare you act like a…a barbarian? And if you touch
me I'll scream…' she warned, backing away in panic as he
moved towards her. If he touched her it would only be a
matter of time—very little time—before she was begging—
and this time she wouldn't be pleading for him not to touch
her…

'As a family our mating rituals tend to be noisy; I don't
think anyone will come running.'

'I'm not interested in your family.'

'Shame; they seem to like you. Of course it wouldn't make any difference if they didn't, but on the whole it makes matters simpler if they like my wife.'

'Ben.'

'Yes?' An odd expression flickered into his eyes as he looked down at her hands curled tightly in the fabric of his shirt. Her head was downbent, as though she couldn't bear to look at him. The tension in her slender body was palpable.

How did you convince someone of your sincerity? She closed her eyes tightly and willed him to hear the truth in her words. 'I'm *not* pregnant.'

'I know.'

Her eyes snapped open. 'What did you say?' Wide-eyed and confused, she finally lifted her eyes to his face.

'I know you're not pregnant.' He deftly untied the ribbon that confined her silky hair at the nape of her neck. 'That's better,' he reflected thickly as he spread it carefully over her shoulders. The delicate friction of his fingers on her scalp fragmented her residual concentration. He gently blew a stray strand that had settled on her cheek.

The warm scent, the teasing reminder of the taste of him made her ache; lips parted, she gasped for air. His fingers framed her face and firmly he pressed his lips to hers. It was all giving, no taking. The tenderness brought the sting of tears to her eyes.

'I tracked Dad down, and he admitted the truth—well, his version at any rate. I suspect I got a strictly censored version. He skated around the stuff that might reflect him in a less than favourable light.'

'That doesn't leave much.'

Was he feeling sorry for her? Was that why he was being so gentle? He realised how much she'd wanted it to be true? God, but she couldn't bear his pity.

This is what I wanted, she told herself. Mission accomplished. That was it, it was over; she could relax. She could get on with her life. Why wasn't she feeling better? Benedict was; he was looking positively smug. He was free. She knew she'd never be free from this love—not ever! It was a life sentence.

'My father has a gift with words,' Benedict admitted wryly.

'You must be relieved.'

'Must I?' The way he was looking at her made her sluggish heart shift into a higher gear. Other parts of her body followed suit and she rubbed the sudden rash of gooseflesh over her upper arms briskly. She dropped her eyes self-consciously from his and laughed lightly.

'It's quite funny when you think about it.'

'The humour escapes me right now.'

'Don't be too hard on him; I think he genuinely thinks he was doing what was best for you.'

'He always does. You seem very forgiving considering what a hard time I gave you because of his manipulative power games.'

She shrugged lightly and realised she was clinging again to his shirt-front. She let go and made an attempt to smooth down the crumpled areas. 'Sorry; it looks like you've been mauled,' she fretted.

He captured her hand mid-pat. 'I've got one or two others.'

'Of course you have.'

'And you can maul me whenever you feel the urge.'

The words turned on that X-rated Technicolor projector in her head and it became necessary to talk. It didn't much matter what she said or if it made sense; she just had to do something to distract herself.

'You can start your new life with a clean slate now. Just the way you planned. You're not...lumbered with excess baggage.' She tried to sound generous and optimistic even if the idea made her feel wretched inside.

'Would it have been so very terrible?' His warm fingers curled around her chin again. His dark, beloved face swam mistily through the fog of hot, unshed tears.

'I don't have the excuse of youth this time.'

'Do you need an excuse?'

'To do what? Be reckless and irresponsible?'

'No, to have my baby.' His hand slid down to rest on her flat stomach. Her eyes were riveted on the warm, intimate image. Her body was screaming out with need. The tears she'd held back successfully suddenly began to fall in earnest.

'You don't know how horrible I am,' she sobbed. 'I wished it was true.' She bent her head and burrowed into the hard, unyielding wall of his chest. The solidity and strength of it were somehow comforting. 'I was actually tempted to let you believe…' She bit down hard on her quivering lower lip and lifted her head, prepared for his scorn. 'Your father is a good judge of character.' There, it was out! Her dark secret was there for all to see.

'So did I.' Benedict was clearly still fixated on her earlier comment.

'You…? I don't understand,' she faltered. The solid ground she was standing on suddenly felt like shifting sand. What he was saying made no sense, unless…? No. She closed her mind firmly against this miraculous, impossible idea.

'I wished it was true too. That's why it took so long for me to see you were telling the truth. I wanted you to be carrying my baby. I thought I could use it as a lever to make you stay with me. Every time I tried to tell you how I felt you pushed me further away. I was so frightened of pushing too hard and losing you completely.' The memory of the pain still lingered like a shadow in his dark eyes.

He caught hold of her cold hand and raised it to his mouth. His eyes were half closed as his open lips moved over her palm. 'Marry me, Rachel,' he said, his voice throbbing with emotion. 'If you really hate the idea of Connor's Creek we could stay here in England. It doesn't really matter where we are so long as we're together,' he said urgently.

'I love you, darling, and I want you, Charlie and me to be a family. Is it the idea of Fauré that stops you speaking?' he demanded roughly. 'You deserve better than some other woman's left-overs!' he ground out passionately. 'Give me the chance and I'll make you happy, Rachel—happier than he ever could!'

Benedict loved her; he was prepared to stay in England and live a life that stifled him. Getting her head around these fantastic revelations required more mental agility than her punch drunk-brain was capable of.

'You can't love me. I'm…'

'The woman who haunts my dreams,' he said fiercely. His arms closed so tightly around her, she could hardly breathe. The compelling message in his eyes distracted her from such mundane necessities. Who needed to breathe when the man you loved looked at you with such fierce, possessive tenderness?

'The woman I want to live with, grow old with—the woman I want to love if she'll let me. Will you?' he growled throatily. She could feel the tension stretching the muscles of his lean body.

She raised a trembling hand to his face. Her fingers trailed with wondering tenderness down his lean cheek before coming to rest against his lips.

'But you didn't come near me after…'

'After you threw me out of your bed—your life? You're

surprised?' he asked, one dark brow lifting ironically. 'I had this idea you might find you missed me more than you thought. Being the optimist, I thought you might be more malleable after a dose of deprivation. I don't know what it did to you, but I've been half out of my mind.'

'I thought you and Sabrina—'

'Despite appearances, I have explained to Sabrina in words of two syllables or less that I'm not interested in resurrecting a very tepid on-off thing we had last year.'

She nodded, accepting his words without reservation.

'I tried to think about the future, tell myself you were just passing through,' she recalled huskily. 'But when I was with you I couldn't protect myself at all. Nobody has ever made me quite so miserable.' Her eyes glowed with a deep warmth as she raised them fully to his. 'Or quite so blissfully happy.' She watched the anguish drain from his face to be replaced by a sensual satisfaction. 'I fell in love with you, Ben, even though I knew there was no future.

'You have to understand that it's a long time since I did anything without considering the consequences. With you I knew what the consequences would be and I did it anyway! If I hadn't been so concerned that Charlie was falling in love too in her own way, bless her, I'd have spent every waking second I could with you before you went away. It wasn't pride or common sense that made me pull back—just a desire to protect her. We come as a package deal.'

'I always did have my father's eye for a good deal. I've got a ready-made family. Besides, Charlie picked me out personally,' he reminded her, resting his forehead against hers and placing his big hands firmly over her rounded bottom. 'She brought me home—home to you.'

'Ben!' What followed was half sob, half husky laugh; translated, it meant rapture and it was lost in the warmth of

his mouth. For several breathless minutes there were no
words at all.

'Someone might come back in,' she mumbled as his lips
nuzzled hungrily at her neck.

'Yes,' he agreed without much interest.

'They'll…they'll…' She twisted her throat to enable him
to complete his self-appointed task of kissing every inch of
her throat.

'They'll be jealous,' he suggested helpfully.

'You need a shave,' she grumbled, rubbing her chin
against his jaw. 'It reminds me of…'

He lifted his head and the devilish glint completed the
disreputable image. 'Who does it remind you of?'

'You know perfectly well who,' she said ruefully. 'I felt
sorry for you,' she added with a sniff.

'And the rest,' he scoffed. 'Your interest wasn't any more
pure and elevated than mine was; admit it.'

'You're so conceited, Benedict Arden.'

'At least you're not dishonest enough to deny that reform
wasn't the only thing you had on your mind,' he teased.

'Just as well, because as it turned out you're beyond re-
demption.' Her expression suddenly sobered. There was
something she had to tell him. 'Talking about honesty…'

'Do I sense a confession coming on? Should I sit down?'

'Maybe.'

Her gravity was contagious; Benedict looked cautiously
down at her.

'About Christophe.'

She felt his hands, which had rested lightly on her shoulders, tighten. 'I know he's Charlie's father but—'

'No, he's not.'

'Pardon?'

She hurried on. 'He's not Charlie's father. He's her uncle;
his brother Raoul was her father.'

'Raoul Fauré.' He frowned, trying to place the name. 'The racing driver?' He rubbed his forehead; there was a dazed expression on his face.

'Yes,' she nodded. 'I met him when I was working for Christophe and his wife as an au pair. I think he was bored one weekend; that's all it amounted to for him,' she admitted. The only thing it hurt to admit that now was her pride. 'I was dazzled by the glamour and you know the rest.' It was amazing that the whole sorry incident could be summed up in two sentences. 'The accident happened not long after.

'Christophe and Annabel never knew; not until Christophe spotted the same family resemblance you did.'

'My God, Rachel, I wanted to kill the man,' he grated hoarsely. 'I thought he was trying to worm his way back into your life, and worse still I thought you wanted him to. I suspected he might even pull some stunt like getting custody of Charlie.' He groaned. 'You have no idea what it's been doing to me imagining...' His dark eyes were filled with pain. 'Why did you let me think that, Rachel?'

'Charlie didn't have a proper family because I was a silly, gullible girl who only saw what she wanted to. I didn't want to do that to her again. She's so fond of you and she kept dropping hints the size of bowling balls about us... I thought you were leaving.' Her eyes pleaded for understanding.

'Like Raoul left you,' he said grimly.

'There's no comparison,' she denied swiftly. 'I've never loved anyone before you.' Lovingly she took his face between her hands and spoke from the heart. 'I didn't have the experience to be able to distinguish infatuation from the real thing back then. I do now. *Nothing*,' she said fervently, 'is more real than the way I feel about you. I needed the excuse to drive you away because I didn't have the backbone to do it by myself.'

'Does Charlie know about her father now?'

'Yes.' She searched his face anxiously for a clue to what he was thinking. What effect had her confession had?

'Everything?'

'Well, I didn't say, Your father wouldn't have remembered my name a week after you were conceived.'

'I can see you wouldn't want to do that. Has he reached heroic proportions yet?'

'You don't mind?' She gave a relieved sigh.

'Mind! I mind all right. But sometimes the truth comes at too high a cost. Charlie needs to be protected from the unvarnished version of this particular truth.'

'I was afraid you'd…'

'I love Charlie,' he said quietly. 'Of course I care about what that bastard did to you! I'd like to climb onto the proverbial old white charger and right all the wrongs that have been done to you if I could. That's what you've done to me, woman.' He shook her gently. 'And if you tell anyone I admitted that I'll never forgive you.'

'My lips are sealed…'

'To every other man but me,' he agreed complacently. The expression on his face as his glance dwelt on the passion-swollen pink outline made her tremble.

'When I think of what you must have gone through. This time it'll be different,' he vowed.

'You want a baby?' She knew she was smiling in a dopey, foolish way, but he didn't seem to mind.

'Don't you?'

Rachel gazed up at the big man she loved. 'Yes, please.'

'Let Charlie's dad be a dashing hero; I can live with it. If you love me I can live with just about anything!'

'I think she's more interested in her real-life hero.'

'And who might that be?'

'He's already spoken for,' she whispered, emotion throbbing in her voice.

'Then you'll marry me?'

'Yes!'

The couple twisted around at the sound of the jubilant cry.

'Nat said you were getting married. She was right!' Charlie was dancing around the room.

'I'm always right,' came the modest reply. 'So where is the bubbly?'

Benedict looked down at his startled bride-to-be, a smile in his eyes. 'Well, you have to say yes now.'

'I thought I did.'

'I might need to hear you say it more than once.'

The idea that Benedict, big, strong, confident Benedict, could need reassurance brought an emotional lump to her throat.

'Can I have a horse? Just a small one. Ben's got loads of money; Nat says so. Nat says—'

'Nat says too much.'

'Excuse my avaricious offspring.'

'She brought me home to you; I'll forgive her anything,' he said with extravagant good humour.

Rachel sighed. He still had a lot to learn. 'That statement will come back to haunt you,' she predicted.

'We've laid to rest the only phantoms that had me worried.'

Rachel returned the pressure of his fingers and nodded mutely back. 'I should have known you were trouble the first moment I set eyes on you,' she teased huskily.

'Forget first impressions.' He dismissed them with a shrug. 'It's lasting impressions that count. Did I make a lasting impression on you, my love?'

'The eternal variety,' she confirmed happily.

EPILOGUE

RACHEL tucked the light sheet over the chubby limbs of the sleeping baby.

'Is he off?'

Rachel leant back into the strong arms that encircled her. 'At last,' she confirmed. 'Turn on the baby alarm, will you, Ben? It went well, didn't it?' she said happily as he returned to her side.

He looked down proudly into his wife's face and nodded. She'd worked incredibly hard organising the christening of their first son and she'd still managed to look good enough to eat all day—and all day he'd been wanting to do just that.

'Isn't it about time you put your feet up? The others are on the veranda knocking back the left-over bubbly. That baby's had enough toasts today to last him clear through till his eighteenth birthday.' He smiled at the small figure of his sleeping son.

'I'll just...'

'No way,' he said, hooking his arm around her trim waist. 'I've already looked in on Charlie and she's flat out.'

'Is it time to worry when you start answering my questions before I've asked them?' she asked, giving one last peek at the sleeping baby before closing the door quietly behind them. Things were good with Charlie right now. She'd got her pony. They were just gritting their collective teeth and waiting for the dreaded teenage hormones which were almost upon them.

'Don't worry, you can still surprise me. Last night for instance...' He let out a soundless whistle.

'Shh!' she said warningly. She reached up and pressed her finger to his lips. 'Someone might be listening.'

He nibbled the finger before saying reflectively, 'That didn't seem to bother you last night.'

'Ben!' she remonstrated, trying to sound angry, but the grin kept peeping out.

She smiled a lot these days. Life wasn't one long party by any means. Ben worked long hours. She could understand his fascination with this land now, and shared it to some degree. Her real passion was reserved for this man who was as complex and demanding as this wild country. Getting to know both better was a rewarding, deeply fulfilling experience. Seeing how much he loved it here made her appreciate how great a sacrifice it would have been for him to stay in London—a sacrifice he'd been prepared to make for her!

They strolled in companionable silence outside to the veranda. The warm night air was soft on her bare arms. Rachel glanced upwards; she didn't think she'd ever take this marvellous night sky for granted.

'So Ruth knew as soon as she heard the name that Rachel was the girl,' they heard Tom Arden say. He was wiping tears of laughter from his face.

'So did most of the legal fraternity in the city,' his wife's soft voice explained.

'So you went to school with this woman who was actually in there when he…?' Natalie asked, her eyes sparkling.

'Did you hear William?' Benedict asked his wife softly. 'I'm sure I…'

'No.' He looked extremely uncomfortable when she waved aside his interruption and leaned forward, her hands on the wooden white-painted rail. With a half smile on her lips she strained her ears to catch the punchline of a story that seemed to be amusing their guests. Between the Ardens and the

Faurés, who had also come over for the christening, they had a full house.

'Yes, I went to school with Carol.'

'Can you imagine Ben of all people rushing into the ladies' after a woman?' Natalie gave a crow of laughter. 'I'd have loved to see his face when the door opened and it wasn't Rachel.'

Rachel turned to her husband. 'You did that?' Her voice alerted their guests for the first time to their presence.

'I thought you were in there. If you laugh, so help me I'll…'

'I wouldn't do that,' she gasped. It was too much; her lips began to quiver and then her face crumpled. 'I wish I'd been there.'

'Me too,' he said with feeling.

The expression on his face made her break down all over again. 'S-sorry,' she hiccuped.

'He threatened to knock down the door,' Tom added.

'Don't,' Rachel pleaded, 'it hurts.' She clutched her aching stomach muscles.

'So does being a figure of fun,' her husband assured her.

'If we're talking pain I'll have you know I lost a tenner to Ruth betting you weren't about to get married. How was I to know she had insider information?' he asked the assembled company in a disgruntled tone.

Sir Stuart Arden got to his feet carefully; he'd spent most of the day appreciating Australian wine. 'To Rachel and Benedict. I always said she was the girl for him, didn't I, Emily?' He looked to his wife for support and she rolled her eyes heavenwards.

'I'll second that,' Ben said, taking Rachel very firmly by the shoulders. 'And if you can stop laughing at me for a second I'll give my own toast—to your lovely lips.'

'Just a second?' she taunted just before he swooped. He made her eat her words in the nicest possible way.

LIVE THE EMOTION

Modern Romance™
...seduction and
passion guaranteed

Tender Romance™
...love affairs that
last a lifetime

Medical Romance™
...medical drama
on the pulse

Historical Romance™
...rich, vivid and
passionate

Sensual Romance™
...sassy, sexy and
seductive

Blaze Romance™
...the temperature's
rising

27 new titles every month.

Live the emotion

MILLS & BOON®

MB3

Next month don't miss -

HER GREEK TYCOON

*An exotic Greek island is the perfect place
for a red-hot affair – and these powerful
Greek tycoons are masters of seduction.
They've made their billions by being
determined and ruthless...and now
they're ready to take a bride!*

Available 2nd May 2003

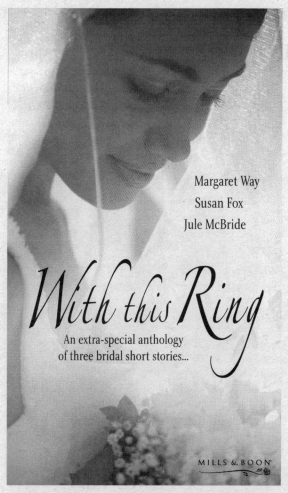

Margaret Way

Susan Fox

Jule McBride

With this Ring

An extra-special anthology
of three bridal short stories...

MILLS & BOON

Available from 18th April 2003

*Available at most branches of WH Smith,
Tesco, Martins, Borders, Eason, Sainsbury's
and all good paperback bookshops.*

0503/024/MB69

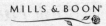

Don't miss *Book Nine* of this BRAND-NEW 12 book collection 'Bachelor Auction'.

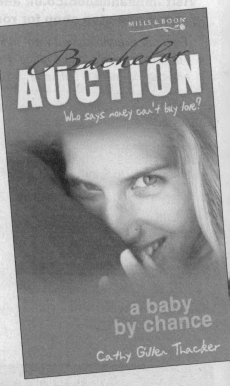

On sale 2nd May

Available at most branches of WH Smith, Tesco, Martins, Borders, Eason, Sainsbury's, and all good paperback bookshops.

BA/RTL/9

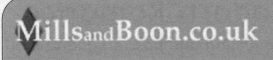

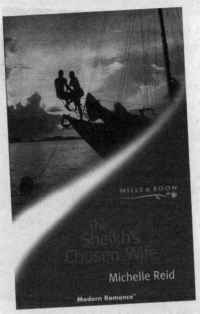

Historical Romance™
...rich, vivid and passionate

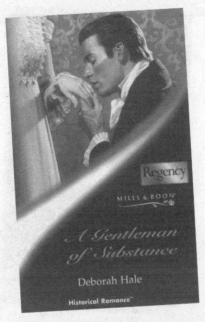

Two brand new titles each month

*Take a break and find out more about
Historical Romance™ on our website*
www.millsandboon.co.uk

*Available at most branches of WH Smith,
Tesco, Martins, Borders, Eason, Sainsbury's,
and all good paperback bookshops.*

Sensual Romance™
...sassy, sexy and seductive

Four brand new titles each month

Take a break and find out more about
Sensual Romance™ on our website
www.millsandboon.co.uk

Available at most branches of WH Smith,
Tesco, Martins, Borders, Eason, Sainsbury's,
and all good paperback bookshops.